CCAR Journal

The Reform Jewish Quarterly

MW01712534

Contents

At the Gates — בשערים

If the Jewish triangle is God, Torah and Israel, let me propose that western civilization's triad has been God, self and world. Over time, within both arenas, the emphasis has gradually shifted from element one to two to three. And yet, nothing is ever completely lost, and we keep knitting things together with new stitches.

Reason and imagination, science and religion, philosophy and poetry, data and intuition, analysis and synthesis—these and other pairings split experience while also challenging us to heal the split. For twenty-first century Jews from modern Orthodox to secular, the first element in each pair probably comes most naturally. And yet, we cover our challot so they won't be embarrassed when we recite kiddush before motzei.

Into this broadly sketched context comes the Winter 2012 symposium issue of the *CCAR Journal: The Reform Jewish Quarterly.* Taking as its topic the pairing of Judaism and Science, this important collection of articles includes a broad range of perspectives. Guest editors Philip Cohen and Hava Tirosh-Samuelson's introductory article begins by explaining that when Israel Jacobson "became the founder of Reform Judaism by creating the first Reform temple in 1810, he did so because he sought to view his ancestral faith through principles of enlightenment and reason." Later, they explain that undergirding Jewish "public behavior was a commitment to the rationalizing and universalizing thinking that, very roughly speaking, began permeating the intellectual atmosphere of the Jews of western Europe in the early decades of the nineteenth century." It seems to me that it is against that background—of the enlightened, rational, and universal—that the Jewish drama has been enacted for the past two hundred years, and still counting.

In addition to this issue's symposium articles, it also contains responses to prior issues and clustered reviews of four poetry volumes, with an introduction by Adam Fisher. As if participating in the Judaism and Science symposium, Adam writes: "Poetry makes an important contribution to our spiritual lives by inviting us to experience the spiritual moment, through the yearning and struggles of the poet. This is very different from theology, which is rational and left-brain. . . . . Science can describe how fog forms, but Sandburg tells us how we can experience fog when he says that it comes in 'on little cat feet.'"

May our lives, understanding, and teaching be enlarged by science and by poetry—both of which manifest God's creative energies, and our own.

Susan Laemmle, Editor

Editors' Introduction: Why Science Matters to Judaism

Philip Cohen and Hava Tirosh-Samuelson

When Israel Jacobson, in Jacob Marcus's felicitous phrase,[1] became "the founder of Reform Judaism" by creating the first Reform temple in 1810, he did so because he sought to view his ancestral faith through principles of enlightenment and reason. That is to say, Jacobson, and his many German Reform successors, struggled to reconceive Judaism in light of the highest conceptions of truth that their contemporary society had to teach. These labors were well received, and, in Reform Judaism's two-centuries history, resulted in a stream within the Jewish tradition that has grown, so that today it claims to be the largest Jewish denomination in the United States.

The Reform Movement may be best known for its rejection of what came to be known as Orthodoxy by its outward manifestations of rejection of halachah. After all, the significant changes in ritual practice wrought by the movement are the most visible manifestations of the movement. The historical rejection of head coverings, of kashrut, alterations in the liturgy, the introduction of organ music—these are what one saw (or heard) when observing Reform worship.

But undergirding this public behavior was a commitment to the rationalizing and universalizing thinking that, very roughly speaking, began permeating the intellectual atmosphere of the Jews of western Europe in the early decades of the nineteenth century. through what came to be known as the Wissenschaft des Judentums, was, inter alia, the search for truth, in this case largely the

RABBI PHILIP COHEN (NY83, Ph.D. Brandeis University) is the spiritual leader of Agudas Israel in Hendersonville, North Carolina.

HAVA TIROSH-SAMUELSON (Ph.D. Hebrew University) is Professor of History, Irving and Miriam Lowe Professor of Modern Judaism, and director of Jewish Studies at Arizona State University.

search for historical truth. The work of such historians as Leopold Zunz, Abraham Geiger, and Heinrich Graetz was first and foremost the application of ideas and techniques of historical scholarship that passionately sought to learn what was true of Jewish history, its people, its ideas, and its literature.

Further, out of that context came one way Reform Judaism conceived halachah: that halachah formed a protective husk surrounding the kernel of a profound idea. This husk protected the kernel, that is, a truth, throughout the Jews' trials and tribulations throughout their history. Now, in modern times, the husk could be cast away, revealing the kernel, the truth of the matter, which can now be unpacked, unfettered by its formerly necessary protective shell. Here, too, we see the notion that the Reform Jewish program contains commitment to the truth.

In the European experience, perhaps the clearest example of the Jewish quest for the truth, here quite clearly philosophical truth, may be seen from the very title of Hermann Cohen's last work, *Religion der Vernunft aus den Quellen Judentums* (*Religion of Reason Out of the Sources of Judaism*) (1919).[2] This great work of Jewish philosophy, the culmination of Cohen's literary career, refracts Judaism through the lens of Cohen's own neo-Kantian thought and seeks to reveal Judaism as the icon of reason par excellence. The result is a highly philosophical Judaism, and perhaps the greatest statement of the method and meaning of Liberal Judaism ever put to paper.

In the United States, four documents, platforms written in a period of over a century, seeking to explicate principles of Reform Judaism, also demonstrate that identical commitment to truth. Note as we briefly examine these documents that their points of consideration are incomplete. By its nature, a platform can only hint at the ideas represented; it cannot give details. Yet, as we focus on specific aspects of these documents, we will see an interesting shift when we arrive at the last of them.

The first plank of the first platform, the Pittsburgh Platform (1885) states: "We hold that the modern discoveries of scientific researches in the domain of nature and history are not antagonistic to the doctrines of Judaism, the Bible reflecting the primitive ideas of its own age, and at times clothing its conception of divine Providence and Justice dealing with men in miraculous narratives."[3] It is clear that the authors wish to express their belief in the importance of "scientific researches" that explicate the "primitive ideas" expressed in the Bible. Science, the plank suggests, will be the tool for the maturing of concepts found in embryonic form in the Bible. This idea is crystallized in the sixth plank, where it says: "We recognize in Judaism a progressive religion, ever striving to be in accord with the postulates of reason."[4] Obviously, this brief statement does not articulate what "reason" means. Nevertheless, it can be inferred that "reason" refers to thinking outside of the Jewish tradition that both judges the Jewish tradition and is an epistemological tool that aids in the understanding of Judaism. These tools enable Judaism to be "progressive."

The Columbus Platform (1937) similarly states: "Reform Judaism recognizes the principle of progressive development in religion and consciously applies this principle to spiritual as well as to cultural and social life. Judaism welcomes all truth, whether written in the pages of scripture or deciphered from the records of nature. The new discoveries of science, while replacing the older scientific views underlying our sacred literature, do not conflict with the essential spirit of religion as manifested in the consecration of man's will, heart and mind to the service of God and of humanity."[5] The main idea here is that the progressive (note that word again) nature of Judaism develops through its history. What is the tool that aids that development? "The new discoveries of science," that is to say, the alterations in our view of the world that Jews receive from scientific research. Again, Judaism judges itself and progresses by the truths put forth by universal culture, whatever that means, and however it occurs.

The 1976 Centenary Perspective, written in commemoration of the centenary of Hebrew Union College and the Union of American Hebrew Congregations, says: "It now seems self-evident to most Jews [beyond the Reform Jewish community]: that our tradition should interact with modern culture; that its forms ought to reflect a contemporary esthetic; that its scholarship needs to be conducted by modern, critical methods; and that change has been and must continue to be a fundamental reality in Jewish life."[6] This somewhat triumphalist statement makes the point that Reform Judaism has taught the Jewish world the importance of interacting with modern culture (whenever "modernity" is taking place). And, presumably, because cultures change, Judaism, continually interacting with culture, will be compelled to reevaluate its intellectual assumptions over and over again. This claim is seen to be the case in the past; we have no reason to assume that it will change in the future.

But a curious thing happens when one views the last of these platforms, the Pittsburgh Platform of 1999. The notion of the necessity of interaction between Judaism and culture is nowhere to be seen. Now, analysis of a worldview based on the absence of an idea is fraught with danger. Perhaps the authors took what we have been discussing here until now for granted. Yet a careful reading of this latest platform reveals no interest at all in philosophical concerns. True, it speaks of God, but tends toward describing experience of God rather than thought about God.[7] It speaks, too, of Torah, and mentions the notion of progressive revelation. "We cherish the truths revealed in Torah, God's ongoing revelation to our people and the record of our people's ongoing relationship with God."[8] However, missing throughout the totality of the platform is the concern for what might be called the encounter of Judaism with wider culture that we have seen manifest in its three earlier sisters. Rather, the authors appear to be concerned with introducing a kind of piety that focuses on experience of God and performance of mitzvot at the expense of the intellectual side of the tradition. It would be too much to claim that this last platform reveals an anti-intellectual bias, but its contours clearly do not embrace the intellectual in the proclivities of its predecessors.

This absence may reflect a turn within Reform Judaism away from those deeper intellectual concerns that historically have been part of the Reform self-image and method since its inception in 1810. And, if so, this issue of the *CCAR Journal* may be seen as a call to return to that intellectual attitude. (Note that this "return" is not necessarily a return to any specific view or method; rather, it is an acknowledgment of the assumption that Judaism has always interacted and grown, that is, benefited, in the interaction with external culture, and as such ought to continue.)

Norbert Samuelson has been engaged in the issue of the interaction of Judaism and science for several decades.[9] He has argued that Judaism must pay attention to contemporary science because today science is the arbiter of truth. He goes even further to claim that Judaism will not be able to survive the twenty-first century unless it rethinks itself in light of the truths of science. Not only should Jews become informed about science, they must realize that their beliefs (as expressed, for example, in the liturgy) are based on outdated philosophy and science that must be rethought. (We mention liturgy in particular because it is the context where Jews encounter Jewish theology in their daily life.) Samuelson's recent book, *Jewish Faith and Modern Science: On the Death and Rebirth of Jewish Philosophy* (2009), explores the issues he thinks are important for Jewish philosophers to consider if Judaism is to reflect the highest intellectual perceptions possible.

In this issue of the *CCAR Journal*, Samuelson has contributed a trigger piece that reflects much of his thinking on this matter found in *Jewish Faith and Modern Science* and several other books. The opening essay is followed by two articles that explicitly respond to Samuelson. The rest of the essays were inspired by Samuelson's lead piece or reflect on the issues that he has outlined in his books. What make the essays in this issue unique is that they come from a diverse audience of academics, rabbis, scientists, and educators. In addition, the contributors identify themselves with diverse streams of contemporary Judaism: Reform, Conservative, Reconstructionist, and Orthodox, indicating that the contemporary Jewish need to engage the sciences is not limited to just one branch of Judaism. All Jews today, regardless of affiliation, need to become familiar with contemporary science and become prepared to rethink the Jewish tradition accordingly. A Judaism that is based on outmoded or even false pictures of the universe will not be able to survive.

About a third of the essays in this issue are written by Jewish academics who hold positions in American universities. Whether the positions are located in departments of Religious Studies, programs of Jewish Studies, or Divinity Schools, Judaica scholars today can access the dialogue of science and religion, a particular academic discourse that has been in existence for about four decades. And yet, the field of Jewish Studies has hardly made an effort to become familiar with the discourse on science and religion. In part, this lack of interest reflects the (somewhat accurate) perception that the dialogue of science and religion is particularly Christian because Christianity is a religion that focuses on belief (*doxa*) rather than practice (*praxis*). By contrast, so many tend to think, Judaism is a way of life in which beliefs are secondary in importance to actions. This perception is historically mistaken and theologically inaccurate: Historically Jews have always engaged in thinking as is evident from the creative legacy of Jewish philosophers and theologians especially during the Middle Ages in Spain and Italy and during the modern period in Germany; and theologically the command to reflect on the meaning of God's revelation is at the heart of biblical religion, and Rabbinic Judaism pondered in great depth how to balance reflection (*iyun*) and action (*maaseh*). This proper balance between the theoretical and the practical was itself a topic that was discussed at some length by medieval Jewish philosophers.

Medieval Jewish philosophers, the most famous of whom is Moses Maimonides (d. 1204), illustrate the balance between *theoria* and *praxis* as much as they illustrate the conviction that Judaism must take note of contemporary science. Rethinking Judaism in light of the science of the day is precisely what Jewish philosophers from Rav Saadia Gaon (d. 940) to Rabbi Hasdai Crescas (d. 1410) have done, showing Jews how science is an integral part of Judaism. In fact, science (or "natural philosophy" as it was called in the Middle Ages) was understood to be the inner meaning of the divinely revealed tradition. To be good Jews as far as Maimonides and other Jewish Aristotelians were concerned required the knowledge of science, especially physics and metaphysics. This thinking resulted in a scientifically informed theology.

For various reasons alluded to in Samuelson's essay, the rethinking of Judaism in light of the natural sciences did not take place in the modern period, even though in the early modern period a small number of Jews did become familiar with and immersed in the study of science.[10] In the nineteenth century, when Jews underwent the process of emancipation and social integration, they separated interest in science from Jewish religious commitment, departing from the medieval heritage. Jews who were now able to enter European universities could become famous scientists, but very few of them cared about rethinking the Jewish tradition in light of the science that they generated. During the nineteenth century Jews excelled in the natural sciences and they were even the leaders and founders of several scientific disciplines (e.g., chemistry, microbiology, and medical anthropology).[11] Yet the commitment to science often came at the expense of commitment to traditional Judaism, and thus the growing separation between Judaism and science became common in the modern period to the detriment of Judaism. To the extent that Judaism was impacted by science, it was the social sciences, especially history, that posed the most serious challenge requiring Jewish intellectuals to respond. All forms of Liberal/Progressive Judaism have manifested the impact of academic study of history on their interpretation of Judaism. By contrast, the natural sciences were considered either irrelevant to Judaism or pertained only to the material level that Judaism transcends.

The dissociation of Judaism and science thus impacted both modern Jewish theology as well as modern academic study of Judaism (i.e., Jewish Studies), and not for the best. This issue of the *CCAR Journal* suggests ways in which the rethinking of Judaism in light of the sciences could begin to take place and revive Jewish philosophy, theology, and ethics. The sciences of physics, biology, psychology, neuroscience, anthropology, and ecology, to list just a few, are all relevant to Judaism if we want Judaism to be believable. In agreement with Samuelson's call, this issue argues that it behooves all Jews today to become familiar with these sciences and to think through their implications for Judaism both as a way of life and as a body of truths. There are many ways to undertake this rethinking, and thus these reflections will be undertaken on many levels. Whether one rethinks Judaism in one's own private study, in the classroom, on the pulpit, in oral exchanges, or in academic writing, one simply cannot remain oblivious to what contemporary science has to say about the universe and about human beings.

Two points emerge from this issue's intriguing essays: (a) the centrality of process philosophy/theology for the rethinking of Judaism and (b) the degree to which the dialogue between Judaism and science can and should be informed by a similar dialogue that takes place among Christians. The two points, of course, are related. The process philosophy of Alfred North Whitehead was adopted by Christian theologians such as John B. Cobb and David Ray Griffin in their rethinking of Christianity, resulting in very innovative recasting of traditional beliefs.[12] Indeed dialogue of religion and science has been most robust among Christian thinkers and the discourse has remained largely Christian; very few Jews take part in it. It is quite telling that several of the contributors to this issue were trained in Christian seminaries, universities, and Divinity Schools, and that they actively engage in interfaith work. It is our belief that a closer interaction between Jewish and Christian theologians can only strengthen contemporary Judaism, by introducing novel ways of thinking and framing traditional theological and philosophical problems.

However, the Jewish engagement with contemporary science is not only unidirectional, when science compels Judaism to reinterpret itself. The reverse can also happen when Judaism's insights can inform how the business of science is conducted, how science reflects about its own procedures, and how language is employed in the theory and practice of science. Between Judaism and science there could be a genuine dialogue, but this dialogue will not take place unless Jews (among whom there are many practicing scientists) wish to effect such dialogue rather than keep the two conveniently apart. The participants in this issue hold that the dialogue between Judaism and science is beneficial for the future of Judaism and that it can take place theoretically and practically, even though the task is challenging.

Reform Rabbis, the primary audience of the *CCAR Journal*, could be at the forefront of the dialogue because of the historic commitment of Reform Judaism to reason. Reform rabbis and those sympathetic to the élan of Reform Judaism should find the contents of this issue of great interest. We have seen that this concern is an ongoing one in the history of the intellectual leadership of the movement, even if, lately, that interest seems to have diminished. We hope that these articles will spur a renewed concern in that interest and its purpose. To those wishing to enter the field of science and religion and engage in greater depth in the discourse on Judaism and science, we append a select bibliography to help direct one's entry into this conversation. If this issue succeeds in its goal, even modestly, then perhaps we can see a return within our own Reform tradition to that particular search for meaning.

Notes

1. Jacob Marcus, *Israel Jacobson: The Father of the Reform Movement in Judaism* (Cincinnati: Hebrew Union College, 1972.
2. Hermann Cohen, *Religion der Vernunft aus den Quellen Judentums* (Leipzig, 1919). English Translation: *Religion of Reason Out of the Sources of Judaism*, 2nd ed., trans. Simon Kaplan (Atlanta: Scholars Press, 1995).
3. http://ccarnet.org/Articles/index.cfm?id=39&pge_prg_id=4687&pge_id=1656.
4. Ibid.
5. http://ccarnet.org/Articles/index.cfm?id=40&pge_prg_id=4687&pge_ id=1656.

6. http://ccarnet.org/Articles/index.cfm?id=41&pge_prg_id=4687&pge_id= 1656.
7. "We regard with reverence all of God's creation and recognize our human responsibility for its preservation and protection. We encounter God's presence in moments of awe and wonder, in acts of justice and compassion, in loving relationships and in the experiences of everyday life." http://ccarnet.org/Articles/index.cfm?id=44&pge_prg_id=4687&pge_id=1656.
8. http://ccarnet.org/Articles/index.cfm?id=44&pge_prg_id=4687&pge_id =1656.
9 See Norbert M. Samuelson, ed., *Creation and the End of Days: Judaism and Scientific Cosmology* (Lanham, MD: University Press of America, 1986); *The First Seven Days: A Philosophical Commentary on the Creation of Genesis* (Atlanta: Scholars Press, 1992); *Judaism and the Doctrine of Creation* (Cambridge: Cambridge University Press, 1994); *Revelation and the God of Israel* (Cambridge: Cambridge University Press, 2002); *Jewish Faith and Modern Science: The Death and Rebirth of Jewish Philosophy* (Lanham, MD: Rowman and Littlefield, 2009).
10. See David Ruderman, *Jewish Thought and Scientific Discoveries in the Early Modern Period* (New Haven: Yale University Press, 1995).
11. Ulrich Charpa and Ute Deichman, eds., *Jews and Sciences in German Contexts* (Tübingen: Mohr Siebeck, 2007).
12. Consult John B. Cobb and David Ray Griffin, *Process Theology: An Introductory Exposition* (Philadelphia: Westminster Press, 1976); John B. Cobb, *A Christian Natural Theology: Based on the Thought of Alfred North Whitehead* (Louisvile: Westminster John Knox Press, 2007 [1966]); *Process Theology as Political Theology* (Manchester: Manchester University Press; Philadelphia: Westminster Press, 1982).

Part I: Responding to Norbert Samuelson

The Challenges of the Modern Sciences for Jewish Faith

Norbert M. Samuelson

A. The Problem

The Hebrew Scriptures present written evidence for what constitutes at least the intellectual content of the culture of those early Jewish people who were the immediate precursors of Rabbinic Jewish civilization. Of course, this civilization did not come into being out of nothing. It has historical, intellectual, and cultural precursors out of which it developed. Solely for the sake of simplification, we begin with this collection of texts as a complete document irrespective of when this codification takes place. Whenever that occurred, the Hebrew Bible describes in broad and usually general terms what were the accepted, maybe even canonical, beliefs of those Judeans who recognized that the new civilization of (for a word) Hellenism was gaining (or possibly already had gained) hegemony over their biblical, Hebrew civilization. Those Judeans recognized that Hellenistic culture contained challenges to biblical culture that, if allowed to pass without address, threatened to destroy Judea, not by physical force but intellectual domination. In this case the challenge was not primarily from armies but from the persuasiveness of Greco-Roman understandings of the nature of the cosmos and everything in it.

The collected texts of at least the *Tannaim* express the attempt of these earliest rabbis to construct a new understanding of the Hebrew Scriptures. This new understanding would enable a

NORBERT M. SAMUELSON (C62, Ph.D. Indiana University) is Harold and Jean Grossman Professor of Jewish Philosophy at Arizona State University.

reconstructed form of biblical faith to make sense out of all the postbiblical changes in history, nature, and in thought about history and nature. These changes in themselves threatened the credibility of the faith put forward by the authors and/or editors of the Hebrew Scriptures. In a word, this is how I understand the significance of the development of Rabbinic philosophy in the corpus of at least tannaitic texts in what had become for subsequent generations of Jews canonical expressions of Jewish faith.

I am not interested in debating here whether or not it is correct to call early Rabbinic writings "philosophy." Certainly it has minimal resemblance to the kind of writings that today, especially in the world of English-language speakers and thinkers, are called "philosophy." However, what British and American academic departments call "philosophy" is not the only understanding of the term. In even this Eurocentric subdivision of Western civilization, it has not been the dominant understanding of what is philosophy, and possibly (in my case I can say hopefully) will not continue to be the dominant understanding of what is philosophy for much longer. For me "philosophy" includes all attempts to make sense out of everything in the most general terms, especially to make sense out of how we human beings locate ourselves in the universe relative to everything else in it. This usage minimally includes other human beings and life forms with whom we interact, all of our physical surroundings both on this planet and in the cosmos, and the entire history of everything insofar as we can understand it, from its temporal or atemporal origins if it has any to its temporal or atemporal ends (again) if it has any.

On this very broad definition of "philosophy" there is nothing special about Jewish philosophy except the specificity of the subject term in its description. Jewish philosophy differs in principle from general philosophy only in the range of the term "we" in the above description. Jewish philosophers in this context attempt to "make sense out of how we" Jews (rather than "human beings" in general) "locate ourselves in the universe relative to everything else in it." Only the subject term in Jewish philosophy is more restricted than the subject term in general philosophy. The rest of the sentence, including the grammatical object related to the grammatical subject, is the same. Jewish philosophy is not reflection solely on the Jewish people and their history. Rather, from the particularistic perspective of the Jewish people with their particular cultural inheritance of texts called "Rabbinic" and "Jewish," attempts to understand as well as it can all of inanimate and animate life in a historical perspective. For the moment let's leave aside the question of what makes this kind of philosophy "Jewish"; let's focus rather on what makes it "philosophy," for with this usage of the term there may today be more academic research and reflection relevant to preserving and/or evolving Jewish faith in schools of the physical sciences (especially in physical cosmology) and the life sciences (especially in evolutionary biology) than there is in contemporary departments of philosophy where the focus of critical attention is increasingly on certain kinds of cognitive use of human language.

The challenges to Jewish faith are not limited exclusively to the encounter between Greco-Roman civilization and the philosophy of the Hebrew Scriptures. As Mordecai Kaplan argued almost a century ago,[1] every encounter of the Jewish people with a new challenging culture has produced major "reforms" in what this people both think and do, and these "reconstructions" probably were critical for it to continue to survive. Briefly, the Jewish people will not and cannot survive solely by military, political, social, and/or economic force. It will survive ultimately because now as in the past it confronted challenges, both ethical (with respect to practice) and intellectual (with respect to belief), that it had to meet and ultimately succeeded in meeting. The Jewish people has found human resources, Jewish philosophers if you will, who in a variety of ways have exhibited sufficient creativity as well as intelligence, to respond with moral and intellectual integrity, and those responses have both preserved what was best in previous Jewish philosophy, providing the basis for what would become a new (hopefully improved) Jewish philosophy (or even philosophies) for the following generations. Thus a new culture or even cultures of the Jewish people have continually emerged.

That has been true in the past, but it is not clear that this evolution of Jewish philosophy is happening today. I argue that the lack of development constitutes a very subtle but nonetheless real threat to the continued survival of the Jewish people, or at least the survival of Judaism as the cultural structure through which the Jewish people express their faith.

Why modern Jewry has failed to reform or reconstruct its philosophy in terms of the challenges from modern Western science is an important question that goes beyond what I am trying to do in this paper. It has to do with the evolution of the physical sciences and the humanistic academic disciplines since the nineteenth century to our day, especially within the institution of the modern university. The sciences and the humanities have evolved in increasingly radically different directions within an institution that itself has evolved simultaneously in contradictory directions—both as the sole institution for purely intellectual speculative activity and in its growing dependence with democratization on capitalistic pragmatic activity. The failure to reform or reconstruct Jewish philosophy has to do with decisions by emancipated Western Jews during the nineteenth century to focus their confrontation with the dominant Western culture on issues that belong to the humanities rather than on challenges that emerge from the sciences. Other factors are also relevant to this complex story, but discussing them goes beyond the topic of this paper. Regardless of the causes, what is clear is that the modern sciences raise serious challenges to continued belief in the traditional and liberal philosophies of Judaism, that contemporary Jewish philosophers are minimally informed of what those challenges are, and consequently that perhaps for the first time in Jewish history committed Jewish thinkers are not succeeding in confronting and dealing with the major challenges of the modern sciences to Jewish faith.

My recently published book *Jewish Faith and Modern Science* addresses this problem.[2] The purpose of the book is not to respond to the challenges, although the second half of the book offers a general strategy for such response. Rather, the primary goal of the book is to call attention to the threat in the hope that raised consciousness in Jewish intellectual circles will lead to a serious encounter of Jewish thinkers with the physical and biological sciences comparable to the rich philosophically informed body of Jewish responses to challenges in modern Western (notably French and German) humanist-directed philosophy in the last quarter of the twentieth century.

B. The Challenges

Following the topology proposed by Franz Rosenzweig in his *Star of Redemption*,[3] questions about Jewish faith center at the most general level on three topics—creation, revelation, and redemption. I want here to summarize my perception of the challenges to Rabbinic faith from the modern sciences around these same three topics. All three are statements about divine relations, viz, how God relates to the cosmos at its origin (creation), to the Jewish people in history (Torah, or Mosaic revelation), and to both the cosmos and everything within it with a focus on its end (redemption and the end of days).

Here are the challenges to Judaism that emerge from the sciences:

A. Issues with Creation

1. From the history and archeology of the ancient Near East: Are academic bible scholars better trained than rabbis to (a) say what the Bible means and (b) serve as moral guides for our lives? Are Bible scholars wiser than rabbis?
2. From quantum mechanics: (a) The moral value of individuals is questionable in God's physical universe. (b) The existential value of individuals also is questionable. Both problems significantly undercut the rationale for a liberal Judaism.
3. From astronomy: Since constellations are not real, how does the God of the universe relate to earthbound creatures? From microbiology and microphysics: How does God govern particles?
4. From relativity physics: What is the relation of God to space-time given that space and time are inseparable?
5. From general physics: What is the soul? Is it a form of energy or is it something spiritual or is it something else?
6. What would a cosmology look like that fits the data of physics and astronomy but assigns reality to morality in the physical universe? Where in the modern conception of the universe is there room for quality and purpose as physically real?
7. Ignorance of physics results in inadequate views of the universe in a number of respects: The universe of humanists and other Jewish philosophers (a) is too small and too shallow (too small from the perspective of the cosmos and too shallow from the perspective of the microcosmos), (b) can make no sense out of the notion of purpose in our purely mechanical/mathematical world view, and (c) cannot account for all changes that occur within our universe.

8. Our universe is too old and human existence is too brief for humanity to provide the reason for the existence of the universe. If we give up this humanist assumption, how can we understand why God created the universe?
9. Especially in light of the principle of inertia, is there a good reason to posit a creator of the universe?
10. Jewish thinking needs to rethink ontological monism and negative theology. For guidance in how to rethink these subjects, models can be adapted from the metaphysics of both Alfred N. Whitehead and Franz Rosenzweig.

B. Issues with Redemption

11. The challenge of standard neo-Darwinism to claim that reality/nature exhibits purpose and design.
12. The need to move beyond the dogma that seeing is believing to a new affirmation of the reality of God.
13. The need to move beyond mind-body dualism to a new monism.
14. The need to move beyond mechanistic science to a philosophy of the soul in terms of grounds for analysis of objective morality and of redemption.
15. The need to move beyond life and death absolutes to redefine humanity in terms of a conception of an asymptotic end of worshiping God.
16. The need to rethink the commitment to preserving human nature and restricting moral responsibility exclusively to human life forms.
17. Understanding halachah more in the modes of Eastern religions as a "way" and less in the modes of Western religions as a "law." Beyond all the confusion of the mostly unintelligible rhetoric of Jewish theologians, this distinction is the bottom-line difference between liberal and traditional Judaism.
18. When and how does life begin and end?
19. What does it mean to be "human"? When do chemical reactions become living things? When do living things become human beings?
20. What role does and should capitalism play in decisions about living and dying?

C. Issues with Revelation

21. Should scholars rewrite Jewish history?
22. Is Judaism "philosophy"?
23. Are the Hebrew Scriptures a "fraud"?
24. Are the Hebrew Scriptures "pious"?
25. Are the Hebrew Scriptures "history"?
26. Are the Hebrew Scriptures "authoritative"?

The most familiar to students of Jewish thought are the issues concerning revelation. Question 21 has been discussed ever since the study of Jewish history emerged in Germany almost two centuries ago as a form of what we call *Wissenschaft*, viz, *Wissenschaft des Judentums*, which here means academic discipline rather than "science" since the modern study of history properly belongs under the academic umbrella of the humanities rather than of the sciences. Question 22, Is Judaism "philosophy"? has already been dealt with above. Finally questions 23–26 all have to do with (particularly) German source-critical approaches to the study of Bible, which properly belong to the disciplines of history and text studies, and both of these, like history, are humanities rather than sciences.

It is not that the issues revolving around revelation are not critical. Quite the contrary. Again no viable commitment to some form of Jewish faith is maintainable that does not deal with these questions.[4] But in at least this case the issues are well known to anyone interested in modern Jewish thought, and there already exists a long list (too long for this paper) of important and relevant efforts by Jewish thinkers (notably by Bible scholars and Jewish theologians) to respond. Instead my attention will be on the first two classifications—creation and redemption—and, since it is too much to discuss all of these points in a single paper, I will here focus only on one. My example will be on Question 9. Especially in light of the principle of inertia, is there a good reason to posit a creator of the universe? I choose it because I think of all the issues raised, its centrality is the least transparent of all the claimed challenges on the list.

C. An Example: The Scientific Principle of Inertia and the Rabbinic Doctrine of Creation

I want to make two points. First, demonstrations in classical (i.e., medieval) Jewish philosophy of the central claims that the purported creator of the universe exists, is one, and is incorporeal (henceforth referred for brevity as "God") presupposes a Platonized-Aristotelianized general understanding of physics and astronomy. Second, these cited scientific premises are inconsistent with central claims in modern (by which I mean post-Newtonian) physics and astronomy. The proper conclusions from the demonstration are the following: One, it is not that the classic proofs are logically invalid; it is rather that their claims are not absolutely valid but valid only within certain ways of conceiving reality scientifically. Two, the first conclusion entails that theology presupposes the physical sciences, so that theological claims are always relative to scientific claims. Hence, three, theology or more generally religious belief presupposes coming to terms with the fundamental claims of the physical sciences.

In my *Revelation and the God of Israel*, I have a section called "The Philosophy of Religion—Proofs that God Exists."[5] There I have argued for this general thesis. Here I want to offer a more detailed demonstration of only a single, although critical, claim in the general argument put forth in the book. I will look specifically at those scientific claims put forth by Maimonides in the *Guide of the Perplexed* as premises for his demonstrations of God,[6] which conflict with the Newtonian principle of inertia in modern physics. I want to tease out the possible consequences for contemporary Jewish theology in this apparent conflict.

In the introduction to the second part of the *Guide*,[7] Maimonides presents twenty-six premises, some of which clearly conflict with the principle of inertia. These are the following: (17) "Everything that is in motion has of necessity a mover."[8] (18) "Everything that passes from potentiality to actuality has something other than itself that causes it to pass, and this cause is of necessity outside that thing."[9] And finally, (25) "The principles of an individual compound substance are matter and form...with regard to this, everything that it is necessary to explain has already been explained. The text of the words of Aristotle is: 'Matter does not move itself.'"[10] Pines cites Aristotle's *Metaphysics* xii.6.1071b29–30 for this reference and comments "The quotation is accurate."

In a word every action by an agent and every state of affairs for a subject requires an explanation, in contrast to the situation in modern physics where no explanation is needed for something to be what or how it is; only to change from being to becoming something else that calls for a cause. Aristotle limits the lack of need for explanation for actually being in some way solely to a kind of being called "necessary." With every other kind of being that is not necessary, there is a need for explanation, because anything that (in Aristotelian language) becomes actual had first to be potential, and as potential required something to cause it to change from being potential to becoming actual. However, in modern Newtonian and post-Newtonian physics the entire conceptual apparatus of potentiality and actuality, including the ontological categories of form and matter, are rejected. Instead, all being is actual being or no being at all, and the kind of things that actually exist are material and not formal.

Newton's first law in his *The Principia: Mathematical Principles of Natural Philosophy* reads as follows: "Every body perseveres in its state of being at rest or of moving uniformity straight forward, except insofar as it is compelled to change its state by forces impressed."[11] I. Bernard Cohen maintains that this law follows immediately from definitions 3 and 4,[12] which state as follows: (Definition 3): "Inherent force of matter is the power of resisting by which every body, so far as it is able, perseveres in its state either of resting or of moving uniformly straight forward"[13] and (Definition 4): "Impressed force is the action exerted on a body to change its state either of resting or of moving uniformly straight ahead."[14] About his third definition Newton elaborates, saying "Because of the inertia of matter, every body is only with difficulty put out of its state either of resting or of moving,"[15] and further, "For a body perseveres in any new state solely by the force of inertia." Hence, clearly the terms "inherent force" and "impressed force" already contain within their meaning the law of inertia. Translated into modern scientific, more mathematical language, what this principle or "law" expresses is the judgment that "a body in uniform motion remains in uniform motion, and a body at rest remains at rest, unless acted on by a nonzero net force."[16] In other words, whatever is true of the state of a physical thing, be it rest or motion or anything else for that matter, it will persist in that state unless some physical thing else causes it to change.

Given this central change in physics, none of Maimonides' listed proofs (what he calls "speculations") of God work. Maimonides presents four distinct arguments for God, all of which were adopted almost word for word by Thomas Aquinas in his demonstrations of God's existence in his *Summa Theologica*,[17] and all of them explicitly or implicitly rest on our listed three premises (numbers 17, 18, and 25). The first proof, which is an argument for God as a first cosmic "mover," explicitly invokes premise 17.[18] The second proof, which is an argument for the causal priority of simplicity over complexity, explicitly names no premises. In contrast, the third proof, which is an argument for the causal priority of necessity over contingency does list premises, namely 19–22,[19] but not the three that concern us. Similarly, the fourth proof, which is an argument for the priority of actuality over potentiality, also lists three premises, namely numbers 23, 24, and 16,[20] but not the three that concern us. Still, even though Maimonides mentioned only one of the three (the seventeenth) by name, and he mentions it only with reference to his first of the four arguments, it is clear from his introduction to this discussion that he intended all three premises to be precisely that, premises, that is, assumptions upon which his four arguments for God depend.[21]

Implicitly, even if not explicitly, an argument can be made that all of Maimonides' arguments in some sense or another presuppose what Maimonides and other Aristotelian philosophers are saying about the nature of explanation that these listed premises assert. Put in nontechnical terms, nothing comes from nothing. Yet, if a set of causes produces effects that are not entailed in the nature of the causes themselves, then the effects can be said to come from nothing. Hence, it does not seem reasonable that something is moving for no reason whatsoever (contrary to premise 17), for otherwise from where does the motion come? Similarly, potentiality is really not in itself anything at all, for what it is depends both on the something actual from which it originates and the something else actual into which it terminates. Hence, any potentiality presupposes something else actual as having at least logical if not causal priority (premise 18). Finally, as Aristotelian physics defines its categories of form and matter, where form is the principle that accounts for what a thing is while matter is the principle that accounts for the temporal-spatial fact that it is, anything that can be materialized must be in some sense informed (premise 25), from nothing can nothing become real, and only some thing can be something.

Yet this Newtonian principle of the new physics overturns past common sense no less radically than the seventeenth century's new cosmology of heliocentrism overturned the geocentrism of the premoderns. In the new physics no explanation is needed for why something is what it is; prima facie all things merely happen to be what they are; the ruling principle of the state of affairs in nature is chance—an implication of modern science that took two centuries of reflection on Newton's revolutionary conception of the physical world to become explicit. Rather, explanation is needed only for a change from any preexisting state to a new state, contrary to the common sense of the pre-Newtonians whose sense dictated the necessary existence, oneness, and incorporeality of their deity.

D. Conclusion

Given this explication of the principle of inertia, let's turn to Question 9 listed above. Especially in light of the principle of inertia, is there a good reason to posit a creator of the universe? How should or may contemporary thinkers respond to the implicit challenge entailed by the above listed ninth issue between modern physics and the tradition Jewish theological commitment to belief in the God of Israel as the creator of the cosmos and everything in it? The religious studies scholar Ian Barbour has argued that there are four possible ways that apparent conflicts between the claims of contemporary sciences and contemporary religions can be handled. [22] The four types of relations are: "conflict," "independence," "dialogue," and "integration." John Hedley Brooke has modified Barbour's claim, saying that usually all four of Barbour's ways are not distinct elements but are joined together in any attempted conceptual encounter with these apparent contraries .[23] For example, let us examine the apparent conflict between the truth claims of post-Newtonian physics that origins in themselves are due to chance and require no explanation to be intelligible and the Rabbinic fundamental or "root" principle (*ikar*) that the universe both has and conceptually requires a creator. Both claims are methodologically independent of each other in the minimal sense that it is solely the business of scientists to determine what they within their disciplines mean by "explanation," as it is solely the business of rabbis to determine what they mean when they say that God is the creator of the universe. Furthermore, this assertion about the proper domains of the sciences and of Rabbinic theology is for Judaism a foundational principle.

However, both claims are made about the same reality, viz., this physical universe, and some dialogue is required by serious thinking Jews (both with each other and within their own thinking) on what a reality looks like about which both claims can be made. It is not sufficient to simply say "science speaks about one kind of universe whereas Judaism speaks about another kind of the universe." If Judaism is to be a reasonable faith for committed Jews who choose not to withdraw from physical reality, Rabbinic thought may not divorce itself from the world of the physical any more than the physical world governed by the laws of physics can be treated as indifferent to Rabbinic law and thought. In the end the initial conflict must be resolved through dialogue in an integrated view of total reality, a reality that takes the laws of the physical sciences (or, the Torah) no less seriously than it takes the laws of the Torah (or, the physical sciences).

One possible solution is to conceive of all of reality in the way that Plato did when he wrote the *Timaeus*.[24] There the cosmos is imagined as a smooth spherical surface that reflects objects of light above it. The sphere is physical space; the objects reflected on the sphere are our physical universe; and the points of light reflected are the deities. As used by the medieval Jewish philosophers and mystics, there is only one point of light (viz., the God of Israel), and the rest of reality is simply a reflection of that single point whose plurality and diversity is attributable not to its source but to the peculiar nature of the reflecting surface. Note that on this model the universe may be said to have an origin, but the origin is not subject to time, which means that it does not reflect any kind of claim that is contrary to the physical law of inertia. However, note furthermore that on this model our world (the reflections) are appearances that have no distinctive ontological status in a universe that contains only two realities—space (the mirror) and God (the point of light)—and of the two it is debatable which has positive being (both, either, or neither), for it could be reasonably maintained (a) that the mirror is space, and space is where beings are located, but space itself is not a being, or (b) that God is here understood as a point, a point is a circle (in two dimensions) or a globe (in three or more dimensions) whose radius is either zero or functionally zero (i.e., infinitesimal), and a circular object whose radius is zero is itself nothing at all.

Plato's *Timaeus* is not the only way that we may and even have imaged a cosmos in which God functions as an origin independent of any notion of efficient temporal cause. The most commonly used world view today is that of Alfred North Whitehead in his *Process and Reality.*[25] Here all of temporal-spatial reality is imaged as a plurality of "actual entities" that have mental and physical aspects but are in themselves neither. Rather they are more "occasions," that is, events or (in the language of modern logic) "states of affairs" that flow in space through time from one occasion into another. Here reality is imagined somewhat as it appears through a microscope—as a sea of fluid beings constantly flowing past, through, and into each other, ultimately coalescing to form new actual entities. The things in the sea and the sea itself together constitute a living, changing being in which everything else is fluid. This fluidity is conceived in terms of a dynamic flow, a flow that exhibits direction but no starting point or ending point. There is no beginning or end in any finite temporal sense, but the flow is conceived in terms of a nontemporal origin and a nontemporal end. That origin is described as containing the seemingly infinite potential of everything that the actual entities may become throughout the flow of physical and mental reality. Conversely the end is described as what it is that everything will coalesce to become when every potentiality is exhausted and reality reaches the idealized, asymptotic end towards which everything is moving. However this end is ideal and not real (to use the mathematical language of Hermann Cohen). It is an end that directs an infinite flow, but the end itself is finite. It functions eternally as an end or ideal (again in Hermann Cohen's language) that is beyond time. Whitehead calls this infinite repository of an idealized universe at its origin "the primordial nature of God," and the idealized universe at its end "the consequent nature of God." Note that, consistent with the law of inertia, what is real (as opposed to ideal) is the directed motion of transitory beings from an infinitely remote past towards an equally infinitely remote future.

I have intentionally built into the above description of Whitehead references to the reasoned cosmic picture of Hermann Cohen, even though I have no basis to believe that either philosopher was familiar with the other. I do so to call attention to the similarity between the envisioned cosmos of Whitehead and its counterpart in Cohen's disciple, Franz Rosenzweig.[26] In his *Star of Redemption,* Rosenzweig images the created world of physical objects as an unending flow of potential nothings changing continuously towards a final end of becoming some-things, an end in a "kingdom of God" where every potentiality will be realized and come together as a single light that replaces all darkness in which, in the words of traditional Jewish liturgy, "on that day the Lord will be one and his name will be one." Rosenzweig images this world as a spatial domain filled with darkness where emerging some-things fill, and thereby enlighten, the empty space. Within the space of this world the emergent some-things are animate and inanimate; the animate beings are human and nonhuman, and the human beings are pagans, Christians, and Jews. In Rosenzweig's conception of the divine kingdom at the end of everything (beyond the traditional Rabbinic "end of days") Rosenzweig images the disappearance of everything into a single universal light. Following Maimonides' negative theology, Rosenzweig tells us that God by definition is not anything that is, so that each thing that becomes something defines God by God not being him/her/it. In the end God is fully defined by a fully emerging universe that is not God, but because this plenitude of light is all that is, at this final asymptotic end, there no longer is any distinction between God and the world.

The parallels between Rosenzweig's Cohenian conception of the cosmos and Whitehead's seem to me to be obvious, and the source of the identity is not any shared historical influence, but shared traditions of Western religion and modern science, which, in both cases, are directed towards integrating the biblical religious traditions of textual commentary with seemingly conflicting modern Western scientific claims, the most important of which (for our present purposes) being Newton's first law of motion, the principle of inertia.

What this discussion of the seeming but no more than apparent contradiction between the modern physical principle of inertia and the traditional Rabbinic principle of divine creation illustrates is how a creative religious thinker of the quality of Rosenzweig engaged modern science with sophisticated religious faith. Despite the many attempts by contemporary commentators on his writings to the contrary, Rosenzweig was not an anti-rationalist who claimed the truth of Judaism despite reason. On the contrary, while he affirmed that the domain of revealed belief transcends the domain of human scientific and philosophic knowledge, a proper interpretation of the former did not and could not contradict a legitimate application of the latter. Both faith and reason had significant feature in the perceived—though false—compatibility of post-medieval Judaism and modern science: the absence, for the Jew, of a conflict between his or her understanding of the Genesis account of creation and the evidence of science, has misled us into believing that the fundamentally important Jewish posit of a purposeful and divinely authored, created universe is consistent with the findings of the contemporary sciences of astrophysics, psychology, and evolution.

In several of his books, Samuelson traces the intellectual history of the Jewish people as it spans the period from the closing of the biblical canon through the dawning of modernity. He speaks of the survival of the Jewish people—and indeed the persistence of Judaism itself—as achieved in a great measure by dint of the capacity of the Jewish people to adapt its religious ideas and practices to the exigencies of various historical situations, and the capacity of Judaism itself to adapt to its historical setting by adopting much from the intellectual climate within which it finds itself. It has historically been of the nature of Judaism to change and develop in response to the influences that surround, assimilating the intellectual material proffered by other cultures, rather than becoming assimilated to the surrounding cultures themselves. The demonstrated dynamic ability of Judaism to adapt is cited by Samuelson as a primary means of—rather than a threat to—Jewish survival, and it is this adaptation that, he argues, is needed more than ever now, in order that the world view represented by quantum physics and the other natural sciences does not come to render Judaism either irrelevant or unbelievable to the modern Jew. If Judaism is to survive in the modern world, it must find a way of adapting its core religious claims and outlook to the demands of contemporary scientific thinking.

My criticism of Samuelson's approach will focus on two distinct but related points. First, when Samuelson uses imprecise and unassuming expressions such as "taking account of" and "coming to terms with,"[3] he moves from arguing that the worldview of modern science represents at least an apparent contradiction in the religious life of the thinking Jew today to the assertion that our Jewish philosophy and theology must ontologically be committed to the worldview of quantum physics. In essence, Samuelson argues that science must become Judaism's metaphysic. In technical terms, Samuelson affirms scientific realism, contending that

Judaism's survival depends on its acceptance of quantum physics *as an ontology*. While this is, to be sure, an arguable position, Samuelson nowhere argues for it, and appears unaware of the ongoing realism/antirealism debate in both scientific circles and within the philosophy of science. It remains unclear that there is sufficient warrant for the acceptance of quantum physics as ontology (and in any case, Samuelson's argument nowhere aims to provide such a warrant), and it is equally unclear that accepting science as ontology is either the only or even the best way to "take account of" modern science in our Jewish thinking.

While Samuelson indeed points to a timely issue in his location of the incompatibility of reality as scientifically construed and reality as envisioned in Jewish religiosity, his assumption that the worldview of contemporary science must be accepted as a metaphysic or ontology is, I contend, an assumption rather than an argument. It is an assumption in need of justification, and it is an assumption with which I, ultimately, will disagree. It is not, I submit, necessary that we understand the quantum worldview ontologically in order to develop a Judaism that is equipped to handle the world in which we live.

Second, Samuelson's argument for a science-compatible new form of Jewish thought is based on the premise that Judaism must or should survive.[4] Again, the wording sounds innocuous: After all, we can assume that the majority of readers of a book on Jewish thought will be in favor of the survival of Judaism. Samuelson's project is mobilized by means of this prima facie convincing assumption, and it is an assumption that has deep emotional appeal. But once again, Samuelson's argument is established by means of equivocation, or at least by a serious ambiguity in terminology. Since he maintains that in order to survive, Judaism must be rendered *true* (i.e., consonant with the truth taught by science), it would seem indeed that truth and Judaism (or at least, truth and Jewish thought) are in some important way connected to each other. Judaism represents something beyond mere culture; it is more than a phenomenon of sociological concern: Judaism has something to do with ideas and truth claims.

However, Samuelson seems unprepared to say that Judaism "is true," either in the sense that it already articulates the truth about the world or at least expresses basic central principles or stands for an orientation that represents a truth that can genuinely be reframed so as to express that inherent basic truth in terms that are relevant to the contemporary scientific understanding of the world. On the contrary, it sounds as if Samuelson is in favor of a project that would *render* Judaism true (i.e., bring it from its current state of untruth into a state of truth by means of replacing even the entirety of its fundamental principles with those of modern science). Thus the question arises as to just why, for Samuelson, Judaism must survive. He does not claim that it must survive *because* it is true, but rather that we might well have to *make it* true so that it *can* survive. Again, if Judaism at its core represents a claim to truth, and (upon Samuelson's criteria) that claim turns out to be false, for what reason should we hold its survival to be of value? If its value is but that of a culture and its folkways, there is no clear urgency to rendering its worldview true (that archaic worldview would be, upon such a model, but an instance of folklore).

Similarly, if Judaism is no mere culture, but a culture based on a truth claim, then the wholesale replacement of its core principles with new "true" ones is the mere investing of science itself with the honorific appellation "Judaism." If, however, we mean to indicate that there is a basic truth in Judaism that can be glimpsed beneath its articulations in outdated theological and scientific language, our task could be construed as a rescue operation—the liberation of Jewish truth from its marriage to archaic theology and its recasting in terms that express its *true meaning* and free it from its apparent contradiction with current knowledge. It is not evident, however, that Samuelson affirms any such decipherable kernels of truth in Judaism, remaining instead silent on the question of whether truth is in Judaism already there to be found, and entirely vague as to the reason why it must be given a truth content if it in fact lacks one. In the end, his glossing over the question of the relation of Judaism and truth leads to a vexing ambiguity regarding the rationale behind his drive to perpetuate Judaism and even concerning the nature of Judaism itself.

Let us begin with consideration of the relation of Judaism and truth as it appears in Samuelson's project. There seem to be two distinct questions at issue, which in Samuelson's assessment are either complementary or simply identical. That is, Judaism's survival of the challenges posed by its encounter with alien cultures, its adaptation to some of the influences of these cultures, and its consequent evolution to its present form, seem to be understood by Samuelson primarily (if not exclusively) in terms of the *sociological* and *pragmatic* concerns presented by the facts of history. We should adapt so as to survive. Yet, the question remains unasked as to whether there is a standard inherent in Judaism itself by which can be measured the acceptability of an idea for adoption by Judaism: Does survival demand the adoption of any idea whatsoever and Judaism's adaptation to any and all intellectual influences? The goal of the survival of the Jewish people qua a *people* is here framed without sufficient reference to the truth of the fundamental beliefs involved or in the meaning of calling that people's worldview "Jewish." It would seem that, in Samuelson's view, Jewish simply is as Jewish does—without reference to any truth that might be inherent in the notion of Judaism itself, as at least a basic orientation toward the universe, reality, and Deity (the latter to be understood in at least a minimal sense of the word). Skipping over the contentious question posed by the existence of the modern ultra-secularist atheistic Jew (as this issue falls well beyond the scope of the present discussion), we remain well within the bounds of reason to question the coherence of a notion of a Judaism that, as a matter of intellectual commitment, either dispenses altogether with reference to (some conception of) the Almighty or so equates God with nature as to reduce all mention of the divine to the subject matter of quantum mechanics.

Samuelson fails to distinguish among the types of reasons one might invoke for the desirability of the survival of Judaism. In so doing, he makes an implicit appeal to the probable emotional disposition of his intended reader (the vast majority of whom, we can reasonably speculate, will themselves be liberal Jews): Of course we want Judaism to survive in the twenty-first century (we might legitimately paraphrase); the question is purely that of by which means we might hope to make this happen. He in essence assumes that the reader is disposed positively toward the goal of securing the continued survival of Judaism, without reference to the reason for this disposition. Yet, as we recall that it is with matters of truth and falsity that science aims to deal, the tacit appeal made in these texts to our personal (or collective) desire to see our (Jewish) mode of living perpetuated is less than legitimate. I take it for granted that as Jews we (hopefully!) desire the continuation of Judaism and likewise desire to aid in its continuation. Yet short of a wholesale reduction of Judaism to culture and its tenets and practices (however these have changed and been manifested) to mere arbitrary preferences, there must be a truth claim of some kind at the heart of Judaism that it is our concern, so to speak, to translate into language that is in conformity with the contemporary world of lived social and epistemological reality. Assuming, against Mordecai Kaplan, that Judaism is inherently something more than just a culture or a civilization, we must not be content to replace the beating heart of its intellectual standpoint. If Judaism is such a standpoint—that is, if there is indeed a truth claim that is integral to Judaism—then it is this truth claim that must be measured against the truth claim of the scientific worldview and either be found acceptable (if in accordance with it) or unacceptable (if it contradicts what Samuelson avers is the best knowledge of the universe at our disposal).

I suggest that we consider the following questions in our examination of Samuelson's proposed method of reconciling Judaism and science: Is there a basic principle underlying the Jewish "stance" toward reality that must be recognized as essential to it? If that principle weighs unfavorably against the basic assumptions of science, does that invalidate its claim to truth? Is the task of the modern Jewish thinker that of replacing the core principles and ideas of Judaism with notions consistent (or identical) with science or that of translating Judaism's core principles into conceptual language that is meaningful within the context of the contemporary lived/social reality? Is the notion of the survival of Judaism solely that of the survival of the Jewish "civilization" (or culture), or does it necessarily also integrally involve the survival of a core principle or principles of belief or attitude toward reality? That is, does Judaism integrally involve a truth claim, or is it in reality "really" a sociological (cultural) designation alone, such as being Irish, Italian, or from Brooklyn? Lastly, does it make sense to continue to call such a body of thought "Jewish" if we have replaced the traditional core principles of Judaism with the principles of a science in contradiction with them?

While not providing a developed philosophical position (i.e., a full Jewish philosophy that is informed by contemporary natural science), Samuelson strives to establish a framework within which, he argues, all valid Jewish thinking on the subject should proceed. He endeavors to sketch a direction through which we might take seriously the claims of modern science while at the same time remaking Jewish belief so as to preserve (or create) the truth of Judaism. Samuelson's overall aim is a noble and timely one: Judaism, he avers, must "come to terms with" contemporary natural science.[5] However, it is his understanding of in what this *coming to terms with* science must consist that should carefully be scrutinized and assessed.

Samuelson evidently understands philosophy/Jewish philosophy to have been replaced by the work of the natural sciences. In both his book and his articles on the subject of Judaism and science, he argues that the tasks once within the purview of philosophy are now being performed in the university departments belonging to other specialties—the work of philosophers has become both superfluous and irrelevant. Philosophy, in Samuelson's view, is dying, and Jewish philosophy—Jewish thought—would do well to separate itself from the methods and direction of academic philosophy entirely and take as its task the reinterpretation of Judaism according to the truths proffered by science.[6]

Samuelson argues that, unlike in the past, contemporary scientists operate independently of philosophy and philosophers: Whereas once natural science was numbered among the branches of philosophy (classified as "natural philosophy"), and often progressed by virtue of the reasoning of philosophers, the problems and paradigms of science are now generated without recourse to academic philosophy at all. Although the de facto claim that scientists do not engage with philosophy departments as a part of their theoretical work might well (as Samuelson asserts) be caused by the inherent irrelevance of current philosophizing and contemporary philosophical methods, this, of course, need not be true. Neither must we conclude that scientists themselves proceed without recourse to philosophical thinking: the generation of paradigms within the particular sciences is arguably a philosophical endeavor (and the scientists engaged in it not infrequently schooled in philosophy of science), albeit of a limited scope. Contemporary science, it may be argued, has less than ever before to do with academic philosophy in part due to its development of a vast and detailed corpus of ideas internal to itself, and because the perspective of modern science is itself an all-encompassing worldview—in other words, it in itself constitutes a *philosophy*. In this and other works, Samuelson quickly dismisses academic philosophy as either concerned entirely with language (and thus replaced by linguistics and other empirical disciplines) or as failing to take account of the truth as presented by science. Philosophy has been replaced by science, just as for Samuelson, religion must be replaced by science. In this regard, Samuelson joins the ranks of those who believe science to have the power of disproving all that which fails to fall into its categories and measurements. Science is presumed to have no need of philosophical justification, but rather to provide its own justification as well as a justification for any legitimate philosophy or religious belief. This is scientific realism, or scientism.[7]

The assumption of scientific realism is that science reveals "how things really are." Although our conclusions will very likely be superseded by new theories, science at any given moment represents the best knowledge currently available of the truth about the universe. The "real" nature of the macroscopic world of persons, places, and things is revealed by science, and that world itself is seen to be in an important sense "unreal" and the result of causes vastly more "real" than itself. Such scientific realism denies the fact, championed by Edmund Husserl, that the realities of science have their basis in an intellectual practice founded in and belonging to the life-world—that macrocosmic world of persons, places, things, knowers, projects, and scientists—itself, which is a consideration that renders problematic our belief in science's capacity to reveal the truth of the universe in contradistinction to the lived world's supposed unreality.[8]

It is clear that, despite (though not because of) his commitment to quantum physics as an ontology, Samuelson is concerned to find a place for the posit of God. While this fact would obviously find a happy reception in the ears of most Jews, we must likewise ask just why Samuelson is moved to affirm this. While early modern mechanistic science ceased to require God as an explanatory principle in its account of the natural order, the universe that it envisioned did not disallow the existence of the Deity, either. Pre-Newtonian physics was more or less able to "accommodate" God insofar as it purported to speak of the workings of the created or natural order, rather than to account for the origin of that order itself: The questions of religion remained outside the explicit purview of science. As Samuelson correctly points out, post-Newtonian, or quantum physics differs from its predecessors insofar as it would seem to provide an account of that very origin itself, in effect ruling out the traditional notion of a Creator God Who brings the universe into existence in time—at least in the Aristotelian sense of bringing potential entities into the actuality of existence as their "mover." The principle of inertia seems to give the lie to even the most metaphorical reading of the Book of Genesis and/or the concept of *b'reishit*.

While it is no doubt true that the world that we inhabit today is vastly different from that of premodern times, in that it is indisputable that our intellectual and social lived reality bears little resemblance to that of our premodern Jewish predecessors,[9] Samuelson's claim that it is not from philosophy but from science that the threat or challenge to Jewish belief primarily comes is less than self-evident. The de facto consigning of philosophy to the sidelines of our society no more demonstrates its uselessness than the relative lack of interest in high culture demonstrates its lack of worth. The influence of the scientific worldview—and its widespread acceptance as the (metaphysical) "truth about the world" reveals not its unassailable and singular "truth," but only the fact that it has indeed been embraced as a philosophy. Science has neither "proven" that God does not exist, nor that the God of medieval theology is but an untenable projection of primitive understanding. It is powerless to do either. The acceptance of a worldview cannot be a result of empirical "proof" or demonstration: Science cannot prove the veracity of science's ability to be the mirror of nature.[10] There is little doubt that science works, enabling us to render accurate predictions and generate technological advances. There is also little doubt that some worldview paradigms "match" the world better than others, insofar as they afford better means by which we might achieve practical and theoretical results and attain successful prediction. Yet such pragmatic success proves neither that the paradigm is a mirror-like reflection of reality as it exists "in itself" nor that it requires no epistemological justification; it does not prove itself as an ontology. Philosophy must necessarily exist in relation and interaction with natural science, as it must not only seek to comprehend the social and technological world that emerges as a result of science's achievement, but also insofar as it seeks to understand the nature of scientific knowing itself. Samuelson is overly hasty in his attribution of the changes in our philosophical concepts exclusively to the changes in science, and in concluding that the work of philosophy is over, its place legitimately to be taken over by science.[11] It could be countered that, despite what is arguably its current state of inadequacy, there is yet much for philosophy to do.

Samuelson presents the reader with an either/or choice: We must either continue to attempt to believe a religious account of reality that integrally involves a scientific account of the universe that is no longer credible (it does not represent our best knowledge of the universe), or we must begin to construct a theology that is based on the account of the universe given by quantum physics (which does represent our best current knowledge). In either case, the assumption is that it is into our account of the universe that our understanding of God is to be fit. God is to be envisioned in terms of our universe (and thus of our scientific understanding of it), and God's relation to the universe and its components is to be understood as a role played by God in the workings of that universe. Not only must our theology be consonant with (i.e., not be in contradiction to) our science, but it must in fact be an extension of that science, if not entailed by it. Samuelson thus seeks a "Quantum God" to replace the "Aristotelian God" in whom we can no longer believe. Samuelson correctly rejects the notion (disturbingly popular among religious believers today, including many Jews) that there are "two truths," an empirical and verifiable truth about the world (coming from science) and a "personal" or "subjective" form of truth in which God is "known." Any suggestion of "two ways" of thinking about the world—a "religious" and a scientific—can result only in the taking of one way as literally true, and the other as at best merely metaphoric and at worst fictional. Such thinking is a sort of last-ditch effort to salvage belief in a God whose existence has become increasingly impossible to affirm in the context of our knowledge of the universe; it serves in our attempt to mitigate the pressure of the cognitive dissonance that is the plight of religious consciousness in the scientific age. It is the apologetic of the modern believer that tacitly attests to the belief that (to quote Mark Twain) "Faith is believing what you know ain't so."

Yet is embracing science as our ontology, is searching for a Quantum God, our only recourse in the attempt to reinterpret Judaism in a way that is meaningful and relevant for the contemporary Jew? Is it actually true that the solution to the problem that its reliance on an archaic science has rendered our old theology unbelievable that of our building a theology based on our current science? Will any future foundational shift in scientific paradigm necessitate yet another complete replacement of Jewish belief? Does, in other words, our ability rationally to believe in God hinge on the possibility of our fitting God into the science of the day?

Samuelson is, of course, correct in saying that the world in which we live is the world as envisioned by modern science: The facts for which one needs to account in formulating a philosophical account of the world doubtless include the facts of science. Yet the dependence of our philosophizing (or of our theology) on natural science is another question altogether, and is, in fact, far from self-evident. Simply because the medieval Jewish (and non-Jewish) philosophers understood theology and metaphysics to be dependent upon natural science does not necessarily entail that this understanding is correct. Samuelson questions much from the medieval philosophical inheritance, but he does not question this assumption. Although he does not present a full philosophy of Judaism and only begins down the road of rethinking the notion of God in the context of the quantum universe, it is evident that Samuelson regards, as did Maimonides, our theology to be consequent upon our science.[12] For him, the choice is between a theology that is in contradiction to our science or one that is, broadly speaking, a part of it and that frames its notion of God in direct reference to the scientifically understood universe and in terms applicable to the universe as scientifically understood.

Samuelson is, doubtless, correct in his claim that the current state of Jewish belief is replete with contradiction, confusion, and perhaps even a portion of disingenuousness. He is also, of course, correct in his assessment of the incompatible natures of past or present Jewish theology and the account of the universe represented by quantum physics. I submit, however, that it is less clear that the correct or rational route to follow is that of embracing quantum physics as the basis of our theology. In its simplest terms, it would appear indeed that to equate the universe with reality *simpliciter* (that is, to decide that the term "reality" as such is exhausted by that which resulted from the Big Bang, including nothing beyond that determination), is to reduce God entirely to nature. The so-called hypothesis of God is not required by the quantum account of the universe—the role of God in creation can no longer be held to be that of Artificer in relation to artefact. Samuelson seems to assume, on the basis of this fact, that anything short of a wholesale identification of God and that quantum universe would necessarily perpetuate the Aristotelian model of thinking and continue the medieval metaphysic that has defined Jewish theology—a metaphysic that, we have seen, conflicts in its foundational principles with contemporary science.

The sort of "Quantum God" suggested by Samuelson brings with it other difficulties as well. What at least appears to be an identification of God and quantum reality seriously conflicts with one of the most characteristic and integral Jewish beliefs of all—that of God's complete transcendence. Judaism becomes indistinguishable from the pagan worship of nature it historically has opposed. Samuelson proposes a reexamination of the idea of ontological monism (the claim that there is but one substance or reality), and in the context of a God identified with the quantum universe, and despite the new quantum understanding of nature, such an identification can result in nothing less than a pantheism.

What might be objectionable to the Jewish consciousness in a proposal of quantum pantheism is twofold: (1) the posit of any aspect of the Deity that transcends its identification with the cosmos will be but an *added belief based not on science at all,* but on a faith that supplements science with unsupportable claims: In philosophical terms, it is unclear how Samuelson's proposal will lead beyond the mere reduction of God to (quantum) nature and result in a pan*en*theism (the posit of a God who, while one with and inseparable from nature, likewise transcends nature and is not exhausted by it).[13] (2) The reduction (identification) of God with (quantum) nature—pantheism—results in the denial of God in anything more than a nominal sense: We opt to call (quantum) nature God (a rose by any other name). The Jew might ask what there is left to worship; the thoughtful Jewish reader might ask what point there might be in the name change—why use the word "God" at all if all one means is (quantum) reality? We here find ourselves suspiciously close to the reductionist philosophy of Mordecai Kaplan, whose reduction of God to the forces of nature and to the natural human feelings of goodwill and moral action sanctifies the retention of Jewish worship practices by lauding them as folkways and, through his use of language, giving to nature a misleading veneer of divinity to which, as mere nature, it is ill entitled. Samuelson's recurrent invocation in his writing of the legacy of Kaplan invites even further suspicion that the Judaism he has in mind is in danger of being robbed of any God save the false God of quantum nature.

We might also observe that whereas Aristotelian science requires some sort of God (Prime Mover) in its account of the cosmos (and in the work of Maimonides that Mover became the God of Abraham, Isaac, and Jacob), the quantum "metaphysics" of contemporary science does not. To paraphrase Laplace, contemporary science has no need of the hypothesis of God. Samuelson rightly observes that modern science refutes the traditional notion of the transcendent Creator God, but in his writings so far gives little indication of how Jewish thought is to contend with a scientific worldview that, in its all-encompassing self-sufficiency,[14] has no room for God whatsoever. We have already seen that any notion of God posited upon a metaphysic of quantum science will have to exist as a supplement to that science: an additional belief for which the theory itself (as a complete account of reality) has absolutely no need. Thus, the question presents itself as to what reasons one might have for positing or believing in God in the first place? If, as it appears that Samuelson believes, reality is limited to what quantum physics teaches, and our legitimate cognition and knowledge are limited to what has a place in contemporary quantum science, would he not be forced to hold not only that we have no reason whatsoever to believe that God (in any way construed) exists, but likewise that any idea of God is but a holdover from a scientific or metaphysical worldview that has been disproven and superseded? If any intuition we might have that there is a God is nothing more than a remnant of an archaic worldview, then Samuelson's desire to rescue the notion of God and to rehabilitate Jewish belief is incoherent.

For Samuelson, it is the inherently purposeless nature of the universe revealed by science that presents the greatest challenge to us in our quest to maintain our Judaism in the face of modern science. Science reveals a universe without moral value: as Samuelson puts it, "Whatever the grounds for moral judgments are, they are not to be found in the physical universe."[15] Ethics, perhaps the core of Judaism, appears impossible in a quantum universe. This is a puzzling statement indeed: For the believing Jew, was ethics ever to be found in the *physical* universe? Samuelson's meaning becomes clear: Jewish ethics is dependent upon the existence of a God Who transcends nature; the acceptance of the metaphysics of quantum physics precludes any transcendence of (quantum) nature, leaving us only the quantum (or "physical") universe to which to turn.

If we are to proclaim the existence of God, then, we are forced to understand God to be synonymous with the quantum ("physical") universe—and no account of nature, quantum or otherwise, can provide us with anything resembling that which Jewish tradition could affirm to be "ethics."

Samuelson indicates that the monism that defines the ontologization of quantum physics might be seen as compatible with the dynamic monisms[16] of Hermann Cohen or Franz Rosenzweig, and suggests that a new Jewish philosophy might take the form of a development of ideas concerning the human being, the nature of the world, and the meaning of redemption from the works of these Jewish philosophers. However, it is unclear that a Cohen-Rosenzweig understanding of reality is in fact compatible with the metaphysical commitment to quantum physics that Samuelson would appear to affirm. The monism of Cohen remains perhaps intractably bound to a philosophical idealism that retains much of the understanding of "spirit" that is rejected in principle by contemporary physics, while Rosenzweig's thinking would surely find itself in opposition to any reduction of ultimate reality/God to identifiable and measurable determinations of energy. Clearly, neither of these philosophers envisioned their monism in terms of a pantheistic reduction or identification of God to or with the quantum cosmos.

Yet even if we were to succeed in establishing a Jewish philosophy in which science were rendered compatible with Cohen-Rosenzweig "New Thinking"[17] it is entirely possible that (despite the Judaism of these two eminent thinkers) we might find ourselves with a thinking so "New" as no longer to be recognizably Jewish. While Judaism has historically featured an emphasis on community and the collective, the reality and importance of the individual to Judaism and Jewish ethics is not to be minimized. Leaving aside, for the moment, the (very real) difficulties involved in maintaining an ontological monism while at once affirming the central Jewish idea of God's Absolute Transcendence, we immediately also are faced with the danger inherent in all forms of pantheism—that is, if there is but one substance, the distinction between God and the world—and the distinction between God and human beings—forthwith is annihilated.[18] A monism—quantum or otherwise—that ultimately proclaims its end in the absorption of the individual into the one true Reality or Substance (God)[19]—even if that absorption remains ever at an infinite remove[20]—lessens the robust reality of the human being[21] and in so doing renders problematic the Jewish understanding of the individual as the inherently valuable *tzelem Elohim*.

Samuelson proposes that an interpretation of halachah after the manner of the Eastern "Way"[22] might represent a fruitful means of understanding Jewish practice and even ethics in the face of quantum monism. While such a view would succeed in reinterpreting revelation in a way consonant with physics, it must fail to vouchsafe the ethical upon Samuelson's quantum ontology. Unlike the philosophies of either Hermann Cohen or Franz Rosenzweig, in which the move of created reality toward the "single point of light"[23] of union with God bespeaks a reality beneath that of quantum mechanics, monism understood as Samuelson understands it—as the "stuff" of quantum reality—is seen by that science ineluctably to be on the move toward that goal. Human life and human action are of necessity irrelevant. Of what significance, then, is the ethical? In a (quantum) universe in which the "true" reality of the human being lies in his or her accidental arrangement as a collection of subatomic particles, the unity of the universe proceeds without reference to human action, as a matter of nonpurposive natural fact. The point of such a "Way," of the development of spiritual or moral perfection, and ultimately of the worship of God, then, is lost. Human action—ethics—can never have the significance in a quantum universe that it has in the scheme of Rosenzweig—namely that of the most important force propelling the union of God and creation.

Is Judaism able to be comfortable with a manner of thinking that, at the very least, so prioritizes the One (in Samuelson's parlance, the universe, or perhaps God) over the many (individual human beings) that the very ethical importance of individuals is only in reference to the One into which they are destined to be dissolved (Samuelson here cites Rosenzweig's idea of creation's trajectory toward utter union in "a single point of light")? One of the most distinctive features of Judaism is precisely its insistence on the robust nature of the difference between and incommensurability of God and God's creation, and the reality and importance of the world and its inhabitants. The remaking of Judaism in such a way as to mitigate that essential claim is arguably a departure from an attitude so integral to Judaism as to be contrary to it. It is difficult, in the end, clearly to discern a difference between this quantum trajectory toward ontological unity and either the ontology of Absolute Idealism or an Eastern mode of thinking that affirms only the All as real (the world of life and of individuality's being but an illusion).[24] Two questions emerge: If this is in fact what Samuelson recommends as the correct future direction for Jewish thought, can we truly say that it is *Jewish* in any more than the nominal sense that it would have been adopted by the Jewish people? The question of an inherent truth content to Judaism asserts itself in this connection: Is Judaism but a "culture" or is it a culture that is in some wise integrally tied to at least a basic principle or set of principles—some manner of truth claim—which may be said to define it as at minimum a stance or a perspective on reality?

Any sort of scientistic reduction of God to the scientifically knowable principles of the universe leaves us with but a force of nature—or, better, leaves us with but the universe, all efforts to revivify religious parlance through painting that universe over with the veneer of sacrality notwithstanding. Kaplan's naturalistic "force that makes for salvation"—the human good will and ethical impulse existing within an entirely natural universe that exhausts reality itself—bears little resemblance to Judaism's transcendent Deity and smacks of atheistic humanism. It is quite likely that the theology of quantum physics suggested by Samuelson's program will ultimately amount to much the same thing, thereby reducing Jewish worship to either cultural folkways or the "worship" of quantum nature. Such a conclusion, we remember, remains speculation in relation to Samuelson's schema, yet the direction he has taken in favor of the ontologization of quantum physics may make these theoretical consequences unavoidable.

It seems a sort of last-ditch effort, and one emitting more than a whiff of desperation, to seek to "plug into" our scientistic conception of reality a posit of a "God" Whose existence that understanding of the universe does not require and can only with a degree of strain even tolerate. The theoretical space available for the affirmation of God's existence upon a view that takes science for ontology is limited indeed. When we, with Samuelson, embark on the quest to unite the Jewish notion of God and the worldview of quantum physics, we seek either to extend the cosmos acknowledged by that physics beyond the power of physics' capacity to know, or alternatively, to reinterpret the scientifically knowable cosmos so as to call it "God." While the second alternative leads us headlong into pantheism, the first smacks unmistakably of a faith that imports a key element of the very archaic metaphysics that Samuelson eschews.

There is more than a trace of such regressive thinking in Samuelson's proposal. I suggest that the most fruitful direction might instead be that of reenvisioning God otherwise than as a component of the reality we seek to know. What is required, I submit, is a *philosophy* that accounts for the existence and efficacy of the science we have, rather than a *science* that can account for (or in some wise render meaningful) our notion of God and our impulse to religious belief.

Is God's reality something entirely different from the being of anything within the spatio-temporal universe? Is God's being other than (or more than) the being of that universe itself? I suggest that the answer—and even the quintessential Jewish answer—to that question must be an emphatic "yes." I would like to suggest that our God is too small precisely when we attempt to fit God into our science as a component or totalizing principle of the universe.[25] I would like to offer for consideration the idea that it is not only the traditional or medieval idea of a human-like Deity Who, through the means of physical cause and effect, creates the universe, but likewise the idea that God is to be understood in terms of natural forces, that has become outdated. I suggest that this is true even if we hold God to be that very Force or Reality of the universe itself.

We are back, once again, to the question—the philosophical question—of why it is we believe that Judaism ought to be preserved and continued. If this is to be for us more than a cultural question, if it is to constitute for us more than a mere matter of subjective or intersubjective preference or sentiment, then there must be some sense in which we find Judaism, as a set of core beliefs and attitudes about reality, to be true. Is Judaism true? Does it contain, in our estimation, some core kernel or kernels of truth that can somehow be reinterpreted—translated, as it were—into conceptual terms that are not only consonant with, but in fact expressive of, the best account of reality that we have? I believe that it does, and that it is the work of Jewish philosophy, rather than of physics, to embark on the business of its translation. I propose that perhaps Samuelson has been too hasty in declaring philosophy to be dead. I suggest that what we should really be searching for is a philosophy—a theology—that as the best expression of our current *philosophical* knowledge is able to accommodate our contemporary quantum science, rather than a way in which we can accommodate our theology (and our God) to the determinations of quantum science embraced as ontology.

Notes

1. Norbert M. Samuelson, "The Death and Revival of Jewish Philosophy," *Journal of the American Academy of Religion* 70, no. 1 (March 2002): 117–34; *Jewish Faith and Modern Science: On the Death and Rebirth of Jewish Philosophy* (Lanham, MD: Rowman and Littlefield, 2009).
2. Cf. Norbert M. Samuelson, *Judaism and the Doctrine of Creation* (New York: Cambridge University Press, 1994), 15, 26. See also Norbert M. Samuelson, *Revelation and the God of Israel* (New York: Cambridge University Press, 2002), 125–27.
3. This manner of speaking in the opening essay also peppers the argument in his *Jewish Faith and Modern Science.*
4. This premise is essential to Samuelson's argument. It appears explicitly in Samuelson, *Jewish Faith*, 3–6 and is developed in greater detail in the essay in this issue.
5. Norbert M. Samuelson, "The Challenges of the Modern Sciences for Jewish Faith," *CCAR Journal* (Winter 2012): 10.
6 See Samuelson, *Jewish Faith*, 23–24.
7. See Samuelson, *Jewish Faith*, 165. Samuelson argues that scientism (or "scientivism") is at work when scientists presume to extend their knowledge beyond that which is scientifically ascertainable, illegitimately concluding that there is no transcendent reality beyond the scientifically knowable—ruling out thereby the posit of God and all theological claims. However, I contend that in Samuelson's own equation of contemporary science and the best available knowledge we have of the universe, as well as in his claim that it is science that tells us the "truth about the world," he likewise strongly embraces scientism.
8. Husserl argues that the "mathematization of nature" is itself a practice engaged in within the life-world, representing but one way of cognizing that world. It is, therefore, impossible to demonstrate its primacy and ability to "reveal" things "as they really are." See Edmund Husserl, *The Crisis of the European Sciences and Transcendental Phenomenology*, trans. David Carr (Evanston, IL: Northwestern University Press, 1970).
9. We might note here that Samuelson claims that it is not merely the social world that has changed in a way that is relevant to our endeavor to know, but the world itself. He employs what is perhaps deceptively ambiguous language designed to give the impression

that not only our changes in knowledge or worldview, but what might in the end be a complete change in Jewish belief, is somehow connected with, if not *caused by*, the constant changes in nature at the quantum level. An example of this is to be found at Samuelson, "Challenges," 12–13, where he writes: "This new understanding would enable a reconstructed form of biblical faith to make sense out of all the postbiblical changes in history, nature, and in thought about history and nature." To my mind, one would be hard-pressed to cite any example of "postbiblical changes in *nature*" (italics mine), or to name any way in which we might attribute the changes in what we believe ourselves to know to the quantum workings of the universe! This loose mode of speaking is intended to reduce in the reader the sense that there is something about knowing (or about the reality we seek to know) that we ought to believe stable and permanent.

10. I use Richard Rorty's apt expression here. I follow Rorty's understanding of science as validated *pragmatically.* To wit, science "works," and the fitness of science and of its paradigms are shown in its success in dealing pragmatically with the world. Although, as Samuelson avers, science may hold the best knowledge of the world that is currently at hand (namely it "works" better than its competitors), Rorty's argument shows that this pragmatic validation is in no way synonymous with its proof—that is, with a demonstration that it provides concepts by means of which we are guaranteed a reflection of the universe "as it is." Put differently, the success of science does not prove that in finding science we have found "the world." Our ontology—and more generally, our philosophy—must provide an account of science and its success, rather than be seen as standing in need of scientific approval. See especially Richard Rorty, *Philosophy and the Mirror of Nature* (Princeton: Princeton University Press, 1979); Richard Rorty, *Consequences of Pragmatism* (Minneapolis: University of Minnesota Press, 1982); Richard Rorty, *Objectivity, Relativism and Truth* (New York: Cambridge University Press, 1991); Richard Rorty, *Contingency, Irony and Solidarity* (New York: Cambridge University Press, 1989).

11. See Samuelson, "Challenges," 15. It becomes clear in the text that the primary reason for Samuelson's contention that contemporary philosophy cannot suffice to provide the intellectual foundation of which today's Judaism stands in dire need is the fact that it is no longer engaged in the development of the physical or natural sciences. Samuelson defines philosophy as "all attempts to make sense out of everything in the most general terms, especially to make sense out of how we human beings locate ourselves in the universe relative to everything else in it." Not only does philosophy, as currently practiced, deal with things other than the natural

constitution of the universe, but, for Samuelson, it is precisely and foundationally the pursuit of knowledge concerning the *natural* constitution of the universe that is required in order to know reality "as it is." For Samuelson, the relevant subject matter for making sense of the world is that of "the physical sciences (especially in physical cosmology) and the life sciences (especially in evolutionary biology)." See also Samuelson, *Revelation*, 120.

12. This is perhaps, in fact, too weak a claim. It is precisely because contemporary academic philosophy does not continue the medieval practice of equating physical science (which used to be called "natural philosophy") with the philosophical disciplines of ontology and psychology that Samuelson finds the method of contemporary philosophy wanting. See Samuelson, *Revelation*, 123–24.

13. While panentheism (as opposed to pantheism) seems to be in which direction Samuelson desires to head in his "process" notion of quantum ontology, it is unclear that his apparent reductionism affords the theoretical space to accommodate it. The reduction of reality per se to the quantum universe allows no room for any posit of transcendent reality (God) save as an unwarranted appendage to the physics that presents a self-sufficient account of the universe. It is for this reason that Samuelson's appeal (*Revelation*, 122) to revelation as a continued valid source of knowledge for philosophical interpretation is anomalous upon his theory.

14 See Samuelson, *Jewish Faith*, 23.

15. Samuelson, "The Death and Revival of Jewish Philosophy," 125.

16. I am using the term "monism" somewhat differently from the way Samuelson uses it in Samuelson, *Jewish Faith*, 32–37. There Samuelson argues that it is traditional Jewish theology that has seen reality monistically (in the final analysis God is the only being), while a simple reading of the *Tanach* implies a plurality of entities in existence. The source of theology's monistic ontological commitment is found to reside in Aristotelian logic, Samuelson argues, while modern linguistics lends itself to a pluralistic ontology. Well and good. It is also to be remembered, however, that Judaism's traditional theological commitment to the reality of the world, the sanctity of individual human beings, and the importance of ethics bespeaks an understanding of creation as ontologically distinct from God, although this theology is ever in tension with that of the mystical proponents of monism. For Samuelson, it might be true that a "quantum" form of Judaism would be "pluralistic," yet I am inclined to denominate the reduction of reality to its quantum natural elements, a monism in which all compelling forms of plurality are dissolved, despite the plurality of atomic components found to comprise that universe. Ultimately, we must find that Samuelson's definition of the universe, as the movement

toward a reality as a single point of light, can be described quite well as a monism. See Samuelson, *Jewish Faith*, 152–54.

17. While the "New Thinking," properly so-called, is that of Rosenzweig alone, Rosenzweig himself argued that Cohen's thought so paved the way for his own, and so embodied its key features, as to warrant the appellation.
18. Although we must remember that Samuelson presents only a sketch of a method and arguments for the issues he holds must be considered, the sort of monism (we might well call it a "quantum monism") that emerges from his considerations are worrisome from the standpoints of Judaism, Jewish ethics, and ethics generally, to name but a few. It is difficult to see how such a monism will, in the end, avoid the monolithic unity of God and the universe characteristic of most Eastern thought and religion (as well as Western Absolute Idealism). From a Jewish theological standpoint, we must wonder about the Jewishness of a doctrine in which the Otherness of God is in essence denied; from the standpoint of Jewish ethics, we must be concerned about the manifest extinguishing of reality of persons and the world; and from the standpoint of ethics as a whole, we must remain on guard in the face of what would appear to be the annihilation of the individual subject and its absorption into the universal concept "humanity" (a la Hermann Cohen) and the ontological (cosmic) "All" implied by Samuelson's monism. For a more detailed discussion of quantum physics and monism, see Samuelson, *Jewish Faith*, esp. 109–11.
19. See Samuelson, *Jewish Faith*, 12: "In the end God is fully defined by a fully emerging universe that is not God, but because this plenitude of light is all that is, *at this final asymptotic end, there no longer is any distinction between God and the world*" (italics mine).
20. As it seems to in both Cohen and Rosenzweig. See Samuelson, *Jewish Faith*, 177.
21. See Samuelson, *Jewish Faith*, 128–31.
22. Samuelson, "Challenges," 17; Samuelson, *Jewish Faith*, 185–92.
23. In "Challenges," 25, Samuelson interprets Rosenzweig's understanding of redemption in terms of "the disappearance of everything into a single universal light."
24. Despite its proviso that union is forever at an infinite remove, it is difficult indeed to envision just how such a monism will prove any more able than Hegel was to avoid reducing reality to "the night in which all cows are black."
25. Cf. Samuelson, "Challenges," 16, Question 7.

Jewish Philosophy, the Sciences, and the Humanities

Zachary Braiterman

The challenge of modern science to Jewish faith as presented here by Norbert Samuelson provides a welcome occasion for all of us interested in modern and contemporary Jewish thought and theology to reconsider the foundational prejudice against science in twentieth century Jewish philosophy. Indeed, it is nothing short of amazing that so few of us have thought so little about the vast potentials for theological rumination opened up by scientific study. Nor is it a coincidence that within the small and isolated world of Jewish philosophy, only a scholar such as Samuelson, steeped in the medieval science of Maimonides and Gersonides, would have thought to call us back to this all-important source for philosophical and theological reflection.

In response to Samuelson's essay, I will say from the start that among Jewish philosophers it is Samuelson's almost unique understanding that the separation between science and the humanities is a modern imposition. Its roots go back to the start of the twentieth century when scholars in the humanities sought to preserve a special domain for the study of history and the arts vis-à-vis the physical sciences. I agree with Samuelson that a hard version of this distinction is an invidious one that has outlived whatever usefulness it may have once offered religious practice and belief. I would maintain, nonetheless, that a soft version of this distinction is inescapable, and that our only option is to stay with and think through it. My own suspicion is that stubborn, irresolvable dualities between brain and mind, matter and spirit will continue to bedevil the convergence between science and the humanities, especially in relation to religion.

ZACHARY BRAITERMAN (Ph.D. Stanford University) is associate professor at the department of Religion at Syracuse University.

About the convergence between the humanities and science that Samuelson wants is, in fact, already well underway, both inside and outside academe. This underscores how out of step the field of Jewish philosophy is with currents in the culture at large. Consider the following:

- We live in a technological world, the ramifications of which effect every sphere of human life, extending from the environmental, to the social, and down to the biological. Deep anxieties about technology found in works by Heidegger and Heschel or in the counterculture of the 1960s have lost almost all of their critical traction, at least for the moment.[1] I do not think anyone can seriously maintain that the problems that impact technological civilization can be solved without input from science itself.
- Even in continental philosophy, perceived by its critics as the bastion of contemporary relativism, there has been a definite fatigue with the "classical" postmodern theory represented in caricature by Jacques Derrida's famous quip, "There is nothing outside the text." The notion has faded that there is nothing real outside of the world of images, words, and concepts in which human consciousness is enmeshed. And there is something tired about continuing to insist with Emmanuel Levinas that "first philosophy" is always constituted as ethics. Most of his critics find this position one-sided and limiting.
- Influenced by Lacanian psychoanalysis, the Slovenian philosopher Slavoj Žižek and the French social theorist Alain Badiou have taken a renewed interest in what art historian Hal Foster has called "the return of the real."[2] Recent work in Affect Theory by Catherine Malabou and Ray Braissier are examples of recent scholars who have taken up the banner of "speculative realism" and pursued continental philosophy into contemporary brain science and astrophysics.[3] While I would not necessarily recommend any of the conclusions advanced by these theorists or their political stances, I consider the direction they propose to be remarkably fruitful.
- In popular culture, the so-called atheist wars led by scientists such as Richard Dawkins, Daniel Dennett, and Sam Harris testify in a negative way to the importance of religion in the

world today and for the need to think about religion in a serious, scientific way.

- Terrence Malick's recent award-winning, critically acclaimed film, *Tree of Life*, represents an important moment in the convergence of science, religion, and art. The movie begins in the beginning at the chaos and creation of the cosmos and the evolution of life on earth; it wends through the quotidian pathos and pain shaping the life-story of a single family in postwar Texas. Its climax is nothing less than a luminous vision of life after death after which a central protagonist, bewildered and buffeted, is thrown back into life. Malick's lushly shot film seamlessly blends nonhuman and human elements, affectlessness and affect. The afterlife is promised without any obvious presence of a god or God; any sense of the divine within the film spools internal to the world-system pictured on screen.
- The indirect impact of science on *popular* religious life and thought is also seen in the works of Jewish authors. I see it in the turn to immanence among authors such as Arthur Green and Jay Michaelson as well as trends going back to the 1970s in Jewish Renewal Movement, eco-Judaism, and the interest in Buddhism and in Kabbalah.[4] The same can be said about the earlier thought of Mordecai Kaplan, albeit without the attraction to mysticism. The causal relation between an interest in science and immanence in theology is most likely simple. In both instances, attention is riveted upon enlarged pictures and conceptions of physical and mental dynamics and values whose locus is this world.

What science has always brought to religion is a sense of scale more vast than both the anthropocentrism and the relatively bounded world-pictures in biblical and Rabbinic religion. Of course, one sees a non-anthropocentric conception of the natural world in Maimonides, for whom the world proceeds according to a logic irrespective of human desires and projects (*ha'olam k'minhago noheig*). The modern and contemporary world-picture of the natural world is still more vast. In fact, "picture" may not even be the right word for it. Radically "acentric" (that is, without a clear, single center) and non-imagistic, it beggars the medieval worldview presumed by Maimonides. The world is too large and too small even to be pictured. Entire stretches and strata of the natural world lie beyond the limits of the human imagination. In this, God is not uniquely unrepresentable, as might have once been thought.

In spring 2011 the continental philosopher, John Caputo, delivered a speech at Syracuse University entitled, "The Future of Continental Philosophy of Religion." The conclusion of the lecture was that modern and contemporary physics has got religion and philosophy beat even where religion and philosophy might have once been able to entertain bragging rights—at the level of the imagination. It is hard not to agree with this conclusion. One might have thought that the fundamental reconceptualization of order presented by quantum physics, string theory, dark holes, and dark matter would require at least a cursory look. However, one cannot find such reflection in the Jewish philosophy as practiced by most university professors (my own included).

The resistance to science in the humanities is not, however, purely arbitrary. What I will call "the problem of different strata" is so extreme, methodologically, that it could very well undermine the "integrated view of total reality"[5] for which Samuelson hopes. The ontological gap between strata relevant to quantum mechanics and strata relative to the domain of human consciousness might be too large for any human thought to bridge; and how to figure God into this gap is hard to imagine. It would seem impossible to make any direct and complete inference from (1) physics, chemistry, and biology to (2) the conscious plane of human experience, and from there to (3) metaphysics. If we cannot be sure about the exact interaction between chemical dynamics and human consciousness, how much more vexed will be any attempt to interpret the physical world and mental image-work in theological terms? The classical dualism between body and soul, matter and mind has been surpassed. In effect, the challenge posed by Samuelson is to think across a vexing intersection defined by *three* irreducible strata.

I understand why Samuelson privileges the microscopic world-picture in his essay here. Solid objects dissolve into "a sea of fluid beings constantly flowing past, through, and into each other, ultimately coalescing to form new actual entities."[6] This picture provides an aesthetically appealing purchase on material dimensions that transcend the limits of the optical eye. But this purchase is only heuristic, as it is in fact given to the naked eye by means of a technological apparatus. It is anybody's guess what an "infinite repository of an idealized universe" might have to do with what Samuelson citing Whitehead calls "the primordial nature of God" or the "consequent nature of God."[7] It is not the internal coherence of the concept that I fail to understand as much as the hermeneutical decision to refer anything having to do with physical properties back to God. Maybe this repository has something to do with the nature of God or maybe it relates more simply to the nature of nature. I do not see any way to resolve this aporia one way or the other.

Related to the problem of different strata is the problem of data. Before this rabbit hole, I would certainly pause, confident that I will never understand the formulas, equations, and arguments that constitute inquiries and debates in the sciences. From the other side of things, I see no reason to commit theology to a dataset with a shelf life of three, five, ten, or twenty-five years. I would maintain, then, that the impact of science on religion and theology will not occur at the granular level or scale pursued by scientists. My guess is that the general impact of science is more diffuse. It works at the level of larger paradigms that reflect the consensus in this or that scientific community and then mediated through technological innovations, popular scientific writing, journalism, literature, and the visual arts.

I for one do not believe that science is self-interpreting. In relation to science, the purpose of all the human arts, including the practice of religion, is to make it possible for us to scratch out a place on the surface of our planet, and to stay committed to the strata of lived life and conscious human perception. In religion, this means to delimit a place in this world before God, and to do so rationally with philosophy. It used to be said that physics has nothing to do with this level of meaning-making, that a physicist cannot tell us how to live or how to pray to God. I am no longer sure this is true, not entirely.

The problems of different strata and data notwithstanding, Samuelson is right to say that it is "not sufficient to simply say 'science speaks about one kind of universe and Judaism about another kind of universe.'"[8] It would be nice if religion could learn how to take its place in the world with the modesty and skepticism with which the best practitioners of science approach data and theory. As Samuelson understands, religion requires the sound and realistic understanding of the physical world that only science can provide, even though I hazard to think that the religious interest in science is affective and existential, not primarily scientific.

Scientists routinely claim that there is nothing outside the physical universe. I do not understand how to adjudicate this kind of claim. At most, scientists writing in a popular idiom will offer up as ersatz spirituality or ersatz poetry a kind of pious awe before the physical world. When they do so, they often sound naïve, at least to scholars trained in the humanities who themselves have also learned to distrust attempts to draw a clear line between facts and values. While these almost apologetic attempts to share their enthusiasm with others are admirable, there are limits beyond which science cannot probe without ceasing to be science. Samuelson is right to argue that theology needs science insofar as religion is understood to have deep roots in the physical world. Nevertheless, I cannot see what science as such might want from religion and theology.

Perhaps this is the place to settle the matter. I doubt it is possible to resolve by means of any integrated, scientific theory the basic quandaries riddling religious life and thought about the transcendence or immanence of God, the absolute or relative reality of material substance, and the moral meaning of life. Unlike Samuelson, I do not think that the Rabbis ever sought to "*determine* what they mean when they [said] that God is the creator of the universe."[9] As I read them, their theological thinking is more loose and associative. While I do not think that science can answer any of these theological questions in terms of definite contents, I am in complete agreement with Samuelson that science will enlarge in a formal way the sense and conception we bring to those questions.

Samuelson opens his essay noting the fear and anxiety with which the Jews in antiquity met the dominant force of Greek wisdom and Hellenistic culture. Their cultural universe was defined by the volatile, super-colliding smashup of civilizations and the transformative impact of new ideas and methodologies on religion and religious experience. With his own immersion in Jewish intellectual history, especially in the medieval period, Samuelson has a pretty good vantage point from which to consider how this all worked out. I get the sense that, having seen it before, Samuelson suffers from no anxiety whatsoever. His approach to the brave new world of contemporary science is recommended for being fearless. The complaint against early modern science in its classical, mechanistic age was that it makes everything "determinate." In contrast, modern and contemporary science tends to make the world less determinate, fixed, and stable, more de-substantialized, pixilated, and "dematerialized."

As I see it, the encounter with science encouraged by Samuelson will *not* make religious belief more rational. The opposite outcome is more likely. My guess is that the encounter with science will underscore just how quirky religious thought really is at heart. What is the relation between spirit, on the one hand, and matter, antimatter, and dark matter, on the other hand? Is God, as Samuelson avers, indeed the God of particles? What does it mean to include particle physics and quantum mechanics into God's creation and the Kingdom of God? Science provides religion heightened levels of high-order fancy at the crossover of disjointed perceptual and conceptual strata. Perhaps we will all come to the conclusion that mater is spirit or spiritual; and that sprit is matter or material, and to finally square religion with Spinoza's famous dictum, "god or nature." My bet, though, is that the view of the world provided for in contemporary science will itself explain or determine nothing. Increasingly, its vision is the vision of a world made more strange and eccentric, not less. The presence of God can only contribute to an intensified sense of strangeness persisting just outside the frame of any scientific world-picture.

Notes

1. See Martin Heidegger, "The Question of Technology," in Martin Heidegger, *Basic Writings* (New York: Harper & Row, 1977). Remarkably, Heidegger's critique of technology is shared by no less than Abraham Joshua Heschel, albeit coming to it from Judaic rather than philosophical perspective. See Abraham Joshua Heschel, *The Sabbath: Its Meaning for Modern Man* (New York: Farrar, Straus and Young, 1951).
2. Hal Foster, *The Return of the Real* (Cambridge: The MIT Press, 1996). The writings of Žižek are two voluminous to list here. For readers interested in religion a good place to start is *The Fragile Absolute: Or, Why Is the Christian Legacy Worth Fighting For?* (New York: Verso Books, 2000). The key work of Alain Badiou, *Being and Event*, may be too difficult for general readers, but a good place to start is his *Manifesto for Philosophy* (Albany: State University of New York Press, 1999).
3. Catherine Malabou, *What Should We Do with Our Brain?* (New York: Fordham University Press, 2008); Ray Braissier, *Nihil Unbound: Enlightenment and Extinction* (New York: Pelgrave, 2010). These titles are indicative of a broad interest in science among

practitioners of contemporary continental philosophy, a field that used to have considerable influence on contemporary Jewish philosophy.

4. See Arthur Green, *Radical Judaism: Rethinking God and Tradition* (New Haven: Yale University Press, 2010); Jay Michaelson, *Everything Is God: The Radical Path of Nondual Judaism* (Boston: Trumpeter, 2009).
5. Norbert M. Samuelson, "The Challenges of the Modern Sciences for Jewish Faith," *CCAR Journal* (Winter 2012): 23.
6. Ibid., 24.
7. Ibid., 24.
8. Ibid., 23.
9. Ibid., 22 (emphasis is mine).

Part II: Judaism and the Physical Sciences

Judaism and Physics

Peter Ochs

For the past thirty years Norbert Samuelson has made serious efforts to reclaim natural science as a serious subject for Jewish philosophy. I am most grateful for this work as well as for the invitation to reflect on these efforts, especially in regard to the physical sciences as a subject for Jewish thinking.[1]

Discussions of religion and science are often global in their reach and quite dramatic in their effects. But I am not going to discuss it in either a global or a dramatic way. Instead, I shall examine only one sampling from the physical sciences: the field of biophysics; within that the study of quantum phenomena within biophysics, and within that only one written account of one series of experiments on the geometry of π electron clouds in cytoplasm. In terms of Jewish thought, I shall examine only the practice of Rabbinic scriptural interpretation, and within that only one account of a disagreement between two recent scholars on what we can learn from *Shir HaShirim Rabbah*. My account will therefore be a bit detailed and dense, but I hope that it will prove beneficial. I want to replace some conceptual theorizing about science and religion with more concrete comparisons of scientific and religious *practices*.

I. Two Case Studies

I want to focus on two types of texts—scientific and religious—in order to illustrate where these practices differ and what they share in common. My scientific text is an essay by Stuart Hameroff published in the edited volume *Quantum Aspects of Life*.[2] My

PETER OCHS (Ph.D. Yale University) is Edgar Bronfman Professor of Modern Judaic Studies at the University of Virginia in Charlottesville, Virginia.

religious text consists of a debate between two Judaic scholars, Michael Fishbane and Steve Fraade, about the structure and meaning of *Shir HaShirim Rabbah*. The debate was published in *Textual Reasonings: Jewish Philosophy and Text Studies at the End of the Twentieth Century* (Radical Traditions).[3] The comparison is not self-evident but its relevance to the relationship of science to Judaism will become clearer as I go along.

A. Stuart Hameroff, "That's Life: The Geometry of π Electron Clouds."

The author of the scientific text, Stuart Hameroff, is an anesthesiologist at the University of Arizona who has teamed up with Roger Penrose, the world renowned mathematical physicist, who has contributed greatly to the dialogue of science and religion by arguing that the laws of physics are inadequate to explain the phenomenon of consciousness.[4] Hameroff, who is the editor of three volumes on the science of consciousness,[5] and Penrose attempted to develop a model of consciousness based on quantum computation in brain microtubules. In the essay under consideration, Hameroff provides evidence for the following theory, whose main components are as follows: (1) biological life is sustained by quantum processes; (2) data gathered from recent studies of cellular metabolism map best onto quantum models; and (3) there is now sufficient evidence that the cytoskeletal material of living cells offers a biochemical environment that could theoretically sustain quantum processes. Skeptics have argued that the aqueous environment of living cells would not sustain such processes. This is true. But recent evidence shows that the cytoskeleton contains oil globules that would protect what is called quantum coherence.

Hameroff reviews laboratory studies over the past one hundred years, including his own work on brain cells, to show that cell physiology does indeed provide the environment needed for quantum coherence. Before reporting on some details of his thesis, let me clarify some of the terms and theories he presupposes. I draw from and highly recommend John Polkinghorne's little introduction, *Quantum Theory: A Very Short Introduction*.[6]

What do we know about quantum phenomena in general? Here are a few crucial points. Classical, Newtonian physicists in the nineteenth century showed that light displays wavelike motion.

The easiest example to picture is that just as ocean waves display interference patterns when crossing each other, so too do streams of light. In 1873 James Clerk Maxwell showed that what was now called electromagnetism displays such waves as well and that they move at the speed of light. So far so good for Newtonian-like physics. As Polkinghorne put it, the catastrophe for classical physics came with new discoveries, in the early 1900s, about black-body radiation. "A black body is one that perfectly absorbs all the radiation falling on it and then re-emits all of that radiation."[7] But a new breed of statistical physicists found that high frequency radiation is emitted from a black body in a way that is not proportional to the radiation that entered it. The results made no sense in classical terms, but Max Planck successfully proposed a quantum model: that energy is not released in a steady stream, but in packets—or quanta—of energy of a definite size that is proportional to the frequency of radiation.

In 1905, Albert Einstein theorized that a comparable phenomenon of light (called the photoelectric effect) could be explained if we assume the light strikes a given body not as a wave but as a series of quanta or particles. As we noted, however, light also behaves like a wave. How can it be both wave and particle? To answer that question we need to refer to the work of Niels Bohr, Werner Heisenberg, and other twentieth-century physicists, whose combined studies on the atom and the electron generated, from 1913 through 1927 and after, what is known as the Copenhagen Theory of Quantum Mechanics.[8] Stated in simplest terms, this theory includes these elements:

1. **Superposition and Probability.** As measured in the laboratory, subatomic particles display features of both waves and particles. As waves, they tend to obey the terms of classical physics; as particles, their energy states and positions are identified only probabilistically, through statistical measures. Quantum mechanics requires duality—adding together these two contradictory methods of measurement: the overall effect is called superposition. The result, in Polkinghorne's terms, is that "(living as we do in the classical world [of everyday experience and meaning]), it is no longer possible to form a clear picture of what is happening in the course of physical processes."[9]

2. **The Uncertainty Principle.** Heisenberg observed that this odd behavior implied that a degree of uncertainty applies not only to predictions about subatomic behavior but also to actual measurements. We cannot simultaneously measure the position and momentum of an electron (or other subatomic particles): The more precisely we measured one of these factors, the less precisely we would be able to measure the other. This is because the act of measurement requires bombarding the particles with whatever particles we use to detect their behavior: The measuring stick must also effect changes in what we measure. In Polkinghorne's terms, "observables come in pairs that epistemologically exclude each other."[10]
3. **Entanglement.** Space limitations allow me to illustrate this feature only by describing the work of my colleague Olivier Pfister, who heads the University of Virginia quantum laser lab.[11] His work is to split a stream of photons in half, generating two streams of photons moving at complementary vectors so that of a given pair of photons, one will spin one way (say clockwise), the other the other way. If we assume superposition and uncertainty, then we can predict that if, at a given time, particle #1 displays one kind of spin, then particle #2 will at that time certainly display the other kind of spin. Schrodinger called this phenomenon "entanglement," indicating that all such pairs of photons or other particles would display such interdependence at however great a distance. This generates the information-theory upon which Pfister builds his quantum computers: that one bit of information (a particle with a given spin) can generate paired bits of information (two entangled particles).
4. **Coherence/Decoherence.** The last argument I will note concerns the environments within which quantum phenomena can be observed. Entanglement is interrupted (suffers decoherence) when a quantum system, such as a pair of entangled particles, interacts with its environment. Measurement is one example of such an interaction. Another example is the kind of radiation that is ubiquitous in most regions of the cosmos.

With this in mind we can return to Hameroff's study of quantum effects in living cells and understand why he cares about the problem of decoherence. Quantum superposition is maintained only in undisturbed environments. Hameroff and his colleagues argue that quantum processes are essential to life and that they take place in the cytoplasm. Skeptics argue that cytoplasm is an aqueous environment whose ionic character will interact with and thus interrupt any quantum system. Hameroff's essay reports that he and his colleagues have identified a nonaqueous, undisturbed environment in the oily globules that inhabit the cytoskeleton. Such an environment could sustain quantum systems, and he and others have measured quantum effects.

B. A Scholarly Debate on Midrash on the Song of Songs.[12]

I now turn to two Judaic Studies scholars, Michael Fishbane and Steven Fraade, who should be more familiar to the readers of the *CCAR Journal* than the scientists mentioned in the previous section. These essays are the written versions of a face-to-face event in a conference on "textual reasoning" held at Drew University in June 1997. By "textual reasoning" I refer to Rabbinic text study plus hermeneutical and historical interpretation and argument. The scholars who participated in the conference constitute the core of the scholarly community of "textual reasoners." The subject of this particular study was *Shir HaShirim Rabbah,* a book of midrashic commentary on the biblical book *Shir HaShirim* (Song of Songs). The scholarly debate concerned the performative force of a redacted book of midrash. Fishbane explained that a midrash collection integrates two forms of discourse: first, a citation from Scripture that introduces an exegetical comment or midrash; and, second, an anthology that orders together a series of exegeses from different time periods. The midrash is stimulated by the letters and sounds of a given citation in a given setting and, by way of the interconnection of many verses, it teaches that all necessary meaning is contained in the biblical canon.[13] By way of illustration, let us consider the first midrash in the collection:

> *Shir hashirim asher l'shlomo*
> *Yishakeini minishikot pihu, ki tovim dodecha miyayin.*
> A song of songs (of/to/by) Solomon.
> Let him kiss me with the kisses of his mouth.
> For your love is better than wine.

The commentary opens with a question: "In what connection was this [Song] recited? R. Hinena b. R. Pappa said, It was cited at the

Red Sea, as it is said, 'I compare you to a mare of Pharaoh's chariots' (Song 1.9)."

Explanation: What is the question posed by the rabbi? If we assume, with the Rabbinic sages, that this apparent love song also signifies a love song between God and Israel, and if Israel says "let God kiss me with the kisses of his mouth," then the question is, when did Israel say this? R. Hinena suggests the occasion was the Red Sea, where the Israelites thanked God for "kissing" them, as it were, by saving them. R. Hinena's proof text is that, by referring to Pharaoh's chariots, the Song alludes to this event.

But another sage disagrees: "R. Judah b. R. Simon said, It was stated at Sinai: *shir hashirim*, the Song of Songs (1.1), [that is], the Song that was sung by the singers. 'The singers go before, the minstrels follow after' (Ps. 68:26)."

Explanation: R. Judah argues no, the kiss of God's direct presence was not at the Red Sea but on Sinai (i.e., the place where God uttered his word from his mouth). The proof text is Psalm 68:17, which alludes to Sinai: "Why do you look askance, you mountain peaks/at the mountain God desires for His abode? Yes, the LORD will dwell there forever."

Then in verse 26, the Psalm refers to a procession of singers, "The singers go before, the minstrels follow after" (kidmu sharim achar nognim), which R. Judah reads as a reference to the Song of Songs.

So that is how a single set of midrash works. The second form of midrashic discourse is the redacted book, an anthology that collects together a series of these interpretations. Often this is a series of contrasting exegeses of a single verse, each one marked as *davar acher* (another interpretation of the verse). Fishbane explains that, while each midrash is "marked by its own literary form and logic,"[14] the collection as a whole is marked by its own form and logic as well. He then delivers the following argument about these two midrashic forms: The redaction as a whole is guided by a single interpretive and theological goal. In Fishbane's words:

> the editor . . . wished to convey a myth of revelation and religious action [teaching] that the written and oral teachings of Judaism were both given at Sinai, and that religious action is constituted by that revelation and its apprehension through study. Eros is the dynamic that links both poles: God's word was sealed through a

> kiss at Sinai, when Israel acknowledged the divine authority of oral teachings that unfold over time; and God's word is renewed through the study of the sages, as they purse their lips in study [one sage in that sense kissing another]...At the same time, the editor wished to express his sense of religious history in terms of spiritual development.[15]

Thus the midrashim move from the revealed word at Sinai to Israel's imperfect ways of receiving the word through several stages that perfect Israel's reception: beginning with the work of angels who deliver God's Word to each Israelite and culminating in the verbal exchange of one Rabbinic sage's words with another.

Fraade celebrates the midrash and Fishbane's presentation. His argument is that the anthology preserves a greater tension than Fishbane reports between the redactor's message and the irreducible hermeneutical power of each individual unit of midrash. For Fraade, the many parts push strongly against the whole; for Fishbane, the whole does more to quiet the independence of the parts. Fraade argues that there remains, throughout, "an unresolved dialectic of intimacy and intermediacy in Israel's revelatory relation to God. Israel desires and is privileged with the 'mouth to mouth' intimacy of God's revelatory kiss, yet also, in fear of the potency of such unmediated divine contact, (Israel)prefers to receive revelation via an intermediary agent."[16]

It is this dynamic and unfinished tension that moves dramatically through the series of "midrashic units," from the fiery words at Mt. Sinai to the debate that issues from the mouths of the Rabbinic sages. As R. Judah states, the Torah that was uttered with one divine mouth is now uttered by many (Rabbinic) mouths. Desire for kisses is transposed to desire to study and share words. The net result, Fraade suggests, may be an interminable and elusive shuttling back and forth between the scriptural text and its Rabbinic interpretations, from one kind of kiss to another.

II. Comparing Practices of Scientific and Jewish Inquiry

What, then, does it mean to examine relations between Judaism and science? My examples above make a methodological argument. To compare science and Judaism we need to look at their practices. Comparison of this kind begins with some form of ethnography. One kind is participant observation of two laboratory activities (in the sense of the science lab and also of the labor of study that takes place between Rabbinic scholars). Another kind—as illustrated in this essay—is reading written reports of such laboratory activity, where we receive the reports as one part of the activity.[17] Now, once having read such reports, what constitutes the actual comparison?

Here is my main point: Comparison is not a neutral or window-like observation of two entities or activities; it is not first-order looking, but a specific, second- and third-order mode of reflection. In our case, this means that the direct objects of comparison are neither the quantum particles and Rabbinic midrashim, nor the contemporary reports we examined on scientific and Rabbinic inquiry. The direct objects of comparison are conceptual models the comparativist must now construct: models of each of the two forms of inquiry and of the activity of comparison itself.

The claim I have just made belongs to the model of comparison I will now construct for you. But, more than that, it also isomorphic with the models of scientific and Rabbinic inquiry I shall also construct. The thesis I am offering stands or falls on this single claim: that what I will label a pragmatic and abductive model of comparison is isomorphic with at least one significant model of quantum biophysics *and* of Rabbinic scriptural interpretation. In other words, these three models are interdependent. This apparent circularity is not a mark of logical error, but of success in the work of comparison. I shall explain why in a moment. But, first, let me begin to illustrate the interdependence to you. I shall begin with a look at the three models I employ.

While best articulated by the logician of science Charles Peirce, the model of comparison I am using was also anticipated by Max Weber as a model of social scientific inquiry. According to two recent monographs by Basit Koshul,[18] Max Weber introduced a triadic model of social science, according to which (1) any claims about the cause of some societal phenomena are warranted only with respect to (2) the inquirer's *Wert-Ideen* (Value-Ideas), with respect to which the inquirer (3) conceives of the phenomenon as an Ideal Type. In Peirce's comparable terms, each stage of scientific inquiry, from data collection to observation to analysis, reiterates a three-part process of (1) attending to some field of data, as (2) displaying some characteristics, properties, regularities, or meanings (corresponding to Weber's Ideal Types), which are identified with respect to (3) some interpretant, or set of conditions and principles of observation (corresponding to Weber's Value Ideas).

With this in mind let me offer a model of Hameroff's study of biophysics. The model is again triadic. Typical of others in the Copenhagen tradition, Hameroff adopts a model of subatomic behavior such that (1) any particle (analogous to a phenomenon in Weber's model), (2) is measured for, say, velocity, position, or spin (analogous to an Ideal Type in Weber's model, or a meaning in Peirce's logic), with respect to (3) a given condition of measurement, including time and/or space, frequency, temperature, and so on and with respect to the macroscopic character of the measurement equipment. (This condition corresponds to the *Wert-Ideen* in Weber or the interpretant in Peirce.) Hameroff might add, for example, that any (1) position of the particle is (2) determined, with respect to (3) its entanglement, its partially concealed velocity, and so on. Quantum features such as superposition and uncertainty are all correlative to the triadic terms of this model.

The skeptical reader might ask: "Why is your model of quantum science so conveniently similar to Peirce's pragmatic model?" My answer explains why I have chosen to examine Judaism in relation to quantum physics (or biophysics) rather than some other model of scientific inquiry. According to one of the founders of quantum theory, Werner Heisenberg, Charles Peirce anticipated quantum theory fifty years before it became an official logic of science. Heisenberg appears to have been thinking in particular of Peirce's notion of abduction and his logic of relatives.

In brief, the theory of abduction showed, against John Stuart Mill, that we do not acquire our understanding of the laws of nature by simple, inductive observation. Instead, we "see" out there only those patterns that we imagine we could see. This is, in other words, the Kantian notion that we see only what we can construct a priori; induction is then not a source of learning new laws, but only of testing the strength of the models that we construct. When applied to his understanding of science, Peirce's logic of relatives shows that the terms according to which we frame sets of data are relative to specific measures we bring to the laboratory. The most bare-bones model of quantum mechanics is correlative to this assumption: illustrated in the claim that the position or velocity of a subatomic particle is relative to its mode of measurement or interference. This implies that deterministic models do not apply to the series of data we acquire about the behavior of subatomic particles. The data is not un-graphable however; after the fact, we can observe for any given stream of particles that a certain series of phenomena is proportional to a given qualitative quantum state, but then there is a gap in the evidence filled only when we observe, after the fact, proportionality between another series of phenomena in another quantum state. In sum, pragmatic logic applies to our model of quantum practices, because it also belongs to the broader resources of quantum theory.[19]

To conclude I shall offer a model of the Fishbane-Fraade dialogue on Rabbinic midrash. According to what I will label the model of "Rabbinic semiotics," each unit of midrash within the midrash collection displays (1) the sense, meaning, and force or effect of (2) a text of *Tanach*, for (3) a particular community of inquiry and practice. In the terms of Fraade's writings on Rabbinic interpretation: The Rabbinic interpreter shuttles back and forth between two dimensions of meaning, so that a midrashic collection reenacts the dialogic character of each Rabbinic reading by juxtaposing each midrash with another reading—a contrary or contradictory one. The words were spoken on Sinai; or no, at the Red Sea; or no, between one scholar and another; or yes to all of them. Fraade emphasizes the potential interminability of the movement, as one generation rereads the scriptural texts in light of yet another layer of interpretation, and then another, shuttling back and forth between two dimensions of two dimensions of meaning and so on. In Fishbane's words, the redactor shuttles between individual units of meaning and that of the redacted whole; in Fraade's words, the shuttling within the whole book of midrash is reenacted in the dialogic process of the reading practices of one's own day. And I would add that it is reenacted here in this dialectic between Fraade and Fishbane's readings of Rabbinic reading. According to the semiotic model, each reading is a reading of a given text (itself a given reading) with respect to a given context and purpose of reading.

Again, the skeptical reader might ask: "Why is your model of midrashic studies so conveniently similar to Peirce's pragmatic model?" My answer explains why I have chosen to examine quantum science in relation specifically to midrashic studies. First of all, my pragmatic model of inquiry emerged initially out of my studies with the Rabbinic thinker Max Kadushin. In books such as *The*

Rabbinic Mind,[20] he offers what he calls a value-conceptual model of classical Rabbinic midrash that is isomorphic with both Peirce and Weber's models. Kadushin cites Alfred North Whitehead as a source for his formal models, and there are only two footnotes to Peirce. But Yohanan Muffs, of blessed memory, told me he used to walk down Broadway alongside Kadushin, who was reading out loud from volume 5 of Peirce's *Collected Papers* (Peirce's volume on pragmatism). I have previously written a lot to show that Kadushin's model of midrash maps directly onto Peirce's logic, not so well Whitehead's.[21] The evidence of Kadushin's work does not prove that pragmatic logics offer the best models of Rabbinic midrash; it only shows this idea is not unreasonable.

Another partial warrant for my model of scriptural comments comes from the historian Robert Markus's studies of Augustine's scriptural semiotic.[22] Markus argues that Augustine's semiotic anticipates and is fulfilled in Peirce's semiotic. In a recent essay, I have argued that Peirce's logic of science may in fact derive its quantum character, in part, from Augustine's scriptural semiotic and that this semiotic resulted from Augustine's reshaping Stoic logic to serve as a logic of scripture.[23] The practice of "textual reasoning" that we observed in the dialogue between Fishbane and Fraade – and that a larger group of us has practiced since the Drew University conference –also provides additional illustrations and warrants for this approach to scriptural commentary.

Concluding Observations

By way of conclusion, let me revisit that circularity we noted among the three models. Consider, for example, how the quantum model attributes superposition to the subatomic phenomenon it is measuring: It will display the contradictory characteristics of both wave-like and non-wave-like (particle-like) behavior, or of particles with both clockwise *and* counterclockwise spin. How about our model of midrashic inquiry? It attributes comparably contradictory characteristics to Rabbinic readings of *Tanach* and Rabbinic academic commentaries on those readings. For the midrash on Song of Songs, the scriptural text simultaneously displays both a plain sense and a non-plain sense (or midrash); a given word or verse of Song of Songs may also display contradictory characteristics—the divine kisses, for example, took place at the Red Sea and no, they did not (they took place on Sinai). According to our essay by Fishbane, the midrash collection displays both a single redacted meaning and a series of atomized, independent, and potentially contradictory meanings. And the academic dialogue between Fishbane and Fraade displays the contradictory claims that, ultimately, the redacted meaning defines the force of a midrash collection and that no, it is does not; the atomized meanings define its force.

And how about our model of comparison itself? Yes, the pragmatic model of inquiry presupposes that its objects of inquiry will display contradictory characteristics: the object I now behold displays the characteristic X (that it will act in fashion A in the space-time ts-1) *and* the contradictory –X (that is will not act in fashion A at that space-time). It must display contradictory characteristics of this kind, since we can attribute noncontradiction only to objects of past actions of a determinate space-time. The pragmatist's notion of contradictory qualities corresponds to the quantum physicist's notion of coherence or superposition and the midrash scholar's notion of the polyvalence of any scriptural text as it is written.

Is my practice of comparison therefore circular? No. I believe it represents the discovery, instead, that quantum measurement, midrashic inquiry, and pragmatic models of observation and comparison represent what we might call three entangled practices of inquiry, three entangled ways of knowing the created world—or the world *as* created. A state comparable to decoherence occurs in so far as these practices are observed as mere windows to certain determinate sets of entities in the world. These sets then appear to us as products of incommensurable ways of knowing the world. In our view, incommensurability is not at all the same as contradiction. The former marks, for example, an ineradicable divide between scientific and Rabbinic or religious inquiries. The latter marks what we might call the entangled states or the interdependence of these inquiries.

Notes

1. A version of this talk was delivered at a special session of the AAR in November 2010.
2. Stuart Hammeroff, "That's Life: The Geometry of π Electron Clouds," in *Quantum Aspects of Life*, ed. Derek Abbott, Paul C.W. Davies, and Arun K. Pati (London: Imperial College Press, 2008), 403–33.

3. Peter J. Ochs and Nancy Levene, eds., *Textual Reasonings: Jewish Philosophy and Text Studies at the End of the Twentieth Century* (Radical Traditions) (Grand Rapid: William B. Eerdmans, 2002).
4. For example, see Roger Penrose, *The Emperor's New Mind: Concerning Computers, Minds, and the Laws of Physics* (Oxford and New York: Oxford University Press, 1989); Roger Penrose, *Shadows of the Mind: A Search for the Missing Science of Consciousness* (Oxford and New York: Oxford University Press,1994).
5. See Stuart R. Hameroff, ed., *Toward the Science of Consciousness: The First Tucson Discussions and Debates* (Cambridge, MA: The MIT Press, 1996); Stuart R. Hameroff, ed., *Toward the Science of Consciousness II: The Second Tucson Discussions and Debates* (Cambridge, MA: The MIT Press, 1998); Stuart R. Hameroff, ed., *Toward a Science of Consciousness III: The Third Tucson Discussions and Debates* (Cambridge, MA: The MIT Press, 1999).
6. John Polkinghorne, *Quantum Theory: A Very Short Introduction* (Oxford and New York: Oxford University Press, 2002).
7. Ibid., 6.
8. For an historical perspective on the Copenhagen Theory, see P. Lahti, K.V. Laurikainen, and J. Viiri, eds., *Symposium on the Foundations of Modern Physics: The Copenhagen Interpretation 60 Years after the Como Lecture* (Turku, Finland: University of Turku, 1988). For a more accessible introduction to the debate in the 1920s between Einstein and Bohr, see Manjit Kumar, *Quantum: Einstein, Bohr and the Great Debate about the Nature of Reality* (New York: W.W. Norton, 2010).
9. Polkinghorne, *Quantum Theory*, 24.
10. Ibid., 33.
11. See http://www.phys.virginia.edu/People/personal.asp?UID=op6n.
12. The texts under consideration are: Michael Fishbane, "Anthological Midrash and Cultural Paideia: The Case of *Songs Rabbah* 1.2," in *Textual Reasonings*, 32–51; Steven Fraade, "'The Kisses of His Mouth': Intimacy and Intermediacy as Performative Aspects of a Midrash Commentary," ibid., 52–56.
13. Paraphrasing Michael Fishbane, "Anthological Midrash," 32.
14. Michael Fishbane, "Anthological Midrash," 32.
15. Ibid., 42.
16. Steven Fraade, "Kisses of His Mouth," 53.
17. My concern with the otherwise very good popular approaches to religion and science is that the entire force of each of these popular books and arguments is strictly hypothetical; they articulate each author's single vision of how certain aspects of religious and scientific practice are similar or different, compatible

or incompatible. But what do these arguments mean about the actual everyday practice of religion and science? How do we see the results of these interactions in the world? And what actual difference will these arguments make for the way these practices continue to interact in the world? I am asking, in other words, a typical pragmatist question: What real difference does it make to compare these two practices? Unless the comparativist not only shows but also contributes to making such a difference, I must conclude that the comparativist achieves only the first of three stages of comparative study. To complete the second stage is not yet to have shown the results of any "living laboratory." It is simply to design a laboratory and then actually to set one up so that we the audience or readers of the comparative study can evaluate the results.

18. See Basit Bilal Koshul, *The Postmodern Significance of Max Weber's Legacy: Disenchanting Disenchantment* (New York: Palgrave Macmillan, 2005); Basit Bilal Koshul, *Max Weber, Charles Peirce and the Integration of the Natur and Geisteswissenschaftern* (Ph.D. dissertation, University of Virginia, 2011).
19. It means to compare certain modes of inquiry in some particular religion and in some sphere of scientific inquiry: say, some mode of inquiry within Judaism and, say, natural scientific inquiry in general or physics in particular or some particular practice of physics such as quantum studies of light.
20. Max Kadushin, *The Rabbinic Mind* (New York: Bloch Pub. Co., 1972).
21. See Peter Ochs, ed., *Understanding the Rabbinic Mind: Essays on the Hermeneutic of Max Kadushin* (Atlanta: Scholars Press, 1990).
22. See Robert Austin Marcus, *Augustine: A Collection of Critical Essays* (Garden City, NY: Anchor Books, 1972).
23. See Peter Ochs, "Reparative Reasoning: From Peirce's Pragmatism to Augustine's Scriptural Semiotic," in *Modern Theology* 25, no. 2 (April 2009): 187–215.

Revisiting Creation, Natural Events, and Their Emergent Patterns

Bradley Shavit Artson

It is fair to say that most scientists today view the laws of physics the way many Dominant theologians view God—as objective, eternal, and unchanging.[1] They hold these laws of nature to exist in some eternal, pure realm, above and beyond the particular manifestations in the lower realm of matter and energy. Physical things conform to these timeless laws, which dictate their behavior and shape their future. This echo of Platonic Forms continues to shape the ideologies and metaphysics of many of today's scientists and philosophers. This presumption can lead to determinism (with enough data we can know all outcomes), to reductionism (explaining the components explains the totality), and to a dichotomy between law and nature. Its classic expression is found in the musings of Pierre Simon, Marquis de LaPlace, whose thought experiment posits a demon in a closed, Newtonian world. He notes that in such a mechanistic system, once the initial conditions are known and specified, all subsequent states are fixed and known as well:

> We ought then to regard the present state of the universe as the effect of its anterior state and as the cause of the one which is to follow. Given for one instant an intelligence which could comprehend all the forces by which nature is animated and the respective situation of the beings who compose it—an intelligence sufficiently vast to submit these data to analysis—it would embrace in the same formula the movements of the greatest bodies of the universe and those of the lightest atom; for it, nothing would be uncertain and the future, as the past, would be present to its eyes.[2]

BRADLEY SHAVIT ARTSON (JTS88, D.H.L. HUC-JIR LA) holds the Abner and Roslyn Goldstine Dean's Chair at the Ziegler School of Rabbinic Studies of American Jewish University.

LaPlace shares today's widespread assumptions that eternal laws, coupled with complete initial data, specify all data for all time. Much of today's science assumes a one-on-one correspondence between idealized mathematical operations and natural phenomena, in which the evolution of physical reality is infinitely determined by differential equations that exist objectively and timelessly. Immutable mathematical formulae and relationships are transcendent and ontologically supreme. The laws are absolute and infinitely precise. They determine all particular states of nature but are themselves prior to, independent of, and unconstrained by nature. The laws are beyond space-time (although they determine space-time), and the laws create and shape creation from the moment of the Big Bang until the present, themselves without change. Furthermore, the laws are posited to be a unity, however much that unity continues to evade theoretical expression and experimental verification.[3] Eternal law precedes ephemeral creation, ontologically and chronologically.

Eternal, static, objective law (somehow) creates and determines contingent physical reality (this leap across categories is the same weak link in the metaphysics of physics as it is in theology). Reality evolves according to the limits and guidelines of these eternally existing, static laws, and those same laws predetermine nature's future. While the laws determine nature, natural phenomena do not modify the laws. Such a view reflects the theological pedigree of physics in a Dominant theology of a timeless, objective, supernatural spirit whose eternal law shapes and constrains all material creation, indeed, it remains its contemporary expression.

Without rejecting the evocative utility (indeed, the majesty) of this metaphoric portrayal of physical laws, might we not profit here by making explicit its metaphoric nature? Embracing this dualistic perspective as if it were literal and objective perpetuates several counterintuitive defects—predeterminism, reductionism, and a constricted view of what counts as real. Recontextualizing this understanding as the metaphor system it is, we are then free to supplement it with other, more dynamic ways of framing the relationship between generalizable patterns (which, in turn have predictive utility) and specific phenomena (which generate those patterns and also instantiate them).[4]

Instead of positing an ideal (and experimentally impossible) priority of timeless law that then generates and constrains natural material phenomena, let us assert what we can indeed know: the priority of events in nature. Matter is energy frozen; energy is heated matter. I shall refer to both matter and energy as natural events or processes. We can know these events empirically. Each natural event manifests certain physical constraints, which we know in the measurement or experience of the particular events. As we measure/experience groups or series of natural events, we are able to generalize patterns of behavior or characteristics from the specific details of the events' individual processes. These generalizations are refined through further measurement and through their predictive utility, but they (the "laws") remain secondary and approximate.[5] Only the events themselves are actual and concrete. The "laws" are composite measurements of these concrete events, expressed as mathematical formulae, generalizations that provide superb intellectual tools for understanding and that generate further research projects in turn.[6]

This reconceptualization of the primacy of natural events that act in patterns, which we label "laws" as shorthand, rejects a Platonic conceptualization of a dualistic reality.[7] No surprise, then, that the biblical/Rabbinic authorities share our conception: In speaking of the biblical/Rabbinic views of miracles, Louis Jacobs notes that they do not involve a suspension "of natural or universal law (of which there was no such conception in their thinking)."[8] With this recalibration, the strict dichotomy between law and nature dissolves—law is the idealized generalization of patterns expressed by natural events.

John Wheeler, Rolf Landauer, Paul Davies, and Gregory Chaitin are some of the voices that provide the tools for this Copernican recalibration. Wheeler[9] and Landauer[10] suggest that the most useful image for conceiving of how matter and patterns relate is to think of information as the beginning of the explanatory narrative of physical reality. Information (what Wheeler calls "bits") is the core data that events (matter and energy) are able to preserve and transmit. Laws emerge from the properties of events, and our perception of these patterns reflects the intersubjective, embodied metaphoric way we conceptualize natural events, explore, describe, organize, and predict them. Our "laws" are neither objective and eternal nor are they subjective and cultural. Instead, our third way, of biologically processing the nature of which we are a part (in which we are embedded, for which we articulate the consciousness) is the human way of discovering reliable patterns in the behavior and characteristics of natural events. This approach allows us to recognize that natural events (processes) are primary, that what we describe as natural law(s) reflects the patterns and characteristics that natural events manifest individually and in groups. There is thus no ontological gap between laws and events. We are able to recognize that as natural events evolve and develop, the laws can and should develop as well— just as there is no absolute time or space. We can see that the laws co-evolve along with the phenomena that generate them. As natural events (including humanity) continue to self-create and to interrelate, they emerge into novel expressions and developing patterns, at once connected to what came before but able to transcend those constraints. The unity we embody and seek is no longer the mystery of transcending dualism (by comprehending how eternal objective law can impact ephemeral subjective material and why these eternal laws should be fundamentally one), but emerges organically from the dynamic interaction of matter and energy at every moment of evolution, at every level of becoming. There was never any time when natural events were in isolation from each other; there was never any place in which natural events were separated completely. Oneness is itself the expression of emergent, dynamic monism—contemplated and expressed through embodied metaphor.[11] And this oneness opens us anew to the marvel of creation—integrating our scientific information and our religious traditions and a unified dance of theopoetic intuition.

Rav Saadia Gaon notes, "There is no means of proving the existence of a Creator other than that of creation."[12] As have others before and after him, he seeks to know the Creator by reading creation. At least since the philosophy of Immanuel Kant, the pursuit of natural theology has been problematic if not impossible. When Kant demonstrated that we are able to know how the mind organizes reality, but not reality as it is independently, he made an ironclad dichotomy intended to sunder forever the simple link between the works of creation and the Creator. Even reconceived as embodied metaphor, Kant's insight stands as a warning against a too facile equation of those attributes of nature a theologian would select to impute to a divine source; the possibility for abuse and distortion remains abiding and real. Nonetheless, if we are no longer constrained by a fact/value dichotomy, and if we understand mind as a process of the universe itself come to consciousness, the laws as the patterns of natural events, then we are no longer seeking to describe a God radically separate from creation and outside space-time. Instead, we are looking for traces of divinity—novelty, relationship, ethics—that permeate creation and become active through our fellow creations and us. In that light, the words of Rav Saadia ring true in a new context: we seek to understand the process that is divine by understanding better the implications of the process that is creation.

Just as facts are already value-laden and values are already steeped in facts, so our consideration of scientific data has articulated values and perspectives to which we can now give more explicit theological consideration. The first of these facts/values is that of evolution and creation, a battle between those who would insist that every detail of material reality was foretold and established in advance and those who see real openness in the process of creation. The battle lines are surprising. For religious fundamentalists, nothing happens in the world without God's prior intention, so real innovation and agency are precluded. For scientific reductionists on the physics side, nothing happens that is not the simple application of each phenomenon's component physics constrained by eternal law (so real innovation and agency are ruled out). Scientific reductionists on the biology side would insist that everything is random, unpredictable, and the expression of an evolutionary process, so that there is randomness without purpose. Our third way beckons between these chastening straits—a cosmos characterized by dynamism, relationship, and openness, a universe in the process of becoming, an open future awaiting the actions determined by our free agency.

The first, and I think, most profound, reality of an evolving, emergent, dynamic creation is that every natural event is related to every other natural event and to all natural events. "God is," as Whitehead reminds, "not to be treated as an exception to all metaphysical principles, invoked to save their collapse. He is their chief exemplification."[13] Creation theology begins with the insight that it is not God alone who is one. All is one. We are related to each and to all, as is the Creator.

That all is one is both fact and value. The Big Bang produced hydrogen and helium, but it was the first generations of supernovae that exploded the other elements into the dark skies, flinging the nitrogen, carbon, and other essentials for building life out into the cosmos. Enough of these elements were collected by the swirling dust that became the solar system and the earth, and the earth was just the right distance from the sun, stabilized by its oversized moon, that it was able to maintain sufficient stability for the emergence of an oxygen-dominated atmosphere, for the emergence of water, for a sufficiently narrow temperature range that the water didn't freeze or evaporate, that organic chemicals could bond, could self-organize in increasingly complex and self-replicating patterns, that single-celled life could commence. That simple life partnered with other single cells (the current theory for the existence of mitochondria and nuclei within cells), and those cells could band together cooperatively to create more complex creatures. Cascading out of this *makor chayim* (*fons vitae*, this fountain of life), some emerged and greened our earth, rooting themselves in sea rock, sand, and eventually risking the dirt. Their children spread as lichen, shrub, and tree, spreading as the great forests and jungles that cradled the Earth, rooting into the very earth they transformed by their presence and stretching toward the light, "the mountains and the hills break forth before you into singing, and all the trees of the field clap their hands. Instead of the thorn the cypress tree shall come up, and instead of the nettle shall the myrtle tree come up; and it shall be to the Holy One for a name, for an everlasting sign that shall not be cut off."[14]

Other children emerged as the soft simple creatures of the sea, some as the myriad bacteria and the swarming insects whose buzzing communities still sustain and pollinate for us all—their distant cousins' progeny. Some of their children's children became the backboned fish, some of whose riskier offspring ventured into the swamps and ponds of amphibian aspiration. A few of these frogs and newts boldly dared into drier parts, and their reptile offspring sprouted sturdy legs for walking the land or erupted in plumaged wings to soar on high. Some of their children's children became mighty ponderous dinosaurs, and some others became the tiny mammals that scurried underfoot until the dinosaurs' demise shoved the timid furry ones onto a path of diversification and growth that produced woolly mammoths, saber-toothed tigers, and also dogs, horses, monkeys, and apes. Some few of those apes descended from the trees and stood up for a better view. We humans have been seeking that clearer perspective ever since.

Life cascades—from the stardust and supernovae that gave our heritage, whose elements comprise our blood, our bones, our skin, our brains, whose electricity powers our nerves and our consciousness. All of the cosmos is our mother/father—we are the descendants and the cousins of the galaxies. And we are also the children and brothers and sisters and cousins of all living things, without exception. Everything everywhere is an expression of oneness. This is both scientific fact—inescapable and inspiring—and theological value—to be is to belong is to be community. Our oneness with all creation impels us to recognize community with all creation. God's oneness is expressed through creaturely solidarity and passion and compassion for all.

Rather than looking for God in some supernatural realm removed from or in opposition to the oneness permeating the living cosmos, our explorations invite us back home, to recognize God as the super, natural one![15] God is found pervading nature's richness, disturbing the still predictability of entropy with eddies and whirls of increasing order, such as to bubble into rivulets of organization and life, which wash into a mindfulness that transcends species and erupts into awareness and self-awareness.

That fecund awareness is one of both boundary breaking *and* of uniqueness, simultaneously. Creation theology is iconoclastic—where some would establish distinctions, our embodied creatureliness also invites commonality across division, as Hans Jonas already stated:

> The *continuity* of descent linking man with the animal world made it henceforth impossible to regard his mind, and mental phenomena in general, as the abrupt intrusion of an ontologically alien principle in the total stream of life. Man's isolation, the last citadel of dualism, disappeared, and he could once again use his knowledge of himself to interpret the totality of which he was a part.[16]

We are stardust—we are all stardust. Seeing all creation as phenomenologically diverse yet ontologically one invites a celebration of the relatedness of all natural events—including each of us and all of us. This evolving emergence of growing complexity never violates the constraints of physics and its component parts. From its very inception, all life emerges from prior life, and life itself emerges from the organic and the nonbiological, so that all of creation is part of a single web, a single interconnected, related, growing process, in which there seems to be a rise in complexity, a rise in experience, ultimately perception, and of consciousness. When we connect with other living things, we tap into a relationship created by shared origins, common organization, overlapping responses to this wonderful planet. Anyone who has ever loved a pet, stood in awe at the shore of the sea as dolphins frolicked, marveled in wonder as salmon returned to their cycle of death and life, stood in silence near a deer frozen in alert attentiveness, or even peered into a microscope at a simple bacterium and reflected on our common cellularity can attest to the profound inviting power of our commonality. Creation invites, "Hallelujah!"

A creation theology takes seriously that emergent evolution simultaneously highlights continuity and discontinuity. Rare are those aspects of nature that do not have some earlier, simpler expression at a more fundamental level. Jonas is most instructive on this point saying: "We can see everything surpassing animality as a new stage of mediate relationship to the world that is already beginning to take form in animals and, in turn, is already based upon the mediate nature of all organic existence as such."[17] Even as a phenomenon can reach toward novelty, it does so on the shoulder of its emergent context. So it is with inwardness, subjectivity, mindfulness, and consciousness, which some take to be the defining traits of humanity, our unique and exclusive prerogative. One need not embrace a full-blown panpsychism to recognize the roots of mindfulness[18] far down into the simplest levels of creation, and scientific evidence is extending mindfulness to the very earliest levels of the biosphere, perhaps even beyond. A few suggestive examples will suffice (note that in each case, I am citing cases that went against what experts "knew" the life form was capable of, and that I am "descending" the ladder of evolution with each example):

- Reports of a chimp that prove that nonhuman primates plan for the future, in this case by stockpiling rocks during the night to fling at unwelcome human visitors at the Furuvik Zoo in Sweden.[19]
- The parrot, Alex, who broke through a series of presumed limits on what birds allegedly could learn: "Birds cannot learn to label objects, they said. Alex did. OK, birds cannot learn to generalize. Alex did. All right, but they cannot learn concepts.

Alex did. Well, they certainly cannot understand 'same' versus 'different.' Alex did."[20]

- Rooks, Eurasian members of the crow family, were able to spontaneously learn to cooperate to move a platform, with each bird tugging on an end of a rope simultaneously to make it possible to get the food on the platform.[21]
- A decapitated rooster lived for eighteen months, fed with an eyedropper directly into its throat; it gained five and a half pounds, walked around and even attempted to crow. This Colorado animal demonstrates mindfulness, but has no brain![22]
- Two neuroethologists, from the University of Toulouse and Australian National University in Canberra, taught free-flying bees to track a trail of colored marks, which they were then able to do in a completely unfamiliar maze. They learned to demonstrate delayed matching-to-sample (DMTS) and were able to generalize to situations never previously encountered, learning an abstract relation.[23]
- A team of Japanese researchers of Hokkaido University demonstrated that *Physarum* slime-mold amoebas demonstrate the ability to memorize and anticipate repeated events. The study showed "a primitive version of brain function" in an organism that has no brain! Biophysicist Toshiyuki Nakagaki noted that this finding "might be a chance to reconsider what intelligence is."[24]

As Hans Jonas teaches, "Whether we give this inwardness the name of feeling, receptiveness, response to stimuli, volition, or something else—it harbors, in some degree of 'awareness,' the absolute interest of the organism in its own being, agency, and continuation."[25] Human consciousness may feel particularly precious, and rightly so. But it is also part of a broader phenomenon that extends across living things, beginning with responses to stimuli that move toward self-preservation and pleasure and away from death and pain. Mindfulness appears to pervade creation—fashioned of the same stuff as humans are. It may differ in kind, but it shares a resistance to obliteration and sameness that is found in matter as well as throughout the biosphere. Matter, it seems, is neither inert nor brute. It upwells, in a rich range of characteristics, responses, reactions, and finally in living things, to intentions and self-awareness.

We are a part of nature. Yet we are also apart from nature, aware of our own awareness, living with an intensity and complexity of feeling and reflection that we do not find in the same degree elsewhere in our natural family. Same yet different, related yet distinct, as we ponder our cousins in creation our awareness of marvel is simultaneously an awareness of our distinctiveness. Only a distinctive creature could summon feelings of marvel, relationship, and connection. And only a particularly mindful creature could think about the wonder of such thoughts and choose to act on them. In true dipolar fashion, a creation theology bids us acknowledge both our embedded commonality and our distinctive uniqueness. Creation asks of us to say, "Amen!" and to choose. An embodied theology of creation invites its children to partake of freedom, to actualize real agency.

Notes

1. By "Dominant theology" I mean the Western integration of Plato's and Aristotle's writings into the Scholastic schools that dominated Christian, Muslim, and Jewish theologies for most of the medieval period, ideas that have continued to dominate much of the field of philosophy in the modern period. According to this approach, there is an objectively true and eternal set of ideas that our minds can track—that God is the supreme example of this kind of eternal, transcendent, spiritual reality vis-à-vis the cosmos, as our souls to our bodies, and that our concepts correspond to these objective categories and that timeless truths are revealed to us largely independent of our brains, bodies, or cultures, because truths rise above particularities and are best distilled through human reason and expressed in language.
2. Pierre Simon, Marquis de LaPlace, *Philosophical Essays on Probabilities*, trans. Frederick Wilson Truscott and Frederick Lincoln Emory (New York: Cosimo Books, 2007), 4.
3. See Brian Greene, *The Elegant Universe: Superstrings, Hidden Dimensions, and the Quest for the Ultimate Theory* (New York: Vintage Books, 2000), for an eloquent and passionate presentation of this unflagging search.
4. In fairness, some recent descriptions of natural laws do acknowledge that the law is a descriptive tool, a conceptual generalization of concrete phenomena, not an objective reality of its own. For example, "In science, a law is a descriptive principle of nature that holds in all circumstances covered by the wording of the law (Daintith & Martin, *Oxford Dictionary of Science* (New York: Oxford University Press, 2005, 464)" or "in logic, a stated regularity in the

relations or order of phenomena in the world that holds, under a stipulated set of conditions, either universally or in a stated proportion of instances." *Encyclopedia Britannica*, s.v. "Nature, law of," Encyclopedia Britannica Online, http://www.search.eb.com/eb/article-9055050 (accessed July 6, 2009).

5. "Secondary and approximate" remains quite significant. Newtonian physics, for example, is also secondary and approximate, yet we continue to rely on it for daily life and for most mechanics.
6. The astute reader will discern echoes of Franz Rosenzweig. See "The New Thinking," in *FranzRosenzweig, Philosophical and Theological Writings*, ed. Paul. W. Franks and Michael L. Morgan (Indianapolis: Hackett Publishing Company, 2000), also found in *Franz Rosenzweig's "The New Thinking,"* ed. Alan Udoff and Barbara E. Galli (Syracuse: Syracuse University Press, 1999).
7. See William R. Stroeger, "Contemporary Physics and the Ontological Status of the Laws of Nature," *Quantum Cosmology and the Laws of Nature: Scientific Perspectives on Divine Action*, ed. Robert John Russell, Nancey Murphy and C.J. Isham (Notre Dame: Notre Dame Press, 1999), 207–31.
8. Louis Jacobs, "Jewish Cosmology," in *Ancient Cosmologies*, ed. Carmen Blacker and Michael Loewe (London: George Allen & Unwin Ltd, 1975), 29. A page later, he observes that the concept of universal law "is anachronistic when applied to the thought of the Rabbis." Ibid., 30.
9. John Archibald Wheeler, in *Problems in Theoretical Physics*, ed. A. Giovanni, F. Mancini and M. Marino (Salerno: University of Salerno Press, 1984).
10. Rolf Landauer, "Computation and Physics: Wheeler's Meaning Circuit," *Foundations of Physics* 16 (1986):551–64.
11. A controversial but evocative expression of this sentiment is Mach's Principle, which states, "The inertia of any particular matter is attributable to the interaction between that piece of matter and the rest of the universe." See John Daintith in *Oxford Dictionary of Physics* (Oxford: Oxford University Press, 2005), 297. Mach's insight, contested to this day, had an important impact on Einstein's formulation of general relativity.
12. Saadia Gaon, *The Book of Doctrines and Beliefs*, ed. Samuel Rosenblatt (New Haven: Yale University Press, 1948), 96.
13. Alfred North Whitehead, *Process and Reality: An Essay in Cosmology*, ed. David Ray Griffin and Donald W. Sherburne, (New York: The Free Press, 1978), 343.
14. Isa. 55:12.
15. The idea for the comma and the term comes from Sallie McFague, *Super, Natural Christians: How We Should Love Nature* (Minneapolis: Augsburg Fortress Publishers, 2000).

16. Hans Jonas, *Mortality and Morality: A Search for God after Auschwitz*, ed. Lawrence Vogel (Evanston, IL: Northwestern University Press 1996), 63.
17. Ibid., 77.
18. The insight of Milton Steinberg is pertinent here: "The entire universe, as I see it, is the outward manifestation of Mind-energy, of Spirit, or to use the older and better word, of God. God is then the essential Being of all beings, though all beings in their totality do not exhaust Him. It is His reason which expressed itself in the rationality of nature, in the fact that all things behave in conformity with intelligible forms, in the fact, in brief, that the world is cosmos not chaos. His power moves in the dynamisms of physical reality. His will is the impulse behind the upsurge of life on this planet. Individualized, He is the soul of man whose thought processes are infinitesimal sparks of His infinite fire, whose moral aspirations are fragments of His vast purpose, whose yearning to create is but an echo of His cosmic creativity. And He is an ethical being, not so much in the sense that He enters into relations with His own expressions, as in the deeper sense that He is the fountainhead, source, and sanction of man's moral life. The human quest after freedom, truth, goodness, and beauty is but the splintered spearhead of the divine drive. So to me, the whole panorama of earth and sky, the tempestuous progress of living things, and the tortuous career of humanity, are the external shell of a process wherein God realizes His character." Milton Steinberg, *A Believing Jew: The Selected Writings of Milton Steinberg* (New York: Harcourt, Brace and Company, 1951), 19.
19. Coco Ballantyne, "Planning of the Apes," *Scientific American* (May 2009), 27.
20. Irene Pepperberg, *From Alex & Me: How a Scientist and a Parrot Discovered a Hidden World of Animal Intelligence—and Formed a Deep Bond in the Process* (New York: HarperCollins Publishers, 2008), quoted in *Discover Magazine* (February 2009), 77.
21. Emily Anthes, "Head Lines," *Scientific American Mind* (August/September 2008), 8.
22. David McFarland, *Guilty Robots, Happy Dogs: The Question of Alien Minds* (Oxford: Oxford University Press, 2008), cited by Nicole Branan, *Scientific American Mind* (August/September 2008), 82.
23. Christof Koch, "Exploring Consciousness through the Study of Bees," *Scientific American Mind* (January 14, 2009).
24. Tetsu Saigusa et al., "Amoebae Anticipate Periodic Events," *Physical Review Letters* 100, no. 1 (January 11, 2008).
25. Jonas, *Mortality and Morality*, 69.

Why We Need Process Theology

Toba Spitzer

There are many challenges to being a liberal rabbi in the early twenty-first century, not the least of which is articulating an approach to Judaism that is meaningful and potentially transformative for the sophisticated, thoughtful people who might be tempted to enter the doors of my synagogue. The issue is not merely one of creating dynamic programming or fostering authentic community, although those are certainly important elements. My larger task, I have come to realize, is articulating a compelling narrative in which contemporary Jews can place themselves. Part of that task is to help Jews experience themselves as living within the mythic narrative arc of the Jewish "master story," the liberation from Egypt and the creation of a Godly covenantal community. For this I have many tools at my disposal, from the lived experience of the Jewish year to the weekly reading of the Torah, as well as a two-thousand-year-old repository of Jewish texts that expand upon and elaborate that narrative.

But there is another part of the task that is more challenging. Central to the Jewish narrative is the notion of a Divine Being that enters into covenantal relationship with the Jewish people. Without a compelling way of talking about how the God so profoundly experienced by our biblical and Rabbinic ancestors is still active in our lives and in the world around us, our master story threatens to become little more than a nostalgic fairy tale. Without a way to conceptualize and talk about the Divine in ways that make both head- and heart-sense, Judaism loses its power to shape our individual and collective lives. And this is precisely what has happened for a vast number of American Jews over the past century. I hear from numerous people that theirs is a "cultural" Judaism, composed of a commitment to the past and some inherited sense

TOBA SPITZER (RRC97) is the rabbi of Congregation Dorshei Tzedek in West Newton, Massachusetts.

of Jewish ethics, happily divorced from the problematics of religious belief. Yet many of these "cultural Jews" are deeply spiritual people who actively desire meaningful forms of spiritual and ethical practice. Judaism's God-problem is keeping them from fully engaging with Jewish life and all that Jewish tradition has to offer.

Religion, Science, and the Problem of Classical Theology

At the heart of this challenge is the prevailing assumption among educated lay people that there is a fundamental tension between religion and science. At worst, they are enemies: The rationalism of science threatens the possibility of religious faith, and religious faith undermines the acceptance of fundamental scientific truths. At best, the two live in a kind of uneasy truce, with science ruling the realm of physical reality, and religion holding sway in the realm of morals and spiritual development. In either case, the disjunction between the two causes many people to feel that a full religious commitment entails some element of irrationality or make-believe.

Yet I am increasingly convinced that the problem is not an essential divide between scientific reason and religious faith, but rather an outmoded frame for religious thinking that relies on the metaphysical "certainties" of an age long past. Beginning with Platonic and neo-Platonic notions of the "perfect" as abstract and unchanging, and continuing through a premodern and Enlightenment dualism of material and spiritual "substances," dominant Jewish and Christian notions of God are shaped by metaphysical assumptions that no longer reflect what we actually know about the world. I cannot imagine any modern person claiming that the actual physical world is less real than perfect "forms" that exist in the abstract—yet that was in fact the assumption of Plato and later philosophers in the Jewish and Muslim world influenced by Aristotelian neo-Platonism. Those "forms" were perfect in that they were eternal and unchanging—a claim that is still made about God.

Another premodern notion that continues to shape how we think and talk about God is the notion that reality is made up of "substances"—entities that are not reducible to anything else. In the philosophy of René Descartes and others, a fundamental distinction is made between material "substances"—the realm of nature and the body—and mental "substances"—the mind and soul.

This profound dualism takes on religious import when the same schema is applied to God: Just as the body and soul are of irreducibly different substances, so too God is irreducibly "other" than the material world that is God's creation. The soul derives from God, and the body from the realm of the material, and the two are ultimately unconnected. Not only are these realms unrelated to one another, an implicit hierarchy is established: the intellectual and spiritual realms, having their source in God, are ultimately of more value, and holier, than the realm of nature and the material world.

These ideas, even if they may have originated outside of the Jewish world, permeate our texts and traditions. Even within Jewish mysticism, which in many ways challenges the rigid dualism of classical theology, there persists the notion that God is ultimately eternal and unchanging, and that the realm of the holy is by definition nonmaterial, with materiality (our bodies, our sexuality, the world of nature) at worst the repository of evil in the world, or at best an "illusion" that merely cloaks God's (presumably nonmaterial) reality.

There are multiple problems stemming from these assumptions. Modern physics has upended premodern notions of reality being made up of eternal "substances." We now know that physical matter is not an enduring, unchanging "thing." Matter can become energy, and vice versa. A static notion of the universe has given way to a dynamic understanding of reality. While one could in theory make the philosophic case for an eternal, unchanging, entirely abstract God that shares no attributes of the universe in which we live, the "usefulness" of such a God is highly suspect. That is, such a God threatens to become little more than a concept, a disconnected divinity, alone and untouchable, with which it is difficult if not impossible to have a meaningful relationship. It may well be that the premodern notions of reality that were projected onto God were in fact meaningful for the people who first articulated them, but that ultimately says more about those thinkers than it does about God. For our own time, we need conceptual categories and metaphors for speaking of God that incorporate reality as we understand and experience it. In addition, as I will argue further on, the static, unchanging God is largely foreign to the Torah and other foundational Jewish texts.

Another significant problem is the dualism mentioned above. Classical dualism promotes a mind-body/nature-soul split that has led to the denigration of our bodies, of the realm of nature, and of women, who in Western culture have been identified with nature.[1] This theoretical degradation has led to very real consequences, whether the plundering of the natural environment or the continued devaluation of women and what our culture labels as "female." As we learn more about the intricate integration of our minds and bodies, as we begin to appreciate the diversity of human self-understanding beyond rigid gender lines, and as we seek to create spiritual lives that embrace our embodied physical selves, a Jewish theology that overcomes the dualism of spirit-matter, male-female, and God-world is an urgent project.

The ultimate problem of classical theology is that of theodicy—the problem of the continued existence of suffering and evil in a world theoretically created and overseen by a God that by definition is "perfect," meaning both impervious to change and ultimately good, and all-powerful as well. It is this conundrum that tends to be most problematic for the people in the pews. If we as religious leaders cannot sensibly articulate a belief in a divine aspect of the universe that is both believably powerful as well as a source of goodness, love, and justice, while at the same time affirming the reality of the suffering in people's lives, then we cannot wonder when those same people decide that the God they have been led to believe in is either a chimera or an outright lie.

A Process Approach

As a pulpit rabbi, as someone concerned with my own spiritual development and that of my congregants, and as someone dedicated to the continuity of Judaism and the Jewish people, I have been searching for ways to think and talk about God that make sense (that is, that are both internally consistent and consistent with our current best understandings of how reality operates), that resonate with Jewish texts and traditions, and that promote wise and ethical behavior. My assumption is that all human attempts to say anything at all about the nature of divinity are both limited and ever-evolving, changing as we gain new insights into the workings of the universe and as our minds gain new understanding. I am less interested in trying to "define" what God is, than to have available a set of concepts and metaphors that provide a frame through which to make sense of my own life and the world around me.

In recent years, I have found the school of process thought, and process theology more specifically, to be a powerful resource in this project. Building on the then-new discoveries of quantum mechanics, the early twentieth-century mathematician Alfred North Whitehead and his followers created new categories with which to think about God and the nature of divinity. The most fundamental claim of process philosophy is that every aspect of our reality is in some way "in process," is constantly being made anew. In the words of C. Robert Mesle, "the world is finally not made of 'things' at all, if a 'thing' is something that exists over time without changing. The world is composed of events and processes."[2] In this understanding, every level of reality, from the molecule to the human being, is a succession of "droplets of experience," which in every moment incorporates aspects of the past while also making way for the new. Whitehead uses the word "experience" to indicate that at all levels of existence, the world consists not of little units of matter, but consequential moments of becoming—moments that combine elements of "choice" (that is, different possible outcomes) with the influence of the past and the surrounding environment.

For process thought, anything that is "actual" is in process. God, in that God too is "actual," must also be in process, ever-changing and incorporating new aspects of experience. In Whitehead's articulation, God is not only *in* process, but is also the Source of novelty, is that which makes possible something other than the eternal repetition of that which has already existed.

The argument of process theology is that the outmoded notions of "perfection" and "omnipotence" that have come to define our sense of godliness are neither compatible with reality nor worthy of adulation. One essential quality of an eternal and unchanging divinity is that it, by definition, cannot interact with its own creation. Meaningful interaction implies some kind of change on the part of both parties to the interaction. In contrast, the process understanding of reality implies ongoing interconnectivity at all levels of being. All life, whether electrons or humans, are "in process" in that they interact with the environment around them, are affected by that environment, and incorporate this experience into the next moment of becoming.[3] So, too, does God interact with God's creation, and thus we can say that God is in process. Far from diminishing God, this inherent relationality is at the very foundation of the notion that God "loves" us and "needs" us, ideas that permeate biblical and Rabbinic theology. God's reality does not stand at an untouchable remove from the created world, but encompasses it, is in process *with* it.

The Process God of Torah

As both Jewish and Christian process theologians have noted, the eternal, unchanging God is most decidedly *not* the deity that we encounter in the Torah.[4] From the very first chapters of *B'reishit*, God is portrayed as a Being that changes Its mind, gets angry and regrets, consoles and berates.[5] Most importantly, this God learns. The Creator of humanity seems to honestly not have a clear idea of what Its creations are going to get up to. The first questions of Genesis—"Where are you?" and "Where is your brother?"—are real questions. Not that God doesn't "know" where these earthlings are physically located, but the Creator seems truly puzzled by their actions. Why are you hiding from Me? Why did you kill your brother? It is indeed possible to read much of the Torah as the story of God's ongoing attempt to learn how to live with, and through, Its human creations.

If God learns, then God changes—and the Torah seems quite clear, and quite comfortable, on this point. *YHVH* is awesomely powerful, but is not static, and the biblical God adapts and changes in response to the needs of the moment.

Even more—at the Burning Bush, God is described as the Power of Becoming itself. When Moshe asks for a name for the divinity that has called to him, he learns that God is called "*Ehyeh asher Ehyeh*," "I will be that I will be." These verses are a kind of biblical proof text for Whitehead's contention that God is the ultimate Source of all possibility and potentiality in the universe. In the words of our liturgy, *Ehyeh* is that which *m'chadeish b'chol yom tamid maaseih b'reishit* (renews each and every day—in every moment—the work of creation). Without this ongoing, dynamic Power, the created universe would be incapable of unfolding and evolving as it has been since the moment of the Big Bang. The God of the Torah, and the God of our daily experience of the world, is not an abstract, unchanging, and immutable Unmoved Mover, but That which allows the universe to unfold in all of its dazzling complexity. Process theology echoes this traditional Jewish notion and gives it resonance with contemporary understandings of the dynamism of physical reality, and the truth of evolution in the biological realm.

Persuasive Power

Another key contribution of process theology is its critique of traditional notions of God's omnipotence. The idea that God is "all-powerful" is problematic on many levels. It implies the existence of a divine power that somehow operates outside of, or over against, the natural laws of physics and biology. Even if God is understood to be the ultimate Source of those natural laws, the implicit meaning of "all-powerful" is that God can abrogate those laws when and if God chooses (which is of course the traditional understanding of "miracles"). The other problem, mentioned earlier, is that of suffering and evil. If God is indeed "all-powerful," presumably able to do whatever God wants whenever God wants to, then why do tsunamis, or genocides, ever happen? To argue, as some do, that God "chooses" to limit God's power for whatever reason leaves us with a divinity that is at best arbitrary, at worst vindictive. To imply, as others do, that certain events only appear problematic from a human perspective, but from God's perspective all that occurs is "good," leaves us with no ability to discern what in fact *is* for the good.

Process philosophers point out that the problem isn't with God, it's with our limited human notions of power. God's power has been mischaracterized as ultimate *coercive* power—that is, the power to get others to do whatever one desires. There are two problems with this notion. The first is that such complete coercive power effectively rids all other beings of any power or freedom. If God truly has the power to control everything we do, then we have no real freedom, no ability to act meaningfully or to exercise our own power in any way. This clearly isn't the truth of our existence, and it effectively renders God's power meaningless—because how powerful does God need to be to exert force over something completely lacking the ability to exert its own will? From a Jewish perspective, human free will is a foundational principle—from Adam and Eve exerting their choice in the garden of Eden, to Moses' challenge to the Israelites to "choose life" on the plains of Moab. God's power, however awesome, is never such that it can erase the reality of human choice.

The second problem is that such a conception of power is immoral. It projects human fantasies of omnipotence—totalitarian fantasies—onto God. It turns power into the ability to control. Why would we want to embrace such a vision of power as ultimate, as Godly, as good?

In place of ultimate coercive power, process theology suggests that we think of Godly power as "persuasive power." In this understanding, God is not only the source of novelty in the universe, but is also That which creates order, and defines the "initial aim" of all of creation. The "initial aim" shapes the trajectory of every created being, establishing its limits as well as the end toward which it is oriented. My own "initial aim" is to come into my fullness as a human being—not as a tree or a frog, each of which has its own "aim." God provides the "lure," acting as the influence that shapes us and urges us on towards our unique end. This urge and influence is experienced as persuasive, not coercive. Just as parents, teachers, doctors, or rabbis guide those in their care not by forcing their child, student, patient or congregant to do what they think is right, but through a combination of cajoling, urging, teaching, and warning, so might we imagine the Persuasive Power of the Universe exerting Its power upon us. This is not to lessen the awesomeness of Godly power, which includes the capacity to create our universe, but rather to reconceptualize how such power operates within the created world, and especially within the human realm.

In biblical language, God's persuasive power is described with terms like *chesed* and *tzedek*, which are understood as Godly powers that human beings can either ignore or live by, in the context of covenantal community. Life lived according to these powers or principles brings blessing; denying or abrogating them causes both ecological and social disaster. Thus we can read the second paragraph of the *Sh'ma* not as the punishment promised by a coercive deity to its wayward charges, but rather as a description of the inevitable consequences of the Israelites' collective failure to uphold their covenantal commitments. This kind of warning is one way in which the Torah describes God's persuasive power, based on an understanding that human actions have consequences, and that only by understanding those potential consequences can we make the right choices. In Hebrew, God's desire is also called God's *ratzon*, often translated as "will." God's will is not something that coerces, but something that desires, that lures, that urges, cautions, and cajoles. We are free to ignore it, but usually at our individual, or collective, peril.[6]

Such a conception of God's power does of course require us to relinquish some things. If there is no ultimate coercive power that controls everything, then we have to admit to a certain element of chance and contingency in the universe. We need to let go of our own fantasies of control, and our need for certainty. Process theology admits this, and indeed embraces it. Chance and contingency are real, as is the reality that with greater complexity comes greater capacity for both good and evil. The ability of an amoeba to suffer, or to cause suffering, is rather limited. But with the development of sentient life and human consciousness comes both the capacity for great joy and great pain, the ability to do good as well as the ability to do evil. The biological process of evolution incorporates accidents and uncertainties, echoed perhaps in the Rabbinic midrash that before settling on this world, God had to make and destroy hundreds of previous worlds. This world is not perfect, and perhaps never will be. Yet out of chaos there emerges some semblance of order, as well as beauty and good.

A Jewish Process Theology

Alfred North Whitehead wrote nearly a century ago, with the explicit intent to reconcile religion and science, to "connect the radical new insights of Einstein's relativity theory and quantum indeterminacy to our living sense of value."[7] The process theology that developed in the wake of Whitehead's insights has been predominantly Christian, with some scattered attempts to incorporate the innovations of process thought into Jewish theology.

Contemporary with Whitehead, Mordecai Kaplan dared to suggest that we think of God as "The Power that Makes for Salvation," that we explore the notion of God as a "process" and not as a supernatural Being.[8] Most recently, Rabbi Bradley Shavit Artson has begun to more comprehensively articulate a Jewish process theology, connecting the insights of process thought to biblical and Rabbinic teachings.[9]

I am hopeful that Jewish theology will be revitalized through the encounter with process thought. Precisely because it is congruent with much of biblical and Rabbinic theology, as well as incorporating the panentheism of Jewish mysticism (while removing the dross of medieval metaphysics), I would argue that a process approach is our best option for shaping a conversation about God that can both make sense to, and provide spiritual meaning for contemporary Jews. I do not know if process theology will do much to convince those who are adamant in their atheism, but I think it can help enormously when it comes to those Jews who want to make sense of their lived experience in spiritual terms, and who seek a way to speak about God that doesn't revert to outdated metaphors or irrelevant metaphysical claims.

There are, in addition, ethical implications of our God-talk. How we think and talk about God says something about how we experience the world and how we live our lives. If we continue to exalt Something that is eternal, unchanging, and exerts ultimate control, how can we accept the reality that life is a constant process of growth, change, and decay, and that ultimate control is an illusion? If God Itself is in process, is constantly evolving and changing, how Godly then to embrace the ever-changing nature of our own existence! If chance and contingency are aspects of a Godly universe, then we can bless the uncertainties in our own lives, rather than bemoaning them. If coercive power is no longer perceived as Godly, we can create a powerful theological critique of ideologies that exalt such power in the human realm, whether we speak of human power "over" the natural world, or the ways in which humans exert power "over" one another.

There is much yet to be done in creating this new approach to Jewish theology. A process understanding of covenant and of mitzvah, of what it means to be "obligated" when we understand God not as Commander-in-Chief but as Something which provides an "initial aim" and a "lure," is a critical next step. A fuller explication of how we can understand God not as "He," "She," or "It" but as Becoming, and yet at the same time meaningfully connect on a personal level to God as "You" in a Jewish idiom is yet another avenue for exploration. We can be humble enough to know that our understanding of That which created and continues to animate this universe will always be limited, while still endeavoring to shape a theological language that helps us discern our place in the world and how we might best align ourselves with God's *ratzon*. May the Process be with us as we do!

Notes

1. I am not suggesting here that philosophical dualism is the cause of women's oppression, which has varied roots across many cultures. But medieval conceptions of the hierarchy of soul-matter and mind-body have profoundly informed and reinforced an enduring hierarchy of male-female in Western culture, a theme that is also prevalent within many strands of premodern Jewish thought.
2. C. Robert Mesle, *Process-Relational Philosophy: An Introduction to Alfred North Whitehead* (West Conshohocken, PA: Templeton Foundation Press, 2008), 8. This book is an excellent, accessible introduction to Whitehead's thought. A good introduction to process theology is John B. Cobb, Jr., and David Ray Griffin, *Process Theology: An Introductory Exposition* (Louisville: Westminster John Knox Press, 1976).
3. "It is impossible for experience to exist independently: Experience arises out of that which is lived. That which is experienced from 'outside' us becomes 'inside' us, or, better, becomes part of us because it is taken into our self as experiencer. Every drop of experience is a novel weaving of the world of preceding experiences out of which that drop arises." Mesle, *Process-Relational Philosophy*, 43.
4. For an in-depth exploration of the resonance of biblical and Rabbinic texts with process theology, see the recent article by Bradley Shavit Artson, "*Ba-derekh*: On the Way—A Presentation of Process Theology," *Conservative Judaism* 62, nos. 1–2 (Fall-Winter 2010): 3–35.
5. A note about pronouns: Where necessary, I refer to God as "It" rather than "She" or "He," because I find that gendered pronouns contribute, even if unwittingly, to an ongoing sense of God as a big Person. If, as some process theologians posit, it is more appropriate to speak of God as "Becoming" rather than as a "Being," then we need to find a way to express this radically nonpersonal sense of divinity. While "it" still has the connotation of a "thing," it does have the benefit of avoiding the connotations of personhood that adhere to the personal pronouns "he" or "she." That being said, I still find powerful the use of "You" when seeking to relate *to* God. For the moment, at least, I am willing to live with the tension of employing a mix of personal and nonpersonal pronouns in an attempt to expand my own conceptual frame.
6. Process theologian Catherine Keller discusses God's power and the notion of "desire" versus control in *On the Mystery: Discerning Divinity in Process* (Minneapolis: Fortress Press, 2008), 87–90. She writes: "The alternative to omnipotence lies in the risky interactivity of relationship. It does not toss the creatures into a deistic void, chilled but autonomous. It continues to call them forth, to invite.

In the language of process theology, it 'lures' them collectively and individually toward self-actualization. The power of God, if it is a response-able power, *empowers* the others—to respond. In their freedom. God's will is indeed God's will! But the term *will* derives from *voluntas,* from which also comes 'voluntary,' which means not control but *desire.* What God *wants.* That wanting, that desiring, has a decisive element, limiting in advance what is possible for this universe. And within those limits Torah, covenant, and the whole apparatus of redemption suggest that God's will seeks to *be done.* On earth. But to *want* is not the same as to *cause.*"

7. Cited in Christine Keller, *On the Mystery*, 23.
8. Kaplan explores these ideas both in *The Meaning of God in Modern Jewish Religion* (New York: Reconstructionist Press, 1962), and in his *The Future of the American Jew* (New York: Macmillan Co., 1948). Kaplan was familiar with Whitehead's work, although he barely references him in his published theological musings, resistant as he was to metaphysics or creating a systematic theology. Kaplan writes, "[Belief in God] is the faith that reality, the cosmos, or whatever constitutes for us the universe in which we move and have our being, is so constituted that it both urges us on and helps us to achieve our salvation, provided, of course, we learn to know and understand enough about that reality to be able to conform to its demands." Kaplan, *Future of the America Jew*, 182–83. In Kaplan's words I hear an echo of the process notion of "persuasive power" and the Godly "lure."
9. Artson, "*Ba-derekh*: On the Way—A Presentation of Process Theology." Other explorations of Jewish approaches to process theology include William Kaufman, *The Evolving God in Jewish Process Theology* (Lewiston, NY: Edwin Mellen Press, 1997) and Sandra Lubarsky and David Ray Griffin, eds., *Jewish Theology and Process Thought* (Albany: Statue University of New York Press, 1996).

Part III: Science and Judaism: Methodological Considerations

A Jewish View of the Evolution of Religion

Allen S. Maller

In 1871 Charles Darwin published *The Descent of Man*, generating an ongoing heated controversy between evolutionists and creationists. The 140-year war between the disciples of Moses and the disciples of Darwin, so to speak, may be drawing to a close with victory going to those who are the disciples of both. In the last few decades genetics has provided us with a whole new source of information about the evolution of *Homo sapiens*. A simple example of this is the answer to the question of when people first began wearing clothing, provided recently by studies of lice genes.

Homo sapiens (HS) is the only living species that clothes itself. Fossilized textiles from more than 20,000 years ago have been found in the cold climates of ice age Europe. However, according to the Torah, the origins of clothing are the not the result of human adaptation to an ice age climate, but the result of human concepts of modesty. Self-aware intelligent minds became moral minds and then became modest minds. Recent DNA studies of body lice that must lay their eggs in clothing show that these lice evolved from head lice that had adapted to clothing that covered the pubic area. According to a 2003 study led by Mark Stoneking, a geneticist at the Max Planck Institute in Leipzig, Germany, this genetic adaptation took place 42,000 to 72,000 years ago. This is a date that would fit in with living in Ice Age Europe and Asia. But a newer study recently published in the January 2011 issue of *Molecular Biology and Evolution* indicates a date of separation between head and body

---

ALLEN S. MALLER (C64) is rabbi emeritus of Temple Akiba in Culver City, California.

lice of 83,000 to 170,000 years ago. Thus, HS may have been clothing themselves for about 100,000 to 150,000 years. If the higher estimate proves to be correct, it will mean that long before HS needed to wear clothing due to living in very cold northern climates, moral rules of modesty and probity became so important that our ancestors, for moral reasons and not simply for comfort reasons, began to cloth themselves. This is precisely the teaching of Genesis 3:7.

A great deal of unnecessary conflict and misunderstanding between the disciples of Darwin and the disciples of Moses has been caused by the careless use of the terms "human" and "man" to describe the increasing number of fossil finds of tool-using biped species, some of them ancestral to HS. Forty years ago, when only about a half dozen *Homo* species were described, they were listed in a straight line and all popularly labeled "humans" and not called human-like or pre HS. Now, paleontologists have about two dozen different species (depending on who is counting), most of them living at the same time as one or two other similar species. When conservationists discuss species, they never lump all mice or tortoises together; but paleoanthropologists routinely call all the different *Homo* species by the same common name, "man" or "human." I shall try to refer to each distinct species by its scientific name only.

Recent fossils found on Flores Island in Indonesia in September 2003 are from a new species of tool-using bipeds named *Homo floresiensis* that lived as recently as 15,000 years ago.[1] HS are not pigmy *Homo sapiens*. They used fire (in use by pre-HS species for more than half a million years) and made stone tools. Yet we do not have any evidence of HF ritual burials, which are the earliest forms of nonmaterial cultural activity, prior to 100,000 years ago. Most people think that the name "human" or "mankind" should be reserved only for our own species. Not using the name "human" and "man" carelessly might help resolve some of the conflict over the theory of evolution.

Another example of genetics bringing the disciples of Darwin and Moses closer together is mitochondrial Adam and Eve. For most of the twentieth century, paleoanthropologists believed that HS evolved from *Homo neanderthalenis* (HN) or some other related species like *Homo erectus*, in various regions around the world. Thus, there was no Eden-like center and no first HS male or female. This belief has been transformed by many genetic studies. Today, with the exceptions of a few regionalists, most paleoanthropologists think there was a historic "out of Africa" homeland. They also think that there was a first individual HS male and female. All men in the world today carry the same Y chromosome and both men and woman carry the same mitochondria. All of today's Y chromosomes were inherited from the same single source, a Y chromosome carried by one individual male. In the same way, we all carry the same mitochondrial DNA because all mitochondrial DNA is passed from mother to child, and passed down through mother to daughter. When a daughter of that first universal mitochondrial DNA female mated with a son of the first universal Y male, *Homo sapiens*, the children of Adam and Eve, were born;[2] none of the descendants of the other premodern HS have survived.

I am more interested in what the disciples of Darwin can teach Reform rabbis—who are the disciples of both Torah (written and oral) and modern science (cosmology and biology)—about the evolution of religion. Darwinists reason that religion is not a maladaptive "illusion" (Freud), nor is religion a manipulative "opiate" (Marx). Darwinists argue that religious behavior is a ubiquitous biological adaptation rooted in HS because religion, like intelligence and language, helps human communities survive. Religion, like intelligence and language, can be used for both good and evil purposes, but this is also true of culture, science, politics, and all other important human activities. Since almost all revealed religions teach that humans have a pre-birth soul that predisposes them to respond to a divine call even before the revelation occurs, I identify the existence of a biological-based, self-conscience spiritual soul, with the evolution of HS spirituality.

A reference to a pre-scriptural, prehistoric period when spiritual evolution was unaided by God appears in the book of Geneses (4:26) where it states, "At that time humans began to invoke *YHVH* by name." Most of the Rabbinic commentators translate the verb *huchal* to mean "profane," taking this as a negative statement. But "began" is the more normal meaning of the verb, and that is the meaning one should try and use first. The Torah asserts that prior to Enosh humans did not practice religion with the divine insight of revelation (i.e., "invoke *YHVH* by name") that later people did. Mystical and spiritual experiences were interpreted by human intelligence without the benefit of prophetic revelation. In the spirit of this Torah insight I offer the following account of the evolution of prehistoric spirituality.

All sentient beings are able to respond to the challenges of life. In each species some individuals respond to new environmental challenges better than others do; and their descendants increase. Some sentient beings that are conscious are capable of learning from the challenges of life. They can improve themselves. A few are even able to show others what they have learned and thus improve their group and their descendants' chances of survival. These species have developed cultural ways of meeting life's challenges. For many centuries it was thought that mankind's ability to use tools was what made us unique. However, we now know that several different species use tools (including birds) and chimpanzees not only use but also make at least three different kinds of tools for different functions. Chimpanzee tool use differs in different locations (a cultural, not a genetic difference). Elephants, chimpanzees, and macaques also show signs of self-awareness by recognizing themselves in a mirror. So what makes us what we are?

First, we are small group, hierarchically organized, social primates. Any genes that enable the group (extended family and/or band) to function better will contribute to individual survival and reproduction. Second, the species that preceded HS and HN have been evolving larger and larger brains for over a million years. Eventually two species, HS and HN, evolved that achieved self-conscious ways of meeting life's challenges through nonmaterial (i.e., cultural and spiritual) behaviors. *Homo neanderthalenis* were a relative of *Homo sapiens* that co-inhabited in Europe and parts of western Asia with anatomically modern humans from about 120,000 to 29,000 years ago. HN were well adapted to the cold and were very muscular. In 2010 a sister species to HN was discovered by sequencing the full genome of a girl's fossil finger bone found in a Siberian cave. This closely related sister group of Neanderthals lived in central Asia about 40,000 years ago. Like Neanderthals, the mysterious group interbred with modern humans, in this case leaving behind a genetic fingerprint in modern-day Melanesians of Papua New Guinea, nearly 10,000 kilometers from where the fossil was found.[3]

Increasing dependence on mental capacities became problematic for those individual HN and HS who malfunctioned mentally or emotionally. Any genes that would help ameliorate individual mental and emotion challenges like stress and anxiety would be selected for and would spread throughout the population. Spiritual activities among HS have evolved over the last 100,000 to 160,000 years. If one takes seriously the biblical claim that humanity was created in the divine image, spiritual evolution testifies to the creation of creatures who are cocreators of purpose-driven, nonmaterial responses to environmental and social challenges. This prepared HS to respond appropriately when divine revelations occurred in historical times.

The evolution of spiritual activities that enhance the successful survival of humanity is not only concerned with enhancing the survival of our own species. With the recent domestication of plants and animals and the very recent industrial revolution, HS acquired a great deal of responsibility for the evolution of many of the species on the planet itself. Thus the behavior of religious people themselves now becomes a factor in the evolution of life on earth. Religious behaviors are evidence of self-conscious creative thought processes most people associate with HS. Religious behaviors are the creative responses of intelligent minds to certain challenges in life.

Homo sapiens faced more than half a dozen different challenges over the last 150,000 years that stimulated spiritual developments that improved survival rates both for groups and individuals within the group. One of the greatest challenges to increased intellectual development is anxiety and self-imposed stress. The more HS can think about things, the greater the ability to produce anxiety and self-imposed stress that are debilitating by themselves, and also depress the immune system. Anything that reduces stress and anxiety increases survival rates for intelligent minds. Also as successful groups got larger it became harder and harder to keep them from internal conflict and splitting. Larger groups and groups with strong emotional alliances were more likely to win when there was intergroup conflict, and had reduced negative effects from inbreeding. Anything that helped larger groups create bonds that were more than family and behavioral norms that were more than mimicking would increase survival rates. Individuals with a mental illness could not contribute much to a tribe or band. Anything that helped heal or integrate these individuals would help survival rates. These are some of the situations faced by a species that began using its mind more and more.

The first challenge is also the ultimate one: death. *Homo sapiens* is the only living species that knows in advance that death is inevitable. Genesis 2:17 teaches "on the day you eat it [the tree of knowledge of good and evil know that you will surely die." Elephants, chimpanzees, and orangutans have been observed to mourn for a dead child, but no other living species practices ritual burial. The intelligent minds of HS responded to the death of loved ones by creating funeral rites and rituals of ancestor worship. Evidence from Qafzeh cave in northern Israel of ritual burial and grave goods (red ocher and mollusk shells of an inedible species) goes back 100,000 to 120,000 years or more. These funeral rituals brought comfort and solace to the mourners. Funeral rituals also had the important effect of strengthening group solidarity at a time when leadership might be challenged and changing. Strengthening group solidarity reduced internal conflict and violence, thus increasing the chances of raising children to adulthood.

Although other species also dream, the intelligent minds of HS creatively concluded that dreams about the dead showed that the dead were still active and could continue to help their descendants. Thus departed spirits ought to be venerated and worshiped. It is possible that nomadic hunter-gatherer bands used the skulls of important individuals in community rituals for many centuries. Two HS skulls from Herto in Ethiopia, well-worn through handling, have been dated to more than 140,000 years ago. These ritual activities strengthened feelings of kinship within and among hunter-gather bands enabling them to be more stable and grow larger. This in turn increased the chances for survival of individuals within the more effective bands and clans. Ritual activities and ideas about help available from deceased ancestors reduced stress and anxiety and so led HS to expand the realm of spirits to the treatment of physical and mental illness. We now know that anxiety and stress weaken the immune system and increase the chances of not surviving an otherwise survivable illness. Anything that reduces anxiety and stress increases survival rates. This is one key reason that religious behavior became ubiquitous.

Illness, especially mental illnesses that tend to be chronic rather than fatal, provided serious challenges to the intelligent minds of HS. Epilepsy, schizophrenia, obsessive compulsive disorder, phobias, bipolar disorders, and other brain diseases occur in at least 2 to 3 percent of the population worldwide. Thus there should be at least one or two cases in every band of fifty to one hundred people. Severe cases are very scary and disabling, but the intelligent minds of HS could react to the challenge of mild cases with a variety of rituals and practices that served to alleviate the symptoms through mind-body interactions that we recognize today as placebo faith healing. Placebo faith healing works primarily by reducing pain through endorphin release and increasing the strength of an individual's immune response, which is weakened by stress and anxiety. Only HS are known to be capable of placebo spiritual healing. Among HS today only a minority of individuals are able to heal themselves with the aid of placebo faith healing. The hope that ritual can heal and the ability to trust a healer are powerful factors that frequently bring about improvement. Chanting, drumming, dancing, meditation, and fasting are widespread ways of inducing an alternative consciousness that helps alleviate pain, stress, and anxiety. With the support of a community of believers, and a tradition that enhances their individual hope and trust, results would be even better. A cure, either short or long term, isn't the only outcome in faith healing. The ceremony itself can reduce many of the side effects of the illness such as depression, stress, anger, and negativity. This often ameliorates symptoms and brings relief. Chronic illness negatively impacts the immune system and eventually increases death rates. Ritual faith healing ameliorates symptoms for many people in these types of situations. This reintegrates the "possessed" into a support group and reduces stress, strengthens the immune system, and reduces death rates.

A tiny charismatic minority, who themselves had struggled successfully to overcome these diseases, may have become guides to others. These shaman guides undertook journeys into a realm of evil spirits who they believed had caused these afflictions and effected cures. A 45,000- to 60,000-year-old site in a cave at Shanidar, Iraq, yielded the skeleton of a badly disabled older HN that the excavator thought might be a shaman.[4] Since this individual could not hunt and thus support himself, the excavator suggested that the man disfigured by his shrunken arm and damaged eye, was thought "touched" by the spirits. Thus he might be able to communicate with them on behalf of the community. So the band had supported him, while he intervened with the spirits on their behalf. The bear skull found next to him, the red flowers piled upon his grave, and a ring of stones around the grave are all evidence of his ritual importance. His advanced age suggested that his HN group revered him for years.

Elders of each family unit, usually in the home, regularly carry on ancestor worship to this day in East Asian religions. Shamans however, were called in as specialists for unusual situations. These shamans were the first professionals. Their disciples were their most successful patients. Shamans in different bands and tribes most likely exchanged experiences and techniques with each other. Recent outcomes of psychotherapy studies have shown that Native American healers have cure rates similar to those of modern clinical psychologists. The growing awareness of positive religious influences on restoring health has even entered medical school curricula. In 1995 only 17 American medical schools incorporated patient spirituality in their curricula; ten years later the number had increased to 101.

Brain diseases may be mysterious and scary but they are not contagious. Infectious diseases are. The intelligent minds of HS observed the spread of disease by contact or proximity and concluded that dangerous invisible pollution could occur. The most obvious source of pollution was a new corpse. It could pollute its surroundings and the people it came in contact with. This pollution is contagious. Even second- and third-hand pollution is dangerous. And very small amounts of pollution are also dangerous. Thus action must be taken to isolate or purify what has become polluted. Fortunately this can be done with specific rituals that serve to alleviate anxieties and stress caused by the spread of contagious diseases. Although newly dead corpses are the most potent source of contagion, fresh blood, especially menstrual blood and the blood of childbirth (a time of great danger to both mother and newborn due to infection) is also disturbing. By extension, other bodily issues like nocturnal emissions and running sores, some activities like slaughter, and breaking taboos can also be viewed as polluting. Those who devoted themselves to restoring ritual purity achieved status and power. Their techniques and personalities were more bureaucratic than those of the charismatic shamans, and so they were more likely to establish a hereditary priesthood. Ritually purifying things that were polluted became important to restoring a positive, hopeful, and therefore healthy balance to society. Quarantining ritually polluted people and objects also sometimes reduced vulnerability to contagious disease.

Without successful reproduction no species can flourish, or even survive. HS were as subject to the biological imperative (commandment) to be fruitful and multiply as all other species. But the intelligent minds of HS knew the dangers of childbirth. Infant mortality rates in most tribes were more than one in four. The maternal death rate for every four births was more than one in ten. Pregnancy was highly desired and birth anxiously awaited. Pregnant women naturally sought the physical help of their mothers and grandmothers who in turn sought the spiritual help of their now departed mothers and grandmothers. Among the earliest gods were birth goddesses. Small stone figures of very pregnant birth goddesses often referred to as "Venus" figures go back 30,000 to 35,000 years. They are the first examples of iconic religion. The worship of spirits within natural phenomena does not need iconic representation. But birth rarely took place in the open or in public. The birth goddess needed to be present in some tangible way in order to ease the anxiety of women in labor. Even today in some African countries the maternal mortality rate is 3 percent per birth. A woman who gave birth to eight children had a one in four chance of dying from giving birth. Any band would benefit even if the presence of goddesses reduced that mortality rate by only 5 percent. Carvings in wood of birth goddesses probably preceded stone statues by many millennia and may have originated more than 50,000 years ago.

Shamans also found that visual aids helped their patients relate to the mysterious struggle that the shaman fought in the foreign spirit world. Since the spirits of animals were often involved both as friend and foe, much of prehistoric rock art (especially in difficult to access caves) probably relates to shamanistic healing rites. Eventually iconic representations of gods and spirits would become almost universal. In historic times these icons would be viewed by increasing numbers of people as representatives rather than incarnations of the Divine.

There was no reason to limit activities of spirits to the realm of the dead or the diseased. All natural phenomena could be motivated by spirit minds. Self-aware, intelligent minds that can read the intentions and motivations of others can also project all kinds of motivations on to other people, animals, objects, and events. The movement of herds; the quantity of animals, fruits, and spring water; thunder, floods, and drought; indeed everything that happens in nature can be ascribed to the will of spirits. Gifts and offerings should be able to influence these spirits (intelligent minds do not like to admit to impotence), and so regular offerings should be made by a group/clan/tribe to keep the natural forces friendly. Western anthropologists influenced by Christian thinking refer to these offerings as sacrifices. The Hebrew term *korban* is both more accurate and more insightful. The verb *Likarayv* means "to draw near" or "come close." A *korban* is a way to attach, engage, or bind the human realm to the spirit realm. When food and drink are offered to another, it is not a sacrifice. Food and liquid offerings are an invitation to a closer relationship. Especially during ceremonial occasions food and drink serve to bring people together, including those who have been estranged from one another because of transgressions that have occurred. Thus, offerings to the gods can help people who feel estranged from the Divine attain rapprochement and return to a closer (*karov*) relationship. Food offered to a god is usually eaten wholly or in part by those who contribute it or by the priests who offer it. The biblical God doesn't want grain or meat offerings (Ps. 40:7). Humans offer them, especially when they feel estranged from the Divine, in order to draw closer to the Divine. Only the sacrifice of humans should be called sacrifice. While human sacrifice was widespread in the past it was usually relatively rare.

Ritual specialists, who unlike charismatic shamans are more likely to be administrator types, usually direct these offerings. As time goes on the rites tend to get more complex and the necessary skills require more training. Those people performing the complex rites easily become a hereditary cast of professional priests. They sometimes also offer an alternative type of leadership to that of the hunter/warrior types. Priests can become the custodians of the customary law of the tribe. Priests can offer advice to help in making important decisions by consulting the gods to determine their will.[5] Fortune-telling enables decision-makers to avoid the backlash of wrong decisions while claiming credit for the good ones. Divination also reduces many people's anxiety about difficult decisions in unclear situations. Even today millions of Americans still consult astrology charts and in Asia people in many Buddhist temples still cast their fortunes.

Most people feel better when they are in control of the important factors in their life. The strong desire for control coupled with belief in good and evil spirits eventually leads some intelligent HS minds to attempt to force a spirit do what an individual wants it to do. Magic is an attempt to subjugate a force in the spiritual world for another person's weal or woe. Magic is always dangerous because people believe that the spirits do not like to be enslaved by humans and power tends to corrupt even those with good intentions. Yet many tribal religions still have lots of room for defensive magic and even those religions that condemn magic have occasional practitioners. Again, the mind-body placebo effect makes magic effective in some societies where belief in magic and superstitions is widespread and well accepted. Accusations of magic and witchcraft are also widespread in some tribal societies. They can be the result of paranoia or scapegoating as often, if not more often, than the actual incidence of magic. Magic and superstitions are the dark side of HS spirituality.

Small groups that lack an incest taboo will be plagued by the ills of inbreeding; therefore exogamy in mating will be selected for. As ancestor worship strengthens kinship ties over more and more generations, it also expands kinship ties over more nomadic bands creating extensive clans and tribes. These clans and tribes gather periodically at a special place to exchange future mates. They also started trading for desirable objects not found in their usual locale. Seashells, obsidian, red ocher, and other materials have been found in campsites and graves more than one hundred to two hundred miles away from their closest source. The stronger the attraction of a special place, the greater the effort that distant clans will make to attend, so gathering spots that are turned into sacred sites of pilgrimage through special seasonal rites will enrich human communities. There are scholars who think that HS advanced trade networks helped them out-compete HN in Europe (recent studies of Neanderthal DNA have shown that they were a distinct species not ancestral to HS). The need for all the clans to show up about the same time leads to fixed seasonal holy days and a religious calendar. The need to mark time for pilgrimage festivals led people to study the cycle of the moon and the movement of the constellations and thus move some of the spirit powers into the sky. Pilgrimage festivals still have major economic impact and serve in most religions as great sources of religious experience and solidarity.

Most but not all, spiritual forces are viewed as personalities. In some cultures an impersonal force (referred to by anthropologists as Mana) is believed to manifest itself in certain individuals or classes of people and accounts for and rationalizes good or bad luck as well as personal, family, or clan/class success and failure. Ritual pollution is usually viewed as an impersonal power and its cure depends upon impersonal bureaucratic techniques. But in most cultures the spirits are personified and ties of kinship relate the various spirits to each other. And in some cultures all or most of the spirits are said to be descendants of an original divine couple, or individual, or egg, or something else. This "creator" god is usually not central to the spiritual realm in later times just as a great-grandmother is recognized as a no longer active progenitor. A monotheism that denies the legitimacy of other gods did not exist before the century of Akhenaten and Moses. This is because the challenges that stimulate intelligent minds are very varied; the range of specific responses is very great and it is very hard to believe that all the variety fits into one very large scale harmony.

In small groups moral values can be based on utilitarian principles like do to others as you want them to do to you, or what goes around comes around. But in larger, more complex societies with diverse classes and castes it may be more effective to root ethics in transcendent terms since there are not enough repeat interactions to validate utilitarian morality. As tribes became larger and villages grew, a judge who rewarded good people and punished evil people helped the community to instill its norms in its members.

With the exception of a sociopath, the intelligent minds of HS also have a conscious, self-evaluating, purpose-driven aspect that needs to be satisfied because groups with a higher percentage of these kinds of minds were more stable and more effective. Guilt arises from many activities and needs to be atoned for. Self-discipline provides many advantages for an individual's survival and success. Most people, and all societies, need the structure of rules, community, and divine discipline to maintain self-control. Hunters needed to kill animals, yet they obviously felt ambivalent about it because almost all human societies have rules either about offering some of the kill to the spirit of the animal killed, or a taboo on killing or eating certain animals. There are much fewer rules relating to eating plants. Spilling blood intentionally is fraught with spiritual ambivalence and tension that needs to be dealt with.

Sex is also never simply a natural act for HS. The mind is always involved. It is not just chance that the first thing HS becomes self-aware of in the Garden of Eden is being naked. The era when sexual modesty became evident is important. The Bible states that the first thing humans became aware of after internalizing the knowledge of good and evil was their nakedness. If this occurred 125,000 to 150,000 years ago it fits right in with increasing evidence of subsequent rapid spiritual/cultural and technological development. There is evidence for body painting and for shells used for ornamentation from over 100,000 years ago. The tool kit of *Homo erectus*, a species prior to HS, changed very slowly over the course of hundreds of thousands of years. Early HS tools changed more quickly over the course of tens of thousands of years. But about 50,000 to 70,000 years ago the pace of change increased substantially for HS both technologically and spiritually. Many paleoanthropologists think that a major improvement in HS linguistic ability occurred about that time. Physically the HS body has not changed much in the last 100,000 years. The HS body 20,000 years before this transition period (50,000 to 70,000 years ago) is not different from the HS body 20,000 years later. But a major change did occur in artistic and other cultural activities. Perhaps the imaginative faculties of HS grew substantially thus causing inspiration and creativity to become more frequent and more rapidly spread. That something very important happened to HS about 50,000 to 70,000 years ago is clear even if we do not yet have evidence of exactly what happened. It should be noted that HN and a sister species recently discovered in Siberia, the *Homo denisova* as well as *Homo floresiensis* all became extinct in a relatively short period of 1,000 generations following the HS transition of 50,000 to 70,000 years ago. Also, many species of megafauna became extinct in Asia, Australia, Europe, and North America during the 40 millennia following the HS transition.

I have not devoted much attention to the development of concepts of God in this essay. It is often said that religion developed to answer the big philosophical questions that still challenge the mind of theologians and intellectuals. However, this applies to only a small percentage of people. The vast majority of people need religion to handle the moral stresses and emotional anxieties of living in an increasing complex society. As Nicholas Wade has argued, while beliefs about God are of great concern to Christians, most other religions focus much more attention on dietary self-discipline, public and private life-cycle rituals, inducing mystical experiences, standards of social and personal behavior, healing sickness and sin, community ceremonies and celebrations, and creating a firm community and individual religious identity. Formal creeds and religious beliefs are a small and recent development within the much larger domain of trust and group loyalty that has been evolving among pre-HS species for hundreds of millennia.[6] Recent brain studies have shown how organic trust and sharing are to human minds. Activities that build group loyalty and interpersonal trust enhance individual survival and promote individual spirituality much more than cognitive beliefs and ideologies. But urbanization, writing, and mass communications may be changing this. Written revelation introduced a tremendous force expanding the power of religion both in space and time. The impact of religions with written revelations on historic human culture is comparable to the impact of modern science and invention on twentieth-century lifestyles. Both together will make the twenty-first century a turning point in human destiny.

What role does God (the One God of the revealed religions) play in all this? According to Genesis 4:26 humans only began to call upon the name of the Lord in the days of Enosh. That could mean that prior to Enosh prehistoric religions evolved naturally. Only with the rise of scriptural revelations did the One God penetrate human consciousness. Or it could mean that human consciousness had finally risen to the level of being able to receive divine communication from the One God. It took over 3,000 years for monotheism to spread worldwide even with scriptural revelations; so it is not surprising that it took over 100,000 years to get humans ready to receive divine revelations.

Spiritually, *Homo sapiens* has been evolving for at least 100,000 to 150,000 years. It is as deeply, if not more deeply, rooted in the HS brain as art or music. Recent studies, especially those on adult twins who were raised apart, suggest genes contribute about 40 percent of the variability in a person's general religiousness. The idea that reason, socialism, or modern science would replace religion has turned out to be a wish fulfillment fantasy of people who bear a grudge against religion. Usually their children or grandchildren return to religion. Religious rituals and ideas are ubiquitous and continue to evolve as the creative intelligent minds of HS encounter changes in their environment. This will most likely continue as long as HS have creative intelligent minds. Or as Albert

Einstein put it: "What is the meaning of human life, or of organic life altogether? To answer this question at all implies a religion. Is there any sense then, you ask, in putting it? I answer, the man who regards his own life and that of his fellow-creatures as meaningless is not merely unfortunate but almost disqualified for life."[7]

Notes

1. See Nicholas Wade, *Before the Dawn* (New York: Penguin Books, 2007), 90.
2. Ibid., 52–56.
3. D. Reich et al., "Genetic History of an Archaic Hominid from Denisova Cave in Siberia," *Nature* 468, no. 7327 (December 23, 2010): 1053–1060.
4. S. Armitage, S. Jasim, A. Marks, V. Usik, and H. Uerpmann, "The Southern Route 'Out of Africa': Evidence for an early Expansion of Modern Humans into Arabia," *Science* 331, no. 6016 (January 28, 2011): 453–56.
5. L. Grossman, N.D. Monro, and A. Belfer-Cohen, "A 12,000-Year-Old Shaman Burial from the Southern Levant (Israel)," *Proceeding of National Academy of Science USA* 105 (2008): 17665–69.
6. Nicholas Wade, *The Faith Instinct: How Religion Evolved and Why It Endures* (New York: Penguin Press, 2009), 101–2.
7. Albert Einstein, *The World As I See It* (New York, 1934), 1.

Dreams: The True Religion-Science Conflict

Russell Jay Hendel

I. Introduction: Overview and Goals

Since the goal of this paper is controversial, I devote this introductory section to a careful defining of the boundaries and parameters of this paper's goal.

The first goal of this paper is to show that the true science-religion controversy lies in the psychological arena, not in the physical-science arena. More specifically, I argue that the goal and raison d'être of organized religion is the development of human dream capacity including human capacity for prophecy, a goal that will be fully realized in the messianic era but can and should be partially realized now. The religious personality should be recognized not only by the religious character of his or her eating and leisure (holidays), but also by his or her spiritual endeavors, which include prayer, learning, and dreams. Dreams as a guiding force of life should not be something therapists use when one seeks counseling, but rather should be an intrinsic part and parcel of our daily activities.

A second component of our main goal is that there are no physical-science religion controversies. I argue that the most famous of these controversies—the apparent contradiction between Genesis 1 and modern cosmology—never really existed. Neither an examination of other Near Eastern cultures nor classical biblical commentaries supports an interpretation of Genesis 1 as dealing with physical creation. Rather, Genesis 1 deals with the creation of prophecy, a theme we find in other Near Eastern cultures.

RUSSELL JAY HENDEL (Ph.D. in Theoretical Mathematics, MIT) is an associate of the Society of Actuaries and teaches mathematics at Towson University in Baltimore.

The third component of our main goal is that this abstract idea of focusing on dreams and prophecy can be applied clinically in a daily setting. The case history of Joseph skillfully shows how to use non-prophetic dreams to achieve emotional fulfillment, personal joy, and divine service.

Each of the above three components of this paper's goals may appear bizarre and contradicted by obvious textual interpretation. Therefore, I must devote separate sections to each component and to its prerequisites. Accordingly, an outline of this paper is as follows. In section II, I review other Near Eastern cultures, showing that they also were not concerned with the creation of the physical world but rather with the creation of prophecy. Since the interpretation of Genesis 1 requires use of symbolism, in section III, I give a brief overview of symbolism: Under what circumstances are we *forced* to interpret a biblical passage symbolically, and, if so, how are we *required* to interpret this symbolism? Then in section IV, I show that Genesis 1 must be interpreted symbolically; it cannot be interpreted literally. In section V, I lightly go over the symbolic meaning of Genesis 1. In section VI, I apply the paper's abstract goals clinically by studying the case history of Joseph. The Bible depicts Joseph as a typical immature teenager. I contrast the modern dream approach to Joseph's dreams with Joseph's prophetic dream approach to his own dreams and offer this as a clinical model for ourselves. Section VII presents the fourth goal of this paper: a response to the three science-religion issues raised in Samuelson's lead essay in this issue.[1] To wit:

1. *Creation*: Our response to the creation problem is that there is not and there never was a serious contradiction between religion and physical science. However, there are contradictions between the goals of the psychological sciences and religion. Secular psychology seeks to enable people to satisfy their physical and social needs and maintain a sense of contentment. Religion, we argue, identifies a deep spiritual need in man, the need for prophetic encounter with the Divine; this emotional need must also be met.
2. *Revelation*: Religion isn't philosophy. Religion comes to enable dreams and prophecies. Modern science does not per se deal with dreams on a spiritual level, though it recognizes them and proposes to interpret them psychosocially. I argue that a

primary goal of religion is to facilitate human use of dreams in one's daily activities and to enrich thereby one's personality and feelings.

3. *Redemption*: Humanity cannot redeem itself if, as modern psychological science claims, humans solely concentrate on physical and social needs. Redemption is only possible when dreams and prophecies flower. And once they are dealt with, redemption automatically follows.

II. Near Eastern Creation Myths

We begin this section with insightful quotes from Tikvah Frymer-Kensky:

> In the past two decades, there has been a tremendous change in biblical studies. The scientific philosophy that prevailed for more than a century has given way, in biblical studies as in other humanities, to a more sophisticated understanding of the interaction between the now and then, the reader and the text. Old ideas of history as "what actually happened" and text as having one correct and original meaning have yielded to a current view of the continual interaction of the viewer and what is seen, of the text and its reader. No longer do we believe that there is a truly "value-neutral" way of reading literature or reconstructing history.[2]

> The last three decades have seen an enormous paradigm shift in our perception of reality and history. The old ideas of "objective science" on which many of us were raised, the old conceptions of History as "what actually happened," of Text as having "one correct reading and original meaning," and of Law as "what is legislated" have yielded to a view of complex interactions of the viewer and the viewed, the text and its readers, the law and its adherents.[3]

These quotes caution against reading the Bible from our own eyes.

To critically understand the consequences of this caution, note that, we, that is, modern humans, are interested in where the physical world came from. Even little children know about the Big Bang. Dreams, to modern humans, have a secondary significance. They are the result of biophysical activity in the brain and body. To modern humans the term "creation" means physical creation, the creation of the physical world.

By contrast, ancient man was not interested in physical creation. The classic creation myths of Babylonia and Egypt deal with the creation of gods, the fight for divine power, and the creation of servants of god. While occasionally creation is mentioned in these myths, it is important not to listen to this word with modern ears. Creation in these myths refers to prophetic creation, not physical creation. To ancient man, dream visions were reality, not something inside man, but something outside him. The gods, visions, and prophetic communications were something real that determined and set reality. To ancient man, the question of where the gods and their prophetic communications came from was very real and meaningful since prophetic visions determined reality.

More importantly, the physical interpretation of Genesis 1, *creatio ex nihilo*, did not bother ancient man because there was no physical law of conservation of mass or conservation of energy that it violated. Indeed, without a well-defined conceptual framework of precise measurement, which ancient man lacked, it would not make sense to speak about conservation laws. And without these conservation laws, a miracle of new matter and new energy had as much believability as a miracle of coincidence.

Although we have not yet defended our view textually, by critically reading Genesis 1 and showing its simple meaning to be the creation of prophecy, it is reasonable that the ancient Jews were no different than other Near Eastern cultures where genesis stories deal with the creation of prophecy and dreams, not with the creation of the physical world.

We also emphasize that Genesis 1 takes place in the context of the Book of Genesis, the book of world-shaping prophecies. Each of the stories in Genesis—Adam, Noah, Abraham, the birth of Isaac, the engagement of Rebekah, the blessings of Isaac, Jacob's escape from Laban and Esau, as well as the Joseph story—are events driven by prayers, dreams, visions, and prophecies that shaped world history. A physical creation story would not fit into such a book; but an account of the prophetic creation of Adam's visions, the first prophecies, would fit into the general book.

III. Symbolism

To clarify the purpose of this section, we point out that merely presenting a symbolic interpretation of Genesis 1 is not sufficient to prove a particular point of view. After all, the simple meaning of the text may be the description of physical creation. Rather, to prove our point, we must follow a precise exegetical methodology that answers the following two important questions:

- *Issue 1*: What criteria must a biblical literary narrative meet to *necessitate* symbolic interpretation?
- *Issue 2*: Given that a certain literary piece *requires* a symbolic interpretation, what interpretive methods *should* be used?

Prior to addressing these two issues we emphasize that for purposes of this essay we use the operational approach to symbolism presented by Hendel,[4] who summarized Samson Raphael Hirsch's symbolic theories.[5] Hirsch's theories were selected because they are simple, extremely comprehensive, operationally defined, and include many features of several symbolic theories. In my previously published essays I cited other approaches to symbolic interpretation and show how Hirsch's theories include them. I also note that Hirsch's operational approach avoids a discussion of the fascinating issue of the difference between sign, symbol, parable, and myth as well as the profound symbolic issues of emotion, evocation, and ambiguity raised so beautifully by the symbolist school. However, an operational approach is needed to ensure objectivity.

It is expositionally easier to address issue 2 first. If the Bible requires symbolic interpretation then that interpretation should be accomplished by one of the following four methods:

1. Function
2. Form
3. Linguistic association in the Hebrew culture; for example, the identical Hebrew root for "almonds" and "hastening" skillfully employed in Jeremiah's vision of almonds, symbolically indicates that God is hastening to bring his decree (Jer. 1:11–12)
4. Explicitly indicated symbolism; for example, the explicit association between wearing tzitzit and remembering God's commandments (Num. 15:37–41)

We can now fully answer issue 1: The bible *requires* symbolic interpretation in the following three cases:

Case 1: The Bible explicitly declares an object or act as symbolic. For example, Shabbat (Exod. 31:16–17) and rainbow (Gen. 9:8–17) are explicitly declared as symbols.

Case 2: The Bible associates one object or act as reminding one of other objects, acts, or events. For example, the tzitzit are explicitly associated with remembering the biblical commandments (Num. 15:37–41). Similarly, matzah, shofar, and sukkah are explicitly associated with commemorating specific historic events (Lev. 23).

Case 3: A biblical chapter requires symbolic interpretation if the biblical chapter has

i. An identified central theme,
ii. Several verses that appear unrelated to the central theme, but
iii. The verses symbolically connect to the central theme using the four methods mentioned above in our analysis of issue 2.

Example: A beautiful illustrative example of case 3 is Ecclesiastes 12:

i. The central theme is declared in the very first verse of Chapter 12: "Remember your Creator in your youth, before the bad days come, [before] years come in which you have no desire."
ii. This central theme, *not waiting for old age*, is unrelated to the many verses in chapter 12 describing darkened windows, shattering beams, etc.
iii. However, if we apply the symbolic methods of *function* and *form* described in our answer to issue 2, we easily symbolically interpret that:
    a. The function of windows is *sight* implying that darkening windows correspond to the *dimmed vision* of old age.
    b. Similarly, beams have the *form* and *function* of bones, so that *broken beams* symbolically refer to the heightened *risk of fracture* in old age.

It is noteworthy that all the Rishonim without exception interpret this chapter as symbolically describing old age. Therefore, in a certain sense, the symbolic methodology described here is semi-objective in the precise sense that independent commentators arrive at highly similar interpretations. There might be some differences with details but the overall picture is agreed to by everybody.

In summary, we have, in this section, presented three criteria necessitating symbolic interpretation, and four criteria by which to interpret symbolically. In the next two sections we apply these criteria to Genesis 1.

IV. Problems with the Literal Interpretation of Genesis 1

Although there are several conflicts between biblical-Talmudic narrative and science, certainly, Genesis is the Goliath that must be defeated for religion to win the war. In this section, I apply the three criteria enumerated in case 3, presented in the previous section, and show that the biblical Author required a symbolic interpretation of Genesis 1.

Recall from the previous section that case 3 of the cases requiring symbolic interpretation, requires (i) a central chapter theme, (ii) chapter verses unrelated to this central theme, and (iii) key symbolic terms in the chapter verses that do relate to the central theme. Let us now examine the presence of each of these criteria.

Case 3(i)—Central Theme: The central theme of Genesis 1 is the prophecies to Adam blessing him with world conquest. To understand this in context, recall that each of the stories in Genesis deal with a lone person changing human history by virtue of prophecy:

- Noah, inspired by prophetic visions, stood alone against a corrupt world and was saved from the flood.
- Abraham, inspired by prophetic visions, stood alone for marital chastity and against idolatry.
- Abraham, inspired by prophetic vision, sought understanding of good and evil when God destroyed Sedom and Amorah.
- Eliezer, inspired by an oath to a prophet, was confident in finding a religious wife in a corrupt world.
- Isaac, inspired by prophetic insights, instituted division of political powers.
- Jacob, inspired by prophetic blessings, stood alone with a corrupt Laban for twenty years and survived.
- Joseph, inspired by non-prophetic dreams, stood up against hostile family and slave owners to emerge as viceroy of Egypt and saved the world from famine.

None of these people achieved their accomplishments through armies. The sole driving force was prophecy. Consistent with this background, Genesis 1, actually Genesis 1–3, presents Adam, the first prophet, who, inspired by prophetic orders, was to retain control of Eden and the world if he obeyed the moral requirements mentioned in Genesis 2. Thus the central theme of Genesis 1–3 is the prophecies to Adam enabling conquest of Eden and the world if he obeyed moral law.

Case 3(ii)—Unrelated Chapter Verses: But now, the rest of Genesis 1, describing creation of the world, has no, or little, relation with the central theme of Adam's conquest of Eden and the world. True, Rashi (Gen. 1:1) argues that Genesis 1 declares God as creator and owner of the world, implying an Authority who can implement His promises. But this comment of Rashi is stretched. Contrast:

a. God caused the flood, enabled Abraham to defeat a powerful military alliance with only 318 soldiers, and enabled Jacob to outsmart Esau and Laban.
b. God created the plants, stars, lights, animals, and birds.

Clearly (a), rather than (b), portrays God as a being of power who can implement His A124uthority. Thus the comment of Rashi arguing that Genesis 1 portrays God's ownership and power is a bit stretched. Primae faciae the chapter verses of Genesis 1 are not, or weakly, related, to the central theme of Genesis 1–3, Adam's empowerment through prophecy.

Case 3(iii)—Symbolic Terms in the Chapter Link to the Main Theme: Every key term in Genesis 1 is clearly biblically used to indicate prophecy. The keywords of Genesis 1—*heaven*, *light*, stars, animals, beasts, *spirit of God*, etc.—have clear prophetic meaning throughout the Bible.

Thus Genesis 1 meets the three criteria of case 3 presented in the previous section; hence, we perceive this chapter as requiring symbolic interpretation by the biblical Author. Previously,[6] I presented further *supportive* criteria against the literal interpretation of Genesis 1 and for the symbolic interpretation. For example:

- A proper translation of Genesis 1:2 is "The earth *had been* formless and void. . . ." The past conjugation (היתה) versus the future conjugation with a preceding vav (ויהי) indicates the past perfect—*had been*—implying an existence prior to creation.
- Similarly, the snake is not a talking animal but a slimy human who attempts to seduce Eve, implying the existence of other humans prior to Adam.
- Also, Cain building a city indicates the presence of other people.

The previous essay concludes as follows:

> Genesis 1 is not describing the creation of the *physical* world; rather Genesis 1 describes the creation of the *prophetic* world. What happened 6000 years ago is not the creation of anything physical since indeed all physical objects already existed, but rather 6000 years ago was the first moment in human history when a human attained prophetic revelation. That human is Adam and that prophetic revelation is recorded in Genesis 1 and 2.[7]

Furthermore, this interpretation of Genesis 1 is not something modern that we are *reading into* the text. The classic commentators treat Genesis 1 this way. For example, Ramban (Rabbi Moses ben Nahman, Nahmanides) does not regard Adam as the first human but rather as the first human with a special soul. We have identified this specialness with prophetic capacity. The Talmud itself sees Genesis 1 not as science but as mystical, the "Works of creation," an esoteric doctrine dealing with prophetic spiritual matters which only the spiritually worthy could study.

V. Genesis 1: The Creation of Prophecy

In the previous two sections I have laid the foundation for rejecting a literal interpretation of Genesis 1 and requiring a symbolic interpretation consistent with the central theme of the chapter, the creation of the first prophet and first prophecy, empowering Adam to control Eden and the world if he observes moral law. In this section we lightly go over the details of this symbolic interpretation.

Genesis 1 describes seven epochs (the seven *days*) needed in the creation of prophecy. Very roughly the seven training epochs for becoming a prophet are:

1. The study of dreams (light—seeing at night)
2. Separation of the physical and the spiritual (e.g., the religious separation of temple/synagogue versus the home)
3. Knowledge of psychology, that is, the awareness of the variety of human approaches to a minimal plant-like existence (i.e., consumption and reproduction)
4. Importance of periodic holidays and commemorations
5. Awareness of the herd nations ("beasts") and the power of flight (birds) (e.g., Egypt and escape)
6. Prophetic animal visions (e.g., Ezekiel 1), human prophecy
7. Shabbat—consolidation and development

These ideas filter into our heritage. Jewish holidays are an example of "Wednesday." The belt worn during prayer separating the lower part of the body from the upper part of the body is an example of "Monday." Although more can be said, we give "clinical advice" useful in daily activities in the next section.

I conclude this very brief section with a word-by-word translation of Genesis 1:1–5. Literal terms (such as "heaven") that have been interpreted symbolically (e.g., "heaven" = "spiritual") have been italicized for the readers' convenience.

> For the sake of the choicest [in man] God created the *spiritual* and *physical* worlds. For [before this creation of the spiritual] the *physical* world was formless and astonishing with the darkness [*of no dreams*] on the brim of man's *unconscious*, but the *spirit of prophecy* hovered over man's *emotions*. And God said let there be the light [*of dreams*] and there were *dreams*. And God saw that *dreams* were good and God differentiated between *dreams* [light] and *no dreams* [darkness—nothing seen at night]. And God called *dreams* day and *lack of dreams* night.

A few comments on our approach should be made:

- My interpretation may appear radical. I would alternatively suggest that we modestly interpreted only half a dozen key terms—*heaven, earth, light, dark, animals, spirit of God*—prophetically. Once we do so, the symbolic interpretation naturally flows.
- In my initial research on this topic, I found resistance and hesitance to this interpretation. But there was an equal resistance to interpreting Ecclesiastes 12 as referring to old age or even to the details in interpreting Song of Songs symbolically. I believe this reflects a deficiency in our education, which emphasizes analytic techniques and avoids symbolic holistic techniques. Had we exposed students to symbolic interpretation in day school these interpretations would be more acceptable.

VI. Clinical Guidance, the Joseph Case Study

Genesis, the book of the prophetic titans, Adam, Noah, Abraham, Isaac, and Jacob, the book of individuals who stood alone against the masses and won through prophecy, this book, ends by devoting 25 percent of its chapters to non-prophetic fantasies of an immature teenager, Joseph. Such a contrast must be explored in context: Adam, Noah, and the Patriarchs are titans to look up to, but are not appropriate role models to emulate since we are not on their level. Contrastively, Joseph is extremely human; he has the fears, fantasies, and non-prophetic status similar to most people. We therefore can turn to the Joseph case study for clinical advice and relevance.[8] Joseph is described (Gen. 37:2) as an immature teenager, a tattletale, who hung around with lower classes. Joseph is one of the first recorded instances of teenage immaturity.[9] The Bible describes how Joseph used non-prophetic dreams to "cure" his immaturity.

Joseph had two significant dreams: He dreamt of sheaves bowing to his upright sheaf and dreamt of stars, the sun, and moon bowing to him. Several features are important in these dreams. First, unlike almost all other biblical dreams there is no hint of prophetic encounter. The dreams do not come from God, do not have a deity symbol, and do not have moral orders. They are ordinary dreams, the type the rest of the world has today. Second, both dreams highlight the activity of bowing.

Before presenting Joseph's treatment of his dreams let us present the alternative non-prophetic treatment. It is tempting to cite modern approaches to dream interpretation. However because of the subjectivity in dream interpretation this would require significant amounts of space. We therefore suffice with his brother's treatment of the dreams. This treatment has many characteristics of modern secular approaches.

Bowing in the bible indicates submission to power. Furthermore, upright objects are universal phallic symbols. Consequently, the dreams echo Joseph's immaturity. The only way Joseph can achieve adulthood is by controlling others; after all, who would share with him if he is immature. Joseph quests adult masculinity (upright sheaves). Joseph's preoccupation with looks and masculinity is a theme through Joseph's life; in fact he went to jail because of this (Gen. 39:6–23). Even on his deathbed, his father still saw the immature teenager questing for masculinity and looks and gave him a blessing that "girls should tiptoe over the walls to gaze at him" (Gen. 49:22). Reuben, the eldest brother, who defended Joseph, nevertheless calls him a child (Gen. 42:22). A less confrontational dream interpretation might use a social versus a physical approach to Joseph's dreams—he sought respect which through his lens of immaturity expressed itself as bowing.

Now we come to Joseph's own treatment of his dreams. Although his dreams were non-prophetic, Joseph's genius, and his contribution to prophecy, was to treat ordinary dreams with prophetic methods. Such a treatment yielded results enabling Joseph to save the world from famine. The prophetic treatment of dreams emphasizes four attributes:

1. A nonsexual interpretation
2. Emphasis on helping the community
3. De-emphasis on short-term transparency and emphasis on long-term non-transparency
4. Emphasis on a project approach involving stages.

Let us now examine these four attributes in detail:

1. *Nonsexual interpretation*: Joseph did not interpret his dreams physically.
2. *Communal benefit*: The word "bow" has four distinct biblical meanings: (i) thanks/gratitude, (ii) submission to power, (iii) greetings, and (iv) worship. Joseph ultimately interpreted "bowing" as indicating "gratitude" for the communal work he intended to do, an interpretation that we see materialize later, when people coming to Joseph for food during the famine bowed (gave thanks) to him (Gen. 42:6).
3. *Non transparency*: Joseph did not impose an interpretation on his dream. Its meaning was non-transparent and enigmatic. He waited. He had no way of knowing that thirteen years later he would be in charge of gathering sheaves and his sheaf gathering would be successful while others would fail.
4. *Project approach*: Joseph did not passively wait for the dream to come true but rather actively participated with the interpretation. While a slave in Potiphar's house and while a prison warden, he acquired managerial experience and leadership capacities. Joseph also continued his dream interpretation while in prison. It is a mistake to see him as passively enduring suffering and suddenly interpreting Pharaoh's dream and becoming viceroy. On the contrary, he prepared for it.

And so, the immature teenager of seventeen blossomed into the mature leader of thirty. This transformation happened because of Joseph's prophetic treatment of non-prophetic dreams. This case study is certainly worthy of our own study and emulation.

VII. Conclusion

To use modern terminology, if religion is to survive in today's competition with science it must market itself properly. The proper approach to marketing is to advertise something unique that you do best. If you try to imitate your competitors you are bound to failure.

The problem with the science-religion dialogue today is religion's passivity; religion defends itself against possible misinterpretation, but I advocate an active, aggressive approach.

Religion is offering something. It is offering dreams and prophecy. Everyone from the immature teenager to the mature prophet can benefit.

Furthermore, dreams should be an intrinsic part of the religious person's life. The religious person eats in a religious manner, has leisure in a religious manner, and does several religious activities such as prayer and learning. Dream interpretation should not be something you do when you have problems and are seeing a therapist. Dreams should be part and parcel of your daily activities and daily approach to life. We should study dreams separately and apply known interpretations to our own problems. I believe such an approach can place religion on an equal or superior footing with science.

I close with my response to the three issues in the Samuelson paper.

1. *Creation*: Religion is marketing prophecy and dreams. Religion (whether Jewish or other Near Eastern religions) doesn't care where the world came from. There never was a contradiction between science and religion on the creation of the physical world. On the other hand, there is a contradiction between science and religion on the creation of dreams. Science believes dreams are psycho-physical. Religion believes all dreams come from God and can enhance the God-man relationship. It is not worth fighting with science over the creation of the world; it is worth fighting with science on the creation and source of dreams.
2. *Revelation*: Religion is marketing revelation. Science does not even acknowledge its existence. The best way to prove revelation is to experience it, to emulate Joseph, to make ones dreams a part of one's life. A person whose life is

transformed by dreams has an adequate basis to believe in revelation.

3. *Redemption*: Science has not redeemed man. Joseph's dreams did redeem him. Had he gone to a modern therapist, taken some drugs, and been taught to live with other people without dominating them ("bowing" = "power"), Joseph would never have been cured or redeemed; rather his symptoms would have been controlled. But Joseph transformed his personality, redeemed himself, and saved the entire world through his prophetic approach to dreams. To achieve redemption we must reactivate our religion's interest in dreams.

Notes

1. Norbert M. Samuelson, "The Challenges of the Modern Sciences for the Jewish Faith," *CCAR Journal* (Winter 2012): 16–18.
2. Tikvah Frymer-Kensky, *Studies in Bible and Feminist Criticism* (Philadelphia: Jewish Publication Society, 2006), 159.
3. Ibid., 255.
4. Russell Jay Hendel, "Genesis 1 Speaks about the Creation of Prophecy, Not the Creation of the World," *B'Or Ha-Torah* 13 (English section) (2002): 71–87; Russell Jay Hendel, "Sacrifice Categories and Personality Types," *Jewish Bible Quarterly* 38, no. 1 (2010): 41–51.
5. Samson Raphael Hirsch, *Grundlinien Einer Judischen Symbolik*, first appeared in German, in his *Gesammelte Schriften*, ed. J. Kauffmann (Frankfurt on Maine, 1902). For an English translation see Jacob Breuer, "Groundlines for a Jewish Symbolism," in *Timeless Torah, An Anthology of the Writings of Rabbi Samson Raphael Hirsch* (New York: Samson Raphael Hirsch Publication Society, Feldheim, 1957). The complete collected works have also been translated into English in *Collected Writings of Rabbi Samson Raphael Hirsch* (New York: Samson Raphael Hirsch Publication Society, Feldheim, 1984).
6. See Hendel, "Genesis 1 Speaks about the Creation of Prophecy, Not the Creation of the World," vol. 3, 3–61.
7. Ibid., 87
8. The material for this section comes from Russell Jay Hendel, "Joseph: A Biblical Approach to Dream Interpretation," *Jewish Bible Quarterly* 39, no. 4 (2011): 231–238.
9. See J. Bigner, T. Grayson, and A. Milevsky, *Understanding Foundations in Human Development*, 2nd ed. (Reeding, CA: Horizon Textbook Publishing), 5.

Rethinking Conjoined Twins

Jonathan K. Crane

In the Beginning

It is a truism that human bodies come in many shapes and sizes. It is no less true that Judaic legal and homiletical sources speak about normal, abnormal, and idealized human forms. Many of the texts addressing abnormal physical bodies wrestle with what it means to be a legal subject, or more precisely, what a human subject *is* and what a human subject *should* look like. This struggle is especially apparent in recent considerations of conjoined twins, a discourse primarily peopled by Orthodox bioethicists. Curiously, this conversation about conjoined twins functions with certain assumptions that appear reasonable at first glance but further reflection reveals dangers—not only to human bodies but also to the Judaic textual tradition itself. These tensions between physical phenomena and Judaic norms reflect a larger, ongoing debate about the interrelationship between science and Judaism generally.

Before turning to the modern discourse about conjoined twins, the famous midrash about the first primordial human merits remembering. According to the Rabbis this first human creature had two faces, one male and the other female.[1] One face looked ahead and the other behind, not unlike the two-faced Roman god Janus who presides over beginnings and transitions.[2] A version claims that not only was the original human diprosopus (two-faced), it also had two spinal columns; or perhaps it was androgynous insofar as it had both male and female sexual organs.[3] Such theories of the primordial human express an early Rabbinic impulse to appreciate the phenomenological diversity of human morphology. Even

---

JONATHAN K. CRANE (NY03, Ph.D. University of Toronto) is Raymond F. Schinazi Junior Scholar in Bioethics and Jewish Thought in the Center for Ethics at Emory University.

more, these theories insist that this diversity was the first manifestation of divinely created humankind. As such they are closer to the divine will than the human singularities with which we are so accustomed, with our but one set of limbs, one torso, and one head. Polymorphism thus raises interesting if not critical theological and legal questions.

Then There Were Two

That human beings are not always born as embodied singularities has long been acknowledged in the Judaic textual tradition, as evidenced from biblical and Rabbinic discussions of congenital deformities.[4] One kind of abnormal birth configuration is that of conjoined twins.[5] Conjoined twins can exist in any number of configurations wherein viscera, organs, and even nervous systems are seemingly shared between what some think as two distinct people. Especially since Ambroise Paré, the famous sixteenth-century French physician, this shared flesh was viewed as an opportunity to develop and practice innovative surgical techniques of separation. Legal and ethical thinking endorsed such interventions primarily because the one, or perhaps two, entities once cleaved apart would better conform to existing notions of human form and function. Indeed, a recent British court endorsed surgical separation because it would promote "the bodily integrity and human dignity which is the right of each of them."[6]

Contemporary Jewish scholarship on conjoined twins has predominantly joined this bandwagon by employing legal and ethical constructs that favor separation of conjoined twins. To support this goal of physical division, such luminaries as J. David Bleich, Mordechai Halperin, Moshe Feinstein, Avraham Steinberg, and Moshe Tendler repeatedly invoke two traditional tropes: the concept of the *rodeif* and the incident with Sheva ben Bichri.[7] Each trope, they argue, is sufficiently similar to that of conjoined twins to be analogous and thus brought into the overall conversation. And moreover, they assume that these analogies can and should have normative suasion in the conversation. This raises the question, however, of whether these tropes are indeed analogous and if it is jurisprudentially appropriate to ascribe to them normative powers when the subject matter is conjoined twins.

Pursuit

Take, for example, the notion of the *rodeif* (a pursuer with lethal intent). The *rodeif*'s roots are biblical, its branches Rabbinic, and its leaves have drifted into myriad of modern ethical and legal deliberations. The upshot of the *rodeif* concept is that if someone pursues another with lethal intent, it is permissible, preferable, and in some cases required to intervene to save the intended victim; this intervention may be injurious and even lethal if need be. A superficial look at the *rodeif* legislation reveals its ready applicability to lethal conflicts between distinct parties, ranging from personal fights to international warfare, and perhaps even to terrorism.[8] The impulse to invoke this concept in biomedical deliberations has Talmudic foundations, as the Rabbis use it when considering whose life to save in a difficult birth—the mother's or the emerging child's.[9] Yet, is it reasonable to rely upon the concept of the *rodeif* to calculate what to do with neonate conjoined twins, that is, twins already outside the womb?

In his discussion of conjoined twins in which he assumes "the girls were separate human beings with their own brains and nervous systems," Moshe Tendler uses the *rodeif* concept to differentiate between a fetus that is completely dependent on the mother for its existence from an independently breathing neonate.[10] In the former instance it would be impermissible to favor the fetus over the mother; the fetus may be eliminated to save the mother. In the latter case, however, the child's independent circulatory and respiratory systems afford the child "full rights and privileges of an adult. The most important of these privileges is the right to life." Tendler reasons that, "surely it is the fetal status of dependency on the mother that justifies the sacrifice of fetal life to save maternal life." Given the situation in which conjoined twins share a heart that cannot sustain both, he concludes: "Without the attempted separation, both would surely die, and therefore in halakhic terminology we classify the baby that had no independent survival, Baby A, as the pursuer [*rodeif*], as if she were pursuing her sister and threatening her life." This therefore justifies surgically separating Baby A from Baby B so the latter could have a better chance of survival. Baby A, the doctors said, could not be saved without and certainly with the separation surgery.[11]

This analogy suffers faulty logic, however. The Judaic legal tradition defines a *rodeif* as a distinct person who intends lethal harm upon another distinct person or persons; hence the term pursuer.[12] Even if we disregard the notion of intent when considering a fetus, a child emerging in the birth canal could be called a *rodeif* only after achieving cardiovascular activity independent of the mother. As Baby A had no independent cardiovascular activity, much less capacity for such, Baby A was wholly dependent on Baby B. Insofar as Baby A's existence was inseparable from Baby B's, Baby A was not and could not be considered a distinct being "full of rights and privileges of an adult," including the opportunity to fit the formal definition of a *rodeif*.

Other scholars offer a different way to utilize the *rodeif* analogy. Mordechai Halperin argues that perhaps Baby A and Baby B were mutual pursuers.[13] If this were the case, medical intervention in favor of one or the other would be prohibited. Yet the case was not of equal pursuers: Baby A was wholly reliant upon Baby B and thus posed a greater threat to Baby B's survivability. Without getting into the details of this or any other case, the calculus using the *rodeif* concept would go as follows. Insofar as Baby A's prospects for living post-operation were negligible compared to Baby B's, Halperin concludes: "then Baby A poses a greater danger to Baby B than Baby B to Baby A. Baby A is therefore considered a pursuer and we may and must separate the twins, thereby killing Baby A, in order to save Baby B." Such draconian consequentialist calculus that maximizes lived life, however, abandons a central and critical principle invoked among contemporary Jewish bioethicists: that every moment of human life is sacred and is of infinite value. This calculus apparently values purported quantity of life over quality of life, that is, the inherent quality—not experienced quality.[14] It remains unstated in Halperin's essay why or whether the *rodeif* concept can or should trump this principle.

J. David Bleich is also suspicious of using the *rodeif* analogy to justify surgical intervention. In his view, because Baby A and Baby B shared a six-chambered heart they were a case of mutual pursuers, which therefore prohibited intervention. The only situation in which one baby or the other could "be judged to be a pursuer [was] if the heart can be shown to belong to one twin exclusively, [then] the second is, in effect, a parasite."[15] But since both Baby A and Baby B shared DNA, it could be said the heart was either's; and since proximity between a head and an organ does not automatically indicate "ownership" among conjoined twins, it was medically inconclusive who "owned" the heart.[16] The only way to salvage the *rodeif* analogy was to declare by fiat that one baby did not have a heart at all and thus was—"in effect" but not in fact—a parasite; excising a parasite would be halachically permissible if not required.

Yet this reasoning simultaneously requires and denies medical evidence. On the one hand it requires knowing if the heart could be successfully located in either Baby A or Baby B. If it could, then ownership would only be clarified in the process of surgery, not beforehand. If it could not, then ownership was clear before operation and the "heartless" twin would be an excisable parasite. And at the same time this logic had to reject medical evidence. Insofar as before operation Baby A and Baby B undoubtedly shared the entire organ, they were joint "owners" of the heart and both benefited from it. Declaring that one or the other was not an "owner" of, or had no legitimate biological claim upon, the heart could only be made by denying medical facts.

Another level of critique may be levied against the *rodeif* analogy. The *rodeif* concept applies both (1) to self-defense against a lethal pursuer, and (2) to intervention to save an intended victim from a lethal pursuer. Obviously it would be unreasonable to invoke rules about self-defense insofar as neonates cannot conscientiously obey (or disobey) rules.[17] In regard to intervention, the question then is whether intervention is justifiable when it cannot be ascertained definitively (medically or halachically) whether the conjoined twins pursue each other in anything but in equal degrees.[18] Since in this case it is impossible to ascertain with any certainty which twin is the greater pursuer, the rule is not to intervene.[19] Moreover, recall that the overarching assumption of *rodeif* legislation is that the pursuer and the pursued are ab initio two distinct beings. So, in fact, the *rodeif* analogy cannot reasonably apply to conjoined twins because they are not distinct and already separate persons; and, in theory, it cannot apply because the nature of pursuit in this case is unclear.

Designate

The other major analogy brought to bear on conjoined twins is a narrative from the Jerusalem Talmud.[20] Heathens encircled a group of traveling Israelites and threatened, "Give us one of your company and we shall kill him; if not, we will kill all of you." The Talmud concludes that the group should rather be killed than send forth any individual for certain death. The story continues: If the heathens specify someone, such as Sheva ben Bichri, the group may deliver him so that the group would not be killed. Rabbi Shimon ben Lakish maintains this deliverance is justified only if the intended victim is already deserving of the death penalty.[21] Rabbi Yohanan disagrees: the guilt of the named victim is irrelevant; that he was singled out by name is what matters.[22]

It is methodologically curious that Orthodox bioethicists would invoke this narrative of social politics to create a bioethical norm. As Bleich claims, there is the principle "that halakhic matters are not subject to determination on the basis of aggadic statements."[23] This principle aside, Tendler asserts that "from this story is derived a halakhic ruling," which is that "it is clear . . . it was permissible to sacrifice one [baby] in order to save the other," and he points to the Rama who links the story of Sheva ben Bichri to a fetus to ground his methodological claim.[24] Insofar as a fetus "did not have a chance to live, there would be no problem about killing it to save the mother, because the absence of any hope that the fetus could survive, and not the mother, makes it as if this individual were designated for death."[25] This logic leads Tendler to conclude that the weaker conjoined twin "has been designated for death, and therefore it is permissible to hasten that death in order to save the life of the sister." This logic equates one of the conjoined twins with a mother and one with an unborn fetus, equations that defy the double fact that neither conjoined twin is a mother nor in utero.[26] And, moreover, Tendler insists that Rambam's interpretation, which follows Shimon ben Lakish's requirement of prior guilt, is the more appropriate analogy than Yohanan's. That is, the weaker twin should be viewed as already guilty of a capital crime, and delivering her to the heathens merely hastens her inevitable demise.[27]

Some scholars salvage the relevance of the Sheva ben Bichri narrative by invoking the notion of mutual pursuit. Just as the heathens are pursuers of Sheva ben Bichri, he is also a pursuer of his fellow travelers. This is because his very presence among them exposes them to the heathen's lethal threat were they not to deliver him over to the heathens. Yet this also means that the group itself is a pursuer of Sheva ben Bichri insofar as the group could deliver him to his certain death. The way out of this threefold mutual pursuit is to focus on life expectancy. Regardless of what happens, Sheva ben Bichri's life expectancy is short; the group's could be long were he delivered. By inversely transposing life expectancy into threat, the logic runs as follows: "Although both parties [Sheva ben Bichri and the group] are pursuers, the [designated] victim [Sheva ben Bichri] poses a threat to the others that is qualitatively greater than their threat to him. Elimination of the designated victim rather than allowing the others to be put to death results in a net gain in the qualitative category of life preserved."[28] Halperin concludes this logic forcefully: The weaker twin "is unquestionably considered a pursuer and in order to save [the other] we may and must separate the twins . . . Therefore her life should be ended in an effort to save the life of [the other]."[29] Akin to the consequentialist calculus with pursuit, this logic adduces to itself the capacity to ascertain different life expectancies and then render a lethal normative conclusion for the lesser of the two. This flies in the face of the fact that even physicians caring for these conjoined twins were uncertain about life expectancy were they to operate and even if they were not to operate; not only was there uncertainty among individual doctors, there was substantial disagreement between them.[30]

Yet the Talmudic interpretation of the narrative of Sheva ben Bichri does not end here. As Bleich notes, the Talmud refers to R. Joshua ben Levi who instructed a town harboring a fugitive to turn that person over to the marauding heathens so that the town would be saved from siege. Whereas beforehand Elijah frequented Joshua ben Levi's, he now absented himself from visiting the rabbi. Distressed, Joshua ben Levi fasted until Elijah finally reappeared with the retort, "Shall I reveal myself to a betrayer!" Ben Levi protested that he was merely acting according to the law, to which Elijah rhetorically responded, "Is this the law of the pious?"[31] This story means to Bleich that although an action may be legally defensible, "it is a course of action that a person possessing a keenly honed moral sensitivity should eschew as repugnant."[32] Put differently, this narrative about Sheva ben Bichri simultaneously establishes a norm that is best not followed. Why, then, do some ethicists invoke this story to construct a bioethical norm?

In addition to these textual difficulties, a more profound challenge is the assumption embedded in the Sheva ben Bichri narrative. Sheva ben Bichri is but one individual, distinct and clearly identifiable from the others who surround him. Not only can he be singled out, he can be separated from the group without harming the integrity of the other people comprising the group. Such assumed human form, however, meets with difficulty the realities of conjoined twins whose morphologies defy clearly identifying one from the other. How reasonable is it, then, to impose this narrative that presupposes certain, singular, human forms upon humans whose bodies would become singular only after surgery? As it stands, applying this narrative to conjoined twins is anachronistic insofar as it puts the proverbial cart before the horse, the conclusion before the beginning, the final—and supposedly idealized—human form before the initial, or given, form.

But Then There Was One

Insofar as it is jurisprudentially difficult to justify invoking either analogy (*rodeif* or Sheva ben Bichri) when considering conjoined twins, might there be other elements of the Judaic textual tradition that could offer normative guidance for these abnormal phenomena? Whereas the *rodeif* and Sheva ben Bichri analogies stretch—even contort—the textual tradition, there are other sources that could better inform contemporary Jewish deliberation about conjoined twins. Just as there are midrashic stories about the original human being that fathom and even commend diverse human morphologies, other texts exist that speak explicitly about conjoined twins that could serve as sources for constructing norms regarding them.

The Rabbis consider diverse human morphologies as early as the Mishnah.[33] Regarding the biblical *gibben* (Lev. 21:20) and why it disqualifies someone from being a priest, the second-century Palestinian *Tanna* R. Chanina ben Antigonus asserts that a *gibben* is someone with two backs and a double spinal cord.[34] The Gemara discusses the plausibility of this understanding of *gibben* by invoking a position articulated by the second-century Babylonian *Amora* Rav in regard to an aborted offspring of a woman that has two backs and spinal cords.[35] There, Rav rules that such a birth does not assign ritual impurity to the woman as would a birth of a normal child. His friend and adversary, R. Shmuel, disagrees: If a woman births an entity with two backs and spinal cords, it is a valid birth and she accrues the appropriate ritual impurity. When these two sages dispute, Rav's opinion trumps in matters of ritual but in regard to civil issues the ruling accords with Shmuel.[36] Returning to the *gibben* debate, it is logical that Rav's opinion and not Shmuel's is repeated because the discussion there is about fitness to serve as a priest.

The disagreement between Rav and Shmuel warrants closer scrutiny, however. They disagree in regard to their contemporary Babylonian *Amora* R. Channin bar Abba's interpretation of the biblical *sh'suah* (Deut. 14:7), a characteristic of animals prohibited for consumption—often understood as cloven hooves. According to Channin bar Abba, the *sh'suah* refers to a creature that has two backs and two spinal cords. In Rav's view, no such creature exists in the world; the eating prohibition must therefore pertain to animals that have such abnormal fetuses within them. Shmuel, by contrast, says that such double-backed creatures do exist in the world, and that the eating prohibition must regard *sh'suah* generally but not to double-backed fetuses found within otherwise normal kosher animals.[37] Rabbi Shimi bar Chiya—Rav's grandson, prodigy, and medical care provider[38]—disagrees with his senior colleagues by reciting the teaching by Chanina ben Antigonus, albeit slightly altered from the Mishnaic version noted above: An animal with two backs and spinal cords is unfit for service. Nonetheless, such a creature can survive. This counters Rav's opinion that no such creature exists, much less persists. Indeed a bit later on, Rav insists that even if such a creature could emerge from a woman, it would not survive even eight days and be circumcised, thus obviating the woman from the *tamei* associated with a birth of a normal, healthy boy.

It is clear thus far that despite Rav's protestations, sages in both Palestine and Babylon had encountered or at least heard of human offspring with two backs and spinal columns. Even if such offspring could exist and survive, it would not be eligible to serve in ritual matters, according to Rav.

The question of survival is taken seriously in another Talmudic discussion regarding *t'fillin*.[39] The second-century Palestinian *Tanna* Pelimo asks Judah haNasi, "If a man has two heads, on which of them does he place *tefilin*?" Judah haNasi responded harshly, "Either rise and go into exile, or accept upon yourself excommunication." While the *Tosafot* defend Judah HaNasi by saying that no such thing exists in the world, the *sugya* immediately recites an incident, itself suggesting historical fact, of a man who has sired a two-headed child and now inquires how much money he is required to give to the *kohein* to redeem his offspring. An elder concludes that he should give twice the usual amount for one child, reflecting a presumption that a two-headed offspring is tantamount to two distinct humans who were born simultaneously. This conclusion is challenged by the observation that neonates who die[40] within the first thirty days do not oblige the parents to pay for their redemption from the *kohein*. The only way to understand the elder's position is that for conjoined twins God based the mitzvah of redemption on head count, not survival of a month.

These questions of *tefillin* and redemption reject the assumption that conjoined twins are automatically two distinct persons, and the Tosafot seemingly agree. After declaring that no such creature exists in the world, the *Tosafot* says, "but, there is a midrash: Ashmedai[41] took from below the earth[42] a man with two heads and brought him before King Solomon. He married a woman and sired several normal children, one of which also had two heads. When it came time to divide his inheritance, the two-headed child requested two portions. The case came before King Solomon."[43] Though the *Tosafot* ends here, the midrash it refers to continues: Solomon constructed a test to discern whether the two-headed child is one person or two distinct persons. He had hot water poured on one head to see if it would evince a response in the other. If there was no response, then the offspring comprised two distinct persons; if there was a cry from the other head, then the offspring was but one. As both heads cried out in pain, Solomon ruled that the offspring was a singleton and warranted only one inheritance portion.[44] The sixteenth-century collection, *Shitah Mekubetzet*, composed by Bezalel ben Abraham Ashkenazi, extracts the norm from this midrash: the conjoined twins "are a single offspring with two heads, and they shall be judged only as a single person."[45]

A conundrum remains. On the one hand the Gemara seemingly insists that conjoined twins should be viewed as two distinct people, albeit with shared flesh. Later tradents would rather view and rule such twins as a single person. One way to reconcile these positions is to observe that the Gemara speaks specifically about redemption from Temple service, that is, ritual matters, and the others—based on Solomon's test—refer to inheritance, or civil matters. It is tempting to relate this to the earlier dispute between

Rav and Shmuel and deduce that Rav views conjoined twins as two people, albeit deformed and thus disqualified from service, and Shmuel sees conjoined twins as a singleton. Such a conclusion, however, projects inappropriately upon Rav, for he does not explicitly declare that the reason for barring conjoined twins from service is because they are two deformed distinct humans. It could as easily be claimed that he views conjoined twins as a conglomerate singleton, as would Shmuel, but a singleton whose deformities disqualify him from service nonetheless.

Indeed, throughout these classic texts the opinion seems to be that conjoined twins—whether they exist only in theory, or only briefly, or in the fullness of human longevity—are to be viewed as singletons, albeit with complex legal ramifications.[46] While this position may not be upheld in every instance of concorporation, of humans living in a combined unit, it would be wrong to presume that it is never appropriate. For there are some twins, like Krista and Tatiana Hogan, whose thalami are connected, enabling one to sense what the other feels and perhaps even think the other's thoughts.[47] In many ways they manifest distinct personalities though their bodily connections suggest a singular, complex, being.

Refashioning *B'tzelem Elohim*

The prevailing Jewish bioethical opinion about conjoined twins favors surgical separation, and it supports this conclusion by invoking rationales that, ab initio, presume human physiques conjoined twins do not already embody. It promotes invasive cutting and severing and sewing physical bodies to conform to the law's preconceived notions of human form and function. In a way it uses the law to cut human flesh as would a cookie cutter. As such, this methodology privileges law over creature.

The Judaic textual tradition, however, does not insist that particular legal assumptions about human form must always prevail. Indeed, the many sources that speak about concorporation neither automatically nor even eventually want to force idiosyncratic human existence into a generic shape and size. The plasticity of human biology, including the rare instances of conjoined twins, is reflected well in the theological notion of *b'tzelem Elohim*. *Elohim*, simultaneously a plural and singular noun, suggests that most any *b'tzelem* would, or at least could, be similarly complex. A close look at Genesis 1:26–27 supports this reading, insofar as the verbs and subjects blur singular and plural. The distinction of human sexes (Gen. 1:27) is subsequent to the initial creation of the conglomerate human (see also Gen. 5:1–2). So, too, does Genesis 2:22–23 endorse this reading, for from the original man woman was surgically separated and fashioned. Though it is biologically impossible for conjoined twins to be sexually different, the force of the biblical text is not lost: Singular divine multiplicity is reflected in human ontological complexity. Human singularity as we now know it is a theologically and ontologically later form of being. Might this suggest that creatureliness should transcend humanly interpreted law?

Then again, it could be argued, and rightly so, that the few sources addressing concorporation are insufficient for all scenarios regarding conjoined twins. Extracting norms from these scant foundations for the ever-expanding array of social, political, and economic complexity—not to mention ritual and medical issues—surrounding concorporation would be akin to hanging a mountainous legal corpus on a thread (*Mishnah Chagigah* 1.8). On the other hand, it is undeniable that these sources do exist in the textual tradition and may, in fact, be better suited to address some of the complex needs of conjoined twins than sources presupposing other kinds of bodies. Why, for example, does Bleich review many of these twin texts but immediately abandons them so as to develop a convoluted apologetic for his teacher's musings? Though the answer may be a matter of deference, it still raises the bioethical question: why rely upon analogies that are *so* dissimilar both explicitly and implicitly to the issue at hand, instead of sources that are obviously relevant in text if not context?[48]

Bioethicists who take seriously both the Judaic textual tradition and the complexities of human existence would do well to do several things simultaneously when thinking about conjoined twins. First, they should defend why certain analogies like the *rodeif* and Sheva ben Bichri are more relevant than others. Identifying the principles (deference aside) that mandate including seemingly farfetched analogies when more similar ones are readily at hand is part and parcel to this effort. Second, once the *relevance* of certain analogies has been reasonably established, the *salience* of certain details therein must also be defended. It is unclear, for example, why some ethicists focus on the Sheva ben Bichri story without considering its conclusion, which, as Bleich rightfully points out, encourages supererogation. Only in this transparent way can the analogical reasoning quintessential to Jewish bioethical discourse be both defensible philosophically and sensitive to the complexities of human existence. Moreover, such a methodology would protect the integrity of the Judaic textual tradition itself from being ripped and contorted to shape abnormal circumstances.

Ontologically, humans are borne—theologically as well as biologically—complex. It makes only reasonable sense, then, to think about humans and to construct (legal) norms regarding them, using assumptions that reflect this fleshy complexity. Perhaps a better bioethical methodology regarding conjoined twins is one that joins together texts that speak *of* conjoined twins as well as those that could speak *to* their circumstances.

Notes

1. See BT *B'rachot* 61a; BT *Eiruvin* 18a; *Tanchuma, Tazria*, 2.
2. Hence, *kalendæ Januariæ*, or *kalends*, a pagan holiday that perhaps even Adam instituted when he witnessed the days getting longer after the winter solstice. See *Mishnah Avodah Zarah* 1:3; BT *Avodah Zarah* 8a; JT *Avodah Zarah* 39c. Of course the Rabbis debated which face looked ahead and which backward. Unsurprisingly, it was unconscionable for a woman to precede a man.
3. *B'reshit Rabbah* 8.1. See also *Yafeh Toar*, ad loc., who would rather the notion of androgyny be divided into two distinct, gender-specific bodies.
4. Such concerns also extend to animals, as will be seen below, for the question arises as to whether physiologically abnormal animals can be sacrificed and/or consumed. Many of the biblical comments about congenital dysmorphology pertain to defining disqualifications for priestly service. See, e.g., Lev. 21:16–24. For Rabbinic consideration of these and other human morphologies, see *Mishnah B'chorot*, ch. 7. See also BT *Nidah* 21a–24b for varieties of (aborted) fetuses and other kinds of births. It could be argued, as does Diego Wyszynski, that even though humans with such abnormalities were barred from priestly service they were not universally ostracized or devalued in society generally. See Diego F. Wyszinski, "Dysmorphology in the Bible and Talmud," *Teratology* 64, no. 4 (2001): 221–25. Such notions of linking disvalue with statistical aberrance came perhaps only with the rise of eugenics in the nineteenth and twentieth centuries.
5. Current scientific estimates locate their prevalence at ~1/50,000 births.

6. Concluding argument by Lord Justice Robert Walker, case no. B1/2000/2696, September 22, 2000, http://news.findlaw.com/cnn/docs/siamesetwins/siamesetwins1.html (accessed June 10, 2011).
7. A third notion was put forward as well. Two people jump out of a plane. Only one parachute opens and the free-falling person grabs the legs of the other. See discussion in Donald D. Drake, "Siamese Twins: the Surgery: An Agonizing Choice—Parents, Doctors, Rabbis in Dilemma," *Assia* 4, no. 1 (February 2001). Reprinted from the *Philadelphia Inquirer* (October 16, 1977). The catalyst for this recent spate of essays was the birth of conjoined girl twins (Baby A and Baby B) to an Orthodox family in 1977. The surgeon, Dr. C. Everett Koop, requested consultation from Rav Moshe Feinstein. What Feinstein advised was not written by him; all that remains are notes of meetings where he spoke or his opinion was aired. In 2000, conjoined twins (Jodie and Mary) were born in Britain, which sparked another round of halachic deliberation.
8. See Jonathan K. Crane, "'With a Mighty Hand': Judaic Ethics of Exercising Power in Extraordinary Warfare," in *Enemy Combatants, Terrorism, and Armed Conflict Law: A Guide to the Issues*, ed. David K. Linnan (Westport: Praeger Security International, 2008), 167–206. See note 18 below for classical sources.
9. BT *Sanhedrin* 72b–75a.
10. Moshe D. Tendler, "So One May Live," *Assia* 4, no. 1 (February 2001), http://www.daat.ac.il/daat/kitveyet/assia%20english/tendler-1.htm (accessed February 14, 2011). All quotes are from the Web version. In Drake (2001) this analogy was raised by Moshe's son, Yaakov Tendler.
11. Catholic Reverend Francis Meehan reasoned that Baby A's "terminal event" had already begun; surgery was therefore permissible because Baby A's death would be "an indirect result" of the attempt to save Baby B. See Drake, "Siamese Twins." While the notion of double-effect has long played a role in Catholic moral theology, a question arises here whether Baby A's medically foreseen and medically certain death from surgery would or should qualify as "an indirect result."
12. Some scholars apply this concept to parasites and other diseases, which also begs the question whether intent, so prevalent in classic Rabbinic sources, can rightfully be jettisoned.
13. Mordechai Halperin, "Siamese Twins: Rav Feinstein's Ruling and the Subsequent Controversy," *Assia* 4, no. 1 (February 2001), http://www.daat.ac.il/daat/kitveyet/assia%20english/halperin2-1.htm (accessed February 14, 2011). All quotes are from the Web version.
14. Halperin seemingly doesn't comment on the fact that both Baby A and Baby B died, one in surgery and one three months later from

complications unrelated to the surgery, respectively. Nor does he seem to contemplate the possibility that the twins could have survived longer had no intervention been tried.

15. J. David Bleich, "Conjoined Twins," *Tradition* 31, no. 1 (Fall 1996): 92–125 (citation on p. 102).
16. Ibid. Bleich, "Conjoined Twins," 119 n. 64.
17. It would also be unreasonable to apply the analogy of the two parachutists (see note 7 above), as that analogy bespeaks of the one with the working parachute defending himself by shaking off the one with the malfunctioning chute. Put differently, that analogy is about self-defense and not intervention, which is the concern here. Bleich, "Conjoined Twins," 101, agrees that applying this parachute analogy to conjoined twins sharing a single heart is misplaced.
18. If it were not a case of mutual pursuit, the rules of intervention stipulate that while lethal intervention is permissible, it is preferable to use non-injurious force to prevent a pursuer from transgression. If non-injurious force would be insufficient to achieve this task, injurious force would be required. And, finally, if injurious force would be insufficient, lethal intervention would be required to save the intended victim. See BT *Sanhedrin* 73a–74b; *Sifrei* to *Ki Teitzei*, 223, BT *Bava Kama* 41b; *Piskei HaRosh* to BT *Bava Kama*, 3:13, 126a; Marashal's *Yam Shel Shlomo* to BT *Bava Kama* 3:9; *Mishneh Torah, Hilchot Rotze'ach Ush'mirat Nefesh* 1.6, 1.7, 1.13, 1.14; *Sifra* to BT *K'doshim* 2:4, 8; *Shulchan Aruch, Choshen Mishpat* 421:13.
19. See Akiva Eiger's Novellae on BT *K'tubot* 33b. Cf. Bleich, "Conjoined Twins," 101–2; Halperin, "Siamese Twins."
20. JT *T'rumot* 8:10. See also BT *Sanhedrin* 72b and Rashi there.
21. As was Sheva ben Bichri for attempting to assault King David. See II Sam. 20:4–22.
22. While most tradents follow R. Yohanan, Maimonides sides with R. Shimon ben Lakish. See discussion in Bleich, "Conjoined Twins," 100–101; J. David Bleich, "The Case of the British Conjoined Twins," *Tradition* 34, no. 4 (Winter 2000): 61–78 (relevant pages, 70–74).
23. Bleich, "Conjoined Twins," 114 n. 32. Bleich makes a similar claim in many of his ethical tracts. Yet later on (106-107), Bleich relies upon Rashi's interpretation of this "narrative" to support his own normative position.
24. Tendler, "So One May Live." See Rama at BT *Sanhedrin* 72b.
25. Ibid.
26. Bleich seemingly argues against this equation when he observes that a fetus is not a neonate, conjoined or otherwise. See Bleich, "Conjoined Twins," 109.

27. Tendler, "So One May Live." Curiously this narrative is absent in contemporary Jewish bioethical discourse about euthanasia where, again, an individual whose life has already been "designated" for death (e.g., a trauma or end-stage disease) is kept from, or hastened to, that inevitability.
28. Bleich, "Conjoined Twins," 108.
29. Halperin, "Siamese Twins."
30. See Drake, "Siamese Twins: The Surgery"; Bleich, "The Case of the British Conjoined Twins."
31. JT *T'rumot* 8.10. See Bleich, "The Case of the British Conjoined Twins," 71.
32. Bleich, "British Conjoined Twins," 72. Nestled in his footnote to this comment, Bleich admits that this Joshua ben Levi narrative qualifies Shimon ben Lakish's requirement that the designated individual already be guilty of a prior capital crime. So at one level Bleich portrays this concluding story as a rebuttal to the whole *sugya*—that is, it would be better not to surgically intervene and necessarily condemn one twin to an immediate death; at another level he disagrees with Tendler's view, based on Rambam and Shimon ben Lakish, that such surgery cannot be justified insofar as the weaker twin is not legally culpable for a capital crime.
33. There are, of course, biblical references to diverse human forms—besides deformities. These are, however, hybrid species that combine human and divine or human and animal attributes.
34. *Mishnah B'chorot* 7.2; BT *B'chorot* 43b. Other Tannaim think a *gibben* has abnormal eyebrows. Unsurprisingly, not all manuscripts of the Bavli have this full mishnah or the Gemara discussion thereto.
35. BT *Nidah* 24a.
36. See BT *Nidah* 24b; BT *B'chorot* 49b.
37. See *Tosafot* and Rashi at BT *Nidah* 24a for more discussion on whether it is acceptable, or even plausible, to eat double-backed animals and/or fetuses.
38. See BT *Chulin* 111b.
39. BT *M'nachot* 37a–b.
40. There is disagreement whether the child dies from being killed or from natural causes. See Rashi and *Tosafot* there.
41. Known elsewhere as the prince of demons. See BT *P'sachim* 109b–112a. Ashmedai probably derives from Zoroastrianism's Ašma, and is found in kabbalistic and other non-canonical Judaic texts.
42. There are seven "earths," each with its own inhabitants and natural order. According to some sources, the fifth-lowest earth—Arka—was given over to the descendents of Cain—a people with two heads who can never reach decisions because of argumentation. See *Haqdamat Sefer ha-Zohar* I:9b; Louis Ginzberg, *The Legends*

of the Jews, vol. 1 (Philadelphia: JPS, 1936), 114. Or perhaps this place was Tevel, the second topmost earth, where inhabitants have two heads, four hands and feet, but only a single trunk. See Ginzberg, *The Legends of the Jews*, vol. 1, 10.

43. BT *M'nachot* 37a, s.v., *o kum gelei*.

44. Adolph Jellinek, ed., *Beit HaMidrash*, part 4, Solomon, end. See also Moses Gaster's *The Exempla of the Rabbis* (New York: Ktav Publishing House, 1968), #113 in the Hebrew (p. 75) and #392.11 in the English (pp. 150–51); Ginzberg's *The Legends of the Jews*, vol. 4, 131–32.

45. BT *M'nachot* 37a, #18. Bleich, "Conjoined Twins," 97, is therefore incorrect to assert that in *Shitah Mekubetzet*'s view, conjoined twins "must be deemed to be separate persons, not only for purposes of inheritance, but for all other halakhic purposes as well."

46. Bleich, "Conjoined Twins," 98-99, recalls a Talmudic discussion of a slave originally owned by two and now manumitted by one, and because of this dual-status is prohibited from marrying either a slave woman or a free woman (BT *Chagigah* 2a–b). Bleich uses this analogy to argue that just as this slave is prohibited from marrying and "dicephalus twins are separate biological entities who physically share a single set of sexual organs . . . the identical result should obtain, *a fortiori*, in instances of shared proprietorship of sexual organs." Conjoined twins are thus prohibited from marrying because of the "dual halakhic identity insofar as legal status of those sexual organs is concerned." Curiously Bleich omits the Gemara's conclusion: the remaining owner should be compelled, for the sake of repairing the world (or social order), to free the slave so that he can freely fulfill the obligations of propagation. Bleich thereby ignores the Talmud's promotion of eliminating legal constructs (or at least this one) for morphologically normal humans.

47. See Susan Dominus, "Could Conjoined Twins Share a Mind?" *New York Times Magazine* (May 25, 2011).

48. For a discussion about the power of dissimilar analogies, see Heidi Mertes and Guido Pennings, "The Force of Dissimilar Analogies in Bioethics," *Theoretical Medical Bioethics* 32 (2011): 117–28.

Part IV: The Human Sciences: Neuroscience, Psychology, and Education

Mystical and Spiritual, Neurological and Theological[1]

Ralph D. Mecklenburger

The human spirit is the lamp of God,
Revealing the deepest self.

—Proverbs 20:27

A non-mystic is someone who believes that when truth is explained to him in words, he should understand that truth. The mystic is someone who believes that real truth, meaningful truth, can never be fully expressed in words.

—Joseph Dan[2]

As my wife and I sit down to dinner on Friday evenings we begin the Jewish Sabbath with the traditional rituals: candles, *Kiddush*, and challah. She lights the candles, praising God for "hallowing our lives with commandments," and I sing the *Kiddush*. Then we sing the blessing over the challah and taste it. Through the alchemy of ritual, more than rational thought is engaged, though if we think about it any particular week we do know that "light is the symbol of the divine,"[3] that "wine cheers the human heart" (Ps. 104:15), and that challah deliciously connects us with the ancient sacrificial worship of the Torah (Num. 15:17–21). Candle flames entrance people in virtually every religious tradition, suggesting, as here, the presence of God, or elsewhere recalling ancient miracles or commemorating ancestors. Whatever the neurological basis, and there must

RALPH D. MECKLENBURGER (C72) is rabbi of Beth-El Congregation in Fort Worth, Texas.

be one, the candles especially, and the whole ritual, effectively set a mood of holiness (*k'dushah*, from the Hebrew root, *kadosh*, something set aside as special), setting this meal apart from other meals. In some families children are blessed by the parents at this time, and spouses sing one another's praises. As often as not we appreciate the symbolism without pausing to reflect on it. It comes up every week, after all, and we have to get to worship services in a little while. But if we were to omit this ceremony some Friday evening, we would miss it. Engaging our minds sometimes more deeply and sometimes less, the ritual employs all our senses to create what contemporary American culture calls a spiritual moment.

Traditional rituals provide religious experience. I like to think of ritual as the flesh on the bare bones of theology. Most obviously, people join in public worship, where prayers, Scripture readings, and, often, sermons, not to mention choreography, silent meditation, and music of all varieties occupy us. All this, moreover, is commonly reinforced by special architecture and visual symbols, and frequently by the special dress of officiants, participants, or both. Depending in part on the skill of the "choreographers" and leaders, and in larger measure on the devotion of the participants, and even on their mood that particular day, for the various worshipers the exercise may be more or less effective, and even sometimes a total failure, in evoking spirituality.

Many other experiences are regarded as worship. Many study, especially sacred texts, together. Religious communities work together in idealistic social projects. Even social activities that may lack any direct reference to God still serve to create community, thereby reinforcing religious identity and a sense of belonging. We can call all that we do individually and collectively in the name of religion "religious experience." But most of us would not call all of it, and certainly not modern synagogues' or churches' endless round of committee and board meetings, "spiritual." Spirituality, it seems, has more to do with God, or at least with some sort of self-transcendence.

Recognizing such obvious religious experiences has pragmatic value, but misses the radical challenge of most religions, and certainly of Jewish-Christian-Islamic-style Western religion. The distinction between religious and secular spheres of life and society is modern, and by traditional religious thought is a false one. While Judaism traditionally counts 613 commandments, we can look more conveniently at the Holiness Code in Leviticus 19, which classic rabbis regarded as containing the essentials of Torah.[4] There we find the text going back and forth indiscriminately between ritual and ethical commandments. It begins with honoring parents, immediately turns to eschewing idolatry and properly offering sacrifices (the prime form of biblical worship), then goes on to a host of ethical injunctions, among them caring for the poor and the stranger, paying laborers on time, and loving one's neighbor as oneself, turning later to farming properly, going to the priests to make atonement when these commandments are violated, and so on and so forth! All these things and more—all of life—is, by the biblical tradition, the province of religion. So if religious experience is what is done as part of religious living, *everything* is religious. Disestablishing religion in many modern nations created a *de facto* distinction between religious and secular, and private and public. This made religious pluralism more workable. But all the religions continue to preach that their ideals and values should shape the behavior of their adherents not only at home and in the house of worship, but in the workplace, the political realm, and so on—everywhere, not only where specifically ritual activities occur.

To complicate matters further, most of us know people who claim to be "spiritual, but not religious." One recent poll found that in America, "The old terms—'atheist' and 'agnostic'—are no longer catch-alls for everyone outside traditional belief. In fact, 24% of respondents put themselves into a whole new category: 'spiritual but not religious.'"[5] Then there are subcategories amongst religious believers who see themselves as more rationally inclined or more mystically inclined. There is great variety even within each major religious tradition, as well as between them. "Religious experience" may reasonably be defined as that which is done in the name of God or religion, but such a definition tells us little. Furthermore, as many have lamented for years, "spirituality" is such a fuzzy term that few are quite sure what it means. We tend to regard spirituality as the sense of being in the presence of God, though that may leave out those who claim to be spiritual without being religious. Even as we remain vague about the meaning of the term, a chorus of voices announces a growing modern "hunger for spirituality."

How nice it would be if the cognitive studies researchers could tell us what is going on in our brains when we say we are having religious experience. This might require the theologically hazardous step of ignoring the classic religious message that religion is for the whole of life. Is someone who is, say, helping the proverbial old lady across the street having a different experience if he thinks of that as a religious obligation, a way to serve God, as opposed to simply a kind deed? I suspect not; but more data is needed to back up that hunch. Could we not at least determine if different regions of the brain are in use, or in use with a different balance among them, when we think we are doing something specifically religious, prayer or other ritual, or Bible study, as opposed to participating in the civic ritual of a Fourth of July parade, or studying for a final exam in grammar? I suspect so, that the balance among brain processes is altered, but, again, this remains speculative. Such studies have begun, however. Together with other aspects of cognitive studies, I suggest they can be helpful in moving us towards a less fuzzy understanding of spirituality.

Direct Experience of God?

Millions of people have a sense of relating to God, and some even of experiencing God's presence. One cannot touch, see, smell, hear, or taste that which is nonphysical. We do, though, experience some of our own thoughts, which are physical, but only insofar as electrical patterns playing on brain circuits are physical. How we might sense God's presence is difficult to say. One logical possibility is that God—as pure spirit or pure intelligence—plants ideas directly into our brains, bypassing the senses. What is more likely, however, and does not require such a supernatural explanation, is that we have certain experiences in the natural course of living that give us that subjective sense. Gazing at the star-spangled night sky, for instance, we feel awe, and, like the Psalmist, exclaim, "O God, our God, how majestic is Your name throughout the earth!" (Ps. 8:10). Rudolph Otto, in this regard, spoke of "the numinous,"[6] and Abraham Joshua Heschel similarly attempted to tease out differences between the experience of the sublime, the wondrous, and the radically amazing.[7] At the beginning of this article I spoke of the difficult-to-express but very commonplace reaction, probably both rational and emotional, to seeing candles burn, and tasting, smelling, and hearing other physical things: bread, wine, and blessings. My wife and I do not get our sense of holiness on the eve of the Sabbath exclusively from these physical acts. We have both experiential knowledge (I loved this as a child) and learned abstract understanding ("light is the symbol of the Divine") of Sabbath rituals. We could not now have the experience, even if we wanted to, without it activating memory circuits in our brains that are also connected with emotional circuits. Our Jewish upbringing, in other words, equipped us with a framework of religious ideas, a paradigm, with which to interpret this and countless other experiences. So we do not need a *deus ex machina* (a divine intervention) to explain why doing Jewish things makes us feel Jewish, even on occasion to the degree that we might say, "What a spiritual moment!" as if we were directly experiencing God. These religious reactions, from the pedestrian but important ("Isn't this a nice, loving, family moment") to the rarer sense of being in God's presence, are conditioned reactions involving both abstract thoughts and emotions. (As we shall see, moreover, thought and emotion are not the distinct categories people often assume them to be.) So by parents and teachers, and then as parents and teachers, we are conditioned to experience these symbols as religious—and not just pertaining to any religion, obviously, but to ours. Others react to different symbols—or in the case of candles to the same symbol!—similarly, albeit through the prism of their own religious/interpretive paradigm. In other words, when we say something is a special religious experience, even to the point, on rare occasions, of thinking "God is with us!" we are almost certainly doing so as a conditioned response. I say this not to trivialize something precious to us, but to point to its neurological underpinnings. The omnipresent God, of course, is present. Past conditioning and present circumstance have come together to heighten our awareness of that at the particular moment.

Because my religious tradition has taught me to do so, I can relate to the ritual itself as sacred because it points to God, or to Torah as sacred because it has taught so many generations, and me, too, about God. The sense of *k'dushah* does not always or even usually require the conviction that one is attuned, directly, to God. Sometimes it does; in my tradition more often it does not. The primary experience is of physical things (sunset, wine, prayer, text, or whatever); the religious content is inferred. An inferred God or other inferred sense of holiness is a secondary manifestation of primary experience. The brain conditioned to do so interprets certain primary experience as religious.

For some in each tradition, though, the desire for direct experience of God persists.[8] So mystics, over the ages, have become convinced that in arcane ways they can directly, as first-order experience, sense God, and thus truth and ultimate reality. In some cases they believe they somehow *merge with* God. There are a great variety of such theories or understandings, loosely lumped together by modern scholars as mysticism.

I would once have said that if you insist that reality as we perceive it is an illusion, hiding a deeper reality within, you are a mystic. Then I started reading about physics, which empirically concludes precisely that what we perceive as solid (or liquid or gas!) is made up of molecules, which consist of atoms, which in turn consist of subatomic particles, and includes more space than anything else. The same could be said of other branches of science, including neuroscience (what we experience as unified self, for instance, is actually many processes going on simultaneously, and more is going on in the brain at any moment than reaches the threshold of conscious awareness). Scientists, though, think they communicate objective facts in words and mathematics. Mystics insist their experience of God is ineffable. So I have come to appreciate Professor Joseph Dan's definition in the epigraph. The mystic believes that ultimate truth cannot be expressed. There may well be a touch of the mystical in all religion, as when I and others argue that God is so far beyond us that we can only speak of God metaphorically. Yet I believe the metaphors are genuinely helpful, that we can express something meaningful about God—stopping short of full mysticism. The point, to reiterate, is that many mystics insist that God *can* be experienced, though people lack the ability to communicate the experience to others.

This is an important digression because for many mystics the goal and highest achievement is not only to experience God, but that merger with God, a *unio mystica* (union with God), and neurological research has shed light on what appears to be the neurological substrate of that phenomenon. The chapter on mysticism in William James's classic, *The Varieties of Religious Experience*, presents passage after passage in which mystics from various traditions speak of the effort to tame and even temporarily eliminate the mystic's private self or ego, ultimately reaching a sense of oneness with God or all being (and of course in pantheistic systems, which mystical theologies often are, everything is God, so union with being *is* union with God). James notes that mystics typically describe their experience and what they learn from it as ineffable.[9] The history of Jewish mysticism shows more complexity. Some mystics—Abraham Abulafia, the kabbalists in Safed, and to some extent modern Chasidism—seek union with God, but others, notably the medieval Spanish kabbalists, do not.[10] This is still mysticism, for even kabbalists not seeking a state in which the boundaries of the self are lost in the vast divine sea of being, the feeling often described as "oceanic,"[11] agree that ultimate reality may be glimpsed but never communicated.[12]

Today science helps us see into the physiological foundation of mystical experiences. Andrew Newberg and Eugene d'Aquili of the University of Pennsylvania received permission to experiment with Buddhist monks as they meditated, attempting to reach a mystical state. They tell us of the meditation of a monk named Robert:

> First, he says, his conscious mind quiets, allowing a deeper, simpler part of himself to emerge. Robert believes that this inner self is the truest part of who he is, the part that never changes. For Robert, this inner self is not a metaphor or an attitude; it is literal, constant, and real. It is what remains when worries, fears, desires, and all other preoccupations of the conscious mind are stripped away. He considers this inner self the very essence of his being. If pressed, he might even call it his soul.
>
> Whatever Robert calls this deeper consciousness, he claims that when it emerges during those moments of meditation when he is most completely absorbed in looking inward, he suddenly understands that his inner self is not an isolated entity, but that he is inextricably connected to all of creation. Yet when he tries to put this intensely personal insight into words, he finds himself falling back on familiar clichés that have been employed for centuries to express the elusive nature of spiritual experience. "There's a sense of timelessness and infinity," he might say. "It feels like I am part of everyone and everything in existence."[13]

Newberg, a neuroscientist as well as a religion professor, used nuclear medicine to take pictures of the monks' brains as they reached what they reported as their deepest meditative levels. They injected a radioactive dye into subjects' bloodstream, enabling them to photograph where blood went in greater or lesser than usual amounts in the brain, indicating greater or lesser use of certain areas. Each of us has what Newberg calls (along with the technical neurological terminology) "a small lump of gray matter nestled in the top rear section of the brain" that orients us in physical space. It keeps track of where we are, our boundaries, so that as we move around we do not bump into things, and appreciate how near or far other things are. "In simple terms, it must draw a sharp distinction between the individual and everything else, to sort out the you from the infinite not-you that makes up the rest of the universe."[14] As Robert went deeper and deeper into his meditative trance, there was less and less activity in this area. The doctors speculate that it was not that the brain area in question was turned off, but rather that it was receiving less data than usual from the senses. Lacking data that showed where the monk ended and the world began, his brain lost track of that distinction. He felt like an undifferentiated part of the vast sea of being.

These results were replicated first with other monks meditating in Tibetan Buddhist style. Then Newberg and d'Aquili repeated the experiment with Franciscan nuns involved in meditative "centering prayers." "The nun begins by focusing her mind on a particular prayer, word, or passage from the Bible. Then she closes her eyes and reflects on the inner meaning and spirit of the text. As [one Sister] explained, 'I open myself to God's presence.'"[15] Since the nuns concentrated on the words of their prayers, their language centers were activated more than those of the monks. But they, too, had a marked decrease in the orientation center, the intensity and length of the prayer experience inducing them to lose track of space and time and seemingly to lose individuality, which was in turn interpreted as being directly in contact with God.[16] In other words, the mystical experience of *unio mystica* was very similar, though the brains of the Buddhists interpreted that experience as joining a universal consciousness and the brains of the Christians interpreted it as communion with God.

In a more recent book, a more secular scientist, Harvard neuroanatomist Jill Bolte Taylor, recounts her experience having a stroke.[17] A stroke is caused by the interruption of blood flow to some part of the brain. Dr. Taylor, it was later determined, had a congenital problem with blood vessels in the left side of her brain—where, among many other things, the orientation area that became less active in the meditating brains studied by Newberg and d'Aquili is located. In Taylor's stroke, instead of receiving less data from the senses as it continued to function, that orientation function itself was impaired, as was much more. The left side of the brain generally handles linguistic, mathematical, and analytic functions, whereas, Dr. Taylor explains: "Moment by moment, our right mind creates a master collage of what this moment in time looks like, sounds like, tastes like, smells like, and feels like." Furthermore, our sense of narrative time is left-brained, whereas for the right brain, "no time exists other than the present moment."[18] The two sides typically work so well together that we cannot introspectively distinguish between them; we feel like one whole person, not two personalities in one brain. Still, some of us (including, quite obviously, this theological writer) are more left-brained and analytical, and some of us (most artists) are more right-brained and spontaneous. Dr. Taylor is convinced that as she had her stroke, and then struggled long-term to overcome the disabilities it caused, more was involved in her altered state of consciousness than just the orientation function that Newberg and d'Aquili emphasize. In particular, impairment of her language and time-keeping abilities were also involved.[19] The important point for the moment, though, is that her experience parallels the mystical experiences we have been discussing:

> I remember that first day of my stroke with terrific bitter-sweetness. In the absence of the normal functioning of my left orientation area, my perception of my physical boundaries was no longer limited to where my skin met air. I felt like a genie liberated from its bottle. The energy of my spirit seemed to flow like a great whale gliding through a sea of silent euphoria. Finer than the finest of pleasures we can experience as physical beings, this absence of physical boundaries was one of glorious bliss.
>
> Without a language center telling me: "I am Dr. Jill Bolte Taylor. I am a neuroanatomist. I live at this address and can be reached at this phone number," I felt no obligation to being her anymore. It was truly a bizarre shift in perception.
>
> When I lost my left hemisphere and its language centers, I also lost the clock that would break my moments into consecutive brief instances. Instead of having my moments prematurely stunted, they became open-ended, and I felt no rush to do anything. . . . I morphed from feeling small and isolated to feeling enormous and expansive.[20]

This and many other passages in *My Stroke of Insight*, Dr. Taylor's enthralling book, sound more like contemporary American "new age spirituality" than classic mysticism. She uses terms such as, here, "the energy of my spirit" and elsewhere "bliss" and even "Nirvana," but not "God." There is little doubt, though, that the phenomenon is the same, albeit interpreted through a different higher-level brain paradigm. For these three examples, Buddhist, Christian, and secular, one could go round and round in chicken-and-egg fashion trying to say whether the experience is primary and the interpretation secondary, or whether the interpretation the brain adds determines what individuals experience, or at least what they express and remember. Either way, we—our brains—assign the meaning. The paradigm we employ to interpret helps shape the experience as well as our understanding of it.

This is important because it explains a widely reported religious phenomenon neurologically, demonstrating that the same brain mechanisms are involved in different religious—and not so religious—traditions. That further demonstrates that the same primary experience takes on different meanings based on the individual's higher-level paradigm or filter. Furthermore, we do not have to assume the nature of God, or even the existence of God, to appreciate that something real is going on in the brain and consciousness of those who report that they have had this "oceanic" experience of oneness with all. The findings do cast into doubt, however, explanations of *unio mystica* as out-of-body experiences as the soul, for instance, rises to higher and higher levels of heaven. (Mystics would probably reply that such language is metaphorical in the first place; the mystic experience—once again—cannot be communicated with any precision.) What remains an open question, however, is of the essence theologically. Is *unio mystica* an illusion, a trick the brain plays on believers? Or, given the scientific understanding of all matter and energy having started in one "big bang" (or even perhaps a series of them as the universe expanded and contracted), are the mystics overcoming an opposite illusion, namely that they are distinct entities when in fact they are, we all are, part of one giant Order? The stroke-stricken scientist joins classic mystics arguing precisely that!:

> Of course I am fluid! Everything around us, about us, among us, within us, and between us is made up of atoms and molecules vibrating in space. Although the ego center of our language center prefers defining our *self* as individual and solid, most of us are

> aware that we are made up of trillions of cells, gallons of water, and ultimately everything about us exists in a constant and dynamic state of activity.[21]

Both are logical, arguable, explanations. It depends on your paradigm for understanding life and the world. That the universe is one vast sea of evolving being subsuming us is basic physics. Within it, though, individual entities come and go, and they, too, from galaxies to microbes, and us in between, are real. A fortunate few have consciousness, which at the human level privileges us with the opportunity to understand much, but still not all, of the rest. That is real, not an illusion. Cosmic oneness, the universe united by the laws of nature, is also real. Since I mean that literally, and the definition of a mystic is that he or she does not believe "that real truth, meaningful truth, can be conveyed in words," I say that without pretending to be a mystic. Reality—thank God—is as wondrous as anything the generations have dreamed.

Do we, then, have direct experience of God? Suddenly we are back to our understanding of that which is beyond our full understanding. Do we experience a Personality who "knows" as we know, "creates" as we create, "rules" as a king or president rules? I have yet to see convincing proof or disproof. If by God, however, we mean the cosmic Order of which we are a part, of course we experience it, every day. Our whole existence depends on it—or, if you will, on It.

Emotion and Spirituality

We should not lose sight of the fact that the mystics, and even the stroke victim, claim as vivid personal experience what I just treated as abstract concepts to be understood intellectually. The example of my wife's and my Sabbath experience with which I began, moreover, and the analogous ritual experience millions of believers have had in all sorts of ritual religions contexts, make no such extravagant claims of divine intoxication (or, at least, do so but rarely). Neither are such examples the same as, but merely to lesser extreme than, the experiences of the monks and nuns in the study, who devote large chunks of time—after years of practice—to achieve what they believe is a spiritual breakthrough to another level of reality. Even with sufficient time meditators do not always succeed, and, when they do, they insist the experience is incommunicable. Much of what most of us more commonly claim as religious experience—prayer and other ritual, text study, the doing of good deeds, awe in nature—may often be difficult, but still not impossible, to communicate. And though the religious feeling in these activities may not always happen when we wish, it sometimes happens when we least expect it. Many a poet or preacher communicates such religious experience quite well, moreover, at least to those prepared to hear it. I suggest that as mystical experience has a neurological substrate, so must our more common and more pedestrian religious experiences. So I hope I have chipped away at the question of what religious experience and spirituality are. But we must press on. What is happening, neurologically, in the more common religious experience so many of us believe we have?

We *Homo sapiens* are distinguished by the sapient, cognitive, ruminative, in a word *rational* part of ourselves. We know that we evolved from the animal kingdom and, as embodied creatures, have an animal nature. But the part of our brains where we do our abstracting, roughly speaking the frontal cortex behind and around the forehead, is larger and more developed in people than in any other animal, and particularly rich in neural connections to other areas so that decisions can be made, in effect, as part of a network. By contrast with this rational part of us, we have tended to think of our emotions as lower and in need of control. Antonio Damasio of the University of Southern California, though, explains that while emotions mostly originate in other parts of the brain, they make vital contributions to our rational thinking. They are in the network, part of, not other than, our thinking. You meet a lot of people in the course of a day and tend to forget most of them. But you will certainly not forget the one you found specially sexy, or generous, nor probably the one whose conversation either specially fascinated you or thoroughly aggravated you. When an emotion is triggered a memory is, as it were, flagged as important for your future reference.

We depend on emotional input to thought in other ways, too. You are walking along when suddenly you see someone or something rushing at you—a raging elephant, a speeding Chevrolet, a menacing character coming out of the alley. This is not an ordinary experience and your mind is seized by a very helpful emotional reaction: fight or flight. This is a matter of survival and there is no time for your big brain to calmly reflect; you must act! We tend to like some emotions, love, awe, and joy, for instance, and might prefer to avoid others, such as fear, anger, and sadness. These and other emotions play a direct role in motivating our attention and proper—in the sense of helpful for our well-being—reaction. We would not want to be blasé when endangered, downcast when the home team wins, or exultant when a loved one dies. Emotions infuse, and often direct, appropriate rational thinking and physical action. As a matter of fact, Damasio demonstrates, our emotions consistently influence us physically; they are "embodied." When you react to threat, blood flows to the muscles and adrenaline pumps so you are ready for action. As readers of body language we instantly distinguish friendly, fearful, and angry faces and postures. If you have autism and do not, you will likely have social adjustment problems. When we speak of fear as a feeling in our guts, and behaving courageously as "having guts," this is by no means purely metaphor. Fear and grief do manifest themselves viscerally ("in the gut"). And without the physical reaction to sexual attraction, the race would not continue. Damasio engagingly speaks of "the motion in emotion." We react both physically and intellectually to our emotions. "Are you having a good day today?"—or a bad one—is less a matter of rational judgment than of emotional reaction to what has happened to you. As the emotions come from older and deeper places in the brain (in terms of evolution) they amount to a parallel system of thought that influences the more abstract and rational system of thought we call "rational." To some extent we learn to recognize rationally, and partially control (inhibiting or magnifying) our emotional reactions, but that extent is limited: We always operate on both levels at once. We keep thinking all the time, but experience our emotions as waxing and waning in response to what we are experiencing (externally) or thinking (internally) at any given moment. Modern neuroscience is not only mapping the several sources of emotional reaction in the brain and how they trigger our reactions, but also trying to explain how we, as humans and thus more sophisticated than lower animals, recognize these states.[22]

What has all this to do with religious experience and spirituality? Everything, I suggest. When we occupy ourselves with specifically religious occupations, however different religious traditions and individuals may define that (most offer prayers, do loving deeds, study inherited texts, while only some offer sacrifices or sit for hours in silence), we call that, in the simplest sense, religious experience. To greater or lesser extent we may intellectualize about it, noting special procedures and symbolic meanings. This is also religious experience. But at some point we sense something more, a shift in subjective feeling, a breakthrough, *spirituality*. At that point some would say, and some would not, that we are sensing God. But our question here is less highfalutin. What is happening neurologically? Emotion is always there at least in the background, but I suggest that when a surge in positive emotion is triggered by an experience, to the extent that it breaks through powerfully enough to become conscious we experience the moment as different, special, set aside—the root meaning of the Hebrew *kadosh* (holy). This experience associated with religion comes to be felt as *spiritual*. We become excited, or awed, feel connected to community, or tradition, or even to God. Another term for this is self-transcendence. Obviously I am not literally connected to the text as, say, the story of Sinai, or Isaiah's throne vision, transfixes, literally excites, my attention. I am not literally connected to my religious community as we sing a powerful hymn together, but I have a sense of enhanced bonding, a quasi mystical feel of being part of something larger than myself. We do not usually mean it literally when we speak of being "inspired," either, though occasionally we may suddenly gasp—inhale—from our sense of wonder or excitement over something. The term inspiration (in-spiration, breathing in) derives from that emotional response. This is all, in effect, "the motion in emotion" in a religious context. It is not purely emotional, for the ritual, prayer, or study takes place in a learned and rationally appreciated context, one's religious tradition, else it is not recognized as religious. Emotion *and* rationality are involved. The issue, it seems to me, is the balance between them. Neuroscientists are beginning to explore this experimentally. A study of mystical experience found enhanced activity in emotional brain centers (not surprising as one "dials down" analytic thought to feel the moment),[23] and a study of six Evangelical Christians and six secularists reading Psalm 23 (and a nursery rhyme and the phone book, with six more secularists as a control group) found the religious subjects had enhanced activity in rational brain centers with the Psalm. (Researchers hypothesized that the religious individuals were placing the familiar text into their established religious "schema"—what I have been calling their paradigm—a more rational function.)[24] My hypothesis about more conventional religious experience echoes Newberg's about meditative practices.[25] Both rational and emotional areas of the brain are involved, but the powerful *feelings* (note the word!) of holiness, spirituality, and transcendence occur when more emotion than usual is stimulated. Psychologists Malcolm Jeeves and Warren S. Brown have summarized the research similarly.[26] Research continues. My hunch is that experiments will show that "Isn't that interesting?" becomes "Wow, how profound, how meaningful!" precisely when emotional arousal becomes conscious.

Spirituality, then, whatever the balance turns out to be as it is further studied, is always emotional as well as rational. We *feel* a bond with community, tradition, or even God, and may think we thereby transcend personal limitations, no longer feeling as small or alone. Spirituality is subjective. Spirituality that is not felt, not subjective, is not spirituality at all. Furthermore, since "all emotions use the body as their theater,"[27] and spirituality has a major emotional as well as a rational component, spirituality is not exclusively in the mind. As emotion has a physical component, spirituality does, too. There is often more than metaphor involved when we speak of being "moved" or "deeply touched" by a religious experience.

Whether felt spirituality is a response to something objectively real is not in doubt where community and ancient texts, as well as ritual items, sacred music, and other aspects of our traditions are concerned. My candles and blessings on Shabbat are very real. They suggest and symbolize, and I respond. But what of that which is symbolized? The Sabbath is real. Tradition is real. But is God, for those who say they sense God's presence, literally, physically, *objectively* and not only subjectively, felt? That is unanswerable until one defines what one understands God to be, and, once again, all God-talk is metaphorical and approximate. Those who think of God as a physical presence (or as all being) will have no difficulty believing, even insisting, that their subjective sense is of Something or Someone objectively real. Those of us who think of God in more abstract, philosophical terms will likely say, as I would, that our spiritual sense is an intellectual excitement, not a direct experience of God unmediated by thought and paradigm.

That the examples of spirituality in this essay are all positive, not negative, experiences is not accidental. In the psalms those crying out in physical or psychological pain, far from feeling God is the source of their woe, feel bereft of God ("How long will You hide Your face from me?" for instance, in Psalm 13:2, and many similar passages). In most religious paradigms, I suspect, we associate God more with good than evil. Still, for monotheists everything comes from God, not only the good, so the theoretical possibility of negative spirituality remains. In a Chasidic tale Rabbi Zusya complains that he loves God enough, but does not fear God enough, and requests that he might fear God as much as the angels do. "And God heard his prayer, and his name penetrated the hidden heart of Zusya as it does those of the angels. But Zusya crawled under the bed and howled like a little dog, and animal fear shook him until he howled, 'Let me be like Zusya again.' And God heard him this time also."[28] One wonders if worshipers hearing Jonathan Edwards preach "Sinners in the Hands of an Angry God," or others whose spirituality includes a major dose of fear, might similarly associate God with negative emotion. "Spirituality" seems too mild a term for terror, but I would not deny the potential for negative spirituality, though I suspect it is far less common than the positive variety.

This notion of spirituality as triggered by an emotional reaction to something, whether something external or even one's own thinking, is worth lingering over, for spirituality is an important aspect of religion. Several years ago I and a local minister led an interfaith group to Israel and one of our stops was the Hill of the Beatitudes overlooking Yam Kinneret, better known to Christians as the Sea of Galilee. Here Jesus is reputed to have given his famous "Sermon on the Mount" (Matt. 5:1–7:29). There is a lovely church with beautifully manicured grounds, and a fine view of the lake. Like so many other groups, we sat everyone down and the minister read the beatitudes, a portion of the sermon (Matt. 5:3–10). I had heard it before and found it, once again, a beautiful, idealistic message. For me, though, that was a largely intellectual response. I was not specially moved hearing the New Testament passage at that particular place. Recently I was talking to a ministerial colleague who had just led a group of ministers to Israel. They stopped at the same place, and her instructions from the tour operator included gathering the group together to read the same passage from Matthew. Her first reaction to the instructions was that the planners were trying to manipulate them; a group of ministers, surely, knew the passage and did not need to have it read to them! But she decided to read it anyway. And in that spot, with the Sea of Galilee below, she said, she could scarcely believe her own reaction to reading that text. "It was powerful!" she said with obvious affect.

Consider: This was not a purely emotional reaction, for without the rational understanding of the place and the text, the religious framework of the experience, it would not have been so powerful. But the knowledge was in her mind whether or not she had read the text. Reading the text triggered an emotional surge. On my trip to Israel I had a similar experience as our group arrived in Jerusalem and we stopped atop Mt. Scopus to survey the city beneath. Taking a cue from a travel book, I had planned on reading ten lines of a famous poem in which the poet, Avigdor Hameiri, in 1922, saluted the city from the same spot and, echoing the millennial yearning of Jews for Jerusalem, exclaimed, "For one hundred generations, have I dreamed of you," and concluded, "Jerusalem, Jerusalem, from your ruins, I will rebuild you."[29] I had been to the overlook before, and had read the poem before. But I had not read the poem there before, and as I was about to recite it I realized I was too overcome with emotion, and asked my Christian colleague to do so for me. It was not even, technically, a prayer, but in this context it was bound up in my religious identity. My colleague found it a meaningful reading (as I found the beatitudes a meaningful reading), but his text experienced in his religious paradigm, and my text experienced in mine, created a Christian spiritual moment for him and a Jewish spiritual moment for me. Spirituality kicks in with the often unconscious and usually irresistible message: pay attention; this is profound!

Similarly, when volunteers go to a homeless shelter to help serve a meal, a not very religiously inclined person, motivated simply to be a good and compassionate citizen, may feel good about the time spent, and may well have some emotional reaction to the scene or to an individual's look or word of thanks, yet not identify that reaction as spiritual. Another person, doing the same thing because she regards it, if Jewish, as a mitzvah or, if Christian, as an act of love (for Jesus instructed that feeding the poor was tantamount to feeding Him (Matt. 25:35–40), may speak of having had a spiritual moment.

Consider a final example, this one of an activity not generally regarded as religious. An atheist friend and I are sitting at the symphony listening to an exceptionally fine performance of a brilliant violin concerto—Beethoven, Sibelius, pick your own favorite! We both love it. It was brilliantly composed and now sensitively performed to evoke emotional reaction. I say to my friend, as the music ends and the applause begins to die down, "That was a religious experience!" And I mean it. My soul has been stirred. He responds (because he likes to needle me!), "I don't know what you mean by 'religious' in this context, but yes, it was glorious!" The point, once again, is that one's higher-level paradigm shapes both the experience and its meaning. It is probably a useful convention of common parlance to reserve not only the term "religious," but also the term "spiritual," for experiences that somehow call God or religion to mind. But recall what I earlier called the "radical challenge" of most religions. God is omnipresent and religion, thus, is about the whole of life. My friend, though loathe to employ the same language, had an experience very much like mine—though not absolutely identical because they were filtered through different mental paradigms. Given the similarity, and given that lots of people these days claim to be "spiritual but not religious," it might be reasonable simply to say that whatever touches the human spirit is spiritual.

Notes

1. This essay, slightly modified, is a chapter from the author's forthcoming book, *Our Religious Brains: What Cognitive Science Reveals about Belief, Morality, Community and Our Relationship with God* (Woodstock, VT: Jewish Lights Publishing, 2012).
2. Joseph Dan, *The Heart and the Fountain: An Anthology of Jewish Mystical Experiences* (Oxford, Oxford University Press, 2002), 3.
3. *Union Prayer Book, Newly Revised* (Cincinnati: Central Conference of American Rabbis, 1940), 7.
4. *Leviticus Rabbah* 24:5.
5. Christine Wicker, "How Spiritual Are We?" *Parade*, October 4, 2009, 4–5.
6. See *The Idea of the Holy* (London: Oxford University Press, 1923).
7. See, for instance, the opening chapters of *God in Search of Man: A Philosophy of Judaism* (Philadelphia: Jewish Publication Society, 1956).
8. In Christianity this desire may be satisfied at least in part by the Eucharist. Those who take that ritual literally as transubstantiation believe themselves to be tasting God. Christians, though, who understand "body and blood" as symbolic, not literal, are in the same position as Jews, Muslims, and others who think of God as utterly nonmaterial. The long history of Catholic mysticism demonstrates that even the Eucharist has not always been sufficient

to satisfy those who yearn for experience of the divine somehow deeper than taste.

9. William James, *The Varieties of Religious Experience* (New York: Barnes & Noble Classics, text based on 1902 edition, 2004), 328–71.
10. See Moshe Idel, *Kabbalah: New Perspectives* (New Haven: Yale University Press, 1988), ix–xix.
11. Sigmund Freud, in *Civilization and Its Discontents*, 11, quotes Romain Rolland using this description of the mystic state. Cited in Matthew Alper, *The "God" Part of the Brain* (Naperville, IL: Sourcebooks, 2006), 131–32.
12. Dan, *The Heart and the Fountain*, 1–7.
13. Andrew Newberg, Eugene d'Aquili, and Vince Raus, *Why God Won't Go Away: Brain Science and the Biology of Belief* (New York: Ballantine Books, 2001), 2.
14. Ibid., 4–5.
15. Andrew Newberg and Mark Robert Waldman, *Why We Believe What We Believe: Uncovering our Biological Need for Meaning, Spirituality, and Truth* (New York: Free Press, 2006), 173.
16. For a more detailed anatomical description, see ibid., 174–80.
17. Jill Bolte Taylor, *My Stroke of Insight: A Brain Scientist's Personal Journey* (New York: Viking, 2008).
18. Ibid., 29–30.
19. Ibid., 68.
20. Ibid., 67–68.
21. Ibid., 69.
22. Antonio Damasio, *The Feeling of What Happens: Body and Emotion in the Making of Consciousness* (San Diego: Harcourt, 1999), especially ch. 2, "Emotion and Feeling," 35–81, and ch. 9, "Feeling Feelings," 279–95.
23. J.L. Saver and J. Rabin, "The Neural Substrates of Religious Experience," *Journal of Neuropsychology and Clinical Neuroscience* 9, no. 3 (1997): 498–510 (cited in Newberg, *Why We Believe*, ch. 7, n. 25).
24. Azari et al. "Neural Correlates of Religious Experience," *European Journal of Neuroscience* 13, no. 8 (2001): 1649–52.
25. "Creating Emotional Realities," in Newberg, *Why We Believe*, 180–83.
26. Malcolm Jeeves and Warren S. Brown, *Neuroscience, Psychology and Religion: Illusions, Delusions, and Realities about Human Nature* (West Conshohocken, PA: Templeton Foundation Press, 2009), 95–97.
27. Damasio, *The Feeling of What Happens*, 51.
28. Martin Buber, *Tales of the Hasidim, Early Masters* (New York: Schocken, 1947), 246–47.
29. Lawrence A. Hoffman, *Israel: A Spiritual Travel Guide* (Woodstock, VT: Jewish Lights, 2005), 158–59.

Neuro-Jewish Education: An Introduction

Justus N. Baird

Not long after my seventh birthday, I found myself lying prostrate on a small conveyer belt, slowly moving headfirst into a late-1970s magnetic resonance imaging (MRI) device. Doctors had discovered a tumor deep in my nasal passage that was putting pressure on my brain. They told me this giant machine could take pictures of the inside of my head. In that sterile white plastic coffin, I lay as still as a seven-year-old can. I remember wondering, "What could they see in my brain? Will those giant magnets hurt me somehow? Could they see what I was thinking?" At the time, that last curiosity —the ability to see a person's thoughts—would have been considered the foolish question of a child. Today, such curiosities drive major research grants.

An Emerging Field; An Exciting Conversation

The emerging field of mind, brain, and education science, also known as neuroeducation,[1] lies at the intersection of three well-established fields:

1. *Neuroscience*: the brain and its functioning
2. *Psychology*: mind and behavior
3. *Pedagogy*: individual education and learning

What began as a cross-disciplinary venture between cognitive neuroscientists and developmental psychologists eventually began to involve educators. Partly in response to exciting new understandings about how brains operate, and partly in response to an explosion of pseudoscience about "brain-based" learning, experts

---

JUSTUS N. BAIRD (NY07) is the rabbi and director of the Center for Multifaith Education at Auburn Theological Seminary in New York.

from the three fields of neuroscience, psychology, and education began a serious attempt at creating shared understanding. Over time, proponents like Kurt Fischer (Harvard School of Education), David B. Daniel (University of Northern Colorado), Mary Helen Immordino-Yang (University of Southern California School of Education), Elsbeth Stern (Swiss Federal Institute of Technology), Antonio Battro (National Academy of Education in Argentina), and Hideaki Koizumi (Hitachi Ltd.) began to call for a deep three-way meeting of the fields.[2] Mind, brain, and education science would form the bridge between them.

To illustrate the inherent challenges involved in such a cross-disciplinary approach to discovery, consider that "neuroscience is focused on the neuron as the primary unit of study while psychology's unit of study is the mind and pedagogy's view is on the society and individual, as manifested through formal educational practice."[3] As neuroscientists, psychologists, and educators came to know each others' fields, they realized that each field can inform the other, and that only when confirmed hypotheses from one field are confirmed in the other two has a real and useful discovery occurred.

The goal of this article is to introduce the fields of neuroeducation and Jewish education to each other, in two ways: firstly, to arouse curiosity among Jewish educators about how we may be able to elevate our practices by applying evidence-based findings from neuroeducation to our own settings; and secondly, to share questions that keep Jewish educators up at night with the field of neuroeducation in hopes that its researchers may soon turn their attention to our vexing problems.

The powerful role that *religious* educators can bring to this cutting-edge conversation came into focus for me when I learned that the entire enterprise of widespread formal education began in religious communities:

> For the most part, churches and temples served as the first classrooms . . . Catholic schools were the first formal educational institutions in Norway around 1152, for example, and the Third Lateran Council (1179) officially mandated free education for the poor of England, though the classes were primarily devoted to religious readings . . . in India in the 18th century, schools and temples were physically one and the same.[4]

Today the field of education is dominated by secular approaches, but the historical roots of education are planted deep in the soil of religious traditions. Perhaps the pendulum is swinging back again. Findings from mind, brain, and education science—such as the critical roles that context, emotions, embodiment, moral support, and the search for meaning play in learning—suggest that religious educators may yet again be poised to influence larger understandings of how humans learn.

Let us turn now to what the field of neuroeducation has to teach religious educators. We begin with a brief overview of the tools of the trade.

How We Know What We Know about the Brain

Since 1979, when those MRI pictures helped surgeons remove my tumor, and especially since the late 1980s, technologies that allow us to see a *functioning* brain (cognitive neuroimaging) have grown tremendously. These new imaging technologies created entirely new ways to understand the brain. What follows is a brief description of the most prevalent imaging tools.[5]

Imaging tools that focus on blood flow in the brain are spatially precise but slow. In positron emission tomography (PET), technicians inject radioisotopes into the bloodstream and then monitor metabolic activity and cerebral blood flow. Another technique, functional magnetic resonance imaging (fMRI), uses radio frequencies and magnets to identify changes in the concentration of deoxygenated hemoglobin. Because fMRI does not require radioactive materials, it is less invasive and safe for use on children. Both fMRI and PET are accurate within millimeters and produce colorful three-dimensional maps of brain activity. Imaging tools that measure blood flow have a relatively slow temporal resolution—measuring changes over seconds—and are used primarily to explore brain activity that is relatively prolonged.

Other imaging tools measure electrical activity. Such tools, called electromagnetic imaging, are temporally precise (with resolution in milliseconds) but spatially coarse (resolution in centimeters). The well-used electroencephalogram (EEG) relies on electrodes placed on the scalp to measure electrical differences. When a stimulus to the brain causes changes in electrical activity, the differences are recorded as event-related potentials (ERP). Researchers have also learned that electrical signals coming from the brain oscillate, like sine and cosine waves, and show a range of frequencies that change when one is sleeping, resting, or makes an error. Electromagnetic imaging tools are sufficiently noninvasive that they can be used with young children, which has allowed researchers to study the brain as it grows and develops. Combining tools that measure blood flow with tools that measure electrical activity can give both spatial and temporal precision.[6]

One additional set of tools for learning about the brain deserves mention: impairments and lesions. Researchers can learn much from a brain that is damaged or injured. The classic example is Phineas Gage and what was long called "the American Crowbar Case."[7] Gage, a railroad construction foreman, was blasting rock to build a rail bed on September 13, 1848, when an iron rod—which he used to pound charges—was propelled by an accidental explosion straight through his cheek and out of the top of the head. Incredibly, the accident was not fatal. The three-foot, 1.25-inch diameter iron rod caused major damage to his left frontal lobe; Gage survived the incident, but his personality did not. Friends said that Gage was never the same again. Thousands of less dramatic cases of brain injuries have given neuroscientists insight into the functional roles of different parts of our brain. Such impairments have also taught us that when one part of the brain goes offline, other parts of the brain can pick up the slack.[8]

I recently asked a group of experiential educators from different countries how they know how well their educational approaches are working. They mentioned facial expressions, body language, response to surveys, and behavioral changes. How exciting it will be for educators to have access to a very different set of feedback tools! What might we discover when we combine the educator's macro-level imaging tools with the micro-level imaging tools of the neuroscientist?

How the Brain Learns: Eleven Findings of Interest to Jewish Educators

The founders of mind, brain, and education science are striving to establish an evidence-based field of study. The following eleven findings have at least one large matched study, or multiple smaller studies with a collective sample size of 250, or are classified as major discoveries that have stood the test of time. In other words, these findings are among the best of what neuroeducators think they know about the brain in 2011.

Alongside each finding, a piece of related wisdom from Jewish tradition is included for comparison and reflection.

WAYS THE BRAIN LEARNS[9]	RELATED JEWISH WISDOM
Human brains are as unique as faces. While the basic structure is the same, no two are identical. While there are general patterns of organization in how different people learn and which brain areas are involved, each brain is unique and uniquely organized. (OECD)	For one [human] stamps out many coins with one die, and they are all alike, but the King, the King of kings, the Holy One, blessed be God, stamped each person with the seal of Adam, and not one of them is like his or her fellow. (*Mishnah Sanhedrin* 4:5)
Experiences change the brain. The brain is a complex, dynamic, and integrated system that is constantly changed by experience, though most of this change is only evident at a microscopic level. (OECD) "You will go to bed tonight with a different brain from the one you had when you awoke."[10]	Elisha ben Avuyah used to say: When a man learns Torah while young, the words of Torah are absorbed into his very blood and issue from his mouth in explicit form. But when a man learns Torah in his old age, the words of Torah are not absorbed into his blood and do not issue from his mouth in explicit form. Hence the proverb: If you did not long for them in your mouth, how do you expect to attain them in your old age? He also used to say: When a man learns Torah in his youth, to what may he be compared? To ink written on a clean sheet. When a man learns in his old age? To ink written on a sheet from which the original writing has been erased. Seeing assures remembering. (BT *M'nachot* 43b)
The brain can rewire itself ("neuroplasticity"). Human brains have a high degree	He [Yehuda ben Taima] used to say: At five [one should begin the study of] Scriptures;

of plasticity and develop throughout the lifespan, though there are major limits on this plasticity, and these limits increase with age. Educational interventions for struggling readers have been able to actually rewire students' cerebral networks. (OECD and Sousa)	at ten, Mishna; at thirteen [one becomes obligated in] the commandments; at fifteen [the study of] Talmud; at eighteen the wedding canopy; at twenty to pursue; at thirty strength; at forty understanding; at fifty counsel; at sixty old age; at seventy fullness of years; at eighty spiritual strength; at ninety bending over; at one hundred it is as if he has died and passed on from the world." (*Mishnah Avot* 5:25)
Critical brain functions are still developing into early adulthood. While emotional areas of the brain fully develop by age 10 or 12, regions responsible for rational thought and emotional control mature closer to age 20 to 24. "You should have known better" may not be a fair intervention for an 18-year-old. (Sousa)	
Connecting new information to prior knowledge facilitates learning, which is a constructivist process. When knowledge is actively constructed by a learner, the learner will be motivated and engaged in learning. (OECD) "Incoming information is constantly compared with what it already knows . . . Human brains seek patterns upon which they predict outcomes, and neural systems form responses to repeated patterns of activation . . . analogies, metaphors, and similes are especially useful in helping students see the connections between concepts."[11] "Humans construct meaning based on their existing knowledge structures."[12]	"Train up a child in the way the child should go (*lefi darko*)" (Prov. 22:6). This means, if you see a child making progress in Bible studies, but not in Talmud, do not try to push the children by teaching Talmud, and if the child understands Talmud, do not push to learn Bible. Train a child in things that they know. (Judah the Pious, *The Book of the Pious*, sect. 208) Repeat them unto your children. (Deut. 6:7) "His delight is in the Torah of the Lord" (Ps. 1:2). Rabbi said: A man learns well only that part of the Torah which delights him, for the verse implies, "[The part of] the Torah of the Lord a man delights in [becomes his]." Levi and R. Simeon Berabbi were

	seated before Rabbi and were expounding verses of scripture. When the book they were at was finished, Levi said: Let the book of Proverbs be brought. R. Simeon Berabbi said: Let the book of Psalms be brought. Levi was overruled, and the book of Psalms was brought. When they got to the verse "His delight is in the Torah of the Lord," Rabbi, expounding it, said: A man learns well only that part of the Torah which delights him. At that, Levi said: Master, you have just now given me permission to get up and leave. (BT *Avodah Zarah* 19a)
Emotions and stress have a major impact on learning and are critical to decision making. "Good" stress (eustress) heightens attention and helps learning while bad stress detracts from learning potential. Educators should understand the biology of emotions, especially stress, and recognize that students cannot focus on the curriculum unless they feel physically safe and emotionally secure. (OECD and Sousa)	A *Tanna* retold this before Rabbi Nachman son of Yitzchak: One who embarrasses another in public, it is as if he shed his blood. (BT *Bava M'tzia* 58b) Hillel said: A bashful person is not apt to learn. (*Mishnah Avot* 2:5)
Context matters. The learning environment, motivation for the topic of new learning, and prior knowledge greatly impact learning. Imaging studies have revealed areas of the brain dedicated to appraising the meaning of an event and deciding what emotional response to use in a social context. (OECD and Sousa)	Eleazar ben Arakh lived in a beautiful area, but he had no colleagues around to learn with. Rabbi Eleazar waited for colleagues to come to him, but none came. He thought about going out to them, but decided that since his colleagues needed his great wisdom more than he needed theirs, he never went. After a while he forgot all of his learning. Years later, when disciples came to

Support matters. Academic, moral, and other support from teachers, peers, or parents are critical for optimal academic performance, which includes learning. (OECD)	ask a question, he was unable to answer.[13] (*Ecclesiastes Rabbah* 7:7; *Avot D'Rabbi Natan* 14) Someone who studies on one's own cannot be compared to the one who learns from a teacher. (BT *K'tubot* 111a) R. Hiyya bar Adda was seated before Rav, who was explaining a matter to him, but he could not comprehend it. Finally, Rav asked him, "Why can't you grasp the matter?" The disciple replied, "Because my she-ass is about to foal, and I am afraid that she may catch cold and die." (*B'reishit Rabbah* 20:6) A disciple was seated before R. Yose, who was explaining a matter that the disciple could not comprehend. Finally R. Yose asked him, "Why can't you grasp the matter?" The disciple: "Because I am away from my home." R. Yose: "Where do you come from?" "From Gobat-Shammai." "What is its climate?" "When a child is born, we crush juicy grapes and smear them on his head so that mosquitoes will not eat him up." R. Yose: "Blessed be He who inspires the inhabitants of a place with love for it." (*B'reishit Rabbah* 34:15) A cultural practice that addresses context and support: *chevruta* study
Movement enhances learning and memory. The brain is more active when learners are moving around. Movement brings	Do not sit too long, for [long] sitting aggravates one's abdominal troubles; do not stand for a long time, because

fuel-carrying blood to the brain and allows the brain to access more long-term memory areas (an ancient survival strategy). (Sousa)	[long] standing is injurious to the heart; and do not walk too much, because [excessive] walking is harmful to the eyes. Rather [spend] one third [of your time] in sitting, one third in standing and one third in walking. (BT *K'tubot* 111a) A cultural practice that addresses movement: *shuckling*, the ritual swaying of worshipers during prayer or study.
There are many stages of memory creation. Immediate memory holds incoming information for a few seconds. Working memory holds information while it is consciously processed, for up to several weeks. Unused information is then discarded (perhaps after a test). Sense, meaning, and relevancy are emerging as major criteria that the brain uses in deciding what to encode to long-term memory. (Sousa)	Elisha ben Avuya used to say: A man may study Torah for twenty years and forget it in two. How? If he sits idly for six months without reviewing, he will find himself declaring that which is unclean clean and that which is clean unclean. If he is idle for twelve months without reviewing, he will find himself mixing up the names of the sages. If he is idle for eighteen months without reviewing, he will forget the substance of whole tractates he had studied. If he is idle for twenty-four months without reviewing, he will forget the substance even of individual chapters. (*Avot D'Rabbi Natan* 24) Why are words of Torah likened to water, wine, and milk? Because just as these three liquids may become unfit for consumption only through inattention, so words of Torah are forgotten only through inattention. (BT *Taanit* 7a–b) It is harder to retain in memory something old than to commit

	to memory something new. The former is like trying to make cement out of cement. (BT *Yoma* 29a)
Sleep is important for memory. The brain is incredibly active during sleep, carrying out processes that help the brain to learn, make connections, remember, and clear out clutter. Sleep deprivation has a negative impact on memory. (OECD and Sousa)	R. Zera said: If a man dozes off in the house of study, his knowledge will become raggedy, for it is said, "Drowsiness shall clothe a man with rags" (Prov. 23:21). (BT *Sanhedrin* 21a) One who accustoms himself to live in a healthy manner . . . who follows this path all his days is considered to be serving God constantly…even when such a person sleeps. If he sleeps with intent that his mind be composed and his body rested so that he will not become ill (for he will not be able to serve God when he is sick), his [very] sleep will be considered Divine service. (Maimonides, *Hilchot De'ot* 3:3)

Implications for Jewish Education

It is regrettable that "most educators spend very little time getting to know the primary organ of their life's purpose: the brain."[14] Can educators practice their profession effectively without knowing more about these learning organs? Would we tolerate a college football coach who did not understand how the circulatory system and lungs work? Or a voice teacher who did not understand how the voicebox and ears work? "Teachers are, after all, the ultimate 'brain changers.' They are in a profession of changing the human brain every day."[15]

The juxtaposition of Jewish wisdom alongside established findings from the field of mind, brain, and education science in the chart above hints at the richness of the mutual exchange to be had between Jewish educators and neuroeducators. The following two topics should serve to illustrate the potential of such an exchange.

Hebrew Learning

Numerous neuroeducation studies have focused on how the brain learns to read.[16] Neuroscientists remind us that learning to *speak* is an ancient evolutionary development, is innate, and is supported by specialized areas of the brain. Learning to *read*, however, is a relatively recent cultural invention; no one was born to read. As one expert noted, "It is unlikely that our brains are genetically predisposed to develop neural systems that support reading-specific processes."[17] Another describes reading as a "remarkable neurological feat [that] involves an impressive coordination of perceptual, attentional, motoric, linguistic, and cognitive components, all performing together at great speed."[18] That humans can learn to read at all is a defining example of the brain's ability to rearrange neural pathways, and there are myriad ways that a learner can get stuck somewhere in the reading process.

When it comes to Hebrew language learning, Jewish educators are often imprecise with terms: for instance, we use the phrase "read Hebrew" when we actually mean "decode Hebrew letters into sounds," or what neuroeducators would call "mapping orthography to phonology." We celebrate a bat mitzvah who can decode quickly and "read" Torah well, even if her ability to process the meaning of the words (semantics) is limited or nonexistent. But we would never say that an American child who can only sound out English words, without any sense of what they mean, can "read" English.

In many American Jewish communities, Hebrew is learned, at best, as a second language in the early elementary school years. From the perspective of neuroeducation, such an approach faces two significant challenges. The first challenge is that when these learners are trying to read words, they cannot map those written words onto previously learned phonology and semantics (sounds and meanings), since, with the exception of a few words from prominent prayers, they know very few Hebrew words by sound.

Second, learning a second language after age five requires much more effort because it uses different neural pathways:

> The results of neuroimaging research indicate that, [when exposed to two languages before age five,] rather than causing confusion in the brain, the brain adaptively uses language areas to process both languages efficiently. More effortful neural processing is required when exposure to a second language occurs after five, as this later bilingual exposure results in a different pattern of neural organization for language processing. The most efficient use of neural resources occurs when language learning happens early.[19]

How might Jewish educators approach our Hebrew language learning goals differently with such knowledge from the field of neuroeducation about how brains learn to read? Should we invest more in early childhood language programs, so that we tap into the automatic language pathways of a pre-five-year-old brain? Could we destigmatize learning through oral memorization—a traditional form of learning that utilizes our brain's ancient ways of processing language—instead of putting so much emphasis on decoding written words? Might we adapt the technology-based interventions that neuroeducators have developed for reading impairments and put them to use for our specific Hebrew language goals? These are the kinds of questions that emerge when we learn more about how the brain learns and attempt to apply that learning to issues in Jewish education.

Interestingly, *Chazal* long ago warned to us to teach Hebrew at an early age, just as a child starts learning to speak. Consider the following texts:

> When a child begins to speak, his father teaches him the Holy Tongue and teaches him Torah. But if he does not speak with him in the Holy Tongue and does not teach him Torah, it is as if he buried him, as it says, "Teach them to your children."[20]

> A pupil who shows no discernible advance in his studies after five years is not likely ever to show it. R. Yose asserted: After three years, for it is said, "To be taught the learning and the language of the Chaldeans . . . they are to be trained three years" (Dan. 1:4–5).[21]

I have been experimenting on my own children in this regard; since my twin boys were one year old, I decided to only speak to them in Hebrew (my wife, also a rabbi, speaks to them in English). The experiment is a few years old now, and I can say that it is much harder for me than for them. They understand me perfectly, even though I am continually frustrated at my own limited vocabulary and imperfect grammar.

Role of Context

A second example—focusing on experiential education and the role of context—will show how explorations within Jewish education could inform the direction of neuroeducation. Evaluative studies as well as sociological studies claim that experiential approaches to Jewish learning like summer camp and educational trips to Israel have solid, long-lasting impact.[22] We have a growing body of evidence that experiential learning does make an impact, but we have only conjecture and unsubstantiated claims about *how* it makes an impact.

In 2003, Barry Chazan articulated core principles behind informal Jewish education.[23] Many of these principles, such as person-centered learning, the centrality of experience, interactivity, the group experience, engagement, and a holistic approach, appear to be strongly aligned with findings from mind, brain, and education science.

Unfortunately, as educators, our claims about educational impact are infrequently rooted in evidence. Chazan's article, for instance, employs the phrase "this educational practice is rooted *in the belief that* . . ." to justify three different principles. By partnering with the field of neuroeducation, we can begin to use statements like "this educational practice is rooted *in evidence that*. . . ." By confirming findings in our own field first, through macro-level studies, and then reconfirming (or adjusting) them in the field of neuroeducation, we can greatly enhance the impact of our work.

Jewish experiential educators, could, for instance, hypothesize which factors may be most relevant to the learning process in a camp environment or Israel trip. We can then partner with neuroeducators to explore the impact of these various factors. Here are sample questions a camp educator might ask:

- How long do brains respond to new contexts as "novel"? When does camp become more like "home" and how does that impact learning?
- How does the brain adjust between dissonant contexts, for instance when returning home after camp? What transition

time or support, if any, is needed, to maximize learning? How does the brain respond if the home context does not support the new learning from the camp context?

- How does the brain process day experiences (e.g., a day trip or field trip) as compared to overnight experiences?
- How does the brain process primarily social or fun experiences (cabin time or waterskiing) as compared to more content-oriented experiential education (an interactive workshop)?
- What signals do brains give that an experience is too challenging, productively challenging, or not challenging enough?

Implications for Neuroeducation

Despite well-established findings about the important role that factors such as context, support, emotions, and movement play in how the brain learns, proponents of mind, brain, and education science still appear to have some biases toward the classroom as the primary location of learning. Rows of desks in secular schools are often seen as the place where education happens. Jewish educators may have a role in helping neuroeducators see the bigger picture.

Because Judaism is a long-lasting, embodied tradition that involves wide swaths of individual and collective experience—including such areas as eating, relations between people, study, language, belief, sex, and appearance/dress, to name a few—Jewish tradition may be positioned to suggest factors beyond the classroom that greatly impact learning. For instance, how can we better study the role of parents and family in the learning process, since the same sociological studies that show the impact of camping show an even higher impact from family and home life? How do repeated or occasional ritual acts affect learning, such as lighting Friday night candles? How does singing and music affect learning and memorization? How does the brain connect food and learning? How do brains process other languages that are used in limited and occasional ways? Why is the Passover seder ritual so successful that even most under-affiliated Jews practice it, and innumerable Christians borrow and adapt the ritual each year?

Were neuroeducators to explore questions like these, which emerge from the context of Jewish education, it could pave the way for secular educators to think beyond the desks in their classroom as they look for ways to create high-impact learning.

Conclusion

Human curiosity and the rigor of the scientific process have brought us a new gift: the capacity to understand how our learning organ works. A rich dialogue between Jewish educators and neuroeducation experts could confirm long-standing practices in Jewish education, call other practices into question, and help address perennial educational challenges like Hebrew language learning. Let us, as Reimer and Bryfman have written, continue to "borrow freely from research and theory in a number of different domains [and] suggest that the time is ripe to rethink how we engage Jewish learners in discovering the power of Jewish concepts and practices to enrich the way they live their lives."[24] At the same time, the wisdom inherent in many aspects of Judaism can serve as 'lights in the darkness' of our grey matter, signaling to neuroeducators new places to look for understanding how our brains learn.

Notes

1. For a brief history of the field, see Tracey Tokuhama-Espinosa's *Mind, Brain, and Education Science: A Comprehensive Guide to the New Brain-Based Teaching* (New York: W.W. Norton & Co., 2011), 4–12. What follows is largely taken from her historical review.
2. Kurt Fischer et al., eds., "Why Mind, Brain, and Education? Why Now?" *Mind, Brain and Education* 1, no. 1 (2007): 1–2.
3. Tracey Tokuhama-Espinosa, *The New Science of Teaching and Learning: Using the Best of Mind, Brain, and Education Science in the Classroom* (New York: Columbia University Teachers College Press, 2010), 31.
4. Tokuhama-Espinosa, *Mind, Brain, and Education Science*, 42.
5. Accessible descriptions of various brain imaging technologies are available in: "Annex B: Brain Imaging Technologies," in Organisation for Economic Co-operation and Development (OECD), *Understanding the Brain: The Birth of Learning Science* (Paris: OECD, 2007), 245–49, and in Michael Posner, "Neuroimaging Tools and the Evolution of Educational Neuroscience," in *Mind, Brain & Education: Neuroscience Implications for the Classroom*, ed. David Sousa (Bloomington, IN: Solution Tree Press, 2010), 27–43.
6. Posner, "Neuroimaging Tools," 34.

7. The Phineas Gage story appears widely throughout brain science literature. See Wikipedia for a list of published materials about the story and a daguerreotype portrait of Gage identified in 2009.
8. Neuroplasticity refers to the brain's ability to "rewire" itself. Neurons and the organization of their networks can change in response to experience or injury. See the chart below for additional information.
9. Except where noted, the findings summarized in this chart were gathered from two sources: Organisation for Economic Co-Operation and Development, *Understanding the Brain: Towards a New Learning Science* (Paris: OECD, 2002), and David Sousa, "How Science Met Pedagogy," in *Mind, Brain & Education: Neuroscience Implications for the Classroom*, ed. David Sousa (Bloomington, IN: Solution Tree Press, 2010), 14–18. For background on the OECD findings, and a comparison of related attempts to classify findings by amount of evidence, see Tokuhama-Espinosa, *Mind, Brain, and Education Science*, ch. 4.
10. Tokuhama-Espinosa, *Mind, Brain, and Education Science*, 33.
11. Ibid., 212.
12. Ibid., 209.
13. Paraphrased for brevity. Also recorded in the *Book of Legends* 213:54.
14. Tokuhama-Espinosa, *Mind, Brain, and Education Science*, 17.
15. Sousa, "Science Met Pedagogy," 23.
16. For reviews of the current research and understanding about how brains learn to read, see the following articles: Maryanne Wolf, "A Triptych of the Reading Brain: Evolution, Development, Pathology and its Intervention," in *The Educated Brain: Essays in Neuroeducation*, eds. Antonio Battro, Kurt Fischer, and Pierre Léna (Cambridge: Cambridge University Press, 2008), 183–97; Usha Goswami, "Reading and the Brain: A Cross-Language Approach," in *The Educated Brain: Essays in Neuroeducation*, eds. Antonio Battro, Kurt Fischer, and Pierre Léna (Cambridge: Cambridge University Press, 2008), 198–212; and John Gabrieli, Joanna Christodoulou, Tricia O'Loughlin, and Marianna Eddy, "The Reading Brain," in *Mind, Brain & Education: Neuroscience Implications for the Classroom*, ed. David Sousa (Bloomington, IN: Solution Tree Press, 2010), 113–37.
17. Gabrieli et al., "Reading Brain,"118.
18. Wolf, "Triptych," 183.
19. Diane Williams, "The Speaking Brain," in *Mind, Brain & Education: Neuroscience Implications for the Classroom*, ed. David Sousa, 101.
20. *Sifrei Eikev* (commenting on the *Sh'ma*).

21. BT *Chulin* 24a.
22. Examples of such studies include "Camp Works: The Long-term Impact of Jewish Overnight Camp," conducted by Steven M. Cohen, Ron Miller, Ira M. Sheskin, and Berna Torr (2011), http://www.jewishcamp.org/static/website/uploads/Camp_Works_for_Web.pdf (accessed June 29, 2011); and "Generation Birthright Israel," conducted by Leonard Saxe et al. (2010), http://www.brandeis.edu/cmjs/researchareas/taglit-birthright.html (accessed June 29, 2011).
23. Barry Chazan, "The Philosophy of Informal Jewish Education," in *The Encyclopedia of Informal Education* (2003), http://www.infed.org/informaljewisheducation/information_jewish_education.htm (accessed June 28, 2011). More recently, some practitioners of informal Jewish education show preference for the term "experiential" Jewish education.
24. Joseph Reimer and David Bryfman, "What We Know About Experiential Education," http://jesna.org/document-manager/doc_download/506-what-we-know-about-experiential-jewish-education (accessed June 29, 2011).

The Science behind *Yetzer Hara*

Geoffrey A. Mitelman

What Is the *Yetzer Hara?*

The *yetzer hara* is one of the most complex topics in Rabbinic literature. It has been variously defined as "the impulse to do evil," "the antisocial impulse," "the sexual urge," "the Freudian 'id,'" and "the desire to be selfish." Yet it is still thought of as something created by God, and the Rabbis even say that "without the *yetzer hara,* man would not engage in business, build homes, marry, or have children" (*B'reishit Rabbah* 9:7).

But the best way to define the *yetzer hara* is to see how it is used in context. So let us look at four texts that refer to it:

1. Who is mighty? The one who subdues his *yetzer hara.* (*Pirkei Avot* 4:1)

Firstly, the *yetzer hara* is clearly something strong, since it needs to be "subdued," and the definition of a "mighty person" is someone who has the strength to conquer it.

2. Rabbi Ammi said: As soon as the *yetzer hara* sees a man making eyes at girls, frizzing his hair, and walking with a swagger, it says, "This one is mine." (*B'reishit Rabbah* 22:6)

Next, the *yetzer hara* clearly has a sexual component to it, and it will push those who are already looking to pursue pleasure towards giving into that urge.

3. The *yetzer hara* yearns only for what is forbidden. (*Talmud Y'rushalmi, Yoma* 6:4)

Here, the *yetzer hara* is what leads us to want things we shouldn't, and if we *do* follow the *yetzer hara,* then we will almost certainly sin if we give into temptation.

GEOFFREY A. MITELMAN (C07) is the associate rabbi at Temple Beth El of Northern Westchester, New York.

4. Rav Assi said: At first the *yetzer hara* is as thin as a spider's gossamer, but in the end, it is as thick as a cart rope. (BT *Sukkah* 52a)

Finally, the *yetzer hara* can exert great power over us if we cannot subdue it. It begins to draw us in with thin strands, but in the end, it develops into a rope that drags us in undesired ways. The unspoken implication of this statement is that we need to find ways to resist the *yetzer hara* early in its pull, since it is easier to escape from a web when it is made of gossamer strands than when it is made of cart ropes!

So the *yetzer hara* is certainly something powerful, and when it remains uncontrolled and allowed to run rampant, it can cause us to do things we'd later regret. My own definition of the *yetzer hara* is "a desire for immediate pleasure that goes against our better judgment."

So why *is* it so hard to resist the urge to give into immediate temptations? Experiments in the field of cognitive science have tried to address that question, and can help us illuminate what the *yetzer hara* is, why it is so powerful, and how we can overcome it—and perhaps surprisingly, it's not by trying to subdue or control it.

The "Self" and "Self-Control"

Cognitive science has been exploring what it means to exert "self-control," wondering why we so often pursue immediate pleasure and ignore our better judgment.

Robert Kurzban is an evolutionary psychologist at the University of Pennsylvania and author of the book *Why Everyone (Else) Is a Hypocrite: The Evolution of the Modular Mind*. As he argues, different parts of the brain (or "modules") have evolved for different functions.[1]

Sometimes these modules work in complement, like our visual and auditory systems, which associate sounds and sights together. Since most of the objects we see on a regular basis occur with sights and sounds occurring in tandem, our brains have evolved to join them together. But in fact, our visual and auditory modules are somewhat independent of each other. When you watch a movie, for example, it certainly seems like the actors' lines are spoken at the same time their mouths move. But if you've sat in a theater where the auditory track wasn't in sync with the visuals, you know that the audio and visuals are coming from *different* sources—it's our brains that bring them together.

So while we tend to think that all the modules of our brains work in perfect harmony, in fact, they are more independent than we think they are. And if there *are* multiple independent parts of our brains, we can ask, "Are there modules that sometimes work in conflict with each other?"

And the answer is, of course there are. As Kurzban explains:

> Some modules are designed to get you to satisfy immediate needs. These are important modules. Some of the needs I have in mind are things associated with the basic necessities of survival and reproduction. In biology, you might hear these referred to as the "four F's": feeding, fleeing, fighting, and having sex. Organisms that didn't have mechanisms that caused them to do the things that enabled survival and reproduction didn't leave offspring. These modules cause you to do things that often get put under the heading of "instantaneous gratification." They're the ones in charge when you eat sweet and fatty foods, stay warm in bed (conserving calories), and have sex with your cute co-worker . . .
>
> But . . . the world isn't going to end tomorrow. Humans have other modules that are more farsighted. These are the modules that cause you to forgo the regular Coke because the sweet taste now is not worth the extra calories you'll have to contend with later. They cause you to get out of the bed in the morning to get your run in, sacrificing snoozing now for feeling better and healthier later. And they cause you to politely decline your co-worker's blatant sexual advance . . .
>
> So, the brain, with all its patient and impatient modules, somehow has to make many trade-offs. The impatient module that "likes cake" (i.e., is designed to motivate the consumption of dense calorie packages) is driving behavior toward consumption, while the patient module that "likes being fit" (i.e., is designed to inhibit behavior with long-run costs) is driving behavior away from it. These somehow must be reconciled.[2]

So "self-control" is really an internal battle between two different modules within our brains—one part of which looks for immediate pleasure, which was good evolutionarily speaking because you never know if today's opportunities will recur tomorrow, and one part of which looks for long-term gains, which was good evolutionarily speaking because tomorrow's opportunities might be much better than today's.

These competing modules help us understand what the *yetzer hara* is about—it's the module that helps us get what we want now, with no thought towards potential negative consequences down the road. And if you are acting for pleasure now and ignore how your actions might affect yourself or other people, you are likely to "yearn for what is forbidden," and fall into the hands of temptation. And the area where there is the most potency and most potential for problems is in the realm where the *yetzer hara* truly lives—the realm of sexuality.

The Power of Sexuality

Harvard psychologist Daniel Goleman notes in his book *Emotional Intelligence*, "There is perhaps no psychological skill more fundamental than resisting impulse. It is the root of all emotional self-control, since all emotions, by their very nature, lead to one or another impulse to act."[3] Obviously, the urges that most require resisting are the ones that are the most powerful—and a desire for sex is one of the most potent.

Sexuality is one of the most powerful forces in nature, for clear evolutionary reasons—it's how we get our genes into the next generation. But when we humans are acting on our sexuality, we aren't consciously thinking about propagating our genes. Rather, we hope that sexuality is the way for two people who love each other to express their intimacy. But if sexuality's power is *not* recognized, it can lead to a wide range of problems—physically, psychologically, and ethically.

Since sexual urges generally begin during the teenage years, Duke University professor Dan Ariely wondered what happens to teenagers at the beginning of their emerging sexuality, especially because teenage behavior tends to be riskier across the board. Indeed, even if sex doesn't lead to an STD, there are emotional issues that come along with sex, and so policy analysts, teachers, and moral leaders have tried to answer the question, "How do we help teenagers avoid the potential harm that sex can cause?"

Some thinkers believe that abstinence-only education is the only effective method, while others believe that informing teenagers about the risks of unsafe sex is the best method to reduce the negative consequences of risky or unethical sexual behavior. But as Ariely shows in his book *Predictably Irrational*, neither of those methods is effective. The problem isn't that teenagers don't *know* the risks of unsafe sex—it's that when they are in a "hot" state, they don't seem to *care*.[4]

In a fascinating study, Ariely asked students a series of questions about whether or not they would engage in either immoral or risky sexual behavior, like, "Would you keep trying to have sex with a woman even after she says 'no'?" and "Would you use a condom even if you were afraid that a woman might change her mind while you went to get it?" In fact, Ariely asked the questions twice—once when the students were simply sitting in a room, in a "cold" state, and once when the students were sexually aroused, and therefore in a "hot" state.[5] He was wondering if, in the heat of the moment, teenagers would ignore the risks and ethical and emotional implications of sex, and instead, "just say yes."

And the results were terrifyingly clear—students were significantly more likely to engage in immoral or risky behavior when they were "hot" than when they were "cold." Ariely claims that it wasn't that the students forgot about the risks or the ethics of sexuality. It's that when they were "hot," their deep, primal urges overtook their analytical brains.

So the natural next question is, are there methods that are effective to curb the power of impulses? A story in *Kiddushin* 81a about Rav Amram the Pious may help shed some light on this issue:

> Certain [redeemed] captive women came to Nehardea. They were taken to the house of Rav Amram the Pious, and the ladder was removed from under them. As one passed by, a light fell on the sky lights; [at which point] Rav Amram seized the ladder, which ten men could not have raised, and by himself, he set it up and then proceeded to go up (*salik v'azil*). When he had gone halfway up the ladder, he spread his feet apart, and cried out, "Fire in the house of Rav Amram! (*nura bei Amram!*)" The Rabbis came and said to him, "We have put you to shame!" He said to them: "Better that you shame Amram in this world than that you be ashamed of him in the next." He then ordered it [the *yetzer hara*] to leave him, and it issued from him in the shape of a fiery column (*amuda d'nura*). He said to it: "See, you are fire (*nura*) and I am flesh, but I am stronger than you."

In its way, this story reflects the Talmudic dictum, "The greater the man, the greater the *yetzer hara*" (BT *Sukkah* 52a). So let us unpack this story.

It begins when certain redeemed women were brought to the house of Rav Amram the Pious. His appellation implies that he was a particularly righteous man, and as he is described as "*the* Pious," it implies that he was the most righteous person of his (or even any) generation. While Rashi tells us that the reason the women were brought to Rav Amram's house was because he himself had redeemed them, I would argue another possibility—given the fact that he was so virtuous, his house was naturally thought to be the "safest" place for the women to remain. However, even Rav Amram was unable to resist the allure of one of the women when the light hit her in just the right way. He was so smitten that he lifted up the ladder separating the lower and upper levels (per Rashi), a ladder that was so heavy that ten men could not have lifted it. And yet the phrasing in Aramaic, *salik v'azil* (he proceeded to go up), might also be seen as encompassing two meanings. On one level, it has the literal sense of "he ascended the ladder," but the phrase might also imply he was getting an erection, with his *yetzer hara* taking control of him.

At that moment, he stopped in the middle of the ladder because he needed "to regain his composure and steel himself against the Evil Inclination" (footnote 35 in BT *Kiddushin* 81a in *Talmud Bavli: The Schottenstein Edition*). It was at that moment that he realized that he could not control his *yetzer hara* by himself, and so created a way to bring in other people to stop him from succumbing to his impulses.

As he stood halfway up the ladder, he proclaimed, "Fire in the house of Rav Amram!" *("Nura bei Amram!")* Now, on some level, this was certainly not true. His house was still standing, and there was no *actual* fire in his house. However, his sexual desire was burning, and the word *nura* is clearly a conscious word choice, as will be shown below. Rav Amram knew that by exclaiming that his house was aflame, his colleagues would come running to assist him, and so even though he himself could not restrain his *yetzer hara*, through a certain level of inventiveness, he was able to overcome it. He ends by telling the *yetzer hara*: "See, you are fire (*nura*) and I am flesh, but I am stronger than you." In other words, though he is only flesh and blood, he can subdue the "fire" (*nura*) in his loins. The ultimate implication is that no matter how strong the *yetzer hara* may be, we have the power to control our impulses—though we may have to be creative and to find some support in order to do it.

An important element in this passage is that Rav Amram was self-aware enough to recognize that he could not control his *yetzer hara* by himself. He sensed that his impulses were taking over, and so used his community to help him alleviate his urges. In the end, he did not give in to sexual desires, because he himself was able to create a way for *others* to stop him from giving in. While he did say to the *yetzer hara*, "I am flesh, and you are fire, but I am stronger than you," he also knew that he could not overcome his urges alone—he needed outside assistance. Perhaps that is the reason why Rav Amram was called "the Pious." It was not because he did not have a *yetzer hara*, but rather, because he devised ways to control and subdue it, even when it was most difficult for him.

A particularly interesting parallel to this idea comes from a modern study that Daniel Goleman describes as "the marshmallow test." In this experiment, a group of four-year-olds were told that if they could wait while the experimenter ran a fifteen-minute errand, they would receive two marshmallows when he returned. If they could not wait, they would receive only one marshmallow, but would get it immediately. It was a "microcosm of the eternal battle between impulse and restraint, id and ego, desire and self-control, gratification and delay."[6] The question before these four-year-olds was the exact same question that continually challenged the Rabbis and Rav Amram in particular—how can we conquer our urges?

These four-year-olds likely had the same difficulty in controlling their desire for immediate gratification as Rav Amram did. And like Rav Amram, the most self-aware used outside help to control their impulses. "To sustain themselves in their struggle, [some of the children] covered their eyes so they wouldn't have to stare at temptation, or rested their heads in their arms, talked to themselves, sang, played games with their hands and feet, even tried to go to sleep."[7] Like Rav Amram, these children "steeled themselves," and when temptation became too much for them to handle by themselves, they invented ways to help restrain their impulses.

What was most surprising about this study, though, was what happened to the children later in life:

> Twelve to fourteen years later . . . these children were tracked down as adolescents. The emotional and social difference between the grab-the-marshmallow preschoolers and their gratification-delaying peers was dramatic. Those who had resisted temptation at four were now, as adolescents, more socially competent...They were less likely to go to pieces, freeze, or regress under stress, or become rattled and disorganized when pressured; they embraced challenges and pursued them instead of giving up even in the face of difficulties; they were self-reliant and confident, trustworthy and dependable; and they took initiative and plunged into projects. And, more than a decade later, they were still able to delay gratification in pursuit of their goals.[8]

As both Rav Amram and the four-year-olds experienced, it is always a struggle to resist our desires for immediate pleasure. But if we are able to find ways to control these desires, we are also that much more likely to be more psychologically stable.

Ultimately, we will never be able to get rid of the *yetzer hara*, and indeed, we shouldn't even try, because we do need it to create children, build homes, and start businesses. But we *do* need to come up with ways to ensure it does not run rampant, and the first step we need to take is to recognize its power. It is often more potent than we think, but, as Rav Amram noted, we can be stronger than it. And the way we do that is not by brute force, but instead, by building a sense of self-awareness so that how we act in a "hot" state doesn't undermine the kind of person we truly wish to be.

Notes

1. Robert Kurzban, *Why Everyone (Else) Is a Hypocrite: Evolution and the Modular Mind* (Princeton: Princeton University Press, 2010).
2. Ibid., 159–60, 162.
3. Daniel Goleman, *Emotional Intelligence* (New York: Bantham Books, 1995), 81.
4. Dan Ariely, *Predictably Irrational: The Hidden Forces That Shape Our Decisions* (New York: Harper, 2008).
5. Ibid., 92–97.
6. Goleman, *Emotional Intelligence*, 81.
7. Ibid.
8. Ibid., 81–82.

The Case for Science Education in Our Religious Schools

Laurie Green

She was a thirty-something mother of two young children with a spectacular level of both secular and Jewish education. She'd lived in Israel, studied Talmud, read Buber and Kaplan, and had once been a daily minyan goer. She should have been our cream of the crop.

She was explaining to me why she wasn't "religious" anymore. Why there was no more Shabbat or shul for her. Why she now considered herself agnostic and culturally Jewish. She explained that she believed in science. Her God was physics. Yes, there was something bigger than herself, she was sure. There must be a reason for existence, a reason why the big bang happened and brought the universe into being. She was now too worldly and educated to believe in the tales of Genesis. "Physics is my God," she said again.

I tried explaining to her that physics was my God too. I shared that I believed that God created the world with the big bang. I explained my view that the Bible was spiritual metaphor. That science answered "what" and religion answered "why." "Well," she said, "I guess our beliefs aren't that different, but I call it science and you call it religion."

Therein lies the trouble. In twentieth-, and now twenty-first-century America, popular culture declares that there is a conflict between science and religion. We have allowed secular voices on the one extreme and fundamentalist voices on the other extreme to set up a false debate. Meanwhile we have remained silent, at least in the popular media most of our congregants read. Contemporary Jewish education has failed to properly address science in its teaching of Jewish belief and practice. We have not addressed science because we see science and faith as two separate things,

LAURIE GREEN (NY07) is assistant rabbi at Temple Beth Zion in Buffalo, New York. She would like to thank Rabbi Drorah Setel for her assistance with this article.

and indeed they are. But that is the thinking of clergy and educators, whereas the average congregant often does not have such an advanced concept. Therefore, when we don't talk about science, they take away the unintended message that science does not have an appropriate place in Jewish thought and Jewish living. We must join in a systematic effort to rectify this problem, or we will continue to lose many more like the woman described above.

This article begins with the proposition that contemporary Jewish education has failed to properly address science in its teaching of Jewish belief and practice. Too many adolescents and adults turn away from Judaism because they "believe in science, not religion," never having been taught how to integrate the two. Similarly, too many look to other religious traditions because they are "seeking spirituality," never having been shown how or where to find it in Judaism. A proper integration of science into our religious curricula can fully address the needs of both groups.

Case Study 1—The Brilliant Atheist

Jacob was a very bright bar mitzvah student. He was a science geek and an avowed atheist at the tender age of twelve. Through our bar mitzvah lessons, we explored his theology and his Jewish identity. Jacob had learned from his public school science teacher, his father, and the television that science and religion are in conflict—that he had to pick one, and that smart, rational people like him choose science. Though Jacob rejected "fundamentalist religion" as he called it, his views of Torah had been clearly influenced by Christian fundamentalist readings of text. I tried to explain metaphor and he looked at me like I was crazy. He had been in Sunday school in a Reform temple for six years. He'd been taught all the Bible stories and like all children he took them literally. He had never learned liberal Jewish perspectives on textual interpretation, nor had science ever been discussed in any of his Sunday school classes. He had learned from the television that "religious people" believed a literal interpretation of Scripture. He told me, "no offense, rabbi, but dinosaur fossils obviously disprove the Bible."

Case Study 2—The Spiritual Seeker

Sarah was seventeen. She had attended Jewish camp, become bat mitzvah, and been confirmed. She was a spiritual seeker. She loved being Jewish. She loved it so much that she kept voluntarily coming to Hebrew high school. Lately, she'd been talking a lot about Buddhism and Hinduism. She was learning Buddhist meditation and going on environmental retreats. I asked her if she was finding spirituality in a Jewish context. She got a guilty expression on her face and told me no. She assured me that she loved coming to services and keeping the holidays. She was very proud to be Jewish. But she wanted to meditate and do yoga and seek other spiritual paths, not just "sit in temple," as she put it. I told her I'd be happy to recommend a few books on Jewish meditation. She looked at me in shock, utterly unaware that such a thing existed. "Why didn't anyone tell me about this before?" she exclaimed. Then she asked me, "Why don't we ever do this stuff in temple?" I didn't have a good answer for her.

It is not immediately obvious what such "spiritual seeking" has to do with science, but that is because our contemporary paradigm juxtaposes the two. For much of Jewish history and human history, science was an inspiration to spirituality. After all, science explains the unity of all existence. Teaching science and teaching spirituality are, at times, related. Sarah came to understand this when I introduced her to Jewish mysticism, and she learned that kabbalistic spirituality developed a cosmology that resembles big bang theory and string theory, stated in spiritual language.[1]

Case Study 3—The Philosopher Scientist

If Moses ben Maimon had not received an excellent education in both the sciences of his time and his religious tradition, he never would have become the Rambam. Maimonides was neither the first nor the last person to integrate science and religion, but he was the most famous Jewish person to do so, and likely the most brilliant. As such he serves as the paradigm of thought on this matter.

Maimonides believed it was impossible for there to be a contradiction between the truth God revealed and the discoveries of human intelligence. As such his goal was to reconcile the wisdom of his time, Aristotelian philosophy and physical science, with the wisdom of the Torah. Today, we think of Maimonides as an Orthodox rabbinical figure, but in his time he was radical in suggesting that Scripture should be interpreted in light of science and not the other way around. As historian David Ruderman writes:

> In the introduction to his *Guide of the Perplexed*, Maimonides argues that Torah must be grounded in reason and that divine science (metaphysics) can only be successfully undertaken after studying the natural sciences (physics).[2]

In other words, religious knowledge rests upon scientific knowledge and the former cannot be obtained without the latter. Furthermore, Maimonides believed the philosophical and natural sciences to be part of the original oral law, and that the exile only later caused the Rabbis to neglect these sciences.

Maimonides even went as far as to introduce the scientific knowledge of his day into his halachic rulings, as has been demonstrated by scholars as Orthodox as Isadore Twersky.[3] As Ruderman demonstrates, in at least one case, Rambam ruled allowing the knowledge of non-Jewish scientists, specifically astronomers, to supersede the Rabbis.[4] Can anyone imagine a great halachic mind of our time doing the same?

Pedagogy

But that was medieval philosophy, and nowadays our brightest minds don't seem as interested in reconciling religious and scientific disciplines. Breaking the "science versus religion" paradigm will require a concerted effort on the part of Jewish educators. I propose integrating science topics into our regular religious school curricula, as part of an overall integrated curriculum.

Surely, with all the other subjects they have to teach, we cannot expect our teachers to teach science. Rather, they should piggyback on the science education students receive in schools, just as they might do so with history or geography. When students study evolution, astronomy, or the big bang in their secular schools, religious educators can also address these topics. I propose that we integrate science education into three areas that we are already teaching: history, Bible, and theology/spirituality.

There are any number of ways that science education might be integrated into teaching Jewish history. For instance, we might teach about Jewish scientists, including but certainly not limited to Albert Einstein. Yet, perhaps the most urgent is to teach about the paradigm of scientific and religious integration, Moses Maimonides.

A fifth grade class studying Jewish history might include a lesson or two on Maimonides. In this way, students will learn that one of the greatest Jewish philosophers and legal scholars was also a physician and astronomer. Students would learn how Maimonides used his knowledge of scientific topics to help him better understand both legal questions and philosophical questions. Teens or adults might take this study to a more intellectually advanced level. Such older students might study the text of *Kiddushin* 30a and explore the idea that scientific knowledge was originally part of the oral tradition. Older students could also study statements on the relationship between science and religion. Quotes from Maimonides, Einstein, and other Jewish thinkers and scientists might be included, along with quotes from Christian and Muslim religious and scientific scholars.

We must also consider scientific views in how we teach Bible. Seventh graders studying *parashat hashavua* might study *Parashat B'reishit* in light of scientific inquiry. For example, since light was created on day one and the sun was not created until day four, the students might be asked where this light was from and what it was for. The teacher could then point out that science also teaches that light existed before the sun in our solar system. Students might then discuss their own views of the interplay between science and religion. The teacher would explain that the two are complementary but different disciplines because science asks "what" and religion asks "why." This might help students to see that believing in science needn't require jettisoning religious belief.

This example demonstrates how teaching science is largely related to bigger questions of how we teach Bible, and specifically how we teach students about metaphor. We must do a better job of teaching students that we are telling them sacred stories, not teaching them actual history. This is a subtle, yet important, distinction for young students, but older students, beginning in the intermediate grades, can distinguish fact from truth.

Audrey Friedman Marcus developed a great lesson that illustrates this point.[5] Her lesson begins by having middle school students read a section of *The Little Prince*, where the prince is speaking with the fox about the nature of friendship. The teacher then asks the students if the story is true. The students inevitable say, "yes," to which the teacher responds, "so animals can talk?" This then leads into a conversation distinguishing truth from fact, which then proceeds to a lesson about metaphor. Students come to see that while *The Little Prince* is not factual, it is a metaphor for certain truths about friendship and life. The teacher then applies these new concepts to biblical stories, such as the exodus and creation stories.

Whether or not one uses Marcus's methodology, a similar outcome is desirable. In this way, we can teach our middle school students that science is about facts. Science seeks to answer "what." In comparison, religion and Bible are about truths. They seek to teach us "why."

Truth is ultimately the realm of theology and spirituality and this realm should not be ignored. Teens and adults should be encouraged to reflect on what role science plays in their own personal theology and personal spiritual practice.

One educational possibility for high school students and adults is to be introduced to Jewish mysticism and its relationship with science. For instance, like Sarah, other students might learn that Lurianic Kabbalah has much in common with certain concepts in contemporary physics. I recently taught a lesson on this subject as part of a creation unit that was part of a Hebrew high school class on "Judaism and the Environment." I watched the widening eyes of several science-oriented students. Students who were frequently disengaged suddenly burst forth with questions. Perhaps, if more Sarahs and Jacobs learned this, they would not feel the need to abandon their Jewish upbringing in favor of atheism or Buddhism, but would be better able to integrate their scientific and/or spiritual passions in a Jewish context.

Even on a less advanced level, questions of science and theology can be addressed. This past year, *Reform Judaism Magazine* published an article entitled "Einstein's God."[6] Following its publication, Susan Goldberg Schwartz, Temple Beth Zion's Director of Lifelong Learning, shared the article with her ninth grade theology class. This led to a very interesting theological discussion amongst the students.

As with any topic, teachers and parents cannot teach what they do not understand. Therefore, I urge my colleagues to consider "science and religion" as a topic for teacher training, family education, and other special programs. This topic might also make an interesting miniseries course of adult education.

A possibility that intrigues me but is beyond my area of expertise is the arena of Jewish day schools. Day schools in particular might serve as an excellent laboratory to experiment with new ways to teach science and religion as complementary rather than competitive disciplines. Wouldn't it be interesting if day schools were to develop curricula in this area? Perhaps we in synagogue-based education programs could learn from our day school colleagues how to better integrate these areas of instruction.

Homiletics

Upon agreeing to write this article, I began more intentionally reflecting upon how I address science (or don't address science) in my own preaching. In fact, my initial idea to write this piece was sparked in part by the struggle I was having writing a sermon about Dr. Stephen Hawking's new book, *The Grand Design*, and the publicity around the book, during which Dr. Hawking pronounced that "One cannot prove that God does not exist, but science makes God unnecessary." [7] Contrast this work with Daniel Matt's *God and the Big Bang: Discovering Harmony between Science and Spirituality*.[8] Perhaps there is a High Holy Day sermon in that comparison. In a society where our brightest minds declare God and religion unnecessary, we rabbis are obligated to preach that bright people can be religious. Otherwise, our congregants who are secularly well educated but comparatively poorly educated in Judaism will take their interest elsewhere. We rabbis have many topics to preach about. Social justice, Shabbat, Israel, spirituality, community, and the environment are all fighting for pulpit time. I have come to believe that science, and what science teaches us liberal Jews about Scripture and spirituality, is also deserving of a week or two a year.

I have discovered that in my efforts to not talk down to my congregants, I have sometimes assumed that they knew things that they did not. I never told them that I believe in a God who is a "sky wizard," but many have assumed as such. In my preaching about Adam and Eve, I have failed to tell them that they weren't really historical people. I assumed they knew this. Yet, apparently, many thought that I believed that everything in the Bible was historically true and that I wanted them to think so too. Similarly, I believe my congregants, and perhaps yours, have made assumptions about science and its relationship with religious thought. If

TV evangelists and atheist physicists are the only voices they hear on the subject, then what can be expected. I plan to start doing a better job of preaching sentences like "I believe that God created the world by causing the big bang," and "Biblical creation stories should be read as metaphor, not as history or science." God forbid I should ever talk down to my intelligent congregation, but God also forbid that I should unintentionally reinforce the destructive populist notions out there.

Conclusion

It has been said that religion is for people who don't know physics. I propose that we suggest just the opposite. Religion is for people who know physics and seek to connect with that expanding universe that is bigger than themselves. For, as the Rambam himself explained, "You will certainly not doubt the necessity of studying astronomy and physics, if you are desirous of comprehending the relation between the world and Providence as it is in reality, and not according to imagination."[9]

Notes

1. The complex kabbalistic theories about the creation of the universe and their parallels with several theories of contemporary physics are beyond the scope of this article. See the work of Daniel Matt and other experts in the field.
2. David Ruderman, *Jewish Thought and Scientific Discovery in Early Modern Europe* (New Haven: Yale University Press, 1995), 30.
3. Ibid.
4. See *Guide of the Perplexed* 2:8, commenting on *P'sachim* 94b.
5. This lesson was never formally published. It was brought to my attention by a colleague. Any errors or misrepresentations of her work are entirely my responsibility.
6. William Berkson, "Einstein's Religious Awakening," *Reform Judaism* 39 (Winter 2010): 67–69.
7. http://abcnews.go.com/GMA/stephen-hawking-science-makes-god-unnecessary/story?id=11571150.
8. Daniel Matt, *God and the Big Bank: Discovering Harmony between Science and Spirituality* (Woodstock, VT: Jewish Lights Publications, 1996).
9. Maimonides, Great-Quotes.com, Gledhill Enterprises, 2011, http://www.great-quotes.com/quote/1442358 (accessed June 24, 2011).

Part V: Rethinking Creation Theology

Science and Judaism in Light of Today's Ecological Imperative

Fred Scherlinder Dobb

In more ways than one, Bacon might be un-kosher: pig meat, of course, but also perhaps the thought and influence of Sir Francis Bacon (1561–1626), a pioneer of the mechanistic worldview that has shaped the development of Western science. At the dawn of the Enlightenment, Bacon argued for empiricism, and for decoupling religion from science so that faith would not constrain research and progress. Laudable as we may deem those efforts, Bacon also bade us to "put Nature on the rack and torture her secrets out of her to the effecting of all things possible."[1] This essay suggests that while empiricism and Judaism may indeed peacefully coexist, mechanism—which views nature purely instrumentally, and thus enables its torture—is truly *t'reif* in the eyes of our tradition.[2] Further, with science now empirically showing how actions rooted in this view constitute a grave threat to creation and humanity and justice, this essay exhorts shapers of twenty-first century Judaism to emphasize the already strong conservationist tendencies within our tradition and place them at the center of our contemporary Jewish experience.

While Bacon was building up modern mechanism in London, the Maharal (Rabbi Judah Loew; d. 1609) was at the same moment tearing it down in Prague. According to the well-known legend, this kabbalistically inclined philosopher used his superior spiritual and scientific knowledge to turn clay into the golem,[3] a

FRED SCHERLINDER DOBB (RRC97; Doctor of Ministry, Wesley Theological Seminary) is the spiritual leader of Adat Shalom Reconstructionist Congregation in the Washington, DC, area.

powerful artificial life-form, to help liberate his oppressed people. But quickly grasping that the unintended consequences of his experiment were too grave, the good rabbi destroyed his prototype and (anti-mechanistically) abandoned the enterprise. He saw the inherent integrity within both science and Judaism but never decoupled the former from the latter's ethical and spiritual call.[4]

The Prague of Loew, his granddaughter, and their golem is the setting for the historical-fiction half of Marge Piercy's powerful 1991 novel, *He, She and It*. The other half, a dystopian future whose protagonists engineer their own golem-like cyborg against the polluting corporations that have overrun the Earth, is perhaps the first great work of Jewish feminist environmental science fiction. Piercy, like all of us who follow Loew and Bacon, inherits both traditions—we live, as Mordechai Kaplan (1881–1983) often taught, "in two civilizations," the Jewish and the Western, with roots in and allegiances to both. Our opportunity and responsibility is to employ the values, assumptions, and norms of each world in questioning and improving (i.e., reconstructing) the other—and to ensure a synthesis that carries forward the best of both.

As Westerners, we expect the "true" narrative of science to make demands on our "mythic" Judaism. Judaism has often been open to this rapid evolution, to the benefit of our tradition. Yet as Jews, who inherent strong arguments against a mechanistic-scientific approach, we must also actively critique the assumptions behind it.[5] This essay considers, in light of both classic Jewish texts and today's climate crisis, what in the larger scientific narrative can be redemptive and relevant, and what remains dangerous and distant. The analysis concludes with a plea for liberal Jews to thoroughly embrace their heritage in this regard and embody the "green" aspects of their tradition outlined here—which may bring their actions in line with the needs of the world in this ecologically imperiled era, even as it may deepen their own spiritual lives in the process.

Norbert Samuelson cites Ian Barbour's theory that "there are four possible ways that apparent conflicts between the claims of contemporary sciences and contemporary religions can be handled. The four elements are conflict, independence, dialogue, and integration."[6] Each element is illustrated here as we address today's ecological challenge (independence), the problematics of scientific mechanism (conflict), the possibilities of science for a Jewish eco-theology (dialogue), and some actions that these reflections might spur us to take (integration).

A. Independence: Today's Ecological Challenge, as Understood by Science

Science alone suggests the pressing nature of many issues, from safe drinking water and environmental toxicology to the extirpation of entire species (itself an affront to the Creator, we must imagine) on our watch. We focus here, as do most current eco-religious efforts, on climate change—the single greatest ecological challenge of our (or any) day. And we recognize the robust scientific consensus regarding climate and energy, which fuels the urgency of so many theological and communal efforts today:

1. Fossil fuels, when burned, emit many pollutants and gases, carbon just one among them; besides climate change they cause acid deposition, respiratory damage (especially in low-resource communities), and broad environmental degradation.
2. Over a third of anthropogenic methane, a potent greenhouse gas, comes from livestock, an industry responsible for fully 18 percent (more than the entire transportation sector) of human-caused climate change.[7]
3. Smokestack and tailpipe (i.e., coal and oil) emissions are mostly carbon dioxide, the atmospheric level of which correlates directly with global average temperature.
4. While atmospheric levels of CO_2 do fluctuate naturally,[8] they have risen steadily from 280 parts per million at the dawn of industrialization to over 390 parts per million today—an increase greater again than that in the many millennia from the last ice age to 1800.
5. Accordingly, the Intergovernmental Panel on Climate Change's two thousand scientists anticipate a global average temperature increase between 2.5 and 10.4 degrees Fahrenheit over the next century,[9] with untold consequences for species, societies, and ecosystems. The extent of the damage will depend largely on the speed of our response.

These points are matters of science, backed by a robust scientific consensus (standing against mostly industry-funded voices, "climate skeptics," on the other side). A sober assessment of this scientific account suggests certain imperatives, moral ones even, to most unbiased observers: that conservation should become a matter of public policy rather than "private virtue"; that mitigation and adaptation[10] should both be pursued with alacrity; and that extant sustainable safe affordable energy sources like wind and solar[11] must be maximized.

Indeed, what we do with that science is an ethical and a religious question. Just as there is no monolithic scientific voice, so we expect a wide array of religious voices, within as well as between faith communities.[12] Christian eco-theologian Sallie McFague celebrates how, on balance, theology has long been "concerned with 'right relations,' relations with God, neighbor, and self; but now the context has broadened to include what has sometimes dropped out of the picture, especially in the last few hundred years—the oppressed neighbor, the other creatures, and the earth that supports us all."[13] It's about time. Moreover, such concerns over right ecological relations must now thoroughly infuse our daily practice, our "lived theology," as well.

Meanwhile, it's worth noting that Judaism alone offers its own cosmology, yet usually makes room for data from the outside (i.e., for science). We see this throughout biblical wisdom literature (Proverbs, Job, *Kohelet*, etc.) in its careful observation of the natural world; in rabbis who were agronomists and researchers as well as Talmudists; in astronomers and doctors who wrote the great medieval Jewish treatises; even in Rav Avraham Yitzhak HaCohen Kook (1865–1935), whose neo-kabbalistic notion that "everything aspires to ascend" intentionally invokes evolution.[14] Kaplan's language, calling Judaism "the evolving religious civilization of the Jewish people," again endorses the Darwinian approach. Since Judaism rarely rejects scientific evidence owing to dogmatic "belief," we can reasonably hope that the urgent science around climate change will indeed drive major salutary changes in contemporary Jewish life and thought.

B. Conflict: Judaism (and Ecology) Versus Science

Of course neither narrative, scientific or Judaic, is monolithic; far from it. Conflict is continual, within as well as between these approaches.[15] Still, the scientific approach of recent centuries has too often been mechanistic, treating nature and its myriad components (and for that matter religion) as "It" rather than "Thou," and paving the way for exploitation. As Christian theologian Dorothee Soelle puts it, "science is a belief system that binds us and rewards its priests and makes hope into a prescientific, unnecessary relic, because there is no space for hope and unpredictability inside its rationally controlled system."[16] Judaism, by contrast, tends toward respect for creation as a whole, and respect for each individual creation as a manifestation of divine creativity and *chesed* (lovingkindness). Science emphasizes knowledge and utility; Judaism emphasizes love and awe. As Heschel writes, humankind "will not perish for want of information; but only for want of appreciation."[17]

We retrospectively side with Galileo, whose "crime" was looking up the truth. Francis Bacon too rebelled against ecclesiastical strictures. But where his Italian predecessor saw beauty in his discoveries, Bacon saw profit. He, with René Descartes and others allured by promises of advances, sought the supremacy of scientific pursuits over all others, advocating that they remain unbounded. "Better living through chemistry," that now-ironic slogan of polluting twenty-century industry, is rooted here.[18] A Jewish critique of scientific mechanism starts here too, with this hubris of boundlessness.

For Jews, giving science or technology carte blanche is folly. Judaism's richest contributions to a modern environmental ethic celebrate that we are indeed bound, commanded, covenantally constricted in our actions, accountable to a greater good. The ultimate example is our Sabbath, whose traditional observance imposes strict limits on our production and consumption; Shabbat's spiritual, communal, poetic nature simply trumps the mechanistic scientific world, each week. Of course kashrut, by delimiting our diet, likewise elevates our boundedness—and it invites "eco-kashrut" and other ethical boundaries upon our otherwise free market and free will. *Bal tashchit*, the law forbidding waste, imposes a different sort of limit on human endeavor, also applicable to modern sustainability efforts.[19] Judaism generally is pro-bounds, proregulation, unafraid to enforce restrictions on private property and private profit—the legal arcana in *Seder N'zikin* directly buttress the communitarian side in current economic and political debates, such as environmental health or protection of endangered species, which pit private good against public good.[20]

These halachic examples point toward a central aggadic value, that of *anavah* (humility). From Moshe ("*ish anav m'od*," a most humble man) to Musar's many *midot* (traits to strengthen in ourselves), humility is a holy goal in Judaism. With humility we become less full of ourselves, and make room for the Other(s). At the *Homo sapiens* level, then, humility translates as the ecological imperative to ensure the continuity of all other life forms, and to limit our own collective footprint. This value diametrically opposes mechanism, or science as license to exploit, "putting nature on the rack" to achieve whatever short-term ends we deem worthy in the moment.

Humility is a virtue across our tradition, one replete with ecological implications. Temporally, the intergenerational nature of the Divine and the central theme "*l'dor vador*" ("from generation to generation") place sustainability at the fore—given the evolving nature of knowledge and wisdom, we should be prudent in our actions, based as they are within our own limited perspective, which soon will likely be superseded. Teleologically, Judaism shares with other traditions the idea that though we are created in the divine image, humans are not the purpose of creation—as Maimonides (1135–1204) wrote, "It should not be believed that all beings exist for the sake of humanity's existence . . . [rather] all the other beings too have been intended for their own sakes."[21] Midrashically, we are reminded of what Job learned so poignantly in the whirlwind (chapters 38–42)—that God's perspective puts ours to shame, and puts us in our place: "Even those creatures you deem superfluous in this world—like flies, fleas, and gnats—nevertheless have their allotted task in the scheme of Creation."[22] Against science's too-common anthropocentrism, Judaism is God-centered (and since creation is holy, a measure of biocentrism pertains as well).

A simple significant teaching from our central story: God created it, and God said it was "good." And this good creation is not exactly ours; rather, "the Earth is God's, and the fullness thereof" (Ps. 24:1; see also Lev. 25, *ki li haaretz*, "for the land is Mine"). Aurora Levins Morales offers a Puerto Rican Jewish naturalist's angle: "I grew up in a place where a tree might fall and, within a week, new seedlings sprang from the dead wood . . . it was never the same place for long. How can you own something that changes under your hands, that is so fully alive? Ecology undermines ownership."[23] Such nature observation, which we can all do, engenders a sense of awe—what

Heschel endearingly termed "radical amazement." Staring agape in wonder is a right response to the splendor of creation, which should in turn recommit us to its protection:[24] "How great are your works, O God, your thoughts are profoundly deep" (Ps. 92:5). This is Judaism's poignant response to scientific mechanism.

C. Dialogue: Science as (Partly) Redemptive in an Eco-Judaism

When science is a handmaiden to technological prowess, in the thrall of mechanism, Judaism rightly critiques it. But advancement of knowledge is inherently good, and Judaism and science (in its more holistic manifestations at least) have much to teach each other. Liberal Judaism is not just open to learning from science, but seeks consonance with it, a concept that Mordecai Kaplan took further than most: "To fail to reconstruct Jewish religion in harmony with the fundamental postulates of modern science is to sin against the light."[25]

Critics assail Kaplan, who spoke of "God Felt as a Presence Through the Natural Universe,"[26] as a pantheist in rabbinic garb. The attack is doubly misplaced. First, Kaplan was more panentheist than pantheist.[27] Consider one of Kaplan's brilliant appellations for God: "the Life, the Love and the Intelligence of the Universe."[28] Spiritual and ethical, even a shade personal, the metaphor remains grounded solidly within nature. Here Kaplan helps us relate meaningfully to a possibly pantheistic God: God may not exist beyond the universe, but all that is good and life-affirming in the universe comprises God. Empiricists and mystics alike might offer prayers to this Kaplanian understanding of divinity.

Deeper, though, concerns about pantheism in general may be overstated—the line between problematic pantheism and kosher "panentheism"[29] is fine, and too much promising theology has been thwarted for fear of crossing it. Arthur Green, recently articulating this concept, still felt it radical enough to title his work *Radical Judaism*: "Here on this smallish planet in the middle of an otherwise undistinguished galaxy, something so astonishing has taken place that it indeed demands to be called by the biblical term 'miracle,' rather than by the Greco-Roman 'nature,' even though the two are pointing to the exact same set of facts."[30]

To say that God dwells within the natural world or even that ongoing revelation comes only from nature is, like any other metaphor for the Ineffable, partially true—and thus worth exploring, even if it turns out to be more partial than most.[31] It may also be a new imperative, one whose time has come, if the universe feels more sacred and more worthy of our love and protection when we assign to it all that previous generations had understood as God. Since science and technology drive much of our collective hubris today, perhaps locating divinity within their orbit would help check their excesses. "Human beings are the stewards of terrestrial creation, not its owners. A most significant aspect of the interaction between science and theology is the latter's provision of a ground for the ethical guidelines within which the great endeavor of science and technology can only rightly be pursued."[32]

Numerous theologians, not just Jewish ones, command our attention here. Jürgen Moltmann's thoughtful observations regarding "God in Creation"[33] don't answer our questions, but deepen them tremendously. Sallie McFague, Arthur Green, Marcia Falk, and other "metaphorical theologians" open up a host of naturalistic images; as Judith Plaskow explains, "God who is the ground of being is present and imaged forth in all beings, so that every aspect of creation shows us another face of God."[34] And the poet-farmer-theologian Wendell Berry, proudly a Luddite for prioritizing community over technology,[35] celebrates God's inherent unpredictability, unknowability, and wildness. After citing King Solomon's prayer from the Temple's dedication ("Behold, the heaven and the heaven of heavens cannot contain thee: how much less this house that I have built?")[36] plus Paul's preaching at Athens,[37] Berry asserts:

> Solomon and Saint Paul both insisted on the largeness and the at-large-ness of God, setting Him free, so to speak, from *ideas* about Him. He is not to be fenced in, under human control, like some domestic creature; He is the wildest being in existence. The presence of His spirit in us is our wildness, our oneness with the wilderness of Creation. That is why subduing the things of nature to human purposes is so dangerous and why it so often results in evil, in separation and destruction.[38]

Though Berry's approach might be deemed anti-scientific, it is really just anti-mechanistic. Ever since Werner Heisenberg's 1927 discovery that science will never be able to tell us everything, the wildness so beloved by hikers and wildlife watchers has been mirrored in the most empirical corners of scientific inquiry. In theology, too, much is gained when we celebrate the wildness in the Creator of this wild world.

Reducing God entirely to the laws of science and nature strays too far from tradition, and from needs of the moment, to be "good theology" for us today. Panentheism, however—seeing the world "as [at least part of] God's body"[39]—maintains the best of pantheism while staying within the fold; it yields a fuller and truer picture.

Science and religion may have competing narratives for the natural world, but our experience of it is unitary, a "natural" blend of awe and utility, of spirituality and physicality, of miracle and everyday. Nature itself serves as a meeting-point for religion and science in our day, as a key resource in our efforts to find a theology for an ecological age: a theology at once philo-scientific, meaningfully Jewish, and green-oriented. At this intersection we can ascribe greater holiness to evolution and to quantum physics alike; we can refine the theological basis for preservation of creation; and we can internalize a host of helpful metaphors for the One, from rock and tree and web to "the Life, Love, and Intelligence of the Universe."

D. Integration: Implications for Today's Jewish Community

So how do we, at a moment of planetary peril, best capture the creative resilience of our evolving religious civilization? How can our Judaism-for-a-warming-world be authentic to tradition, helpful to the biosphere, and a healthy step in the further evolution of our deepest commitments? A few brief considerations follow.

We can emphasize the green strands of tradition, maximizing Judaism's contribution to the needs of the hour and helping it speak most powerfully to the rising generation. Jews in every era lift up aspects of our wide-ranging tradition that speak best to their moment, and in every era other Jews say the first group goes too far, too fast. This is healthy. Within whatever reasonable limits come from our movement affinity and our ideology, let us help make Judaism relevant in this generation—not so much by imposing a green agenda from the outside, but by highlighting the green themes that have long inhered within.

Since Judaism's communitarian and conservationist messages feel countercultural in today's America, more secularized adherents may not necessarily embody and act on these traditional values. Here is an opportunity for liberal Jews to join a needed effort and help the Earth simply by becoming "more religious," more thoroughly infused with their heritage in this regard. It's an opportunity too for liberal religious leaders to be defenders of the faith, to call their flock toward a remarkable alignment between traditional observance and the world's needs. Doing so should yield green dividends, even as it helps these Jews deepen their spiritual journeys.

We can connect with other faith experiences and communities, to the benefit of each tradition and of the Earth. Just as science knows no borders, ecology is a field that unites Jews and others in remarkably close ways: at the grass-roots level via IPL (Interfaith-PowerandLight.org), GreenFaith, etc.;[40] and at the leadership level through the Coalition on the Environment and Jewish Light (www.COEJL.org), which is one of four groups in the National Religious Partnership for the Environment (www.NRPE.org). Not only is interfaith cooperation itself a key civic and social good today, it also mirrors environmental awareness in how each individual and each species/faith is in turn part of and responsible to a larger whole.

With our presence, we can ensure that Judaism plays a vibrant role in the great sustainability struggle that will define coming generations' experience. *L'dor vador* is a newly relevant and multivocal expression: We pass down the tradition from generation to generation, out of love for Judaism and for the Jewish people; we pass down a healthy balanced planet from generation to generation, out of love for creation and for our future. And as this exploration of science and eco-Judaism has shown, those efforts are mutually reinforcing—thinking and acting in Jewish-inspired ways is good for the Earth, even as our robust defense of creation today is good for Judaism. May we be both scientific, and religious, about sustaining all that is dear to us.

Notes

1. David Orr, *Resurgence* 247 (March/April 2008), http://www.gratefulness.org/readings/rhythm_gratitude_orr.htm.
2. Norbert Samuelson, among the challenges presented in the opening essay, gives as number 14 the "need to move beyond mechanistic science to a philosophy of the soul in terms of grounds for analysis of objective morality and of redemption." Norbert M.

Samuelson, "The Challenges of the Modern Sciences for Jewish Faith," *CCAR Journal* (Winter 2012): 17. I would emphasize, rather, "The need to de-center mechanistic science in favor of love-of-creation and love-of-the-Creator, since respect and awe for nature and the imperative to protect it are both core Jewish stances, and urgent contemporary obligations."

3. The golem story first appears with certainty only in the early nineteenth century, close in time to Mary Shelley's parallel (with or without golem influence) 1817 cautionary tale at the start of the scientific-backlash, *Frankenstein*.
4. According to Rabbi Shlomo Aviner (an extremist settler rabbi who nonetheless accepts evolution and dinosaurs), "the Maharal says that the purpose of science is to describe reality, while the Torah describes what reality should be, i.e. what is good and what is bad. What exists is interesting, but it is not Torah." Quoted in J. J. Goldberg, "Science Meets Settler Theory, or How Frankenstein Embraced Godzilla," *The Jewish Daily Forward*, November 13, 2009, http://blogs.forward.com/jj-goldberg/118873/.
5. The scientific story is of course itself a "myth" (in the literal sense of a master story that strives to make sense of our reality) no less than Jewish tradition. Samuelson seems to envision philosophy the same way, as he extends the term to include "all attempts to make sense out of everything in the most general terms, especially to make sense out of how we human beings locate ourselves in the universe relative to everything else in it. This usage minimally includes other human beings and life forms with whom we interact." Samuelson, "Challenges," 13.
6. Ian Barbour, *Religion in an Age of Science* (San Francisco: Harper, 2000 [1990]), 4.
7. Http://www.fao.org/ag/magazine/0612sp1.htm (UN Food & Ag. Org.).
8. Obfuscators overstate these fluctuations. Recent ice core samples prove that despite wild gyrations in global climate over the last eight hundred thousand years, natural cycles explain every shift—except our present, unprecedented spike. See Ed Brook, "Palaeoclimate: Windows on the Greenhouse," *Nature*, May 15, 2008, http://www.nature.com/nature/journal/v453/n7193/full/453291a.html: "The fundamental conclusion that today's concentrations of these greenhouse gases have no past analogue in the ice-core record remains firm . . . The data further reinforce the tight link between greenhouse gases and climate."
9. The IPCC's most recent comprehensive summary (http://www.ipcc.ch/pdf/assessment-report/ar4/syr/ar4_syr_spm.pdf) highlights the scientific consensus estimates. The then-most-recent figure for atmospheric carbon dioxide was for 2005, at 379 parts per

million, but increasing steadily at about 3 parts per million per year; come 2012 we approach 400 parts per million.

10. Adaptation is relatively simple in developed nations that can afford complex seawalls, early-warning systems, urban relocations, etc. It is much more challenging in the developing world, which will be hit hardest by the impact of emissions they largely did not generate. Incrementally, in a small but very real way, each measure of fossil fuel that the developed world does not burn not only prevents more lives lost and more destroyed ecosystems, but it also helps correct the inherent injustice of today's energy gap between developed and developing nations.
11. Wind and solar are emphasized here over other supposedly "sustainable" sources, since while hydropower and biomass (burning wood, etc.) are relatively carbon-neutral, they bring other environmental and social concerns in their wake. And though nuclear energy causes no air pollution when produced normally, the average forty-year lifespan of a nuclear plant leaves millions of tons and many acres of highly radioactive material for tens of thousands of years—so even leaving accidents (Fukushima, Chernobyl) and weapons proliferation concerns aside, nuclear energy is hardly "sustainable" on the basis of intergenerational justice alone.
12. Ideological differences may in fact be greater within than between faiths—the fault line, common to most faith communities, lies between an insular fundamentalism and a self-critical pluralism. See Arthur Green, *Radical Judaism: Rethinking God and Tradition* (New Haven: Yale Press, 2010), 141, for a poignant "confession" of this reality. The status of women is among the bellwethers of this divide; though efforts have been made to include here many women's and explicitly feminist voices, quotations preserve the language and pronoun choices of the original text, however problematic.
13. Sallie McFague, "A Square in the Quilt," in *Spirit and Nature*, ed. Steven Rockefeller and John Elder (Boston: Beacon Press, 1992), 46.
14. Rav Kook, *Orot Hakodesh* (*Lights of Holiness*), I:220–21: "The doctrine of evolution that is presently gaining acceptance in the world has a greater affinity with the secret teachings of the Cabbalah than all other philosophies. Evolution, which proceeds on a course of improvement, offers us the basis of optimism in the world. How can we despair when we realize that everything evolves and improves?…Evolution sheds light on all the ways of God. All existence evolves and ascends…not a spark will be lost from the ensemble. All will share in the climactic culmination."
15. Conflicts like those within science and within Judaism can be useful, even holy, per Ovadia m'Bartenura on Avot 5:17: *mitoch havikuach nitbarer haemet* ("from the struggle/disagreement, the truth emerges").

16. Dorothee Soelle, with Shirley A. Cloyes, *To Work and to Love: A Theology of Creation* (Philadelphia: Fortress Press, 1984), 160. Irving (Yitz) Greenberg offers his own blistering critique (as summarized by Marc Ellis in his *Toward a Jewish Theology of Liberation* [Maryknoll, NY: Orbis Books, 1987], 20): "For the past two centuries an allegiance has been transferred from the 'Lord of History and Revelation' to the 'Lord of Science and Humanism,' but the experience of the death camps asks whether this new Lord is worthy of ultimate loyalty."
17. Abraham Joshua Heschel, *Man Is Not Alone* (Philadelphia: JPS, 1951), 22. Eilon Schwartz argues in *Judaism and Ecology*, ed. Hava Tirosh-Samuelson (Cambridge: Harvard University Press, 2002), 100, that "the theme of radical amazement," developed thoroughly by Heschel but present since the wisdom literature, "is the closest that classical Jewish texts come to a wilderness tradition." And Sallie McFague in *Models of God* (Philadelphia: Fortress Press, 1987), 186, adds that "If one can say that the basic religious apprehension is the wonder at being, wonder that there is something rather than nothing, then the ecological evolutionary sensibility is . . . religious."
18. Of course the counterargument, that we should live *with* nature rather than over against it, has a venerable pedigree too—Sir Francis lived long after his coreligionist and namesake Saint Francis of Assisi, who by contrast counseled that we respect animals and walk lightly upon creation. Our "Western" tradition still incorporates elements of each Francis, in an uneasy detente.
19. Rooted in Deut. 20:19's prescription against cutting down an enemy's trees in wartime, tradition extended *bal tashchit* in numerous directions, including energy efficiency. As Rav Zutra opines (*Shabbat* 67b), "whoever covers an oil lamp or uncovers a naphtha lamp violates" this mitzvah—thus it is a halachic imperative even to use the most efficient available approach when burning fossil fuels.
20. For instance, Talmudic-era threshing floors and tanneries were like today's noxious factories or power plants—where do these get sited, and who do they impact the most? "We keep a fixed threshing floor . . . carcasses, graves, and tanneries 50 cubits away from the town. We only put a tannery to the east [downwind] of the town. Rabbi Akiva says in any direction except west, and distanced 50 cubits" (*Mishnah Bava Batra* 2:8–9). Similarly, public areas are like today's national forests—should logging, mining, oil production, and other extractive industries be allowed on public lands, despite the damage they cause? "The one who sets down a vessel in a public area, and another comes and stumbles on it and breaks it—that [latter] person is not liable. And if they are injured by it, the owner of the cask is liable for the damage. The one who draws water from a public place and another is injured by it . . . or

the one who hides thorns or glass, or the one who makes a fence of thorns which falls into a public area and injures others, is liable for the damage. The one who puts their straw and their stubble into a public area for disposal . . . or the one who turns over a heap of stones in a public area, and these injure another, is liable for the damage" (*Mishnah Bava Kama* 3:1–3).

21. *Guide of the Perplexed*, 3:13. The same logic is advanced by Ibn Taymiyya, a century later, who observed in his *Majmu Fatawa* regarding the Quran's many anthropocentric *suras* that "it must be remembered that God in his wisdom brought into being these creatures for reasons *other than serving human beings*. In these verses God only explains the [human] benefits of these." S. Nomanul Haq, "Islam and Ecology," cited in Mary Evelyn Tucker and John Grim, eds., *Daedalus* 130, no. 4 (Fall 2001): 154.
22. *Sh'mot Rabbah* 10:1, circa eighth century C.E.
23. Aurora Levins Morales, "Nadie la Tiene: Land, Ecology, and Nationalism," in *Torah of the Earth*, ed. Arthur Waskow (Woodstock VT: Jewish Lights, 2000), II:188–89.
24. "'We know to the extent to which we love', said Augustine. Through this form of astonished, wondering and loving knowledge, we do not appropriate things. We recognize their independence and participate in their life. We do not wish to know so that we can dominate. We desire to know in order to participate. This kind of knowledge confers community . . . It lets life be life and cherishes its livingness." In Jürgen Moltmann, *God in Creation*, trans. Margaret Kohl (Minneapolis: Fortress, 1993), 32.
25. Mordecai Kaplan, *The Meaning of God in Modern Jewish Religion* (NY: Berhman House, 1937), 356.
26. Kaplan, *Meaning of God*, table of contents—among the many aspects of divinity he locates in various points along the Jewish year, he associates this "scientific" aspect with Sukkot, the fall harvest festival.
27. Arthur Green, in RRC's *Raayonot* (1984). Green has since expounded on how Herschel and Kaplan unite in pantheism (defined two endnotes hence) in "A Kabbalah for the Environmental Age," in *Judaism and Ecology*, ed. Hava Tirosh-Samuelson (Cambridge: Harvard University Press, 2002), 315, and in his *Ehyeh* and *Radical Judaism*.
28. Green, in *Raayonot*; Kaplan, 1929 diary, in Mel Scult (ed.), *Cummings of the Spirit* (Detroit: Wayne State University Press, 2002), 300. This appellation for God comes at the end of a lengthy journal entry about Jewish demographics in the Midwestern communities through which he was touring on January 3, 1929: "It is now 11:20 P.M. I want to note that with the help of God, the Life, the Love and the Intelligence of the Universe, I have been able to turn to good account the hours I am spending on this train. I thank

thee, O God for the blessings which I enjoy. Amen." Scult identifies Kaplan's 26-volume journal as the most prolific diary extant in English, besting Pepys, Johnson, and other well-known diarists by a wide margin.

29. "Panentheism" is defined and evaluated by Norman Lamm in *Torah of the Earth*, ed. Arthur Waskow (Woodstock, VT: Jewish Lights, 2000), I:117; he attributes the "felicitous term" to Charles Hartshorne, and defines it as "God includes the world within Himself, but is not limited to or by it. He is immanent, but also remains transcendent to it. 'He is the place of the world, but the world is not His place' [*B'reishit Rabbah* 68:9, *Hu m'komo shel olam, v'ein olamo m'komo*]."
30. Green, *Radical Judaism*, 21.
31. Hava Tirosh-Samuelson forcefully rejects what smacks of pantheism: "A Jewish environmental philosophy and ethics cannot be based on a simplistic version of pantheism that acknowledges only the world and nothing beyond the world. From a Jewish perspective, 'biocentrism' is just another form of paganism that must result in idolatrous worship of nature. An environmental philosophy that merely reveres what is, while ignoring what should be, is not viably Jewish...It is precisely because humans are created with the capacity to transcend nature that they are commanded by God to protect nature. Therefore, a Jewish environmental philosophy and ethics cannot give up the primacy of the human species in the created order." Hava Tirosh-Samuelson, "Nature in the Sources of Judaism," in Tucker and Grim, *Daedalus*, 116–17.
32. John Polkinghorne, *Science & Theology: An Introduction* (New York: Routeledge, 1998), 132.
33. Moltmann, *God in Creation*, 53: "Every natural theology proceeds from the self-evidence of nature as God's creation. On the other hand, every theology of nature interprets nature in the light of the self-revelation of the creative God. So what is the relation between natural theology and the theology of nature? By asking this question we are turning the traditional interest in natural theology upside down: the aim of our investigation is not what nature can contribute to our knowledge of God, but what the concept of God contributes to our knowledge of nature." Perhaps, following Moltmann, a comprehensive Jewish theology of nature is long overdue.
34. Judith Plaskow, *Standing Again at Sinai* (HarperSanFrancisco, 1990), 165. Marcia Falk has since popularized the use of *Ein HaHayyim* (Wellspring of Life) in contemporary liberal liturgies, including the Reconstructionist prayer book series as well as her own *Book of Blessings*.
35. "To this day, if you say you would be willing to forbid, restrict, or reduce the use of technological devices in order to protect the

community—or to protect the good health of nature on which the community depends—you will be called a Luddite, and it will not be a compliment. To say that the community is more important than machines is certainly Christian and certainly democratic, but it is also Luddism and therefore not to be tolerated." Wendell Berry, "Christianity and the Survival of Creation," in *Sex, Economy, Freedom & Community* (New York and San Francisco: Pantheon, 1992), 131.

36. Heschel, who was no pantheist, cited the same scripture to make his panentheistic point: God "includes the universe, but, to quote Solomon's prayer in dedicating the Temple: 'Behold, the heaven, and the heaven of heavens cannot contain Thee' (I Kings 8:27). The awareness of God as the dwelling-place of the universe must have been very poignant in post-Biblical times, if *Makom* ('place') was a synonym for God."
37. "God made the world and all things therein, seeing that He is Lord of heaven and earth, dwelling not in temples made with hands" (Paul, Acts 17:24).
38. Berry, "Christianity and the Survival of Creation," 101.
39. Sallie McFague, *Models of God*, 72.
40. "Etcetera" covers a lot of wonderful work being done by green Jewish groups such as The Shalom Center and Hazon in frequent concert with their counterparts across the religious spectrum.

Not Playing to Empty Benches: The Role of Mind in the Search for Meaning

Lawrence Troster

The Challenge to Mind and Meaning

The late biologist Stephen Jay Gould, in attempting to disabuse us of our belief that humanity is the inevitable result of a progressive evolution, quotes Mark Twain that if the history of life were the Eiffel Tower, then humanity is the paint on the top, and if anyone thought that this paint was the purpose of the tower this would be the greatest arrogance.[1] Gould bases his perspective not only on the age of life on earth but also on the contingencies inherent in the evolutionary process. He has also famously said that humanity is a "glorious accident," the result of a long series of evolutionary contingencies stimulated by large-scale environmental changes. If it were possible to "rewind" the evolutionary "tape" and replay it, it would be unlikely that humanity would be the result.[2] Gould's perspective is a common one amongst not only evolutionary biologists but also physicists summed up by Steven Weinberg's famous comment, "The more the Universe seems comprehensible, the more it also seems pointless."[3]

In his trigger article, "The Challenges of the Modern Sciences for Jewish Faith," Norbert Samuelson lists among his challenges that modern science brings to Judaism the question: "Our universe is too old and human existence is too brief for humanity to provide the reason for the existence of the universe. If we give up this humanist assumption, how can we understand why God created the universe?"[4] This question goes to the heart of the problem for

---

LAWRENCE TROSTER (JTS82) is rabbinic scholar-in-residence for GreenFaith, the Interfaith Environment Coalition in New Jersey. He is pursuing a Doctor of Ministry in Ecological Ministries at Drew Theological School in New Jersey.

Judaism that scientists like Gould and Weinberg assert: How can we consider humanity to be "created in the image of God," and thus the center of divine purpose and concern.[5] The challenge to this important Jewish value comes from two elements that modern science asserts about the universe and the evolution of life and consciousness: time and the contingent character of cosmic and biological evolution.

Catholic theologian John F. Haught has explicated further on how evolutionary science and modern cosmology create critical problems for Western religion. First, Darwinian theory shows that all living creatures share a common ancestry and are historically and organically interconnected. Therefore, the traditional ontological discontinuity between humanity and the rest of creation, which was a central feature of Jewish and Christian theology, no longer exists. From a traditional perspective the universe consists of a hierarchy of distinct levels of being and meaning. The lowest levels consist of inanimate objects followed by the level of living things, in ascending value: plants, animals, humans, and, finally, God. But now we know, for example, that humanity shares 98 per cent of its genes with chimpanzees.[6] Secondly, Darwinism, as it is now understood, sees no major distinctions between life and non-life. Life arises from dead matter as a result of the laws of physics and chemistry enacted over billions of years. Thus evolutionary science collapses and reverses the sacred hierarchy: What is lowest becomes what is most fundamental, and matter is the ultimate source of all things living and non-living. Any emergent features of the universe, like mind, are only "epiphenomenal derivatives": the accidental combinations of its lowest elements. Lastly, according to Haught, the theory of natural selection states that the variety of life in the natural world is a product of completely random forces undirected by any intelligent agency or divine providential intelligence. Therefore the universe is an impersonal structure without any essential meaning.[7] These are the conclusions drawn by scientists like Daniel Dennett and Richard Dawkins: Darwinism proves that there is no intelligent designer of the universe and that evolution is a meaningless process.[8]

This paper will attempt to deal with this challenge by considering two writers who see the existence of mind as having a significant role in the universe: the philosopher Hans Jonas and the physicist John Wheeler. In their own distinctive way that considers two different sciences—biology and physics respectively—these two thinkers have much to teach all of us who are pondering how to bridge science and religion. I will reflect on the ramifications of their ideas for contemporary Jewish religious life at the conclusion of the essay.

Hans Jonas

The German-Jewish philosopher Hans Jonas (1903–1993) is one of the most original Jewish thinkers of the twentieth century, but most Jews are still unfamiliar with his works.[9] Jonas rejected the stance of many scientists that mind is only an epiphenomenon. He saw the existence of mind as a significant datum in the universe and disputed many of the materialist assumptions of mind in scientific materialist thinking. Jonas felt that much of modern philosophy and science created new perspectives of nature and humanity, which "imply the negation of fundamental tenets of the philosophical as well as religious tradition"[10]—that is, the biblical/Jewish tradition. The universe is no longer "creation" with a divine order and purpose, but rather is a process determined by mindless law without purpose, values, goals, or ends. In this kind of universe there is no special status or place for humanity.[11]

Jonas responded to what he considered modern nihilism by his understanding of how a living organism actually exists. Every living creature, from the smallest microbe to humankind, shows concern for the continued existence of its own being: They connect to the world around them in a constant effort to stave off death and nonbeing. This is revealed through metabolism, the exchange of matter with the environment, which all organisms must exhibit in order to survive. It is the most basic expression of an organism's struggle for life. Every life form also has what Jonas called "needful freedom," because it consistently exhibits a dynamic unity beyond the sum of its parts while still being dependent on constant exchanges with its environment in order to avoid dying.[12] Jonas believed that the polarities that humans find in themselves—being/nonbeing, self/world, form/matter, freedom/necessity—are also to be found in the most primitive organisms and thus are an essential part of life itself. And these polarities reveal the existence of mind.

As evolution gives expression to a new level of complexity, there is an increase in mind. This new level includes greater freedom but also greater peril in the potential for pain and suffering. For example, while all life requires nutrition and the possibility of reproduction, animal life also has the capacities for movement, desire, and sensitivity to its environment that most plants do not exhibit. But with these increased capabilities, animals also have the ability to feel pain, fear, and abandonment. When humans evolve, being now becomes self-reflexive, attempting to understand its place in the whole of which it is part. As a result, the particular human anxieties of existence, unhappiness, guilt, and despair also arise.[13]

Jonas asserted that if lower life forms are viewed as not having a trace of mind, then this perspective is not a scientific fact but a metaphysical prejudice, a form of mechanistic or reductionist materialism, which is not a neutral description of the physical world.[14] In response to modern nihilism, Jonas asserted that there is purpose and meaning in the universe and by interpreting the facts of biology existentially and seeing the inherent value in the natural world beyond ourselves, there is an ethical imperative for humanity to accept the role as guardians and stewards of the natural world. The biosphere has become "a human trust" with a moral claim on humanity and must be cherished not only for utilitarian requirements but also for its own inherent value.[15]

Although Jonas felt that it was not philosophically necessary to posit a divine creation to the universe to counter modern nihilism he nonetheless felt that theology responds to human spiritual needs: We want to know that there is a loving God who created the universe and still sustains it and we hope that goodness is not lost or forgotten in this universe.[16] Jonas felt that only through theology can these needs be met. In order to suggest the existence of such a God, Jonas shows how the material content of the universe as described by science from which life and subjectivity emerged to become mind can be said to originally come from a "creative ground," which can be called "God." In other words, from the evidence of the universe, the material content that is deduced reveals the existence of subjectivity. This subjectivity leads to mind, which in turn comprehends the existence of God.[17]

The central issue for Jonas is how the development of the universe from its beginning to the emergence of mind can be explained since the universe moved in a physically improbable process, one that was an anti-entropic direction from disorder to order. Does this improbable process prove that there was a program or a design inherent in matter from the time of the big bang? If so, this design would be a "cosmogonic logos."[18] Jonas rejects the idea of a logos on the ground that if there was information in the primordial matter of the universe, it would have been the result of some kind of organization that did not exist at the time of the big bang, when there was only a primordial chaos from which order emerged. For Jonas, the existence of such a logos would also be too deterministic. Instead, Jonas believed that the laws of nature emerge in a kind of cosmic natural selection as only a self-conserving reality would survive. Order is more successful than disorder and regularity replaces arbitrary multiplicity: Protons become the law of gravity and mechanics, hydrogen becomes the elements, and the four basic physical forces emerge from the original "chaos." But why did the universe continue to develop order after the basic laws emerged? In a Darwinian process there is always enough disorder left over to allow for new characteristics by random events, which would then itself be subject to natural selection. Therefore a logos is not necessary and it can be assumed is that there is a "susceptibility" to order that codes the surrounding disorder for "information."

This would not, however, explain the evolution of mind. For Jonas, subjectivity, or inwardness, is ontologically a fact of being and must be an essential part of the evolution of life. Even though the arrival of life can be explained from nonliving matter this does not explain life's subjectivity—life could have been only a kind of chemical reaction. Yet subjectivity in life does exist, interacts with matter, and is inseparable from it.[19]

In order to come to a solution, Jonas rejects both the dualistic and monistic explanation for subjectivity and mind. Dualism is logically rejected because an independent thinking substance that cannot prove its own existence is stupid, and phenomenologically it is rejected because the experiences of the body, such as pleasure, pain, perception, desire, and feeling, are part of thought. Therefore Jonas rejects the existence of an individual immortal soul. Classical monism or materialism is also rejected because it turns the soul and mind into instances of "epiphenomenalism," which is self-contradicting. Instead Jonas posits a different kind of monism. Since matter finds its voice in subjectivity, it is necessary to revise the concept of matter beyond its external qualities that can be measured and abstracted by physics. There is a need for "a metaphysics" of the material substance of the world, which must include the idea that the matter that emerged in the universe must have had the possibility of inwardness even though it did not yet exist.[20]

Jonas then asks: "Who (or what) 'endowed' matter in this way? What share did this 'endowment' have in the course of cosmic events?"[21] Given Jonas's theology of God and rejection of a logos, he believed that this arising was "an entirely neutral contingency whose occurrence involved no favoring preferment of any kind."[22] The arising of subjectivity must be inherent in matter itself; therefore there is no "plan" in the universe for the arrival of mind. There is what Jonas called a "cosmogonic eros"—a tendency or a yearning instead of a logos. Even with this "eros," there is large measure of contingency. The existence of an Earth where there are favorable conditions for life arising came about only by chance circumstances in the universe. Then the "readiness is there and subjectivity receives its opportunity." Matter is "subjectivity in its latent form, even if aeons, plus exceptional luck, are required for the actualizing of this potential."[23]

When mind does finally arise, thought adds a transcendental dimension that is expressed in three freedoms of thinking that go beyond matter: the freedom of thinking for determining itself through choice of object; the freedom to transform the sensations into self-created inner images (imagination's freedom to invent); and the freedom carried by language to transcend the images of the imagination and thus allow the mind to gain the ability to grasp the idea of the infinite, the eternal, and the absolute. Only through language does mind still remain bound to the world of the senses. For Jonas, this ability of the human mind is what makes us different from the animals.[24] These characteristics of the human mind allow humans free will of conduct and moral choice: It moves humans from the "is" to the "ought." Moral freedom is both the most transcendent and the most precarious of human freedoms because it can also lead to evil: "The knowledge *of* good and evil, the power of discriminating between them, is also the capacity *for* good and evil."[25]

For Jonas all of this was *cosmological evidence*, the characteristics of the universe as it is now seen. From the cosmological evidence he believed that it was possible to deduce something about the beginning of the universe (cosmogony). Subjectivity cannot have been foreign to matter from its very beginning: There must have been a possibility of subjectivity. While Jonas admitted that this speculation may be a matter of faith, it is a rational faith given the evidence. Matter "from the very beginning is mind asleep, so we must immediately add that the really first cause, the creative cause, of mind asleep can only be mind awake." Here Jonas referred back to his earlier ideas about God after the Holocaust.

In that earlier work creation begins with God's self-limitation, a version of the kabbalistic doctrine of *tzimtzum* (the contraction of the divine for the purpose of creation). While in *tzimtzum*, the contraction is followed by the insertion of divine creative energy into the space provided, for Jonas the contraction is total: "The Infinite ceded his power to the finite and thereby wholly delivered his cause into its hands."[26] After the initial act of creation, God allows the universe to continue to develop on its own: "Having given himself whole to the becoming world, God has no more to give: it is man's now to give to him."[27] The divine direction of creation has ended and the universe proceeds in a completely naturalistic way on its own. For Jonas, God could only be one that "abandoned Himself and his destiny entirely to the outwardly exploding universe and thus to the pure chances of the *possibilities* contained in it under the conditions of space and time."[28]

Why God created the universe in the first place is unknowable, but once it occurred, creation proceeded only immanently with no outside intervention. One of Jonas's rational proofs for such a process is in the size of the universe and the apparent rarity of life and mind. "Only a universe colossal in space and time, in accordance with the rule of mere possibilities and with no intervention of divine power, offered any chance at all for mind's coming to pass at any time or place whatsoever."[29] The rarity of life and mind in the universe imposes upon humanity in the present time the duty to preserve creation: "We must protect from ourselves the divine cause in the world that has become threatened by us, that we must come to the aid of the deity who has become powerless for Himself regarding us. It is the duty of power that knows, a cosmic duty, for it is a cosmic experiment, which we can wreck along with ourselves and spoil within ourselves." [30]

Evaluating Jonas's theory of mind and creation there is a problem with his acceptance of such a high level of contingency in cosmic and biological evolution. While his "creation theology" is positioned within modern cosmology, he would be forced to agree with Gould that if the "tape" of evolution were replayed there would a high probability that sentient life would not emerge even with a cosmic "eros" towards mind. There would be those who would argue that this limitation on God's action is too high. One can still accept a high level of contingency while having a stronger sense of cosmic direction from chaos to order with a much higher probability of conscious life appearing somewhere in the universe even if it is not human life. Nonetheless, in his philosophy of life and in his theology of God and creation, Jonas provides a new way to utilize science to establish meaning, purpose, and value in the universe.

John Archibald Wheeler

Another, albeit very speculative, way to posit the importance of mind in the universe is articulated by the theoretical physicist John Archibald Wheeler (1911–2008) in his version of the Anthropic Principle known as the Participatory Anthropic Principle (PAP). Wheeler worked with Niels Bohr on explaining nuclear fission and with Albert Einstein on unified field theory, and during his long tenure at Princeton University he trained two generations of leading theoretical physicists. In the 1950s Wheeler formulated a program of geometrodynamics, whose goal was to explain all physical phenomena in terms of the geometrical properties of curved space-time. In the early 1970s Wheeler abandoned this program and turned instead to focus on general relativity theory, which up to that time was detached from experimental physics and was not taken too seriously by other physicists.

The Anthropic Principle was first proposed by theoretical physicist Brandon Carter in 1973, as a reaction to the Copernican Principle, which asserts that humans do not occupy a privileged position in the universe. The Copernican Principle underlay the Steady State theory of the universe, which had been refuted by the mounting evidence for the big bang theory. In its most basic (or "weak") form (WAP), the Anthropic Principle states that:

> The observed values of all physical and cosmological quantities are not equally probable but they take on values restricted by the requirement that there exists sites where carbon-based life can evolve and by the requirement that the Universe be old enough for it to already have done so.[31]

While this idea may sound obvious, its implications are extremely far-reaching. As George Gale pointed out, it is quite easy to imagine a universe very different from ours in which the physical laws would not allow for the emergence of conscious life. Therefore this universe must exist within certain cosmological quantities.[32]

There are several other versions of the Anthropic Principle that go beyond WAP. In the Strong Anthropic Principle (SAP) as defined by Barrow and Tipler, "The Universe must have those properties which allow life to develop within it at some stage in its history."[33] This means that a universe in which there exists conscious observers *had* to come into existence. The Strong Anthropic Principle is an attempt to deal with the large number of cosmological constants and other factors found in the universe that seems to make it particularly fit for conscious life. The scientist George Wald in a speech given in 1983[34] and published in 1984[35] pointed out several of these factors: the ratio of the weight of protons to electrons, which makes the chemistry and physics of solids possible; the abundance of carbon in the universe without which life could not emerge; the fact that water is one of the only substances that can float when it is in a solid state, which allows life to survive in the winter and the existence of consciousness itself. There are many more such physical qualities that the universe exhibits that make it seem particularly fine-tuned for conscious life.[36]

There are three main versions of SAP to explain why the universe is so amenable for conscious life: (1) there is only one universe intentionally designed to allow for the emergence of conscious observers; (2) observers are necessary to bring the universe into being; or (3) there exists an infinite number of universes and as such one must exist in which there are conscious observers.[37]

The first version of SAP is usually rejected by scientists because it recapitulates the classical teleological argument for the existence of God. The third version has many variations and is currently the most accepted because it removes any element of teleology and fits certain models that have been developed in quantum physics and/or modern cosmological theory. In the multiverse theory what is commonly called the universe is only one domain of a larger structure in which there are an infinite number of domains. If so, then by definition there must be at least one domain that will have all the conditions for emergence of conscious life. One of the problems with this theory is that there is likely no way to prove the existence of other domains.[38]

The second version of SAP is John Wheeler's Participatory Anthropic Principle (PAP) which he once summarized as: "Physics gives rise to observer-participancy; observer-participancy gives rise to information; information gives rise to physics."[39] Wheeler, like Wald, sees the existence of mind as a central principle of the universe, and he derived his perspective from quantum mechanics in which the observer and the observed universe are deeply interconnected. Therefore conscious minds observing the universe can be said to have participated in its creation and existence or as Paul Davies explained it, "It is only through acts of observation that the physical reality of the world becomes actualized."[40] This theory is what is known as a "cosmic causal-loop theory," in which the universe is created in the past by the observers in the present who have been created by that universe. But this theory, according to Davies may require that the universe itself must become in some sense self-aware through a final merging of mind and cosmos.[41] This is a conclusion that Wald also came to, but for Wald there is a purpose to the universe coming to this final state. In Wald's version of SAP, mind is fundamental to the universe from the very beginning:

> the recognition that a universe in which mind can eventually achieve such overt expression as in science, art and technology must be at its core, from its inception, in some sense a knowing universe; that it must in some sense possess mind as its pervasive and enduring attribute. The stuff of this universe, then, is ultimately mind-stuff. What we recognize as the material universe, the universe of space and time and elementary particles and energies, is then an avatar, the materialization of primal mind. In that sense there is no waiting for consciousness to arise. It is there always. What we wait for in the evolution of life is only the culminating event, the emergence of creatures that in their self-awareness can *articulate* consciousness, can give it a voice and being also *social* creatures, can embody it in culture, in technology, art and science.[42]

And what is the reason that the universe "wants" conscious life to evolve? In the speech version of Wald's article he is reported as saying, "The universe wants to be known . . . Did the universe come about to play its role to empty benches?"[43] One can interpret this idea theologically and say that God needs conscious observers in creation in order to actualize God's existence and not play to "empty benches" or as it says in *Pirkei Avot* 6:11: "Everything that the Holy Blessed One created in the world was created solely for God's glory." And there is also the midrash to Isaiah 43:12: "'You are my witnesses says the Lord and I am God'—when you are My witnesses, I am God, but when you are not my witnesses, I am not God, if one may say such a thing."[44]

Conclusions

The age of the universe and the many contingencies in both cosmic and biological evolution can indeed be, as Norbert Samuelson has pointed out, a serious challenge to classical Jewish concepts of a meaningful creation with a special role for humanity. But, as I have shown in this essay, it is possible to construct a theology that takes into account modern science while still leaving room for meaning and purpose in creation. Hans Jonas's philosophy and theology shows how mind is a fundamental characteristic of the universe that allows for a critical and meaningful role for humanity. Wheeler and Wald's versions of the Anthropic Principle can be theologically interpreted to assert that although the specific form of the human was not necessarily divinely ordained, the existence of conscious observers was one of the goals of creation in order to actualize God's existence in the universe. While these perspectives do not guarantee a solution to this particular challenge, at least they may allow for a deeper discussion of the relationship between mind, matter, the universe, and our conception of God.

This kind of discussion I believe is essential for Jewish theology and ethics in the twenty-first century. The lack of attention by Jewish theology to the modern scientific worldview has made Judaism seem, for many Jews, to be simplistic and irrelevant. As Arthur Green has observed, during the nineteenth century the study of Jewish philosophy was confined to rabbinical seminaries and the study of Kabbalah was discredited as being outside of mainstream Judaism. Nonetheless, most Jews' contact with Jewish theology, even in the liberal denominations, came through the prayer book (whether traditional or revised), which had retained many of the Rabbinic ideas about God, revelation, and redemption, including the nexus of sin and punishment. It was therefore not surprising that many Western Jews, now trained in the new scientific worldview, thought of Judaism as childish and unsophisticated. Judaism no longer spoke to the world they lived in, and this was one of the factors that contributed to Western Jewry becoming highly secularized.[45] This situation is still often the case today. Most modern Jewish theological writing does not address the critical challenges that modern science poses for theology, and many traditional sources are used uncritically without consideration of the worldviews that produced them.

For example, it has been my experience that many of the authors of Jewish environmental writing continue to utilize biblical and Rabbinic sources uncritically; even when the writers are affiliated with Conservative, Reconstructionist, or Reform movements they feel a need to cite these sources in order to sound Jewishly authentic. This attitude to tradition was criticized by Gordon Tucker when he confronted the Conservative Movement's responses to the status of gays and lesbians in Judaism. Tucker asserted that Conservative Judaism must be true to its own theology, in which "the text of the Torah is not necessarily God's word, and thus not an infallible expression of God's will."[46] Jewish environmental theology (and by extension the rest of modern Jewish theology) must also be true to a non-fundamentalist perspective on revelation along with the implications of the modern sciences of biology, ecology, evolution, and cosmology in order to create an eco-theology that will engage the depth of the modern environmental crisis.[47] In my own experience, the work of Catholic theologian and environmental visionary Thomas Berry opened my eyes to the possibility of a new Jewish eco-theology inspired and informed by modern cosmology and ecology.[48]

Given what we know now about the origin of the universe (as theoretical as some of that knowledge is), contemporary Jewish creation theology must be formulated within the perspective of modern science. Hans Jonas, Norbert Samuelson, and to a lesser extent Arthur Green, are examples of those who have attempted to do that and there a few others who have taken the same path.[49] I too have been thinking for many years about John Wheeler's Participatory Anthropic Principle and its implications for Jewish creation theology, and I hope to continue to do so for many more.[50] I do agree with Samuelson's key conviction that contemporary Judaism requires science in order to reconstitute itself.

The relationship between science and religion, which has produced rich and sophisticated Protestant and Catholic theologies that are integral parts of seminary curricula have been virtually absent from Jewish seminary learning, where Jewish theology, ethical theory, and philosophy are usually given a backseat to the study of Bible and Rabbinic sources.

I was fortunate that during an undergraduate course on Maimonides, the teacher introduced me to the work of the historian of science Thomas Kuhn, where I learned about how shifting worldviews developed from the "paradigm shifts" in the history of science. While at the Jewish Theological Seminary, I was encouraged by two great teachers, Rabbi Seymour Siegel z"l and Rabbi Neil Gillman, to pursue interests in bioethics and modern cosmology, and my first published essays grew out of my work with them. Since then I met and studied with many scientists and Christian theologians who motivated me to consider these issues from a Jewish perspective. This is why I believe that the writing of many scientists and Christian theologians who have been actively involved in the dialogue of science and religion can inform Jewish theology. Many of the issues they consider are our issues: divine providence, evil and suffering, free will, the doctrine of creation, etc. They have elected to engage modern science while most Jewish theology assumes that science and religion are either in conflict (agreed to by both fundamentalists and atheistic materialist proponents) or reside in two separate realms of truth, or two "non-overlapping magisteria" (as Steven Jay Gould put it) and "never the twain shall meet." The separation between science and religion is also affirmed by existentialist philosophy, which has shaped much of Jewish theology in the twentieth century. These approaches to the relationship between science and religion are the ones that most people encounter in the media, even though there is a long and sophisticated literature on the historical and theological models of this encounter that shows that a much deeper paradigm is possible, as documented by the work of Ian Barbour, John Hedley Brooke, and Philip Clayton among others.[51] I have also found that is a real lack of theological courage in many of my colleagues to face the really difficult questions that the modern world presents.

It can be asked whether the average synagogue member would really care about or understand the scientific and philosophic perspectives discussed in this article. Since most Jews today have at least a college if not graduate education, I believe that they can absorb and learn from many of these issues. For example last year I gave a sermon for the *Yizkor* service on the last day of Passover. I used that occasion to deal with my own beliefs in the afterlife and how I had theological problems with the traditional concepts of the soul and resurrection. These problems stem from the conflict between the traditional Jewish eschatology that sees the eventual negation of death with the ecological/biological necessity for death in the natural world.[52] While admitting that I could not be sure what would happen to me after my own death, I used Hans Jonas's thought to assert that I did believe that at a minimum everything and everyone in the universe would be remembered in the mind of God long after we would be forgotten in the land of the living. I said how this gave my life some ultimate meaning and that was good enough for me. Many people told me that it was the best *Yizkor* sermon that they ever had heard and how much it appealed to their own spiritual positions.

I believe that if rabbis, theologians, and scholars of modern Jewish thought would more deeply engage in this discussion their input would be welcomed by Christian theologians and they would be taken more seriously by the rest of the Jewish world. But they must learn the science, and given the general lack of science knowledge in the general public (especially in environmental issues) they would become part of an important educational project.

Jews today, like many other people, are searching for meaning in a world where shallow ideas and political bombast predominates. The discourse has often been dominated by atheistic scientists who have tried to remove any sense of purpose or meaning to the natural world. But the need for meaning continues and the relationship between mind, matter, the universe, and God should be a central issue for Judaism in the twenty-first century. I was attracted to Hans Jonas because he faced these issues honestly and bravely; Jewishly centered but not afraid to deal directly with the challenges of science. Norbert Samuelson has done the same and we need to continue to take up his challenges.

Notes

1. Stephen Jay Gould, *Wonderful Life: The Burgess Shale and the Nature of History* (New York: W.W. Norton & Co., 1989), 45.

2. Stephen Jay Gould, *The Flamingo's Smile* (New York: W. W. Norton and Company, 1985), 431. See also Wim Kayzer, *"A Glorious Accident," Understanding Our Place in the Cosmic Puzzle* (New York: W.H. Freedman & Co., 1985), 86–87.
3. Steven Weinberg, *The First Three Minutes: A Modern View of the Origin of the Universe* (Glasgow: William Collins, 1977), 148.
4. Norbert M. Samuelson, "The Challenges of the Modern Sciences for Jewish Faith," *CCAR Journal* (Winter 2012): 16.
5. For a discussion of this issue from an environmental perspective see Lawrence Troster, "Created in the Image of God: Humanity and Divinity in an Age of Environmentalism," *Conservative Judaism* 44, no. 1 (Fall 1991): 14–24.
6. John F. Haught, *God after Darwin: A Theology of Evolution* (Boulder, CO: Westview Press, 2000), 57–59.
7. Ibid., 23–24.
8. Daniel C. Dennett, *Darwin's Dangerous Idea: Evolution and the Meaning of Life* (New York: Simon & Schuster, 1995); Richard Dawkins, *The Blind Watchmaker* (New York: W. W. Norton, 1986).
9. For a comprehensive study of Jonas's life, works, philosophy, and ethics consult Hava Tirosh-Samuelson and Christian Wiese, eds., *The Legacy of Hans Jonas: Judaism and the Phenomenon of Life* (Boston and Leiden: Brill Academic Publishers, 2008).
10. Hans Jonas, "Contemporary Problems in Ethics from a Jewish Perspective" in *Judaism and Environmental Ethics: A Reader*, ed. Martin Yaffe (Lanham, MD: Lexington Books, 2001), 250–63.
11. Jonas, "Contemporary Problems," 252.
12. Hans Jonas, *Mortality and Morality: A Search for the Good after Auschwitz*, edited and introduced by Lawrence Vogel (Evanston, IL: Northwestern University Press, 1996), 66–67.
13. Jonas, *Mortality and Morality*, 70–74, 88–92; see also Hans Jonas, *The Phenomenon of Life: Toward a Philosophical Biology*, 2nd ed. (Chicago: University of Chicago Press, 1982), 186.
14. See editor's introduction to Jonas, *Mortality and Morality*, 11.
15. Hans Jonas, *The Imperative of Responsibility: In Search of an Ethics for the Technological Age* (Chicago: University of Chicago Press, 1984), 8, 136–42.
16. Jonas, *Mortality and Morality*, 36.
17. Ibid., 165–97
18. Ibid., 167.
19. See Paul C. W. Davies, *The Fifth Miracle: The Search for Origin and the Meaning of Life* (New York: Simon and Schuster, 1999).
20. Here Jonas parts company with Whitehead. See *Mortality and Morality*, 211 n. 4. Jonas finds Whitehead to be "overbold" and

"not covered by any datum of our experience, which allows us to discover or suspect traces of subjectivity only in high-level formations of organisms." For a comparative analysis of Jonas and Whitehead see Sandra B. Lubarsky, "Jonas, Whitehead, and the Problem of Power," in Tirosh-Samuelson and Wiese, eds., *The Legacy of Hans Jonas*, 397–417.

21. Jonas, *Mortality and Morality*, 172.
22. Ibid. Unlike Jonas, John Haught, in *God After Darwin*, 168–84, believes in a kind of logos that existed in the universe even before the emergence of life. He accepts and follows Teilhard de Chardin and Whitehead, whom Jonas explicitly rejects. See Haught's Boyle lecture, "Darwin, Design and the Promise of Nature," available at http://www.stmarylebow.co.uk/docs/BoyleBooklet.pdf.
23. Ibid,173.
24. Ibid, 75–86.
25. Ibid., 175.
26. Ibid., 142.
27. Ibid.
28. Ibid, 189.
29. Ibid, 190.
30. Ibid, 191.
31. John D. Barrow and Frank J. Tipler, *The Anthropic Cosmological Principle* (Oxford: Clarendon Press, 1986), 16.
32. George Gale, "The Anthropic Principle," *Scientific American*, 245, no. 6 (December 1981): 154.
33. Barrow and Tipler, *The Anthropic Cosmological Principle*, 21.
34. Reported in Dietrick E. Thomsen, "A Knowing Universe Seeking to Be Known," *Science News* 123 (February 19, 1983): 124.
35. George Wald, "Life and Mind in the Universe," *International Journal of Quantum Chemistry* 26, Quantum Biology Symposium 11 (March 1984): 1–15. See also Paul Davies, *Cosmic Jackpot: Why Our Universe Is Just Right for Life* (Boston: Houghton Mifflin Company, 2007).
36. A list of some these factors can be found in George Greenstein, *The Symbiotic Universe: Life and Mind in the Cosmos* (New York: William Morrow & Co., 1988), 256–58.
37. Barrow and Tipler, *The Anthropic Cosmological Principle*, 22.
38. Davies, *Cosmic Jackpot*, 151–90.
39. Quoted in Paul Davies, *The Mind of God: The Scientific Basis for a Rational World* (New York: Simon and Schuster, 1993), 224.
40. Ibid.
41. Paul Davies, *Cosmic Jackpot*, 251–55.
42. George Wald, "Life and Mind," 12 (italics in original).

43. Thomsen, "A Knowing Universe." See also George Wald, "Life and Mind," 13.
44. *Sifre: A Tannaitic Commentary on the Book of Deuteronomy*, trans. Reuven Hammer (New Haven: Yale University Press, 1986), 359; Piska 346. See also Abraham Joshua Heschel, *Man Is Not Alone: A Philosophy of Religion* (New York: Octagon Books, 1972), 241–44.
45. Arthur Green, *Radical Judaism: Rethinking God and Tradition*, (New Haven: Yale University Press. 2010), 71.
46. Gordon Tucker, "*Derash ve-Kabel S'char* [Seek and Receive a Reward]: Halakhic and Metahalakhic Arguments Concerning Judaism and Homosexuality," http://www.rabbinicalassembly.org/sites/default/files/public/halakhah/teshuvot/20052010/tucker_homosexuality.pdf, 19.
47. I have attempted to write Jewish eco-theology with these issues in mind. See Lawrence Troster, "The Book of Black Fire: An Eco-Theology of Revelation," *Conservative Judaism* 62, nos.1–2 (Fall/Winter 2010–2011): 132–51.
48. Thomas Berry, *The Dream of the Earth* (San Francisco: Sierra Club Books, 1990 [1988]).
49. See the reference to Green above. For a review of some Jewish writing on creation see Lawrence Troster, "From Big Bang to Omega Point: Jewish Responses to Recent Theories in Modern Cosmology," *Conservative Judaism* 49, no. 4 (Summer 1997): 17–31.
50. Lawrence Troster, "The Love of God and the Anthropic Principle," *Conservative Judaism* 40, no. 2 (Winter 1987): 43–51.
51. See, for example, the work of Ian Barbour: *Religion and Science: Historical and Contemporary Issues* (San Francisco: HarperCollins, 1997); John Hedley Brooke, *Science and Religion: Some Historical Perspectives* (Cambridge: Cambridge University Press, 1991); Philip Clayton, *God and Contemporary Science* (Grand Rapids, MI: Eerdmans, 1997).
52. See my "The Promise of Creation: A Jewish Environmental Theology of Redemption," in "*'The Mountains Shall Drip Wine': Jews and the Environment*," *Studies in Jewish Civilization*, vol. 20, ed. Leonard J. Greenspoon et al. (Omaha: Creighton University Press, 2009), 183–98.

Judaism and Science: Selected Bibliography

A. Religion and Science

Alper, Matthew. *The God Part of the Brain*. Naperville, IL: Sourcebook, 2006.

Barbour, Ian. *Religion and Science*. San Francisco: Harper Collins Publishing, 1998.

Beauregard, Mario, and Denyse O'Leary. *The Spiritual Brain*. New York: Harper, 2007.

Boyd, Robert, and Peter Richerson. *The Origin and Evolution of Cultures*. Oxford: Oxford University Press, 2005.

Boyer, Pascal. *Religion Explained: The Evolutionary Origins of Religious Thought*. New York: Basic Books, 2001.

Brooke, John Hedley. *Science and Religion: Some Historical Perspectives*. Cambridge: Cambridge University Press, 1991.

Brooke, John, and Geoffrey Cantor. *Reconstructing Nature: The Engagement of Science and Religion*. New York and Oxford: Oxford University Press, 1998.

Clayton, Philip, ed. *The Oxford Handbook of Religion and Science*. Oxford: Oxford University Press, 2006.

_____. *The Problem of God in Modern Thought*. Grand Rapid, MI: Eerdmans, 2000.

_____. *God and Contemporary Science*. Grand Rapids, MI: Eerdmans, 1997.

Drees, Willem. *Religion, Science, and Naturalism*. Cambridge: Cambridge University Press, 1996.

Dunbar, R., C. Knight, and C. Power, eds. *The Evolution of Culture*. New Brunswick, NJ: Rutgers University Press, 1999.

Ferngren, Gary B. *Science and Religion: A Historical Introduction*. Baltimore: Johns Hopkins University Press, 2002.

Grassie, William. *The New Sciences of Religion: Exploring Spirituality from the Outside in and Bottom Up*. New York: Pelgrave Macmillan, 2010.

Harrison, N. *The Bible, Protestantism and the Rise of Natural Science*. Cambridge: Cambridge University Press, 1998.

Haught, John F. *Science and Religion: From Conflict to Conversation*. New York and Mahwah, NJ: Paulist Press, 1995.

Hefner, Philip. *The Human Factor: Evolution, Culture, and Religion*. Minneapolis: Fortress Press, 1993.

McClennon, J. *Wondrous Healing: Shamanism, Human Evolution and the Origin of Religion*. DeKalb, IL: Northern Illinois University Press, 2002.

Peter, Ted, ed. *Cosmos as Creation: Theology and Science in Consonance*. Nashville: Abingdon Press, 1989.

Polkinghorne, John C. *Belief in God in the Age of Science*. New Haven: Yale University Press, 1998.

_____. *Quantum Physics and Theology: An Unexpected Kinship*. New Haven: Yale University Press, 2007.

_____. *Quantum Theory: A Very Short Introduction*. Oxford: Oxford University Press, 2002.

Rolston, Holmes III. *Science and Religion: A Critical Survey*. Philadelphia and London: Templeton Foundation Press, 2006.

Ruse, Michael. *The Evolution Wars: A Guide to the Debates*. New Brunswick: Rutgers University Press, 2002.

Tattersall, Ian. *Becoming Human: Evolution and Human Uniqueness*. New York: Harcourt Brace, 1998.

Wade, Nicholas. *The Faith Instinct: How Religion Evolved and Why It Endures*. New York: Penguin, 2009.

_____. *Before the Dawn*. New York: Penguin, 2006.

Whitham, Larry. *Where Darwin Meets the Bible: Creationists and Evolutionists in America*. Oxford: Oxford University Press, 2002.

Wilson, David Sloan. *Darwin's Cathedral: Evolution, Religion, and the Nature of Society*. Chicago: University of Chicago Press, 2002.

B. Judaism and Science

Cantor, Geoffrey, and Marc Swetliz, eds. *Jewish Tradition and the Challenge of Darwinism*. Chicago: University of Chicago Press, 2006.

Cohen, Naomi W. "The Challenges of Darwinism and Biblical Criticism to American Judaism." *Modern Judaism* 4, no. 2 (1984): 121–58.

Dorff, Elliot N. *Matters of Life and Death: A Jewish Approach to Modern Medical Ethics*. Philadelphia: Jewish Publication Society, 1998.

Efron, John. *Defenders of the Race: Jewish Doctors and Race Science in fin-de-siecle Europe*. New Haven: Yale University Press, 1994.

_____. *Medicine and the German Jews: A History*. New Haven and London: Yale University Press, 2001.

Efron, Noah. *Judaism and Science: A Historical Introduction*. Westport, CT: Greenwood Press, 2007.

Fisch, Menachem. *Rational Rabbis: Science and Talmudic Literature*. Bloomington, IN: Indiana University Press, 1997.

Freudenthal, Gad (ed.). *Science in Medieval Jewish Communities*. Cambridge: Cambridge University Press, 2011.

Hart, Mitchel. *The Healthy Jew: The Symbiosis of Judaism and Modern Medicine*. Cambridge and New York: Cambridge University Press, 2007.

Harvey, Steven, ed. *The Medieval Hebrew Encyclopedias of Science and Philosophy*. Dordrecht, Boston, London: Kluwer, 2000.

Jonas, Hans. *The Phenomenon of Life: Toward a Philosophical Biology*. Chicago: Chicago University Press, 1982.

Langermann, Tzvi Y. *The Jews and the Sciences in the Middle Ages*. Aldershot: Ashgate/Variorum, 1999.

Plaut, Günther W. *Judaism and the Scientific Spirit*. New York: Union of American Hebrew Congregations, 1962.

Ruderman, David B. *Kabbalah, Magic and Science: The Cultural Universe of a Sixteenth-Century Jewish Physician*. Cambridge, MA: Harvard University Press, 1988.

_____. *Jewish Thought and Scientific Discovery in Early Modern Europe*. New Haven: Yale University Press, 1995.

Samuelson, Norbert M. *Judaism and the Doctrine of Creation*. Cambridge: Cambridge University Press, 1994.

_____. *Revelation and the God of Israel*. Cambridge: Cambridge University Press, 2002.

_____. *Jewish Faith* and *Modern Science*. Lanham, MD: Rowman and Littlefield, 2009.

Swetlitz, Marc. "Responses of American Reform Rabbis to Evolutionary Theory, 1864–1888." In *Interaction of Scientific and Jewish Cultures in Modern Times*, edited by Yakov Rabkin and Ira Robinson, 103–25. Lewiston, NY: Mellen, 1995.

_____. "American Jewish Responses to Darwin and Evolutionary Theory, 1860–1890." In *Disseminating Darwinism: The Role of Place, Race, Religion and Gender*, edited by Ronald L. Numbers and John Stenhouse, 209–46. Cambridge: Cambridge University Press, 1999.

_____. "Responses to Evolution by Reform, Conservative and Reconstructionist Rabbis in Twentieth-Century America." In *Jewish Tradition and the Challenge of Darwinism*, edited by Geoffrey Cantor and Marc Swetlitz, 47–70. Chicago: Chicago University Press, 2006.

Tirosh-Samuelson, Hava, and Christian Wiese, eds. *Judaism and the Phenomenon of Life: The Legacy of Hans Jonas*. Boston and Leiden: Brill Academic Publishers, 2008.

Troster, Lawrence. "Love of God and the Anthropic Principle." *Conservative Judaism* 40, no.2 (1987/1988): 43–51

_____. "From Big Bang to Omega Point: Jewish Response to Recent Theories to Modern Cosmology." *Conservative Judaism* 49, no. 4 (1997): 17–31.

Response to the Spring 2011 Symposium

The discussion regarding the perilous condition of Reform Judaism (*CCAR Journal*, Spring 2011) prompted me to reread Dr. Alvin J. Reines's z"l article, "Crisis, Polydoxy, and Survival," as found at www.polydoxinstitute.org under "Jewish Survival." In 1978, he identified the state of American Jewry to be in crisis, "a turning point for better or worse," and advised the adoption of a crisis mentality, a "crisis consciousness...so that the urgency of our situation penetrates the deepest recesses of our minds and hearts."

Lance Sussman reflected this point of view in his critique of the CCAR for placing "tens of thousands of potential Reform Jews 'outside the camp.'" He echoed Reines's emphasis on personal autonomy when concluding how that very autonomy was limited "by promulgating a religiously more traditional second Pittsburgh Platform."

During a long academic career at the College, Reines labored on the philosophic and theological foundation necessary to clearly define the phenomenon of Reform Judaism. He focused our attention on the concept of personal religious authority and produced a vision of Reform Judaism as a religion of freedom **from** authoritarian theistic religion. It is no wonder that he constantly worried about his students' success in the field when the major institutions of Reform, designed to support them in caring for the needs of liberal Jews, continued to promote a vision of Reform that he coined "traditionoid." With this, I believe he meant to provoke the movement's leadership to awaken to the reality that their vision was not coherent with the existential experience of Reform's constituency.

Reines argued for the immediate and requisite implementation of a strategy to provide the Reform Jew with a concept of religion that could be embraced as authentic. And in so doing, he offered us a definition of Reform Judaism unique among the extant Judaisms due to its consistency with science and the emerging consciousness. Polydox Reform Judaism acknowledges open theological opportunities for creative responses to finitude with a Covenant of

Freedom that protects personal religious authority in mutual support, respect, and understanding among co-religionists.

Dr. Reines's legacy endures as an inheritance and a challenge. His extensive writings have been carefully catalogued in the Web site of the Polydox Institute. With a crisis consciousness we can hopefully move forward for the good of all.

MICHAEL P. PERELMUTER (C75) is president of Jewish Freedom Covenant, former Hillel director at California Institute of Technology and Occidental College, and founding educator of the Catholic-Jewish Educational Enrichment Program.

Responses to the Summer 2011 Issue

Modern vs. Postmodern Jewish Thought: A Hidden Theme of *CCAR Journal*, Summer 2011

When it is not devoted to a single theme, the CCAR *Journal* is generally an amalgam of papers on a variety of topics. I was intrigued, however, to find a hidden theme working its way through the Summer 2011 issue.

The subject was introduced in the first article ("An Outsider's Look at *Mishkan T'filah*"). Marc Brettler pulls together some personal observations regarding the content of the Reform Jewish prayer book, particularly in the area of its continuity and discontinuity with a traditional siddur. He notes especially a current of ambivalence running through prayers, mostly but not exclusively in their English rendering. He means no criticism in this observation, but nonetheless points to an important development in Reform Jewish thought.

Although certainly recognized by many readers of this paper, I think it is valuable to note that a siddur has purposes that go beyond the organization of worship. The siddur is the most heavily used text in Jewish life, and thus, far more than any other scholarly or authoritative work, serves as a formal articulation of Jewish theology. What should a Jew believe about God's relationship to Israel, humankind, the natural world, and the world-to-come is expressed in the prayers and readings of the siddur.

Nineteenth-century prayer book reform both greatly reduced the length of worship services and made definitive changes in theology. The idea of a personal God Who also had an active role in nature was substantially eliminated. Specific images of a messianic future, including the advent of a Davidic messiah, the ingathering of the exiles, restoration of the Temple service, and resurrection of the dead, disappeared as well. It would certainly be incorrect, however, to assert that Reform Jewish thought was simply not Orthodox. Rather, it was a theology built around a wholly transcendent deity whose firm directing of history was progressively (and irresistibly) moving toward a universal messianic ideal.

There have always been discordant elements in the prayer book. In the 1940 edition of the *Union Prayer Book*, the phrase *mikol haamim*, denoting Israel being chosen by God from among the world's peoples, has been removed from the Shabbat eve *Kiddush* (p. 93), but is retained in the blessing over the reading of Torah (pp. 145–46). The subsequent *Gates of Prayer* (1976) articulates a somewhat wider range of theological assertions, but nevertheless remains true to the main elements of classic Reform. God remains distant and nonpersonal. Of particular note, the weekday *Amidah* in the "traditional" service (pp. 37–47) makes a point of eliding the so-called nineteenth benediction that calls upon God to condemn the wicked.

As Dr. Brettler aptly notes, *Mishkan T'filah* departs from the theological boundaries of classic Reform Judaism, but by no means wholeheartedly. Both the Hebrew and English rendering of prayers open the worshiper to the concept of a personal God Who might intervene on behalf of the sick, of a Jewish return to Zion, and of the possibility of surviving one's death. Yet, all of these apparent reversions to traditional Jewish thought are presented equivocally. As a self-professed outsider, Dr. Brettler tactfully restrains from drawing any conclusion from this ambivalence. I, however, would note that *Mishkan T'filah* is a formal concession that Reform Jews and Judaism no longer adheres to any consensus of what characterizes its theological assumptions.

The absence of consensus is then exemplified with two submissions that are placed near the end of the issue. Seymour Prystowsky's "It Is Time to Change Our View Regarding Miracles, Rituals, and Prayers" is separated only by a review essay from the symposium organized by Laurence Edwards on Michael Fishbane's *Sacred Attunement*. (I need to state at the outset that I have not yet had the opportunity to read Fishbane's monograph. My comments here rely on the essays solicited by Rabbi Edwards.) The fault line that runs between Rabbi Prystowsky and Prof. Fishbane, at least as filtered through the insights of the essayists, is precisely, in my opinion, that which creates ambivalence in *Mishkan T'filah*. The line, however, is not between classic Reform and tradition, but rather between modern and postmodern.

Philosophy as epistemology—the problem of how we know what we know—has always consisted of two components: the input of one's senses and the application of reason. The first component has never been particularly controversial, although the reliability of certain technical extenders of our sense perceptions has been challenged through the ages. The second part has been more problematic. What makes reason reliable? The ancient Greeks posited that it was part of the metaphysical realm of the natural world. Medieval philosophers placed reason in the mind and will of God. Modernity sought it in the fundamental structure of the human mind.

Sim Prystowsky is a modernist. In his confidence that the human mind is the source of a rational ordering of the knowable world, he is distressed by any suggestion of active divine intervention as a form of medievalism, or more fashionably put, magical thinking. Although modernity has mounted a sustained challenge on God's existence, Prystowsky, particularly in reference to Heschel's radical amazement, remains a pious believer. The issue for him is not whether one can attest to the reality of God, but rather what is the God one believes in? Prystowsky concludes that it is the Sovereign Ruler beyond Time and Space, the object of our wonder and blessing, but otherwise incapable of having any direct impact on our lives.

Michael Fishbane demurs. The contours of his approach are indicated especially in the first two essays that comment on his book, those of Kenneth Seeskin and Elliot R. Wolfson. Both scholars put Fishbane's philosophy in direct confrontation with Plato. One is reminded of the quip of the British philosopher-mathematician, Alfred Whitehead, to the effect that all of Western philosophy can be viewed as footnotes on Plato. It was, after all, the seminal Greek thinker who created the formula that knowing is perception plus reason in the first place. The question Prof. Fishbane poses is: Is this formula, however enduring, really the case?

The problem with Platonism, and all its iterations through the centuries, is that reason, in whatever way it is construed, must be *assumed* to be reliable. What is there outside the rules of logic that can show that logic is logically true? Metaphysical Nature, Universal Mind, God; they are all variations on the effort to establish an objective foundation upon which the propositions of unchallenged Truth can be built.

A fateful crossroad has been met. Without an unshakable foundation no Truth can be reliably asserted. Yet, if there is an unshakable foundation, how can one talk meaningfully of a God Who intervenes in our personal lives? Further, without Truth, how can any sense of order or community be maintained outside the brute exertion of force?

For centuries, the solution to these fundamental questions was not to think much about them. Believers simply accepted logical contradictions, such as God's simultaneous immanence and transcendence. Order was maintained by subtle forms of coercion, often backed up by the sword when appeals to tradition and ecclesiastic authority failed. To this day, magical thinking is often greatly preferred to any serious examination of reality.

To their credit, neither Rabbi Prystowsky nor Prof. Fishbane chose to evade these questions. Prystowsky upholds the Platonic standard in its modern form. Doing so, however, leaves him and us with an unbridgeably distant God. Even Heschel's radical amazement or Buber's Thou cannot be much more than a mental disposition: not the Presence of the Divine, but only the sense that there is a Presence lurking at the edge of knowable existence. God is ultimately an idea. The Christian theologian, Paul Tillich, commented that one should not say "only an idea," but "nothing less than idea." Nevertheless, as my teacher Eugene Borowitz put it, it is hard to warm up to an idea.

Is this all there is? The question can be asked from two standpoints: Is there a valid approach to the evaluation of truth that is not essentially Platonic? Does Jewish thought offer an alternative? Michael Fishbane wishes to answer both of them in the affirmative. His contribution places him among a growing group of scholars who have picked up this challenge. The late French-Jewish philosopher Emmanuel Levinas was among the first to struggle within himself over the competing strands of the "Hebrew" and the "Greek." See, for example, his lecture titled "The Temptation of Temptation" in *Nine Talmudic Readings* (Indiana University Press, 1990). Eugene Borowitz offered one of the first systematic efforts at describing a postmodern approach to Jewish thought in *Renewing the Covenant* (JPS, 1991). Bradley Shavit Artson contributed a valuable paper on just this point, "Life of the World: Beyond Mind/Body Dualism to Embodied Emergence," in volume 79 of the *Hebrew Union College Annual*, which was issued only a few months before the Summer 2011 issue of the *CCAR Journal*.

Something is gained, and something lost. Postmodern thought opens out the opportunity for a richer encounter with the Divine. It creates the possibility of worship being more than hymns and prayers sent out into the void. These longings, resisted for over a century in Reform worship, are tentatively brought back into the liturgy. Yet, can we keep our equilibrium and not tip over into otherworldliness and magical thinking? Can we preserve our confidence in what we hold to be true, what we cherish as ideals? Rabbi Prystowsky is doubtful. Prof. Fishbane holds out hope. And *Mishkan T'filah*, we can see, has hedged its bets.

PAUL GOLOMB (NY75) is the rabbi of Congregation Achim Yisrael, the Vassar Temple, in Poughkeepsie, New York.

Response to *Revisiting the Jewish Law on Intermarriage: A New Response to Today's Challenge*

Katherine A. Abend's article (Summer 2011, "Revisiting the Jewish Law on Intermarriage: A New Response to Today's Challenge") is fascinating. A central point of her article is "keeping Jews and their children connected to Judaism." She points out that currently "it is the Jewish community's *reaction* to intermarriage that is largely responsible for the tendency of the Jewish partners and their children to disengage from Jewish life" (p. 79, emphasis in original). She notes that with rare exceptions the Jewish person and the intended partner/spouse feel rejected and rebuffed when the question of intermarriage arises. Though there are success stories with Jewish Outreach, on the whole statistically, increasingly people are being lost to Jewish life because presently there is no mechanism halachically to integrate *gerei toshavim* into Jewish life, and to recognize children of such a union as Jews.

Abend does a fine job presenting her case for reinstituting the category of *ger toshav*, in this case understood as the spouse/partner of someone who is Jewish, and who will actively support the concept of a Jewish home and the rearing of their children as Jews. She sets out her arguments clearly and provides a brief overview for each section.

In its own way, this is a marvelously controversial idea. I believe that Abend makes a good case for both a more Orthodox and a more progressive approach: that is, the more Orthodox would argue that the older the sources (i.e., closer to Sinai) the more important the authority, whereas a more liberal view sees an ongoing revelation. Abend deals with this in her endnotes 126ff.

Abend cites both Jewish and secular legal sources for the acceptance of an evolved halachah that would allow for the reintroduction of the category *ger toshav*. She references Rabbi Ishmael's rules of interpretation, and cleverly supports this with arguments based on the teaching of Rabbi Meir Leibush ben Yechiel Michal (the Malbim, see endnote 143). While I cannot evaluate the secular sources, her Jewish sources, if I understand her correctly, make a case for an updated *ger toshav* that could, in principle, be acceptable to the Orthodox, and for the reasons she lists, be acceptable for the more liberal wing of Judaism. The process would be "contingent on certain commitments by the couple that would help achieve the goal of keeping the Jewish partner and the couple's children connected to Judaism. The non-Jew could agree to take a course about Judaism and then formally commit to raise his or her children as Jews." For those who only accept matrilineal descent, the non-Jewish woman "might be asked to agree that any resulting children will be converted to Judaism" (p. 79).

Abend reviews some of the traditions regarding the *ger toshav* and notes that since the Jubilee year no longer exists as a functioning reality, "it is no longer possible to become a formal *ger toshav*. However, many people, especially intermarried Jews, could make an informal claim to this status" (p. 83). She argues convincingly that "a practical approach calls for granting the broader rules of acceptance to modern *gerei toshavim* who swear to live by the Noahide laws before a *beit din*" (p. 84).

While some may quibble over specific sources that Abend lists in her detailed endnotes, this is an article that will be read primarily by liberal rabbis and those sympathetic to that position. I would hope that the broad concepts she suggests will provide the basis for serious discussion throughout the Jewish community, for our own sake, and for the sake of the generations to come.

DAVID J. ZUCKER, Ph.D. (C70) is retired rabbi/chaplain and director of Chaplaincy Care at Shalom Cares, Aurora, Colorado, www.davidjzucker.org.

Response to *Alternate Views for Tishah B'Av*

I enjoyed Allen Maller's article in the Summer 2011 issue titled "Alternate Views for Tishah B'Av." He makes an intriguing suggestion in his conclusion, "Tishah B'Av should become a day devoted to understanding Reform Judaism's view of Judaism" (p. 48).

Reform Judaism has redefined holidays twice. Shavuot and Yom HaAtzma-ut. Have we been successful?

Shavuot has become reinvented as confirmation and it works more or less okay. The major parallel is the receiving of Torah at Sinai with the receiving of Torah as a graduate from religious school. And the special food for the holiday, dairy, has been fully incorporated. I can say to any Jew (who knows what Shavuot is) that I celebrated Shavuot and he or she knows more or less that I commemorated receiving Torah and I ate some blintzes, cheesecake, or ice cream!

The failure has been Yom HaAtzma-ut. At the 1988 convention of the CCAR, the Reform Jewish rabbinate passed a resolution elevating the status of Yom HaAtzma-ut to *chag*.[1] An article published in the *CCAR Journal* pointed out that unlike all other Jewish holidays, there is no similarity in how it is celebrated in Israel versus how it is celebrated in the Diaspora:

> Yom HaAtzma-ut in Israel = barbecue and picnics.
> Yom HaAtzma-ut in the United States = falafel and craft shows.[2]

And the article concludes, "The Reform movement has not developed a set of home/community celebrations that will lead to a common experience with our Israeli counterparts and Jews over the entire world."[3]

I think the fate of Tishah B'Av was sealed in the Reform World when the Holocaust received its own commemoration rather than being included in the concept that Tishah B'Av commemorates Jewish tragedies. In my twenty-eight years in the rabbinate, I have never led or participated in a Tishah B'Av service or event.

In quoting from Graetz on the founders of Reform Judaism, specifically Rabbi Holdheim, Graetz said, "Since Paul of Tarsus, Judaism has not known such an enemy in its midst, who shook the whole edifice to its foundation."[4] I suspect the Orthodox Community would be amused if we did select Tishah B'Av as a day devoted to understanding Reform Judaism's view of Judaism. Given the Graetz quotation, they might well regard such a celebration of Tishah B'Av as a tragedy consistent with both their understanding of Reform Judaism and Tishah B'Av.

Notes

1. Elliot Stevens, ed., *CCAR Yearbook*, vol. 98 (New York: CCAR, 1989) , 151.
2. J. Segal, "*Arbah Regalim*? The Impediments to Yom Haatzmaut as a *Chag*," *CCAR Journal* (Spring/Summer 2002): 69.
3. Ibid., 70.
4. H. Graetz, *History of the Jews*, vol. 5 (Philadelphia: JPS, 1895), 680.

JOSHUA SEGAL (C83) is the rabbi of Congregation Betenu, Amherst, New Hampshire. He is best known for his work on Jewish cemeteries; see http://CemeteryJewish.com.

Book Reviews

Poetry Feeds the Jewish Soul: Introducing Four Reviews

Adam D. Fisher, Poetry Editor

Voices Within the Ark, a collection of poems of Jewish interest from dozens and dozens of modern Jewish poets, was published in 1980. Since then, one would have hoped to find a great deal of poetry in Jewish periodicals as well as many books of poetry published by Jewish publishers. Unfortunately that has not happened. Poetry has either been ignored or is an also-ran in most of the Jewish world as it is has been in the general culture. I suspect that poetry has been looked upon as opaque, requiring both a PhD and infinite patience to unravel its meaning.

And yet, whereas twenty years ago it was hard to find a poetry reading on Long Island, where I live, today a person can attend several readings every night of the week. Why? First, there is a considerable amount of poetry being written that is accessible to the average reader. Second, poetry speaks to our inner experience. It attempts to relate that experience as freshly as possible and invites the reader/listener to enter that experience.

Poetry also makes an important contribution to our spiritual lives by inviting us to experience the spiritual moment, through the yearning and struggles of the poet. This is very different from theology, which is rational and left-brain. Theology attempts to explicate religious belief and fit it into a philosophical frame. That of course is valuable, but it is only half of the spiritual search. The other half is actually finding a way to the religious experience itself. For example, while Heschel can tell us that wonder is a gateway to God, poetry can help us experience that awe and wonder. Science can describe how fog forms, but Sandburg tells us how we can experience fog when he says that it comes in "on little cat feet."

It is a source of pride that the *CCAR Journal* has published poetry and reviewed books of poetry for many, many years. In this issue the work of four contemporary poets is reviewed. Of course their work ranges over many aspects of the Jewish experience, but each of them, to one degree or another, addresses our spiritual yearning.

Ruthie Gelfarb speaks of Merle Feld as a poet and teacher, and as "a midwife of spiritual writing." Jim Rosenberg tells us that Yehoshua November writes of the fragility of our relationship with God, which to me implies a need for constant renewal and *t'shuvah,* in the sense of returning to a relationship. I see a yearning for God when Jim Rosenberg pleads, "if only I could hear the echo/Of Your cry of absence/Calling me." And Rachel Barenblat reminds us that "God hides in plain sight/veiled by the textures of creation."

It is clear that the poetry in these books has much to contribute to our Jewish spiritual journey. Each of these books makes a real contribution to helping us understand and deepen our Jewish lives.

Finding Words
by Merle Feld
(New York: URJ Press, 2011), 86 pp.

I confess. I am a huge fan of poet Merle Feld. Her earlier poem "We All Stood Together" expressed my and many women's critique and sadness at being overlooked in our people's central narratives, such as the Revelation at Sinai. Feld also helped me to find words, my words. And she has done the same for and with many rabbinical students. While studying for the rabbinate, I participated in the inaugural group of the Rabbinic Writing Institute, of which Feld is the founding director. Biweekly, Feld guided and prompted me so that I could develop and explore my inner life and thus serve more effectively as a spiritual leader. In other words, Merle Feld has been an active midwife of spiritual writing.

After much anticipation, *Finding Words,* a collection of fifty-seven Feld poems, has been published by the URJ Press. *Finding Words* is written with great sensitivity, a caring heart, recognizable human frailty, and at times painful honesty. The book is divided into four parts: "What's Known and What Needs to Be Studied," "Leah's House & After," "Practice," and "Recognizing a Moment of Happiness." The first section's twelve poems touch on lessons learned through experience, the passage of time, and perspective. In the poem "Burning," the poet recognizes that now, at age fifty-seven, she could be a good mother, and she can now "see clearly/through the rear view mirror/the daily anger that burned, burned." Such honest revelations prompt one in early stages of life to consider what we will regret in the years to come about our present attitudes and actions.

In "Leah's House & After," seventeen poems explore relationship dynamics and single moments—the silences between people, the pain of holding a deceased brother's sweater, the awkwardness of friendships that wither. In "Prolonging Silence" Feld notes, "The one who prolongs the silence/is the one with the power,/ and as the silence expands/and extends, the power/expands and extends." Feld shares that she enjoys it. With refreshingly atypical honesty, Feld expresses and describes her shadow side and baser qualities.

In the last part, "Recognizing Moments of Happiness," Feld revisits her youth, her family, and her relationships. At last, she recognizes and describes the joy and the sacredness of her mundane everyday life. Really, it is all our lives—family birthday rituals, visiting aunts, and nine-ounce Nestlé bars. In the book's final poem, "Recognizing a Moment of Happiness," Feld writes of "the happiness shining through/special moments and moments ordinary./Only now do I finally understand/that all along the choice was mine,/even on terrible days remain a prisoner of terror,/or dare to celebrate the sunlight on the grass." These choices are ours to make, and clearly our Jewish tradition with its recommendation of one hundred *b'rachot* per day is striving to wake us up to the miracle of the mundane.

As a rabbi, I frequently seek out poems that I can use in services; poems that in their extreme specificity touch on the universal. *Finding Words* offers the opportunity to share individual poems about death, broken relationships, and the experience of Jewish holidays. With the collection, one can purchase a study guide written by Susan Ain. *Finding Words*, read and studied in conjunction with the study guide, would be an excellent choice for a synagogue book group. Congregants could present groups of poems and discuss the thematic sections of the guide (e.g., "Rituals, Secular and Holy"). Or, *Finding Words* and the study guide can be used as a basis of a congregational spiritual writing group. In this way, each of us can have the chance to find words, our words.

RABBI RUTHIE GELFARB (NY07) focuses her rabbinate on *tikkun olam* and *tikkun atzmi.*

God's Optimism
by Yehoshua November
(Charlotte, NC: Main Street Rag, 2010), 65 pp.

Yehoshua November, a Chabad Chasid in his early thirties, lives with his wife and four children in Morristown, New Jersey. He teaches composition and creative writing to secular students at Rutgers University, and on weekday evenings he travels to Flatbush in Brooklyn to teach mostly observant Jewish students at Touro's Lander College.

November's recently published first volume of poetry, *God's Optimism*, pulses with the creative tension between the secular and the observant worlds. Thus, November begins his wryly ironic "A Jewish Poet" with the observation that "It is hard to be a Jewish poet./You cannot say things about God/that will offend the disbelievers." While November seems to be at home in his Chabad community, his poems are suffused with allusions to a secular culture in which he appears to be equally at home. In "Night," for example, the reader—the listener—meets the renowned German writer "Goethe/scrubbing his undergarments in the sink." In another poem November celebrates Harpo Marx, "the most lighthearted of five brothers," the "master of improvisation,/with your baggy travel coat/of useless goods/and your wild curly blond wig."

To my way of thinking, the autobiographical "Billboards" is one of the strongest and most imaginative of the forty-six offerings in the collection. November is driving home on a weeknight, having taught one of his college classes, and is "merging onto the ramp/beneath the nearly naked supermodel/advertising a watch." Other billboards lead to a meditation on the complexity of marriage:

But how, to begin with,
do two people never related by blood
unpack everything they have separately collected
into shared rooms?

The very next line reflects upon the complexities of divorce:

And then, with what strength do they repack
and empty the rooms they have filled?

The poem comes full circle when November hears "over the radio/that the model has just separated from her third husband."

> But in the billboard,
> she continues to look out at the world
> with her careless smile,
> as cars drift into the darkness of the interstate.

"Billboards" is one of many poems in *God's Optimism* that touches on the subject of divorce. I suspect that for November the threat of divorce, in addition to lurking in some dark corner of even the healthiest of marriages, is a metaphor for the ever-present threat of a disruption of his up-close and personal relationship with God. Indeed, some of November's most poignant poems—poems filled with angst and longing—sound a sense of resignation, a sense that there can be no certainty in any relationship—whether between one person and another or between an individual and God.

In many ways *God's Optimism* is a youthful book; the poems speak a wistful gentleness, an absence of guile. At times, the poems sound like prayers, but prayers that permit, even encourage a necessary doubt. Perhaps, what makes November's poems seem so fresh, so pure, is their lack of the bitterness, the hurt, the anger that come from being subject to the slings and arrows year after year, decade after decade. In his title poem, for example, the poet links his own youthful optimism with the optimism of God Himself:

> [This world] remains
> only as long as God pushes it into existence.
>
> Think of the optimism of God, then,
> how, every second, He recreates our lives.

Only time will tell how November weathers his transition from songs of innocence to songs of experience.

All the poems in November's first collection are written in free verse; there is not a single sonnet, villanelle, or pantoum, not a single example of terza rima or blank verse form, not a single rhymed couplet. Moreover, November employs a limited palette in choosing his words, so that at times the music of his lines seems rather flat. This is not to deny that he is capable of creating gorgeous images—as in "The Meditation of Travel," which concludes by comparing a traveler's memories of "home" to "carrying a cello/ through a winter night,/the dark wood rotting/in the snow." I would hope that in his next volume November, who clearly has the heart of a poet, will devote more attention to broadening the range of his poetic expression.

In her glowing introduction to *God's Optimism*, Liz Rosenberg, one of November's professors during his undergraduate years at SUNY Binghamton, writes that "I am in the presence of a young master—as honest and witty as Kafka, as visionary as Doestoevski, but with a voice and presence all his own." From my perspective, Rosenberg's accolades, however well intended, do not help either this poet or his readers. To compare this young poet to such giants of world literature places an unfair and unnecessary burden upon him. It is enough that Yehoshua November continues to mature in his art, so that he will one day fulfill the considerable promise of his debut collection.

JAMES B. ROSENBERG (NY71) is rabbi emeritus at Temple Habonim in Barrington, Rhode Island. He was poetry editor of the *CCAR Journal* from 1997–2006.

70 Faces: Torah Poems
by Rachel Barenblat
(Montreal: Phoenicia Publishing, 2011), 81 pp.

Rachel Barenblat, a rabbi living in Western Massachusetts, has given us a real gift—a poem for each *sidrah*. They are beautifully written; accessible; and perfect for reading on a Shabbat afternoon or sharing with a community in a sermon, *d'var Torah*, introduction to a Torah reading, or in a study group.

There are so many good poems with so many important insights it is hard to know where to start. Take "First Step" (*Lech L'cha*) in which she understands the command to Avraham to be addressed not only to him, but a mission that all of us undertake. "It's not going to be easy./All of our roadmaps are wrong . . . /This right here is holy ground . . . /listen to the voice from on high/and deep within, the one that says//I'm calling you to a place/which I will show you//and take the first small step/into the surprising sun." Does she mean that our roadmap, Torah, doesn't work but that we should listen to the voice deep within us? Probably not. I think she means that the roadmaps provided by society are all wrong and that we should attend to our own spiritual truth and let it guide us.

Later, in "Travelogue" (*D'varim*), when Moses addresses the people from the other side of the Jordan, Barenblat has Moses say, ". . . but you were afraid of the prospect/of entering somewhere new, maybe/being changed by the experience?" And at the end of the poem Moses says, "After a journey like this one/no one is exactly the same/as on the day of departure/from that other home so far away." The unknown is frightening for many—one of the things most frightening is not only what might happen but how we might change.

She gives us ten poems for the *Akeidah*. In the fourth she humanizes Avraham: "We'd always had a good relationship,/God and I,/Avraham says, leaning back/and puffing on his pipe." And in a wonderful image of closeness to God she says, "God was right there//whispering in my ear/as near to me as the thrumming/of blood in my veins,/as the hopes in my heart." She soon has Avraham tell us that, "I'd like to say/I knew what I was doing/I knew Yitzchak would never/meet my eyes again."

After Jacob and Esau embrace, Jacob ignores Esau's invitation for them to travel together. In "Encounter" (*Vayishlach*), Barenblat comments, "And again the possibility/of inhabiting a different kind of story/vanished into the unforgiving air." Talk about missed opportunities due to fear! And in "Unrecognizable" (*Mikeitz*), Joseph sees his brothers and turns away to weep, "not ready/to show my true face//or how I had yearned/for the relationship we still/didn't know how to have." In both these poems, she uncovers the truth of our own lives as we struggle with broken relationships.

Rabbi Barenblat writes a wonderful midrash on *Sh'mini* where it tells us to break any earthen vessel into which something unclean falls. In "Vessel," she writes, "The heart is an earthen vessel,/the body an urn." She then provides us with beautiful images of ourselves when she says that we are "made from dust . . . and patched with slip,/divine fingerprints everywhere." After pointing out a few of the unsettling things that happen to us she says, "each of these charges the heart/with uncanny energy, untouchable.//All you can do is break the clay/wide open, crack the very housing.//What hurts is what draws you/ever nearer to what we can't reach."

Barenblat also helps us with some of the most difficult-to-explain passages. In "Like God" (*Tazria*) she begins, "When a woman carries a grain of rice/invisible inside her rounded belly" then tells us some of the difficulties of pregnancy, and "when a woman gives birth to an infant—/even the air around her crackles . . . /changed by the enormity of being like God/and shaping new life in her compassionate womb." She gets us beyond the sacrifices and the ritual uncleanness, and gets to the heart of the matter: the wonder of pregnancy and childbirth. Barenblat, who has a son, doesn't romanticize pregnancy and childbirth but she does understand *Tazria* in terms of its most fundamental meaning.

She is especially inventive and playful in "Red Heifer" (*Chukat*): "Could Moshe have imagined/the Red Heifer Steakhouse/of King George Street/in Jerusalem? He never crossed//the Jordan, a Diaspora Jew/to the last of his days...The heifer was a koan/in hide and bone . . . Do the diners at the Red Heifer/contemplate death's mysterious power/to linger on our clothes/and in our hearts . . .?" Who among us has not tried to imagine a biblical character in a modern setting?

Nitzavim tells us that concealed acts are God's concern but that overt acts require us to apply God's teaching in the text. In "Secrets," Rabbi Barenblat reminds us that "God inhabits our secrets,/nestles in our fantasies." Then she insightfully reminds us that, "God hides in plain sight/veiled by the textures of creation... on Yom Kippur/when we knock on our hearts//we don't have to be afraid/to throw our screen doors wide open."

Not every poem will strike a chord within all of us—no book could do that—but there are such riches here that everyone will find many, many poems that will help him or her see these passages with new eyes.

ADAM D. FISHER, D.H.L. (NY67) is the poetry editor of the *CCAR Journal* and rabbi emeritus of Temple Isaiah, Stony Brook, New York.

Until the Blue Kingdom Comes
by James B. Rosenberg
(Bloomington, IN: Xlibris, 2011), 158 pp.

I've known Jim Rosenberg for over twenty years and during that time I've read many of his poems. I always knew he was a fine poet, but his new book left me breathless. It is wonderful—his best work yet.

First, he loves words and has a good ear using alliteration and other sounds so that his poems sing. Second, he has a great deal to say—there is valuable content in his work. Third, he doesn't pull punches. He writes from the gut and it shows.

The first section of his book is mostly poems of Jewish interest and it is here that his poems will be of great help to Jewish leaders of all kinds who look for material to embellish stories, *divrei Torah*, and sermons.

In a poem that just sings, Rosenberg uses a quote from Job as the title of his poem: "When the morning stars sang together." There he says: "Sing aloud for the coming of the light!/Clap your hands for the dawning of the day!/Shout for joy at the passing of the night!" This of course reminds us of the Psalms, and the rest of the poem is just as musical and is more than a poem; it is a prayer.

One of my favorites is "God's Toolbox" (see Spring 2011 issue of this Journal), in which he quotes from Yehuda Amichai who says that "God is lying on His back under the world . . . repairing." Rosenberg takes that image and runs with it. He pictures God lying on His back repairing the world and complaining like a parent whose teenage son or daughter has just wrecked the family car: "I've given them a Cadillac,/And they leave me this jalopy." He describes all the tools God has assembled and in desperation God turns to us and says, "*Oy vey iz Mir*!/I cannot fix this by My Self." It is an engaging, stunning poem with many applications.

In "The Pit," Rosenberg speaks of reaching out to God, "If only I could hear the echo/Of Your cry of absence/Calling me calling me,/The echoing cry of your absence,/The echoing cry." In this call he speaks to the yearning for God, which is in so many of us.

"Uncle Amos" is different altogether. Here Amos is the eccentric uncle, who shoots barbs at the current "cows of Bashan" (Amos 4:1). He sees Amos as performing street theater when he "storms into Bonwits on a Saturday afternoon/In loin cloth and sandals." He ends the poem by claiming that Uncle Amos is a Chippendale dancer. How's that for midrashic imagination!

In "Glasses," he turns serious again, struggling with a way to speak of God: "God is neither the object nor the subject.//God is the glasses the world wears to see." In "Allen's Lion," he takes a line from Ginsberg and in a great riff on that line imagines a lion in his living room, which, after comments from a cast of characters, "exits left,/Straight through the closed screen door,/Trampling the dandelions on the front lawn." What Rosenberg's fabulous imagination gives us is delicious.

These are just a few examples of the riches to be found in this book. I could turn to almost any page and find additional examples of wonderful musical and insightful lines.

Another aspect of Jim Rosenberg's poems, which is notable, is that he enriches them with references to both Jewish and general culture. He mentions figures as diverse as Salvador Dali, John Berryman, Allen Ginsberg, Diego Rivera, and Maya Angelou as well as Cain, Esau, Isaiah, and Isaac Luria.

This is not to say that this collection is without flaws. It has a few, very few; but, they are rare and more than made up for in lines that sing like Walt Whitman. Couldn't you find lines like these in Whitman? "In the distance, Long Island Sound, a strip of blue/Dotted with white sails puffed by the four o'clock breeze."

Jim Rosenberg's poetry is so well done, so Jewishly attuned, and so accessible that it deserves a place in your library and on your nightstand.

ADAM D. FISHER, D.H.L. (NY67) is the poetry editor of the *CCAR Journal* and rabbi emeritus of Temple Isaiah, Stony Brook, New York.

Call for Papers: *Maayanot*

The CCAR Journal: The Reform Jewish Quarterly is committed to serving its readers' professional, intellectual, and spiritual needs. In pursuit of that objective, the Journal has created a new section to be known as *Maayanot* (Primary Sources). The new rubric will have its debut in the Spring 2012 issue.

We invite the submission of proposals for translations of significant Jewish texts, accompanied by an appropriate introduction and annotations and/or commentary. These texts can represent fresh approaches materials from any period of Jewish life that would be of interest to our readers. When appropriate, we will include the original document in the published presentation.

Please submit your ideas and proposals to *Maayanot* editor, Daniel Polish, dpolish@optonline.net.

Along with submissions for *Maayanot*, the *Journal* continues to welcome the submission of scholarly articles in fields of Jewish Studies, as well as other articles, poetry, and book reviews that fit within our Statement of Purpose.

The CCAR Journal: The Reform Jewish Quarterly
Published quarterly by the Central Conference of American Rabbis.

Volume LIX, No. 1. Issue Number: Two hundred thirty-one.
Winter 2012.

STATEMENT OF PURPOSE

The CCAR Journal: The Reform Jewish Quarterly seeks to explore ideas and issues of Judaism and Jewish life, primarily—but not exclusively—from a Reform Jewish perspective. To fulfill this objective, the Journal is designed to:

1. provide a forum to reflect the thinking of informed and concerned individuals—especially Reform rabbis—on issues of consequence to the Jewish people and the Reform Movement;
2. increase awareness of developments taking place in fields of Jewish scholarship and the practical rabbinate, and to make additional contributions to these areas of study;
3. encourage creative and innovative approaches to Jewish thought and practice, based upon a thorough understanding of the traditional sources.

The views expressed in the Journal do not necessarily reflect the position of the Editorial Board or the Central Conference of American Rabbis.

The CCAR Journal: The Reform Jewish Quarterly (ISSN 1058-8760) is published quarterly by the Central Conference of American Rabbis, 355 Lexington Avenue, 18th Floor, New York, NY, 10017. Application to mail at periodical postage rates is pending at New York, NY and at additional mailing offices.

Subscriptions should be sent to CCAR Executive Offices, 355 Lexington Avenue, 18th Floor, New York, NY, 10017. Subscription rate as set by the Conference is $75 for a one-year subscription, $125 for a two-year subscription. Overseas subscribers should add $36 per year for postage. POSTMASTER: Please send address changes to The CCAR Journal: The Reform Jewish Quarterly, c/o Central Conference of American Rabbis, 355 Lexington Avenue, 18th Floor, New York, NY, 10017.

Typesetting and publishing services provided by Publishing Synthesis, Ltd., 39 Crosby Street, New York, NY, 10013.

The CCAR Journal: The Reform Jewish Quarterly is indexed in the *Index to Jewish Periodicals*. Articles appearing in it are listed in the *Index of Articles on Jewish Studies* (of *Kirjath Sepher*).

ISSN 1058-8760

ISBN: 978-0-88123-180-9

GUIDELINES FOR SUBMITTING MATERIAL

1. The *CCAR Journal* welcomes submissions that fulfill its Statement of Purpose whatever the author's background or identification. Inquiries regarding publishing in the CCAR Journal and submissions for possible publication (including poetry) should be sent to the editor, Rabbi Susan Laemmle, in electronic form via Laemmle@usc.edu. Should problems arise, call 323-939-4084.

2. Other than commissioned articles, submissions to the *CCAR Journal* are sent out to a member of the editorial board for anonymous peer review. Thus submitted articles and poems should be sent to the editor with the author's name omitted. Please use MS Word format for the attachment. The message itself should contain the author's name, phone number, and e-mail address, as well as the submission's title and a 1–2 sentence bio.

3. Books for review and inquiries regarding submitting a review should be sent directly to the book review editor, Rabbi Laurence Edwards, at *LLE49@comcast.net*.

4. Inquiries concerning, or submissions for, *Maayanot* (Primary Sources) should be directed to the *Maayanot* editor, Rabbi Daniel Polish, at *dpolish@optonline.net*.

5. Based on Reform Judaism's commitment to egalitarianism, we request that articles be written in gender-inclusive language.

6. The *Journal* publishes reference notes at the end of articles, but submissions are easier to review when notes come at the bottom of each page. If possible, keep this in mind when submitting an article. Notes should conform to the following style:

a. Norman Lamm, *The Shema: Spirituality and Law in Judaism* (Philadelphia: Jewish Publication Society, 1998), 101–6. **[book]**

b. Lawrence A. Hoffman, "The Liturgical Message," in *Gates of Understanding*, ed. Lawrence A.Hoffman (New York: CCAR Press, 1977), 147–48, 162–63. **[chapter in a book]**

c. Richard Levy, "The God Puzzle," *Reform Judaism* 28 (Spring 2000): 18–22. **[article in a periodical]**

d. Lamm, *Shema*, 102. **[short form for subsequent reference]**

e. Levy, "God Puzzle," 20. **[short form for subsequent reference]**

f. Ibid., 21. **[short form for subsequent reference]**

7. If Hebrew script is used, please include an English translation. If transliteration is used, follow the guidelines abbreviated below and included more fully in the **Master Style Sheet**, available on the CCAR website at *www.ccarnet.org*:

"ch" for *chet* and *chaf* "ei" for *tzeirei*

"f" for *fei* "a" for *patach* and *kamatz*

"k" for *kaf* and *kuf* "o" for *cholam* and *kamatz katan*

"tz" for *tzadi* "u" for *shuruk* and *kibbutz*

"i" for *chirik* "ai" for *patach* with *yod*

"e" for *segol*

Final "h" for final *hei*; none for final *ayin* (with exceptions based on common usage): *atah, Sh'ma*, but *Moshe*.

Apostrophe for *sh'va nah*: *b'nei, b'rit, Sh'ma*; no apostrophe for *sh'va nach*.

Hyphen for two vowels together where necessary for correct pronunciation: *ne-eman, samei-ach*, but *maariv*, Shavuot.

No hyphen for prefixes unless necessary for correct pronunciation: *babayit, HaShem, Yom HaAtzma-ut*.

Do not double consonants (with exceptions based on dictionary spelling or common usage): *t'filah, chayim*, but *tikkun*, Sukkot.